THE STERLING FOREST

JOHN FENZEL

Breathe Press

Published by BREATHE Press

BREATHE is a registered trademark of BREATHE, Inc.

This is a work of fiction. Names, characters, places, and incidents either are the product of the author's imagination or are used fictitiously, and any resemblance to actual persons, living or dead, business establishments, events, or locales is entirely coincidental.

Dust jacket design by Kate Handling Creative

Printed in the United States of America
Library of Congress Cataloging-in-Publication Data
Fenzel, John
The Sterling Forest / John Fenzel.—ed.
I. Title

ISBN 978-0-9822379-1-5 (acid-free paper)
1. Congressman—Fiction. 2. War—Fiction. 3. Russia—Fiction.
4. Cold War—Fiction.
6. CIA—Fiction. 7. Baltics—Fiction
8. Switzerland—Fiction. 9. Lithuania—Fiction.
10 9 8 7 6 5 4 3 2 1
First Edition

For Ciri—For making everything possible.

Acknowledgements

The Sterling Forest is a product of the encouragement and support of many people—first and foremost, to the men of A Company, 2nd Battalion, 10th Special Forces Group, who conducted the first U.S. deployment to the Baltic States; and to all of the Lithuanians, Latvians and Estonians we served alongside—you and your extraordinary—often harrowing—stories inspired this novel.

I am grateful to all of those who have provided their ideas and support along this rather incredible journey.

Without the constant encouragement, wisdom and hard work of my extraordinary wife and first editor, Ciri, this novel simply would not have materialized. From weaving together the initial story idea through the process of writing, revising and publishing—her constant support and help were instrumental throughout.

I am extremely grateful to Tammy Thorp whose wise counsel and tremendous insights helped immeasurably in creating a story that was both compelling and plausible.

Thank you to Robert Marek—editor to Robert Ludlum, Thomas Harris and many other great authors—as the beneficiary of his candor, coaching, and decades of experience, I am very fortunate.

My mother—Muriel Fenzel—who has been listening to my stories for over a half century, remains one of my most valued editors and enthusiastic supporters, always pushing me toward a higher standard.

Finally, I could not be more grateful to Dr. Ronald Chudd whose tireless efforts and amazing eye toward detail and discerning vision were crucial from beginning to end.

Sincere thanks to Kate Handling—an extraordinarily talented designer—for creatively bringing *The Sterling Forest* to life on these pages and on the worldwide web.

Each of these magnificent people read the manuscript as it evolved, and I am eternally grateful for the guidance, ideas and support. Because of their help, I know *The Sterling Forest* is a better story.

PROLOGUE

"IN THE OLD DAYS," my Uncle Jonas would shout at full volume, as if he was delivering a toast: "life was good!"

"Do you hear me, Danno?" he would bellow again in his thick Lithuanian accent, pointing over at me with his massive index finger so I would remember.

But it wasn't the pointing or bellowing that made me remember. It was the repetition.

It was always like this at the Chicago Lawn VFW Post back in the '70s. First, the shot glasses came out, the Krupnik—a kind of sweet, honey-infused vodka that Lithuanians loved so much it had become a national tradition. And there were the cigarettes and cigars, and the wistful, drunken remembrances and laments of a time long past. All but forgotten, except by them.

The theme song from *Hawaii Five-O* would be playing—so now, looking back, I figure it had to be around eight on Friday nights. I'd look up from the television, nod at Jonas and smile. The Krupnik was in full flow by the time the first body was falling out of a random Honolulu high rise—every single episode. Steve McGarrett would get the call first, and his band of elite cops would spring into action.

"We had jobs!" My uncle's fist would pound on the table, nearly tipping some of the glasses over. There would be an eruption of curses in Lithuanian, and then laughter.

"We had food on our table!" one of his friends would agree. "To Freedom!" Another would shout, toasting the good old days, but also goading Jonas on. Everyone loved Jonas, and many revered him.

1

When he entered a room, everyone stood and made the effort to shake his hand.

Heads would nod in unison with every statement. Grumbles of agreement fueled by nostalgia for a time and place as ethereal as the white rings of smoke hovering overhead.

"Our life was good," they would repeat to themselves in a practiced, subdued chant. And I knew they always meant it.

As a joke, I would absently repeat it to them in unison, "Life was good!"

Our life was good. The implication, of course, was that the good times were long over. Never to return. It was a depressing thought if you were to take it seriously. But I came to realize it just meant that things were different now. And yet, I always suspected there was more behind that chant.

The garish camaraderie—if not comedy—of it all amused me, and every so often it would also fascinate me. After all these years, the same group of men who were friends so many years ago were still just as close, like brothers. The Krupnik and smoke mingled with their voices, providing comfort, and giving credence to their individual recollections of events only they understood. *When life was good.*

Right about when the second body fell out of another Hawaiian high-rise, another old-timer would shake his head solemnly and remind everyone, "Until the Bolsheviks came."

More drunken murmurs of agreement followed, and the discussion would shift to the war in Lithuania—and the dead.

Always the dead.

You could set your watch by it. Like clockwork, they'd begin talking in reverent, subdued, respectful tones.

Every so often, one of the men would point at me and shake his head. "You just don't know...you kids will never understand what it was like." ·

Maybe not... I thought.

"Life was good!" someone else would repeat loudly.

And then another voice would remind everyone from across the table, "Until the Soviets came." "And the Nazis invaded," said another.

"And until the Soviets *came back*," Jonas added, clarifying.

Heads would nod again, this time with a vengeance, and someone—usually my uncle, would pour more Krupnik in the glasses.

Always at that point—when the Soviets came back—I noticed the conversation at the table would become hushed. There was one reason for Krupnik at that point: to drown out the past, not to bring it back. The men would lean back in their chairs, cigarettes would light up, and the room would quickly fill up with cigarette smoke—mostly from unfiltered Camels. And then everyone would watch as Steve McGarrett and his cops would close in on the bad guys in a classic, high-speed car chase, and Chief McGarrett would be right there, always, to make his arrest—always showing Danno how it was done.

Steve McGarrett always got his man. And crime never pays. Those were the consistent *Hawaii Five-O* themes from a simpler time. And yet, I always got the feeling that Steve McGarrett wasn't really the one in control. Secretly, I though, Danno was the man behind the curtain, with his hands firmly on the wheel.

A commercial break would come on and then Jim Rockford's answering machine would play:

"This is Jim Rockford. At the tone, leave your name and message. I'll get back to you."

"Jimmy, old buddy. It's Angel! You know how they allow you one phone call? Well, this is it."

And the theme song from *The Rockford Files* would play. Just around then my mother would call the VFW, asking whoever was behind the bar to send me home.

I never seemed to make it very far on those Friday nights on the Southwest Side. The area was called "Chicago Lawn," in a neighborhood called "Lithuanian Plaza." It's where all the Lithuanians started to settle back in the late 1800's.

The neighborhood boys would shout at me to join their street hockey game in progress, because—as Jonas would say—I ran "like a rabbit being shot at." We would play under the street lamps, and as dusk thickened into night, it was easy to feel like you were playing in a well-lit stadium. To complete that effect, Jonas and his friends would watch us from the sidewalks, shouting and stopping traffic, until the game was over.

All of the men would stagger back to their red-bricked bungalows, loudly singing songs in Lithuanian that ranged in tempo from victorious marches to Slavic funeral dirges. Fireflies would light the night, and I would imagine they were our Lithuanian ancestors dancing around us.

My uncle would call for me just as I'd be walking home, and in his slurred raspy voice, from all the Krupnik and cigarettes, "Daniel!" sounded a lot like "Danno!" My friends would hear him and from then on, everyone called me "Danno." That's how I got my nickname. I didn't mind, because after all, it was Danno who did all the work. And Danno was the one who was *really* in control.

I would walk with my uncle back to his house down the street, often holding him upright when he began to stumble.

"Danno!" he'd announce loudly, holding up both of his massive arms. "Someday, you will be President of the United States!" And then I'd catch him as he stumbled again. We'd end up on his porch, looking out into the night, talking like men well beyond their years. He was the father figure in my life. He'd light another of his Camels, and the words came out in clouds of smoke.

He'd talk to me about my father who died in a Soviet prison in 1962, just as the Cold War was heating up, right after I was born—often mixing past and present tenses.

"Danno, your father is proud of you," he would say. *"You be proud of him. No one else like Lucas Tory!"*

"I wish I had known him," I would say, meaning it.

"He knows you," Jonas would answer. *"Don't you worry…."*

My mother never remarried, and I never once saw her with another man.

"Daniel, I will always love your father. There will be no one else on this earth for me," she told me more than once.

Jonas was a gregarious personality—always laughing, always smiling. He dominated a room. Everyone knew him, and everyone admired him. He was a Green Beret who served in Vietnam, in 1968, when he only had a green card. I've been told by a few of his friends that he had also worked for the CIA, going back and forth between Laos and Cambodia targeting the North Vietnamese infiltration routes with Montagnard counterinsurgency forces. Among his awards, I found a Distinguished Service Cross for his actions in defending his firebase against a Viet Cong attack. When Jonas returned from Vietnam, he would often be gone for weeks and sometimes months on end.

I went to Marmion Military Academy—a Benedictine-run military high school in Aurora, Illinois. I was a boarding student there, and Jonas would always come over on weekends to visit my friends and me when he was home. We'd sit on the bleachers of the football field at night eating hot dogs he'd imported from Wally's Hot Dog Stand on Diversey and Central Avenue in Chicago—the largest and best hot dogs in Chicago at the time. Wally's is gone now, and Marmion is now just called 'Marmion Academy,' but those memories are indelible.

For me, those were the days when life was good.

Most often, when Jonas wasn't around—I never knew where he was. One evening, I went by the VFW to see if he was there, and one of his friends whispered to me that he was in Afghanistan fighting the Soviets. I didn't take that too seriously—I just assumed he was on a business trip. Then a week later, Jonas would be home, as if he never left—not skipping a beat. I'd know he was home, because he'd call me without fail, and have me pick up his lottery tickets at Bruno's Bakery, along with a loaf of Sour Rye and his Lithuanian newspapers from the newsstand. I'd sit on his porch for hours, listening to his stories about the old days in Vilnius, interspersed with war stories from Vietnam; and in those moments, I knew that in the day—in his day—Jonas Tory had to be a real force to be reckoned with.

When crime started rising in Chicago Lawn in the '80s, we moved out to Lake Forest—one of the most picturesque suburbs of Chicago. I got accepted at Harvard, and then Yale Law School. When I graduated from Yale, I worked at the Supreme Court as a clerk for

Chief Justice John Roberts.

I lived in DC, but I'd go back to visit Lake Forest whenever I possibly could. During one visit, as my clerkship was ending, Jonas talked me into running for Mayor of Lake Forest. I hesitated at first, thinking my future was in a big New York City law firm, but he persisted, and so did my mother. Ultimately, I ran, and won by a landslide. At 30 years old, being Mayor of Lake Forest was a great place to serve and build a record of public service, while also gaining some name recognition. Being in Lake Forest also allowed me to be with that "Greatest Generation" of first generation Lithuanians.

Growing up, and through adulthood, Jonas and his friends were my touchstones—who kept me grounded no matter what the event or circumstance. But I started noticing that there were fewer and fewer of them left. My mother would call me up more and more frequently to deliver a eulogy or be a pallbearer. It was always sad for me to see the old timers go, because they were all one-of-a-kind, and they were a big part of my childhood. Eventually—and far too late—I realized that they were the ones who raised me, and who define me today.

After I finished my term as Mayor, I went back to Washington as a White House Fellow, working directly for the White House Chief of Staff. While I was there, I gained some valuable experiences that made me start thinking about a long-term political career.

On those nights I came back home to Lake Forest to visit, the phone would inevitably ring, and I'd hear Jonas' distinctive voice, asking me to pick him up at the VFW post. He would ask me how everything was in the White House, and I'd get plenty of policy advice from him on a full range of political issues.

Jonas was 92 years old when I first told him I was running for Congress.

"Shoot the bastards," he said matter-of-factly, pulling out a bottle of Krupnik and two shot glasses. "The first thing you do when you get to Washington is you shoot the goddamned bastards who are ruining my beautiful country! I tell you, Danno—you bring me there, you don't have to worry—I'll do it!" It went on like that—irrational and bombastic, but always highly entertaining. Before I knew it, he'd switch to Lithuanian without realizing it, and I'd have to struggle a bit to keep up with the conversation. I understood the language, but I couldn't speak it well.

"You're going to give yourself a coronary, Jonas," I'd say to him.

Jonas would shake his head and point to the sky and say, "No one gets off Planet Earth alive, Danno! Remember that!"

Getting back to Lake Forest was my own way of reconnecting with real people, in the real world. Their grievances and concerns became my own political platform. And I always left there with my batteries fully recharged. If I won that congressional race, I told myself, I wouldn't let Jonas and his friends down—I'd fight for them. Because they fought for us.

Beyond the political issues, though, if I'd had any idea then of what I know now, I would have listened more closely to the stories of those men sitting around that table smoking unfiltered Camels, and drinking Lithuanian Krupnik. I would've listened more closely to my uncle, walking unsteadily in the middle of the street, and sitting on his porch—talking and singing about the old days—and I would have listened to them eulogizing their dead. My father among them.

Had I known then what I know now, I would have asked more questions, and I would have turned the television off. I would have listened. Closely. And then I would have known that I was never really in control of anything.

CHAPTER 1

THEY SAID IT COULDN'T BE DONE. An Independent victory in one of the most traditionally Democratic districts in the country. We made history that day. I'll concede that the redistricting and government shutdown didn't hurt, nor did that FBI sting that led to my predecessor's resignation. The stars aligned properly, and you couldn't have scripted it better for us. At the end of the day, we were just plain lucky.

There I was, a former Mayor of a small Chicago suburb, struggling to campaign for a congressional election that no one thought I could realistically win, especially as an Independent. No one was really paying much attention to my candidacy. I drove around in my Volkswagen from town to town on my own dime, but the only support I was *really* getting was moral support:

"We're behind you, Danno!" "Danno you can do this!" "Book 'em, Danno!"

It was great fun. But no financial support whatsoever—no real money to keep a successful campaign going. Jonas taught me to never quit if you believe in what you were doing, so I just kept going.

You could say it was a disadvantage being an Independent, but we just saw it as an opportunity to call out the failed policies of both sides.

Our campaign was all about fighting the corruption that was so rampant in Illinois politics. There was unprecedented unemployment in Chicago, jobs were going south to Mexico *and* east to China, energy prices were through the roof, and our taxes were so high that all of our corporate partners...Amoco, American Airlines, Inland Steel... they were getting swallowed up lock, stock and barrel and moving to London, Atlanta and Shanghai.

Part of the trouble was our attitude as a city. We had this kind of superiority complex—an "Us-Versus-Them" attitude, and it was palpable: "We're better because we're Chicago." You know, all I could do was shake my head when I heard people say that. It tends to ring hollow when your State is regarded as the most corrupt in the Union, has the highest murder rate in the nation, and is practically bankrupt— when you have one of the highest tax rates, when your pension funds are depleted, and when your businesses are running to the States next door to escape the chaos. So, maybe you're not better after all.

That's what I campaigned on. Restore safety and security to our town. Bring back the jobs we lost, lose the attitude, be fiscally responsible, lower taxes and start being friendly again! That's how we won. "Keep it simple," Jonas always told me, and that's what we did.

Just when you think you're chasing an unobtainable goal, *People Magazine* randomly says you're one of "50 Hot Guys in 50 States," and *that day* the money starts coming in. It wasn't a ton of money, but enough to do some direct marketing you wouldn't ordinarily be able to do with mail and TV. Oprah wants you on her show. Diane Sawyer is on call waiting. And Lara Logan is there from 60 Minutes—*actually there*, interviewing Jonas on his front porch! Lara spent an entire Sunday afternoon there with him, and they went on for hours talking about Lithuania and the Cold War. I guess they got along famously— because I heard stories about their meeting for weeks afterward.

The messages from Jonas that night were classic:

"Brad, this is Jonas. You've got Angelina. I've got Lara. Come over and we have a party!"

The calls started coming in for me to appear on shows, like *Today* and *The View*.

And yet, still, it was a tough campaign and a close race.... until we proved the Silver Star of my incumbent opponent was a fraud, and in the face of Stolen Valor accusations, the Democrats were left reeling for a suitable replacement at the eleventh hour. It didn't end there. When my Republican opponent got caught in a corruption scandal involving undocumented workers in his mansion, suddenly our campaign had a glimmer of hope where none previously existed.

All that, combined, won that election for us.

I was happy to win, but on November 3rd, I was exhausted. Completely, utterly spent. I felt like the dog that just caught his tail. And that day, *Cosmopolitan* Magazine dubbed me "Bachelor of the Year."

Suddenly, TV crews and photographers were crawling all over Lake Forest, and actually staking me out.

At first, I thought it was funny. I mean, *Paparazzi!* Following *me!*

Jonas laughed at that too when I'd told him and he started leaving messages for me on my cell phone, calling me Brad Pitt.

"Brad, this is Jonas Tory, when you go to Washington don't you forget us veterans, okay? Say hi to Angelina, okay?"

"Brad, this is Jonas Tory, keep the communists out of Lithuania, okay? Tell Angelina she should come with you and me to Vilnius!"

Aside from Jonas' comments about Angelina Jolie and Brad Pitt, it was all a bit surreal for me to even consider.

A week after the election, I desperately needed a break. So I begged off from all of the media appearances and decided to go back to my old neighborhood, see my mother, my Uncle Jonas and all the old timers—the ones who were still around.

I arrived at Jonas' home, expecting the door to be left ajar, as it normally was. I rang the doorbell, and then knocked, but no one answered. The door was locked. I searched around remembering he left an extra key in a nearby planter, but instead found it under his doormat. I let myself into the house that had remained essentially unchanged as long as I could remember.

I absorbed the warmth of the radiators, and looked around. The house was small and modestly furnished. It smelled faintly like cigarette smoke, but it was clean and stood around me in a familiar and comforting way. He still had the original turquoise and Sunbeam Yellow appliances from the 1960's and 70's—the KitchenAid Custom 21"Harvest Gold" portable dishwasher. Some, like the Wedgewood Double Oven, were older than that. But somehow he kept them in good working order and the place was spotless.

They don't make them like this no more. Everything they sell now? Junk!

I pulled the bark cloth draperies open. Jonas was a fanatic when it came to keeping things clean and organized. I attributed it to his Green Beret training. The only sign of slight disorder were the occasional coffee stains on the burnt-orange carpet.

"Everything has a place, Danno," he would always say to me. *"That way, you can always find what you're looking for when you need it. Remember that."*

I called his name again, but no answer. Upstairs, I found him in his room, in bed, face up. His mouth was open slightly, and he looked like he was asleep. But I knew right away something was wrong. He was too still, with an ashen white, waxy complexion; and his chest wasn't rising or falling. His hand was cold to the touch. I checked for a pulse and found none.

I sat down on the side of the bed and looked at Jonas, asleep forever. My heart sank, and I broke down beside him. I felt a rush of regret that I hadn't gotten a chance to say goodbye to him. But it seemed fitting that it was me who found him, and not someone else.

Beside an old 1960's style black rotary telephone, was a wireless version of the same phone. As I dialed the police, I saw the photograph that had fallen out of Jonas' hands. It was that photo that started my journey—and what led to all of the events that followed.

CHAPTER 2

THE PHOTOGRAPH WAS A FRAMED old black and white 8x10 that looked like it had been kept in his nightstand. The drawer was opened. All of the photos in his room were familiar to me except this one: two men in Soviet Russian uniforms and a young woman in a grey uniform standing in front of a large brick building with two long scarlet banners with a red, gold-bordered star over a large gold hammer and sickle hanging in front and on each side. Cars appeared to be coming and going on the adjacent street as they stood there smiling, casually posing for the camera.

At the time it struck me as odd that Jonas would keep a photograph of Russian officers, framed. But as I studied the photograph more closely, I began to recognize the officer on the far left.

The broad smile, the hard jaw line and his barrel chest quickly gave him away. I looked over at his body on the bed to confirm what I already knew. The resemblance was unmistakable.

It was Jonas.

Jonas Tory, a Russian officer?

I didn't recognize the other male officer, standing to the far right. The woman standing between them wore a basic service uniform—a grey double-breasted wool suit with white blouse, black tie and side cap. Over her shoulder, a leather handbag and long strap. She stood in a suggestive model's pose, arms akimbo, knee out. Her features were refined, hair was pulled back into a bun—she was by any measure, strikingly beautiful, even in a Soviet Army uniform.

I recognized her smile first, and then her eyes. They were dark and playful, cunning…the same eyes I'd grown up with—that could read me so well when I failed to tell the truth after a fight on the playground, or when I attempted to conceal a bad grade. It was the same bemused smile that greeted me when I found my way home after the street hockey matches outside the VFW.

My head was spinning.

Why was I only seeing this photograph now? What was Jonas saying in death that he couldn't tell me when he was alive?

I looked again at the photograph closely, just to confirm what I already now knew.

The woman in the photo was my mother.

CHAPTER 3

WHEN I EXPLAINED TO MOM that Jonas had passed away, she closed her eyes for what seemed like a very long time. When she opened them, she shifted her gaze to the kitchen window and just kept staring outside, as if she were looking back into a different time. Tears were rolling down both of her cheeks.

Mom's kindness and compassion were always well known and writ large, but so was her toughness. Raising me as a single mother was always what I admired most about her growing up, and she did it seamlessly and without the slightest complaint. Now, at 92 years old, she had already survived a few minor strokes; and yet, she still had all of her wits about her, and she had retained her natural beauty, even in her old age. She was still thin and her posture was still good. Her hair was white, not grey; and although her skin had wrinkled, her complexion still had plenty of color in it. But now she appeared more fragile, even vulnerable, and she seemed to have withdrawn socially.

The house had the same furnishings, the same smells, and the same creaky hardwood floor. After Mom's previous stroke, I bought one of those hospital beds that came with all the controls and elevations, and put it downstairs in the living room so she wouldn't have to climb or descend the steps.

I was actively searching for a live-in nurse to care for Mom, and ound Elena Litvina. She was a nurse, and she was a Godsend. Elena was in her late forties or early fifties—the daughter of a retired Lithuanian diplomat, who studied nursing in the Czech Republic before settling in Chicago. A graduate of Loyola University's nursing program who was relocating from Holy Cross Hospital after her husband died, she was a natural choice to be mom's private nurse. She and mom got along well—she read the paper to my mother, cooked for her, brought her to church, gave her all the meds she needed, and lived upstairs in my old bedroom.

"Mom, I need to show you something," I said softly. "This photograph—I found it in Jonas' bedroom."

After a few seconds she turned to face me with a pained, yet inquisitive expression but said nothing. I set the framed photograph on the table and I saw her quickly glance at it. Her hands rose to the table and her fingers touched the frame but did not grasp it. Instead, she slowly and wordlessly pushed it off the table. It crashed facedown to the floor, the glass shattering into shards around our feet.

"*Mom!*" I exclaimed, jumping back in my chair and quickly bent down to pick up the frame. Elena rushed into the room to assist, picking the shards of glass off the floor.

Initially, I thought it was an accident, but when I looked back up at her, she was again staring out the window. She was breathing more heavily, and yet she was silent, which was totally uncharacteristic.

Tanya Tory always had something to say.

I placed the frame back on the table, and Elena finished sweeping the glass into a dustpan. Mom refused to look at the photograph again.

"I'm very tired, Daniel," she said simply.

Based on her reaction, I hesitated at first to say anything further. After her last stroke, the doctors had warned against exposing her to anything that could upset her and cause another stroke. But this was just too important, and the revelation simply too dramatic to ignore.

"Okay, Mom, listen to me. I just have to know," I began again quietly, sitting back down beside her. My tone was insistent: "Please tell me, and I won't ever ask again."

She shook her head slowly and finally she turned to meet my eyes. Her words came in her native Lithuanian, slow and halting: "*Sunki situacija ...Dievũ mìško padángėj.*"

I had heard her say the first part before, albeit in a different context, *sunki situacija…. A difficult situation.* But my Lithuanian was not good enough to translate the other half: …. *Dievū mìško padángėj.* Something philosophical, I thought, about God.

"We should let your mom rest—she's had quite a bit of trouble sleeping lately," Elena said, dustbin in hand.

I nodded absently, and walked out of the house with many more questions than I'd come with.

CHAPTER 4

"IN NOMINE PATRE, et filius spiritus sanctus...."

I barely heard the priest concluding his final blessing over Jonas' casket at St. Casimir Lithuanian Cemetery in Chicago. It was a cool spring morning, the kind I knew Jonas loved to spend sitting on his porch, filling out his lottery cards and reading *Respublika*, the Lithuanian daily. The dew was still on the grass and there was a slight chill in the air. It seemed fitting that we would be saying goodbye to him on such a day. The thought crossed my mind that he'd engineered the weather himself.

I held on to my mother's arm as we filed past. Mom placed her hand on the smooth grey metal and kept it there as she walked along its full length. As she separated herself from the casket, she leaned her weight into me and started sobbing quietly.

I never quite understood my mother's relationship with Jonas. For as long as I can remember, there wasn't much interaction between them. Even when we were at neighborhood events and Jonas was there, Mom never really talked to him. And there were times she'd actively avoid him.

One of Jonas' friends once told me that it was because Jonas and my father, Lucas Tory, we're so similar in appearance, and their voices were almost identical. But Jonas was the only living link I had to my father, so that's why I think she let me go over to his house.

I put my arm around my mother and walked her back through the grass and past the other headstones to the waiting limousine.

A baritone male voice called out behind me as I opened the door and helped Mom inside. "Daniel, hold on for a second."

It was Darius Zemaitis, our family attorney.

He greeted my mother, kissing her hand and expressing his condolences on behalf of his family.

Darius was also a Lithuanian émigré, and trusted by all of the Lithuanian families in our neighborhood. He still had lots of contacts in Vilnius and throughout the Baltic states too. It had been years since I'd seen him, and he'd aged considerably and put on quite a bit of weight. He practically waddled toward me. He had the same thick brown mustache that covered most of his upper lip. I shut the car door as he approached.

"Darius, it's been a long time," I said, shaking his hand, and thanked him for coming.

"He was a great man, Daniel. And he was very proud of you... what you accomplished. We all are."

"I loved him very much."

Darius gazed down, nodded, then looked back up at me. "Jonas assigned me as the executor of his will. We should go over that whenever it's convenient for you."

I nodded, not yet thinking about wills and inheritance—nor, for that matter, was I anxious to deal with the legal aspects and logistics of it all. I was already fully aware that my schedule was becoming more and more packed with events in Chicago and Washington, D.C.

"Why don't I stop by your office in the morning?" I suggested. "Would that work for the others?"

Darius shook his head. "There are no others, Daniel. You're it."

My head started to swim at the revelation. Honestly, I was floored. "But Jonas had so many friends. That can't be...."

Darius turned back at the Jonas' casket, waiting to be lowered into the ground. "He left all he had to you," he said with finality. "Tomorrow morning's fine. Stop by any time. Just a few documents to sign."

CHAPTER 5

I DIDN'T EXPECT TO INHERIT anything from Jonas. In fact, it was the furthest thing from my mind. I mean, if you love someone, you don't really give any thought about inheriting anything from them, do you?

I wasn't rich when I won that congressional seat. To be honest, I was living off credit cards and I was drowning in debt. Eventually, I reasoned, I'd dig myself out. Jonas' words always stuck with me: *Money...it's a renewable resource, Danno. But don't forget—pride isn't renewable. Pride is forever....* Going into that meeting with Darius, it occurred to me that this must have been Jonas' own way of helping me out.

I arrived at 9am, and Darius was waiting for me. He shut the door behind us, sat me down in front of his desk, and had his secretary bring me a cup of coffee. His office wasn't large, but it was tastefully decorated with nautical paintings, models of ships and artifacts from shipwrecks that he had acquired on his own dives. He had several large pieces of amber with large insects embedded inside, scattered on end tables around the room. The walls were a dark oak, giving the office an aura of a Captain's quarters on an expensive yacht.

Darius sat down and shuffled through a few papers. He appeared to be a bit nervous, I thought. Not really himself. Finally he looked up at me as I sipped the coffee.

"Well, Danno," he said, inhaling. "As I said to you yesterday, Jonas left everything he had to you." He paused and lifted the paper in front of him off the desk. He shook his head. "But I didn't expect..." Darius' voice trailed off.

"Didn't expect what?" I asked a bit impatiently.

He gave me a bemused look. "Did you know that Jonas was rich?"

Before answering Darius' question, I did my own flash survey of Jonas' life as I knew it. I shook my head and shrugged. I had no idea my uncle was wealthy—he displayed no outward signs of wealth whatsoever. "He lived off his military pension," I said softly. "He probably banked his salary from UPS. And he told me he had some stock options...."

Darius leaned back in his chair, and scratched his eyebrow. I got the impression he was in a quandary. He leaned forward, put his reading glasses on, and handed me a financial spreadsheet. The heading read simply, **Summary of Assets.** Underneath that header it read, "*Bank of Chicago: $26.5 million.*"

He continued to rattle off several more assets from UPS, and account balances, but after the first or second one, it was all a blur. Nothing was registering and at that moment, I must have looked like I'd been struck by lightning.

"Jonas Tory—your uncle—was a millionaire, Danno," he said in summary. "And now, thanks to him, even after the inheritance taxes, so are you."

"I had no idea," I said wide-eyed, but doing my best to appear calm.

Darius stood and walked around his desk, picking up a large envelope. "None of us did. It appears he kept that fact hidden from everyone. Even me."

"But how—?"

"He had a high-end attorney in Baltimore do his will, establish a series of iron clad trusts and offshore accounts that allowed him to avoid Federal and State taxes. I've never seen anything quite like it— it's been managed brilliantly and meticulously over years." He handed me the envelope in his hand. "Here... the legal papers you'll need to sign.... Jonas' will...it's all in there. Take your time and review them in private. You can do it here or at home—whatever you prefer."

"I think, right now, I'd like to go home," I said, staring at the envelope. It suddenly felt like a lead weight in my hands.

He nodded. "I understand. When you're ready we'll go over the legal documents together."

I rose to leave. My head was swimming and I felt a little dizzy. No matter how hard I tried, I couldn't make sense of it.

Jonas, a millionaire?

But in retrospect, it shouldn't have surprised me. Jonas Tory was, in many ways, exactly what you would expect of the closet millionaire: a patriotic veteran who volunteered to fight for his adopted country, and who settled with the rest of his fellow Lithuanians in Chicago, saving every penny he earned. He was the gregarious Teamsters member with strong arms and a strong back; always with a story that would make you laugh or cry, and often times simultaneously. And he was always ready to pass a five-dollar bill to the homeless guy on the street, with strict instructions to bypass the liquor store, and buy himself a good lunch.

Darius met my eyes with an understanding, sober expression. I think I may have thanked him and shook his hand at that point—I don't remember. He walked me to the door, and then as I was walking away, he called after me, pulling out two sets of keys from his pocket. He handed them to me.

"Jonas left his house and his Town Car to you too, Danno. These are spare keys."

CHAPTER 6

I SAT IN JONAS' DINING ROOM, staring out the window, searching the memories of my childhood for clues that might help make sense of it—the photograph of my mother, and Jonas and the other officer wearing Soviet Army uniforms...and the money I'd just inherited from Jonas.

I looked over at the envelope on the dining room table that Darius Zemaitis handed to me in his office. It sat there, unopened. Reaching over, I picked it up, tore through the seal, and pulled out the sheaf of papers inside. The top document was Jonas' last will and testament, dated a year ago. The opening statement was simple:

I, Jonas Tory, a resident of Lake Forest, Illinois, being of sound and disposing mind and memory, and not being actuated by any duress, menace, fraud, mistake, or undue influence, do make, publish, and declare this to be my last Will, hereby expressly revoking all Wills and Codicils previously made by me.

I will, give, and bequeath unto Daniel Orion Tory, the Property described below:

The bungalow appeared at the beginning of the list accounts from banks in Chicago and Lake Forest. And the Lincoln Town Car was at the very end of the list of accounts, both appearing as odd bookends to Jonas' financial estate—or misplaced punctuation marks to a life I thought I knew, but didn't.

Yeah, tell that to the media, I thought. I could see the headline now:

"Freshman Congressman's Family Tied to Financial Corruption and Violent Past."

I heard a siren passing loudly outside. Suddenly, I felt sick to my stomach. And angry—angry at Jonas, angry at my mother for never telling me about our family, and raising me in complete ignorance of our past. Never preparing me for the day it would all hit me squarely between the yes.

And now that that day had arrived, Mom refused to explain it or even to discuss it with me.

Why?

I looked around Jonas' living room. The bookshelves were neatly racked and stacked with all of the *National Geographic* videos and *Time-Life* books on the Wild West, World War II, Korea and Vietnam that he'd ordered off the television ads and accumulated over the years—all organized chronologically and sequentially, and all of them in mint, unread condition. On the top shelf, one of the books in the World War II series appeared to be missing, but the rest of them were there. On each of the shelves, he had model fighter airplanes dating back to the biplanes of World War I up to the Stealth Bomber and the F-35 Joint Strike Fighter.

If Jonas had left any clues to his past, they weren't visible to me. I kept glancing back at the will. The bank accounts were organized by largest account balance to the smallest. So the placement of the Town Car and the bungalow, sandwiching all of those international accounts seemed strange to me, given Jonas' penchant for keeping everything organized.

Everything has its place, Danno. Remember that.

As I recalled Jonas' words, the ring of my cell phone interrupted.

When I answered it, I heard Elena, my mother's nurse, telling me Mom had another stroke and the ambulance had just left the house.

CHAPTER 7

RUSHING INTO THE EMERGENCY ROOM, I saw Elena standing there by one of the interior entryways, talking to one of the hospital nurses. As I approached, she looked over at me with a worried expression.

"Daniel, your mom is in the operating room. They think she has an aneurysm…it's in her brain, but they don't know exactly where or how serious it is yet."

As she spoke, all I heard was "aneurysm," and I felt like the floor had just collapsed beneath my feet. Suddenly, I felt responsible. Of all people, I knew how fragile mom was, and so I knew better than to confront her with an issue from the past that was potentially so controversial—and *especially* right after telling her about Jonas' passing.

"I was in the kitchen when I heard her fall in the living room," Elena continued. "She was on the floor, unconscious."

I mumbled my thanks to her for getting her to the hospital so quickly and for calling me. It occurred to me that the siren that I'd heard pass by Jonas' bungalow was the ambulance that was carrying my mother here, to the emergency room. Suddenly, I no longer felt like a successful congressional candidate, but a failed son.

I closed my eyes and held the bridge of my nose in an attempt to stave off the onset of a migraine.

"Daniel…" Elena said after an extended pause.

I looked up at her and my vision was starting to blur from my headache. The bustle of the ER swirled around me.

"She was holding this when I found her." Elena handed me a 5x8 white-bordered black and white photograph of a smiling baby, maybe two or three months old, lying down on a dark blanket, dressed in what appeared to be girls' clothing. I hadn't ever seen the photograph before. I flipped it and found my mother's distinctive European script on the back:

Tatyana Tory - Kaunas, Lietuva, 6 gruodis 1958

Tatyana Tory – Kaunas, Lithuania, 6 December 1958

1958... *Four years before I was born.*

"Do you know who this is in the photo?" Elena asked in a curious tone.

I shook my head. But Mom's words returned to me. *"A difficult situation,"* I remember her telling me.

A day had passed, and I had been by my mother's bedside the entire time, working on my laptop, making phone calls, and doing my best to coordinate and build a Congressional staff. Honestly, though, with my mother in that condition, my heart just wasn't in it.

I heard someone enter the room and I looked up to see Elena standing there. I stood and hugged her. Her eyes were big and kind.

"How is she, Daniel?" Elena asked softly.

I shrugged and put my hands in my pockets. "They say it's too early to tell, but they're 'guardedly optimistic' about her full recovery," I answered quietly. "Her hip is badly bruised, but not broken."

Elena sat down and I looked over at my mother lying there in the bed. There was the systematic beeping from the machines and the steady sound of oxygen being pumped through her mask. There was an undeniable connection between both women, and that was one connection I was proud to have made. In some ways, I sensed that Elena knew my mother better than me—she understood Lithuania, and was fully conversant in its history and culture. It produced a connection that only "First Generation" immigrants from Vilnius with a fluency in their native language could share.

"Elena," I said, turning to her. "Yesterday, Mom said something in Lithuanian—*Dievu mìško padángèj*...can you tell me what that means?"

Elena nodded. "Under the skies of the forest of the Gods," she said simply, standing up and walking around to my mother's side. She looked up at me and continued: "Balys Sruoga, a famous Lithuanian intellectual, wrote a memoir with that title: *"Forest of the Gods,"* about the Stutthoff concentration camp in Poland, near Danzig, where he was held by the Nazis."

"Why would she use those words?"

Elena shook her head thoughtfully. "I don't know. After her stroke, she could be fully lucid one moment and confused the next. But, the book is in the house. I know she's read it because I've put it back on the shelf a few times after finding it on her bedside table."

I nodded my understanding, repeating the words to myself so I would remember them: "Under the skies of the forest of the Gods...."

CHAPTER 8

JONAS' LINCOLN TOWN CAR probably would have stayed in his garage if my own Jetta hadn't broken its timing chain right there in the hospital parking lot. It had 189,000 miles on it, and this appeared to be the culmination of a lot of problems that kept piling on over time. I pushed it into one of the parking places reserved for doctors, and called the shop to get it towed.

The Town Car was under the carport next to the bungalow; and even though it was nearly ten years old, it only had 20,000 miles on it. Like everything Jonas owned, it was clean and in impeccable condition—gleaming black. I chuckled and shook my head, hearing Jonas' voice, as if he were standing next to me, *"A congressman shouldn't drive an import, Daniel. You drive an American car now!"*

And who was I to argue? Especially when I didn't have enough money in the bank, or credit to pay for the repairs to the Jetta.

Until learning of my inheritance from Jonas, that is—none of that had quite settled in; and even if it had, I had no idea how to access those funds. So, I may as well have been dead broke at that moment. The Congressional campaign had played a big role in my financial situation, because I had put a second mortgage on my house to pay for additional TV and web advertising.

The Town Car started right up when I turned the key. It still had that new car smell to it—I think because he had the detailers work on it every couple weeks whether it needed it or not. I looked down and that's when I saw the book on the floor below the passenger seat. Just lying there.

Everything has its place, Daniel. Remember that.

Jonas' words echoed. So it was especially odd to see the book here in his Town Car, completely and definitively out of place. My heart began to pound even before I picked it up. *Why would he put it here?*

When I did, I realized it was the *Time-Life* book on World War II that was missing from Jonas' shelf, with the distinctive black and white photo on the front and rear boards of the smooth hardcover binding. But it was the photograph on the book that immediately caught my attention. There was the same 8x10 photograph I had found in his room—with Jonas and another man, dressed in the Soviet Army uniforms, and my mother in a Russian woman's auxiliary uniform. Above, in bold red, almost gothic script was the title of that particular volume:

The Cold War Resistance

"What—?" I must have been shaking, because I could barely open the book's cover. Eventually, I managed to turn to the copyright page. On the bottom left of the page there was the blurb entitled: **About the Cover.** Reading those words that followed was the first remnant of an explanation I'd been seeking:

> *Lithuanian resistance members, 1960 (left to right), Jonas Tory, Tanya Klimas, Lucas Tory, disguised in Soviet Army Uniforms, standing in front of the NKVD Headquarters in Vilnius, Lithuania, after emplacing powerful satchel bombs inside, only minutes prior to its destruction.*

Klimas, I knew, was my mother's maiden name.

And Lucas Tory was my father.

CHAPTER 9

I SAT IN JONAS' TOWN CAR for an hour or even more—I don't remember. What I do recall is sitting there thinking about the three most important people in my life, and realizing with a sudden clarity that I didn't really *know* any of them.

There was a bookmark midway through the *Time-Life* book. I opened it to that spot and found an entire page highlighted in dark brown with white text and several photographs. One of the photographs was a "before and after" shot. The "before" shot was the same photograph of Jonas, my mother and father in front of the NKVD headquarters in Vilnius. The "after" shot showed heavy black and white smoke billowing from all of the blasted out windows. Papers and debris scattered the sidewalk and road in front of the building's ruins.

The caption underneath the photographs read: *(Left) Members of the Lithuanian Resistance, posing as Soviet Army officers in front of the NKVD Headquarters in Vilnius, Lithuania after infiltrating and successfully emplacing timed explosive charges throughout the building, on each floor. (Right) Moments later—a Resistance photograph depicting the immediate aftermath of the explosion.*

I kept wondering why Jonas left the book in his car. I was certain of one thing: he meant for me to find it here. Not in the house, not through Darius Zemaitis—but here…in his Town Car, underneath his carport.

I started looking under the seats to see if he'd left anything else and I nearly fainted from the powerful new-car scent that had been sprayed on the carpet. I tried to open the glove compartment, but it was locked.

Locked.... That, also, I found odd. *Who locks their glove compartment?*

I took the keys from the ignition and found the key to the glove compartment. It popped open and underneath the owner's manual and warranty folders, I found the envelope—white, legal-size—with Jonas' handwriting on the front:

Personal for Daniel Tory

Opening it, a smaller, brown envelope rectangular in shape, several inches long, and an inch wide—the kind used to store buttons or keys—fell out onto my lap. I pulled the sheet of stationary out. It was personalized with Jonas' name on top, and his thick European scrawl in blue fountain pen beneath:

Dear Daniel,

There were things I could not tell you. Things that happened long ago before and after you were born. The bank accounts they are yours now. The key it is for a safe deposit box in your name at the Lake Forest Bank and Trust. You will know what to do. You must be careful who you can trust. Take care of the car. Keep it clean. Think of me when you drive it! Always remember you are from Lithuania! I am very proud because you will be President!

Jonas

I sat in Jonas' Town Car, dumbstruck—holding that note in one hand and the envelope with the safe deposit box key in the other in complete disbelief.

Jonas wrote like he spoke. His punctuation and grammar weren't perfect. He jumped from subject to subject in run-on sentences. I

31

couldn't help but smile as I read it; and while I was intrigued, I was also taken aback by what he'd written, and in such a cryptic way.

I read his note again. The only new information was sandwiched between the Jonas "Toryisms" in his note:

...The key it is for a safe deposit box in your name, at the Lake Forest Bank and Trust. You will know what to do. You must be careful who you can trust....

The existence of a safe deposit box didn't surprise me, but why hadn't it been mentioned in his will? With so much money—a few million dollars-plus already in the mix, the last two sentences about me knowing what to do, and being careful who I trusted...well, that's when I started to get nervous.

CHAPTER 10

I SAT IN THIS DINER on Western Avenue in Lake Forest, thinking about Jonas and my mother and father…the photograph of them all together. It was from a different time that seemed completely foreign to me. Back when my father was alive, and when my mother and Jonas were actually communicating with one another.

I found myself wondering again why Mom and Jonas never talked much. For me, it was a recurrent question. Whenever I would ask either of them, they would shrug and manage to change the subject to something else—usually they would talk about my father—how much he loved me, what a good man he was, and the sacrifices he made to bring us here, to Chicago. But neither Jonas nor Mom would ever say anything critical about the other.

As I sat there contemplating their relationship with one another, I realized that the only thing that connected them at all was my father, Lucas Tory: Jonas' older brother…my mother's only husband…and the father I never knew.

That thought was interrupted by the sudden flashing and clicking of camera lights by two paparazzi in the diner—point blank—as I sat there with my coffee. I wasn't prepared for them, and for a moment I sat there a bit bewildered, and the whole diner was looking back at me wondering what the commotion was all about. When I finally realized who those folks were, I got up, put a five-dollar bill on the table, and rushed out to the Town Car as they followed me, cameras snapping and flashing in rapid succession.

I drove for a while, past Jonas' house, past my mother's house, and eventually ditched all of the paparazzi following me. That's when I ended up in the parking lot of the Lake Forest Bank and Trust.

CHAPTER 11

"This way, Mr. Tory," the tall bank officer said with a smile. Her eyes were bright green, and friendly. A brunette with short, dark brown hair, she walked in long, fast-paced strides. "Jonas has told us about you."

"He did?" I asked, visibly surprised.

She nodded. "When he put your name down as an authorized key holder to his box."

"And when was that?"

She shrugged lightly. Her smile was easy and open. "About a month ago, I suppose," she said, walking beside me with a larger key. "He keeps trying to connect us, you know."

I was surprised, but shouldn't have been. That was just like Jonas, using his nephew as an excuse to meet a beautiful girl. But I had to admit; in this case, I couldn't blame him. I guessed she was in her early-thirties, elegantly dressed in a black designer business suit. Her features were soft. Refined. As she walked, she carried herself professionally and confidently.

"Sorry about that," I answered. "Sometimes Jonas couldn't help himself."

She stopped in mid-stride and looked over at me with a concerned look. "You're talking about him in the past tense."

She didn't know.

"I'm sorry, what's your name?" I asked her quietly.

"Robin," she answered. "Robin Nielsen."

I nodded slowly and spoke softly. "Robin, Jonas died a week ago." I saw her eyes widen with distress and genuine surprise.

"I had no idea—" Robin Nielsen exclaimed, and I could see her tears beginning to well up. "I'm so sorry, I—"

No one reads the obituaries any more, Danno! Jonas' always said that every morning I would bring him the paper.

I stood there feeling pretty helpless—right there, in the middle of the bank, breaking the news of Jonas' passing to a complete stranger, albeit a strikingly beautiful one, and consoling her. Jonas had to be looking down and laughing. *"You see, Daniel? You see what I do for you? I save the best for you for last! Ha!"*

"It was sudden, he died in his sleep…he didn't suffer at all."

Robin Nielsen nodded, and continued to walk slightly ahead of me, toward the bank safe in silence, doing her best to conceal her tears.

"We would have coffee together sometimes at the diner across the street before the bank opened," she said, still composing herself. "In fact, that's where we met." She inserted her key into the barred gate and opened it. "He was my friend, Mr. Tory. I always enjoyed his visits."

"Daniel," I heard myself say. "Please call me Daniel."

She nodded and smiled. "He talked about you often, you know. He was very proud of you."

"Well, I was proud to be his nephew. He was like a father to me." I paused for a second and turned to her. "Can I ask you how often Jonas came here? To access this box?"

"Just about every day," Robin said matter-of-factly. "Throughout the week and on Saturdays. Every time, he would tell me that he had something new for you to put into it, for safekeeping"

She led me inside the safe lined with safe deposit boxes. There was a large table in the center. She pointed at one of the large boxes directly in front of me.

"That's it. Box 1754. You first," she said, gesturing to my key.

I inserted the key and turned it, and Robin reciprocated with her bank key. She pulled the box out effortlessly, like a drawer and handed it to me.

Unprepared for the dead weight, I nearly dropped the box. Robin's eyes betrayed some level of amusement, as she caught hold of the box and assisted me in placing it on the table.

"Okay. I'm impressed," I said, meaning it.

She laughed and shook her head. "I've been lifting this box for Jonas for quite a long time—I know how heavy it is," she said with a soft laugh, then pointed at a series of three doors opposite me. "We have several rooms here in the vault to provide you some privacy."

I lifted the box, intrigued by its weight and what could possibly be inside it. But I also found myself distracted—and captivated by Robin Nielsen.

CHAPTER 12

AS I LIFTED THE LID on that safe deposit box, I felt like I was being transported to another place and another time. The familiar dusty, musty scent of Jonas' attic wafted up toward me. Looking down, I saw the mass of antique medals, all pinned to a cloth-covered piece of cardboard. Many of the medals were crosses, suspended by colorful striped ribbons. I touched one at random. It was a silver cross with an anchor forming the letters "P" and "W". Flipping the medal over, I found the inscription, *1939 ARMIA KRAJOWA 1945.* Another had a red ribbon bordered in white, with a circular bronze medal and Maltese cross.

Many more. Row after row of them. The thing that immediately struck me was that they weren't all from Lithuania, but from Poland, Estonia, and Latvia and probably a few other countries.

I carefully set the medals on the table, to the side of the box.

The next layer, underneath those medals, was a legal size book bound in what was now well worn, if not crushed, reddish suede. Hesitating only a moment, I opened the cover and saw the handwriting in an old-style Lithuanian script—all in a faded blue fountain pen. The date on the first page, as best as I could tell, was June 15, 1940.

Glancing over at the inside cover, I saw a photo of a man holding a Thompson Submachine Gun in a field, with a forest and bunker as the backdrop. There was a name printed boldly at the top left: **Lucas Tory.**

The features of the man in the photo were angular. His eyes were steady and self-confident. I stared at the photo in disbelief for a very long time, but the resemblance to Jonas…and to me was unmistakable.

Reflexively—suddenly—I shut the book. With my hand still on the cover, I sat back in the chair. My heart was racing and my skin was tingling. I'm not sure what I was expecting, but I can say with certainty that I wasn't ready for this. And at that moment, for the first time in my life, I felt a personal resentment build up toward Jonas. If this was what I thought it was, there was simply no excuse. All these decades, I'd known him, asking him and my mother about my father, they'd never told me about a journal, or a diary, or a personal record of any kind from the man himself.

Never.

I sat there in disbelief. How could you reconcile an omission like that?

Whatever it was—diary, journal or just a bunch of notes—it was sitting right there beside a mass of World War II medals and decorations that, I also suspected, belonged to my father. I felt a kind of sensory overload overcome me. I honestly just wanted to lock that box back up, run away from it forever, and go back to life as it was only a week ago. Jonas must have anticipated that reaction because when I looked down I saw an old black and white photograph in a wax paper envelope as the next layer.

Sliding the photograph out of the envelope, I recognized the face of my mother first. She was smiling, standing beside a child, a year or so old, and two other men, one was Jonas—the other was my father. No Soviet uniforms, no guns. They were standing outside in front of a large cathedral. Flipping the photograph over, there was a faded inscription in Jonas' handwriting:

Lietuvo, 10 Juni 1960

Well, any thought that the child could be me was immediately eliminated with that inscription because I was born a year and a half later, in 1962. December 7, 1962, to be exact. And the clothing the child was wearing looked distinctly like a little girl's.

My world was spinning. *Hard.* The revelation that I might have a sibling out there—somewhere—was just too much for me to fathom. A whole host of thoughts raced through my mind—maybe the baby didn't survive? Was it a boy or girl? Why didn't my mother tell me I had a brother or sister?

Perhaps the answers to those questions were in the safe deposit box, I thought. A single manila envelope was the only thing that remained in the box. The final layer. My hands were shaking as I pulled the envelope out and opened it. Five small books of varying dimensions and colors fell onto the table. All seemed brand new, in contrast to the other contents in the box. The embossed labels on the books should have been the first indicator of what these books were, but I really wasn't thinking straight at the time, so I failed to make the correlation.

> *The Swiss Credit Bank, Zurich*
> *The Union Bank of Switzerland*
> *The Bank Leu (AG), Zurich*
> *The Swiss Bank Corporation, Basel*
> *The Swiss Volksbank, Berne*
> *Lombard Odier - Geneva Private Bank*

I opened up the first book and it was then that I realized I was staring at a passbook for a bank account. A Swiss bank account, to be exact. And it was made out in my name as the account holder. Flipping the page, I saw the account balance and suddenly felt all of the air being pulled out of that small room.

CHAPTER 13

1,500,000,000 EU...
1,750,000,000 EU...
1,250,000,000 EU...

I flipped each passbook furiously, in complete disbelief...

2,250,000,000 EU...
1,350,000,000 EU...

This was some kind of joke, right? It had to be, because even the idea that any Tory was a billionaire many times over, complete with Swiss Bank accounts, seemed completely ludicrous.

We were Lithuanian émigrés, residents of Lake Forest: hard-working, everyday Americans who played Bingo on Friday nights, Backgammon on our porches and the lottery on Wednesdays and Saturdays. That's about as wild as we ever got, so sitting there in that room surrounded by billion Euro Swiss bank account balances, old photos, and a hand written journal explaining the secrets of a family I thought I knew, was well beyond the fray of being remotely conceivable.

What made it all worse was that I really had no one to talk to about any of it. I had a very small campaign staff that I was trying to transform into a congressional staff, and a ton of campaign donors who I didn't really know. Jonas was gone, paparazzi were trying to find me around every street corner, and my mother was in the hospital in an induced coma. Truth be told—I was a complete mess.

I shoved everything into my briefcase and walked out of the room. For a moment I just stood there, and everything was swirling around me—customers, tellers, conversations, the giant bank safe, desks, security. I began to feel faint, and just as I was about to collapse, I heard a voice.

"Mr. Tory?" It was Robin Nielsen. She was smiling, and somehow, I realized, she had a calming effect on me. "Are you okay?"

I tried to smile back and managed a slight nod, trying not to embarrass myself by collapsing on the floor. "Yeah," I said. "I'm fine." She was obviously concerned, and in her concern I saw a real beauty that transcended the physical. "I'm fine," I repeated. "Thanks."

"Would you like us to secure your safe deposit box?"

I shook my head. "No, you can close the account. But..."

I hesitated, and Robin looked at me to finish the statement, as I struggled to find the words. When they came, the delivery seemed awkward and desperate.

"I was wondering...would you have dinner with me tonight?"

She shook her head slowly, with a genuine, apologetic smile. "I'm afraid I can't."

I nodded and smiled briefly. "Of course, I understand."

That "Bachelor of the Year" title isn't helping me much...

I thanked her, and walked out the door, as quickly as I could.

I set the briefcase down in the backseat of the Town Car, and sat there for a while, trying to breathe normally.

After a minute or two, I heard Robin Nielsen's voice calling my name. I looked up and saw her walking to the curb.

"I am free tonight, after all, Mr. Tory—if the invitation still stands?"

I smiled with a measure of relief that, I think, took me by surprise. She handed me a business card:

Robin Nielsen Translations
English-Lithuanian-Polish-Russian
847-555-1212

"Languages are my first love," she said, anticipating my question. Gesturing at the bank, she continued. "The day job pays the bills."

I held up the card. "I'll call you," I replied.

CHAPTER 14

WE WALKED IN TO Chicago's Alinea Restaurant, Paparazzi-free. It was the first time I'd been there, but it's always been listed in the "Best Restaurants" and I wanted to go. Getting a same-day reservation at one of the world's best restaurants was a different story though.

"I'm afraid we have no open tables this evening," the scheduler answered, when I called.

When you don't get what you want, never take "No" as the final answer.

Jonas' advice was what guided me to run for Congress as an Independent when the other two parties turned me down.

"This is Congressman Daniel Tory, could I speak to the owner?"

"One moment, please, Sir," came the immediate response.

A male voice this time. "Congressman? I'm very sorry for the delay. We have a table reserved for you at 7PM. We look forward to seeing you tonight."

That was really the first time I experienced the power of a congressional seat, and the effect was both instantaneous and impressive. Somehow, I didn't think things would always be that easy, but I was grateful that it worked this time. My world, or at least its facade, had been turned around, and I looked forward to a much-needed distraction, as well as having someone genuine to talk to that night.

There's a good reason why Alinea is rated as one of the world's best restaurants. From the moment you walk in, you feel like you've been placed into a cocoon—your own private universe where you're safe and well taken care of. Our Maître'D greeted us at the entrance and expressed his condolences for Jonas' passing, in Lithuanian. I didn't answer at first because I was so surprised—so Robin did, in fluent Lithuanian.

"*Jono konservatorių buvo didis žmogus. Mes praleisti jį labai daug.*" Robin said, and then repeated in English for my benefit, "Jonas Tory was a great man. We miss him very much."

"I'm impressed," I told her. "Jonas would have been too."

"Thank-you," Robin replied, with a smile. "That's very high praise—from both of you."

As we were seated, I asked the Maître D' to bring out two of their better bottles of wine in their inventory, one red and one white.

Order a red and a white, Danno, and you cover all your bases. The wines help you travel in time...they make dinner an event to remember.

We talked about Jonas throughout dinner. Jonas was the common ground between us, and she was genuinely interested in hearing about him. She listened to all of my stories, and asked questions. And, of course, the wine didn't hurt. A 1984 Romanee Conti and a 2000 Marquis de LaGuiche Chassagne Montrachet. Exceptional and very expensive, but, as Jonas promised, they did indeed helped to make it an evening to remember. In many ways, it marked the beginning of a series of cascading events that I could never have predicted.

We ordered the tasting menu and over the next seven courses, I learned about Robin Nielsen. I learned that as a young girl she and her parents had emigrated from Lithuania in 1990 as soon as the Berlin Wall came tumbling down. And that she had graduated from the University of Chicago with degrees in Russian Studies, and in Bank Administration.

"My mother raised me to love languages, and my father insisted that I study business. So dual Russian Studies-Banking Administration majors were our compromise." She smiled with green eyes like liquid crystal, sipping the wine from her glass.

"A romantic mother and a pragmatic father," I observed.

She nodded. "My father was never in a hurry for me to get married. Independence and freedom were always the family mantra growing up. I suspect it was the same for you?"

I hesitated—turning the stem of my wine glass several times. It smelled wonderful. "My family has always been rich on old world philosophy, but I'm only now learning that transparency was never their strong suit."

"Well, you know, we East Euros are always more opaque than we like to admit."

I pulled out the old journal that I found in the safe deposit box and set it on the table. "It's some kind of diary that Jonas left for me. I think it was my father's."

"You haven't spoken about your father tonight."

I shook my head. "I never knew him. But I get the distinct feeling Jonas is introducing him to me now." I handed the book to her. "It's all handwritten in Lithuanian."

"This was in the safe deposit box?"

I nodded. "Among other things."

She shook her head and smiled. "Every time he would come to the bank to access the box, he would tell me he was bringing more things for you." She carefully opened the cover of the journal. After a moment of looking through the pages in the dim light, she looked up at me, eyes wide. "This was written sixty-five years ago!"

I nodded. "I saw it for the first time today at the bank. I never knew it existed."

"Would you like me to translate it for you?" she asked directly.

"All afternoon I've been debating whether to ask you," I answered. "This has been sitting with Jonas' for half a century, and he doesn't show it to me until now, after he's gone."

Robin nodded. "I'm sure he had a reason for waiting."

"With Jonas, who knows?" I said. "Honestly, it scares the hell out of me."

"I'd be honored to translate it," she said. "Whenever you're ready."

The sommelier approached again with a bottle of Chateau d'Yquem, and after presenting it to me, poured a small amount to sample.

Jonas used to call this Sauternes, *Liquid Gold*, and after tasting it, it was perhaps the perfect description. I asked the waiter to pour himself a glass.

"Simply the best there is," the waiter stated matter-of-factly, as he poured both glasses.

Robin and I touched glasses again. She proposed the toast in Lithuanian, *"Su šeima."*

"To family," I repeated, in English. "When times were good."

"Pardon me?" Robin asked.

"Something Jonas would often say," I explained.

"Well, if Jonas were here, I'd tell him times are pretty good right now," Robin said, laughing. Her smile and laugh were relaxed, like everything about her.

"Oh, he's here with us," I said with a smile. "He definitely hears you. And he approves of the wine, as well as the company."

Robin raised her glass. "To the best of times, then."

CHAPTER 15

WE BOTH HAD MORE WINE than either of us anticipated that night. We left my car parked at the restaurant, and Uber'd back to Lake Forest. As we pulled up to her apartment, I stepped out and reached out for her hand.

"Thank-you for a great evening," I said.

"You're stealing my lines," she scolded with a smile.

I held out the journal to her, and put it into her hand. "If you could translate this, I'd be grateful."

She put her other hand over it. "Of course."

"And just so we're clear, you're not doing this *pro bono.*"

"Now you're sounding like an attorney," she replied, with a laugh. "It may take a little while, but I'll start right away."

I handed her a card with my personal contact information, normally reserved for the large financial contributors to my campaign. "It's all a plot to get you to go out to dinner again."

"I'd like that very much," she replied, holding up the book and the card, and walking away. "Goodnight."

I admit that, at that moment, I was intrigued. Intrigued and intoxicated—not necessarily a great combination as far as leveraging the best judgment. When I got back into the Uber car, I must have given the driver my mother's home address rather than my own, because that's where I ended up—at her house, fumbling around the porch for the spare key she kept under a flower pot there. There were three flowerpots, and as fate would have it, I found it under the last one—the one I dropped, and that shattered in a thousand pieces in front of the doorway.

The next morning, I awoke in the living room, still in my suit and with the kind of headache God would smite you with in the Book of Leviticus.

They say your life is punctuated with seminal moments— moments that spur you into action. Life-defining, scare-the-shit-out-of-you moments that you never forget. Well, I can say with certainty, this was one of them.

Maybe it was waking up with the same familiar surroundings, where nothing had changed since I had left home to go to college.

I stood up and walked into the bathroom. Glancing at the mirror, I winced. My haggard appearance only touched the surface. All of the money I just found out I'd inherited didn't matter to me—what really mattered was that I had no real understanding of my family's past, and there was the additional guilt of having been on a date the previous night while my mother was in a coma a few miles away. Waking up in her house in a complete, hung-over state only added to the surreal events of the past two days.

"Who are you?" I muttered out loud, looking into my own bloodshot eyes.

That was the big question that nagged at me now, following Jonas' death; and yet, what really frightened me was that I didn't have a good answer. So, at that moment, I made up my mind to learn about my family's past, and to find out who I really was.

CHAPTER 16

MY CELL PHONE RANG during my drive home. I was surprised to hear Robin Nielsen's voice on the other end. I thought I'd be the one calling to apologize for conduct unbecoming a future Congressman. In stark contrast to my own pounding headache and nausea, though, she sounded fresh and upbeat.

"Sorry for all the wine last night—it was way too much."

She laughed. "It was a great evening, and the wines were incredible."

"While I'm sure Jonas would have approved of their quality, even he would have stopped before we did."

"All night, I had the feeling he was with us, and was also enjoying our conversation," she replied, laughing. "A fitting way to celebrate his life."

"Yeah, lately, I feel like he's been communicating to me—in riddles."

There was an extended pause on the other end of the line, and I thought we'd been disconnected.

"I woke up early this morning and began translating the book you gave me. I'm only several pages into it, and not all of it is legible, but I think you should read what I've been able to translate so far."

"Can you give me a preview?"

"I wouldn't do it justice," Robin replied. "But you were correct. It's a journal, and it's an amazing story."

CHAPTER 17

SITTING THERE AT MY KITCHEN TABLE, her fresh appearance stood in stark contrast to my own. While I managed to change clothes, that was all I'd done. I brewed coffee with my French press.

"You look a bit rough, Congressman," she laughed.

"Coffee has been proven to solve all known problems," I replied, serving her. "One cup at a time."

"Indeed," she smiled, taking a sip. "Can I ask you something?"

"Sure," I said, sitting in the chair across from her.

"Why don't you have a hundred people here getting you ready to go to Washington?" She asked. "You don't act like you're in a hurry. Most people would be."

"I think I'm trying to figure out for myself how to go from campaigning twenty four hours a day to actually being a member of Congress," I answered.

"They're two entirely separate skills, I suppose."

I nodded. "I can campaign in my sleep, but legislating is completely different, and don't tell anyone, but I have no idea where to begin."

Robin smiled. "You seem to have a pretty good idea of who you are, and you have your priorities in place. That's all you need. You'll figure the rest out."

I looked out the window, still feeling the pounding in my head. "Well, that's the problem," I replied. "The truth is, I really don't know

51

who I am, because everything I thought I knew about my family was based on incomplete information."

"So how can you possibly say, 'this is what I stand for,' when you have no idea who you really are?" she asked rhetorically.

"Yes," I answered. "Exactly."

"The good news is that you've already been elected."

"Obviously, I put the cart before the proverbial horse," I said, taking in the coffee.

"It's true," Robin said. "That our families are pretty central to who we are— their history, their values, their struggles, successes and their failures—they're our foundation. I know mine is."

"Tell me," I said.

"About what?" She asked, momentarily confused.

"Your family."

She paused. "Nothing like yours, I'd say. What they have in common is that they're Lithuanian émigrés who came to Chicago because they had extended family already here," she explained. "Dad was a finance professor, and my mom was one of his students." She laughed. "They don't talk about it much, except that when the Wall came down, they took the first opportunity to come to America to start over. Dad took a job as a bank teller, and Mom stayed home and took care of my brother and me."

"Finance and banking run in the family then?" I asked.

She shrugged. "I grew up around it, so I suppose it came naturally."

"How much did your parents share with you about their lives growing up?"

"Some—but I know not everything," she answered. "I've been able to pick up a lot of their history by tracing our genealogy. A lot of what I've learned are in conversations, stray comments, and photographs that turn up. You can't completely erase the past."

"That may be my own issue," I said. "All this time my family history was hidden around me, in plain sight—I just didn't pay attention."

Robin pointed at the pages she had translated. "That should provide you with some insights at least."

June 15, 1940 – *Today, Russia's tanks entered Vilnius. Their planes flew low over our farm. Dark smoke billowed in the distance from targets we could not see. Artillery pieces ring our beloved city. Only yesterday, Germany invaded Paris and with such a coincidence we cannot help but believe that these invasions are connected. Vilnius radio says Russia has also invaded Latvia and Estonia. The Bolsheviks are invading Poland, and all of the Baltic states—Estonia, Latvia and Lithuania. I see mother cry and father consoling her, telling her that everything will be fine for us, that this is something that concerns the politicians, not us. Mother does not answer him, she only continues to sob and ask how it will affect us, the children. She asks him: How can the politicians protect us?*

June 17, 1940 – *We hear the sounds of artillery and tank fire echo through the countryside. A bomb landed not far from us at an intersection on the roadway and left a large crater. We see refugees on the road, coming from Vilnius. A few at first, but now there are many more on foot with horse drawn carts and baskets, and a few trucks and cars.*

July 26, 1940 - *Father tells Jonas and I to help him fill the storage rooms with food that will keep for a long time. When those above ground are filled with beets and potatoes and corn, we build more underground storage rooms where more food and canned goods can be kept. Father tells us that they can also act as shelters to protect our family if the war reaches beyond Vilnius to our farm. I start to believe that he knows more about what is happening than he tells either myself, Jonas or Mother because when we believe we have built enough shelters, he finds another spot to build one. But the others we build are in the forest, far away from our farm. Spread apart, always by a riverbed, dense with brush. My hands become blistered and more calloused every day as we work into the night, and our backs ache from digging and carrying earth and supplies constantly. We smell like raw earth and our hands are sticky from the tree sap. Some of the storage rooms are nothing more than shallow holes. Others are large rooms with timber frames that take much longer to build. We camouflage them all so they are undetectable. I am worried about Jonas because he has a cough. I tell father, but he tells me we have no choice. We must continue to work. Not just for ourselves, but for Lithuania, he says.*

It's the first time I hear any mention of fighting for Lithuania. And the first time I hear of a larger purpose than protecting our farm and our family.

July 30, 1940 – A group of men have come to the farm today to visit my father. They are speaking for a long time in the barn. Neither Jonas nor I have ever met or seen these men before. They are not soldiers or farmers. Listening to them when they introduce themselves to father, I tell Jonas I believe they are Lithuanian and Polish, and one of the men is American. We are both very glad that they aren't Russian. In the evening, the men leave. Father tells us that they will return tomorrow, and that we will have much work to do when they arrive, so we should rest.

August 1, 1940 – When the men show up this time, they come in the nighttime with trucks—six of them. After a short conversation, father directs Jonas to guide the first two trucks to the closest storage locations we had built over the previous weeks. He tells me to guide the next two trucks to the eastern locations. Father brings the last two trucks to the western locations. We do not ask questions. His final order to us is to be back at the farm by midnight. I drive in the truck with two men, one Lithuanian, and the other from Boston in the United States. They do not talk much, but they are friendly. I notice that both carry pistols behind their belts. I point out the turns and soon we are in the forest. The first storage site I guide them to is a hidden cave. When they open the back of the truck, I see the boxes. Long and short wood boxes. The American tells me what these boxes contained and the caches that we created would help us regain our freedom. "Compliments of President Roosevelt," he says. From curiosity, I ask him what is inside the boxes. Without saying another word, he takes a lever and removes the wooden top from some of the boxes in front of me.

And then I understand what he is telling me: the long boxes are filled with rifles, wrapped in wax paper and a kind of sticky oil, and the short ones are packed with grenades—hundreds of them, stacked like eggs.

I set the notepad down, and looked over at Robin, in what must have been a shocked expression.

"Your family has lived quite a life," she said, simply.

"Jonas used to tell me, 'we are all a product of our past. Remember always that you are Tory. Tory's are tough.'"

"But you didn't realize just how tough you were?" she smiled back at me across her kitchen table.

"Something like that." I ran my fingers through my hair and thumbed randomly through my father's journal. I was amazed at how neat the handwriting was, all in faded ink—some entries in black, some in blue. There were smudges here and there and the ink was faded, but there were very few scratch-outs or corrections to his almost perfect cursive handwriting. "Would you continue translating it?" I said, turning to her again. "I'll pay you."

"Of course," she replied, smiling. "But this is *pro bono*."
In the midst of everything that was happening it came to me as a sort of epiphany then that I needed help. And I needed it now.

Robin sat down beside me, and looked at the journal and back up at me with sympathetic eyes and an understanding voice. "I'd like to help, if I can."

I was somewhat embarrassed that with a family of native speakers, I had never learned to speak Lithuanian fluently. I could understand it reasonably well when my mother or Jonas spoke it to me, but that was about it. And yet, I still hesitated—the knowledge that I was possibly holding several *billion* dollars in Swiss bank accounts, with no knowledge of their origin, or how to access them—was strange, if not worrisome. It occurred to me that because everything was in a safe deposit box, no one else around me knew about that inheritance, but me. And whom exactly can you trust with something like that? I wasn't really sure, but it seemed Jonas had arranged for me to meet

Robin for a reason. Like everything was scripted by him.

"Feel free to say 'No' at any time—okay?" I began haltingly. "I just got elected to this congressional seat a little over a week ago, and in the midst of everything that's happened, I haven't even begun to hire a staff. If you'd be willing, I was wondering if you'd be the first?"

"A cast member in, *Daniel Tory goes to Washington?*" Robin Nielsen said with a wry smile. "Sounds entertaining."

"Well, it's hardly destined to be a Frank Capra film, and I'm no Jimmy Stewart," I replied. "But that's one thing I can promise you—it won't be boring."

She laughed. "I have no political experience to speak of."

I shook my head. "There's an argument out there that lack of political experience is actually an advantage in Washington."

"Special Banking Assistant to the Congressman from Illinois?" She said laughing. "I'm not sure you need one of those."

"Chief of Staff would be a good title," I said.

Robin shook her head slightly, looking down. "I've never worked on the Hill."

"It's not a requirement," I replied. "Right now, I'm honestly more concerned about operations than policy. "More than a few folks have told me that it's easier to run for office than to run the office. I'm under pressure from campaign donors to hire their sons and daughters and cousins by marriage, and what I need is someone who can create good clear decision-making and communications processes, while keeping me organized and moving forward."

"Can an Independent ever be organized?" She countered, smiling.

"*Touché*," I answered, raising my index finger. "Keeping me organized is a full-time job, and maybe an impossible task. But you could begin by helping me navigate one slight detour."

"Detour?"

I lifted my father's journal from the table. "This journal, and a few other things over the last few days have all made me realize I really don't know my own family—at least the way I thought I did." I paused and put the diary down. "So, I'm going to hop on a plane to Europe to find out what I can before my swearing-in."

"You want me to arrange your trip?" she asked.

"I'd like you to come along," I answered, shaking my head and taking a sip of wine. "I'm not sure how to do this by myself—and your genealogy skills would come in handy."

"I'll have to think about it." Robin's eyes were wide. In her voice I detected not only surprise, but also a level of measured excitement.

"Of course," I answered.

"Okay," she said after a moment.

"Okay?" I asked.

"I've thought about it," Robin said, smiling broadly. "When do we leave?"

CHAPTER 18

WE ALL HAVE CHOICES IN LIFE. *Our choices help us grow.*
Jonas told me that more times than I can count. But those words
never meant much until I made the choice to drop everything that I
was required to do as a newly elected United States Congressman.

Those tasks far exceed anything I was prepared for—mainly
because I hadn't given them much thought: search for a place to live
in D.C., make the move from Lake Forest, and set up congressional
home offices in Illinois. What I really found out was that there's no real
roadmap to how you go about being a congressman.

So, I felt as if I was the dog that just caught his tail.

Congratulations. You're a congressman. Now what?

The truth is, you're on your own. I received a large package in
the mail that provided me with lots of information—only some of it
very useful. What it did tell me is that each Congressman has an office
budget of about $3 Million or so when you count it all up, including
travel. You have a set amount of money you can spend on your staff,
and there aren't any left and right limits on how you spend it. In the
House of Representatives, you can't hire more than 18 people, and you
can't pay any one person more than $170,000. Beyond that, you can
divvy up the money any way you like. You can give some staff higher
raises than others. You can hire fewer staff and pay all of them more;
or you can hire more staff and pay each less. It's all left up to you as
the congressman-elect to decide—just don't blow your budget was the
clear implication.

The rest of the package was filled with rules and regulations about ethics, legislative procedure, committees, the layout of the Capitol—essentially, Congress 101. While I'm sure it was standard procedure and a desire to be efficient, it was all just bureaucratic overload for me at the time. I had hundreds of resumes from people looking for jobs, with more flooding in daily. I had a few hundred emails in my inbox that I hadn't even looked at. It was overwhelming. So, I just stopped answering my phone. I kept up appearances, but behind the scenes, I felt like I was drowning.

There was also the small matter of inheriting all of that money from Jonas, most of which was apparently sitting in Swiss bank accounts. The question that kept nagging at me, in addition to where the money came from, was why those accounts weren't mentioned in Jonas' will? So, before I was sworn into Congress, I thought it might be a good idea to find out, rather than risk becoming tomorrow's headline in *The Washington Post* or *The Drudge Report*:

Freshman Congressman and Most Eligible Bachelor is World's Richest Man.

At the end of the day, I just needed to get my head straight. Hiring Robin Nielsen as my Chief of Staff, and buying those plane tickets to Zurich were only the beginning steps.

CHAPTER 19

AS IT TURNED OUT, we didn't need airplane tickets to go to Geneva. When I went through all of the contents of the safe deposit box again, an envelope fell out of one of the Swiss bank passbooks. Inside, I found a pamphlet and business card for the Chicago Executive Airport and a bill of sale, made out in my name, for a Boeing 787—paid in full, and dated only three months previous. When I called the number on the card, I was placed on hold for several minutes before a confident, professional voice belonging to the manager of the airport, Frank Ippolito, answered.

"Congressman, we've been expecting your call."

I didn't immediately respond, more out of plain ignorance than from the shock I was already experiencing from the previous days' revelations.

"Please help me understand," I began. "I just found a bill of sale in my name for a jet that appears to be parked at your airport, that I had no idea existed, until now."

I heard Frank Ippolito's calm, slightly amused voice on the other end. "Jonas warned me I might get that kind of reaction from you—he said the Dreamliner was going to be a surprise gift to you."

"Well, he achieved that goal," I answered. "Is this a fractional ownership—what exactly?"

"Full ownership, Congressman," Frank replied immediately. "It's all yours, for your exclusive use, anytime you want to use it, notwithstanding the weather. And it comes with a pilot, co-pilot and jet fuel on contract, purchased for a full year."

"Can it fly internationally?"

"Depending, of course, where you'd like to go and the time it takes to secure flight clearances— it's meant to fly intercontinentally," he answered. "It's brand new and fully customized by Lufthansa Technik. The best in the business."

"Can it fly to Geneva, Switzerland?" I asked.

"We'll need a few days to get the country clearances, but Geneva has the longest runway in Europe, so it's likely doable. We'll begin work on those now, if you want to go there."

"Okay, you gotta tell me," I said finally. "This isn't some kind of elaborate joke, or initiation ritual on Candid Camera?"

"No joke. You're really the proud owner of a Boeing 787 Dreamliner," he replied enthusiastically. "And we're honored to be maintaining it for you."

We left two days later, once the pilots were able to get all of the flight clearances to Europe. Privately, I had done my own due diligence to ensure that the Dreamliner really was mine, and not a favor from someone else who would be expecting some kind of payback. It still seemed far too bizarre to accept—but so did everything else over the past week.

Robin took a leave of absence from the bank; and that morning, she thought we were heading to Chicago's O'Hare Airport. As we got closer, I told her that we'd be taking a private jet. I knew I'd have some explaining to do once we arrived at the smaller Chicago Executive Airport.

The first thing I heard from Frank was an apology for not realizing that Jonas had passed away, and how genuinely sad he was for losing one of their best clients. That statement alone was interesting to me—*Jonas? One the jet center's best customers?* I conveyed my own apology for not first informing him during our telephone conversation.

Inside the jet center, Frank introduced us to our pilots, Pat Moroney and Mike Ryan. They led us through a side door to a large, gleaming hangar with its bay doors open. Once we stepped inside, Robin and I both gasped.

CHAPTER 20

ABSOLUTELY INSANE, I THOUGHT.

The Dreamliner took up the entire expanse of that hangar. The gleaming, polished concrete floor made the jumbo airliner even more impressive as it reflected its image from below. It had a flowing tricolor red, white and blue scheme to it. Despite my great surprise, I had to smile, because I wouldn't have expected anything less from Jonas, with his patriotic approach to everything in life. But seeing a red, white and blue 787 that I had suddenly inherited, right in front of me—well, that familiar feeling of sensory overload returned, with a vengeance. I saw Robin looking over at me with a rather shocked expression that begged for an explanation. But at that moment, I really couldn't speak.

"It's a beauty, isn't it?" Frank said. "We're proud to be on your team, Congressman."

I nodded and pointed up at the behemoth in front of us. "Did Jonas ever fly in it?"

Frank shook his head. "The renovation was only recently completed, so unfortunately he didn't ever see it in its completed state, but I think he would've been pleased."

Robin grasped my arm as she walked beside me and whispered. "Daniel, this jet *belongs* to you?"

"So I'm told."

As we walked up the stairway, Robin was silent at first. "And *Jonas* had it built for *you*?"

I turned to her just before we walked through the cabin door.

63

"There's a lot I should be telling you right now, and I will once we're in the air."

Frank Ippolito's voice came from inside the cabin. "Come in!"

If there is such a thing as "New Airplane Scent," that's what we were greeted with as we entered the cabin.

Jonas would've liked this too, I thought.

Stepping onto the two-tone woven grey and black carpet, the first quarter of the interior had been transformed into a small movie theater and meeting room of sorts. An oversized TV screen hung on the wall with a line of single lie-flat leather swivel seats in front, and custom sofas upholstered with a modern dual blue and white swirl design. Mahogany circular tables were situated on each end with cushioned leather seats.

There was an extravagant white and wooden accented dome ceiling with recessed lighting and custom rectangular shaded slat windows on each side of the airplane. The next quarter of the aircraft had parquet flooring and a long conference table surrounded by black leather executive seats.

"This room was designed to be both a dining room and a conference room," Frank said. And then pointing up at a TV set that was rising up through a hidden compartment at the end of the table, he continued. "That's a Planar screen. It has full secure video teleconferencing capability while we're in the air. We're equipped with satellite Wi-Fi, so we can access any movie that is showing instantly through the Internet."

"And all supported by a full, world class galley at the front of the airplane near the cockpit—it can serve snacks, drinks or a full gourmet meal—whatever's required," Frank said.

As we continued to make our way to the rear of the aircraft, we passed by one of the bathrooms on the far end of the conference room. Equipped with a Sitka Spruce bowl sink, crystal mirror, enclosed by white marble walls, it bore no resemblance to any of the commercial airlines I was accustomed to flying.

The master bedroom was the *coup d' grace.* I never knew airplanes had bedrooms, but there it was: a queen bed, with a beige throw spread diagonally across one corner. The bedroom walls were padded with tapestry fabric and maple hardwood borders.

Behind a false wall, we walked into the master bathroom, fully equipped with "his and hers" sinks on very fancy Quartzite countertops, surrounded by custom maple cabinetry. The mirrors and lighting made the bathroom seem much larger than it was. A fully enclosed shower separated the sinks.

As we walked back to the front of the airplane, Frank stopped us in the conference room.

"All of this is impressive," he said. "But most impressive is the avionics package that was installed—it has all of the upgrades—an active gust alleviation system, forward looking infrared radar, and more. Jonas didn't spare any expense and what that translates to for you is a smooth, comfortable and very safe ride tomorrow."

I thanked Frank for the tour. He signaled to the pilots that we were ready to depart to Zurich. "4,000 miles and change to Geneva, Congressman. Your bags are in the master bedroom. You have two flight attendants that are available to you throughout the flight. They'll have you there in less than ten hours, and you'll have a car waiting for you upon your arrival. Enjoy!"

"I wasn't expecting this, Daniel," Robin said, sitting down beside me on the sofa of the airplane.

"Neither was I," I replied, trying to smile. "After all that's happened this past week, I wasn't sure what to expect—definitely not this."

"You asked me to work with you—I'm ready to do that, but for me to be effective you might want to share with me the things you haven't yet told me." She took a glass of ice water from the flight attendant. "Judging from the journal and this airplane, I suspect Jonas left you with a few surprises."

I nodded, and reached over to my briefcase and opened it. "This," I said, holding my hand out at the surrounding cabin, "is only the most recent surprise."

I handed her the pile of bankbooks, and pointed at them in her hand. "That's the biggest shock of all, and the real reason we're flying to Geneva."

She flipped open the first book, and turned a few of the pages before the balance fully registered, and the shocked expression he had been anticipating arrived.

"Daniel?" She suddenly began opening up each of the books with increasing speed. *"Oh .... My .... God."*

CHAPTER 21

"I THINK YOU NEED a Chief Financial Officer more than you need a Chief of Staff," Robin said directly.

"I'm not sure what I need at the moment," I answered, reaching over to the bar. "Except maybe some Scotch."

"Jonas really gave all this to you?" Robin asked in a loud whisper.

"So it appears," I answered.

I explained what I could of my family's history, and the false impressions that my family had either actively cultivated or passively allowed—to include the distinct possibility that I had a sister living somewhere in Eastern Europe, who I'd never met or known about. Robin listened intently, and I think what impressed me most was that she didn't speculate or judge—she just listened, asking simple questions along the way to help her understand, or to clarify.

At one point, I stopped talking just to find out what Robin was thinking. She leaned down to her backpack and lifted out her notepad and my father's leather-bound journal.

"Your father's journal entries read like something in a movie, Daniel," she said, handing the notebook to me. "I was able to translate a few more pages."

I leaned my head back in the leather chair and stared at the notebook. Sensing my anxiety at what those pages would contain, Robin got up to talk to our flight attendant and take another tour around the airplane.

I opened the notepad to the page she had marked.

August 14, 1940 – *An armed Lithuanian resistance is being formed, my father tells us. Jonas and I are excited that we will be partisans, but mother says it is too dangerous for us because we haven't had any military training. Father and she argue, he tells her that we are old enough to shoot and so we are old enough to resist the Russian invaders. Last night there was a meeting of the Lithuanian Freedom Army. Father is placed in charge of one of the regions in our district. He asks Jonas and me what we should name our detachment of partisans. We give him many names, but the name we like best is "Hawks," because we will attack aggressively and move swiftly. Father tells us we are his lieutenants, that [illeg] we must build our own band of partisans, and create our bunkers and command posts. Our farmstead is our first command post, our base, Father says, but soon we will need to abandon it and move elsewhere, into the woods. Mother does not know this yet, he says. He will be the one to tell her. Not us.*

August 24, 1940 – *Over the past week, we have had many men and a few women join our partisan unit. Over the radio, the news tells us that Lithuanian men born between 1908-1926 are subject to conscription in the Russian Army. Many of the men who join with us are Lithuanian soldiers who have hidden their weapons and find us once they learn that Father is leading the resistance in this district. We receive reports that the KGB have rounded up many of our government workers, reporters, teachers, and Army generals in Vilnius and jailed them. Father says he knows some of them. Today, we count more than 170 partisans who have joined us, and are awaiting orders to fight the Soviets. Mother is constantly cooking with the other women, peeling potatoes, preserving beans and making jam from raspberries and wild strawberries.*

August 30, 1940 – *Today we attacked the Zarasai jail to liberate our fellow Lithuanians who the Soviets had imprisoned there. With our group of 160 partisans, we killed the 12 Russian guards. Once inside the prison, we captured 28 automatic rifles, 40 grenades and a large amount of ammunition. 45 of our fellow Lithuanians who were in the cells are now partisan members. As we make our way back to the farm, we see a Soviet convoy approaching on the road. Father orders us to stop our trucks on the roadside. With hardly any time to prepare, we ambush them right there—killing the Soviet militia chief, another militiaman and four Soviet soldiers. As the leader of the Hawks, the men he liberated are now calling Father "The Wholf". Other partisans I meet have code names like "Diamond," "Black Peter," [illeg] and "Green Devil." Today was the first time I have killed another man. Jonas said he saw me kill at least five of the Russian soldiers. He tells everyone I am good at killing the enemy, a "natural Hawk." Father says he is proud of me. But when I think about it tonight, I feel a little bit sick and I can barely write this because my hands are still shaking. One of father's friends tells him that the NKVD know about us, and are now hunting us.*

September 1, 1940 – Father wakes us very early in the morning, and tells us that Jonas and I must leave the farm right away. He tells us that he has received a warning that armed Russian and militia units are conducting searches on the farmsteads, detaining Lithuanian men for conscription in the Soviet Army. When we get out of bed, ten of our Hawk partisans are waiting for us outside. We dress quickly and gather up our arms and ammunition. When it comes time to go, father says he and mother will meet up with us later in the forest. He explains that he is not of conscription age, and that he has to convince mother to leave the farm. Both mother and father hug Jonas and me, and we say goodbye. All four of us are crying when we leave. Tonight, we are deep in the forest, where we built our caches two months ago. Mother and father are not here yet, and I am very worried.

I took a deep breath and exhaled. Sensing that I had finished reading, Robin sat down in the sofa across from me.

I closed the notebook. "You know, I grew up in Chicago Lawn before moving to Lake Forest. Lived in a bungalow with my mom, grew up around all of the first generation, blue-collar immigrants from Lithuania and Poland. Went to an Ivy League school, became a lawyer and got elected to the United States Congress," I paused and took another sip of Scotch. "Whenever I'd see them, sitting around their poker tables, Jonas and the rest of his friends told me how proud they were of me. As a group, they were what defined 'Normal" for me."

Robin crossed her legs. "Your father's journal tells me that nothing about your family quite fits into what the rest of us would see as normal." She leaned forward, smiling and holding my father's leather diary in both hands. "And what's most surprising to me is that we're only at the beginning of his story."

That's when we felt the plane's wheels hit the runway at Geneva International Airport.

CHAPTER 22

AS WE STEPPED OFF THE AIRPLANE onto the air stairs, we looked down to see a small welcoming committee waiting for us on the tarmac.

Beside the Swiss customs agent, were two men in suits, a black Mercedes CL600 Coupe and chauffeur.

"Welcome to Geneva, Congressman Tory," one of the men announced, hand outstretched. "I am Rémy Recordon, Mayor of *Genève*."

The other man stepped forward, "Welcome, Congressman. I am Andre Vaissade, Manager of JetAviation. We are honored to host you."

I introduced Robin to both men as my chief of staff, as our bags were loaded into the Mercedes.

"You are staying at the Hotel President Wilson, Congressman," Vaissade said. "It is a marvelous hotel, and the Presidential Suite is known as the finest in the world."

I nodded. "Who made that reservation, may I ask?"

"The Tory Foundation has taken care of everything," Vaissade replied cheerfully. "They arranged for your car, as well. It will take you to the President Wilson directly."

I watched as our luggage was being loaded into the trunk of the Mercedes.

Rémy Recordon handed me a large envelope. "Congressman Tory, my wife and I would be honored to have you and Miss Nielsen to our home for dinner tonight, if you are available?"

I looked over at Robin, who was looking at me with an amused smile. I nodded slightly and shook his hand. "We'd be delighted, Mayor."

Recordan nodded. "Your driver knows the way. We will see you at 7 tonight then?"

Absently, I thanked him for the invitation as the Swiss customs agent approached and requested our passports. Following a cursory review, he stamped both passports and handed them back to us without comment.

Inside the car, I noticed Robin conducting a Google search on her cell phone. "It may interest you to know that the Tory Foundation has very good taste!"

"Well," I answered. "That's good to know, since I didn't have any idea we even had a foundation."

"Also good to know," Robin said with a tinge of sarcasm. "The hotel suite we're staying in is normally reserved for celebrities and heads of state."

"Obviously, they make exceptions during their off season," I quipped.

She continued to read the online description:

> "...The modern glass and steel suite occupies the entire top floor of the President Wilson Hotel, is just five minutes away from the United Nations Building and has spectacular views out over Lake Geneva toward Mont Blanc. There are four bedrooms, six bathrooms, a 26-seat dining room, a grand piano and a billiard table. At $73,000-a-night, the suite is a modern-day fortress. It has panic buttons, bulletproof windows and armored doors. Its features include a private elevator, internet Wi-Fi and a mini bar."

"Thank God for the mini bar," I replied dryly.

Robin continued the Google search on her iPhone. "And, Daniel?"

After a few moments, she looked up at me. We were passing by the United Nations Office. "There's no record of any 'Tory Foundation'—here, or anywhere."

CHAPTER 23

IF IT'S POSSIBLE FOR A FORTRESS to make you feel less secure, that's how I ultimately felt at the President Wilson Hotel.

Make no mistake, it's a great hotel and the suite is something to behold—an entire floor encased in bullet-proof glass, with 360-degree views of the lake and the surrounding pre-Alps. Nothing less than spectacular. And it had its own safe room, just in case everything went south quickly.

But I've always thought there's a difference between being protected and feeling secure—the physical doesn't always translate to the psychological. After 9-11, Jonas told me, *"Danno, one thing to remember about security. It's like oxygen—you only miss it when it's gone."*

As our luggage was being delivered, I heard a knock on the door to the master suite. It was Robin, and she had an envelope in her hands with "Tory Philanthropy, Ltd" emblazoned in bold black letters on the upper left corner.

"A message from our sponsors?" Robin asked smiling. "It was on the dining room table."

I looked at her with a curious expression, and took the envelope, hesitating only a moment before opening it.

The Tory Foundation
P.O Box 1002
1211 Geneva 12
Switzerland

Dear Congressman Tory:

Welcome to Genève! We are honored that you have taken the time to visit with us.

Please accept our deepest condolences for the passing of your uncle, Jonas Tory. Jonas was a great man—he was greatly admired, and we all miss him. We are delighted that he arranged for your visit with us.

You should know that Jonas spoke of you often, and was very proud of you.

We hope the accommodations are to your liking. Whenever Jonas would visit Geneva, he would stay in the Hotel President Wilson, in the same suite as you are now staying.

We look forward to meeting with you tomorrow at the Foundation's headquarters. A car will be waiting for you and Ms. Nielsen at 9:00AM tomorrow in front of your hotel.

Sincerely,

Laurent Abraham
Executive Director

I sat down on the corner of the bed, wanting to collapse from exasperation as much as from jetlag-induced exhaustion. I could practically hear Jonas now: *Danno! Welcome to my favorite hotel! Try the bed! Try the minibar! See the big lake!*

I exhaled and looked up at Robin. I handed the letter back to her. "What has Jonas gotten me into?"

When Robin finished reading, she looked over at me and smiled faintly.

"My mother always tells me, 'Shopping is cheaper than therapy.' I need a dress and shoes for tonight. Want to come along?"

CHAPTER 24

WE TOOK THE HOTEL'S SEDAN across the river to Geneva's version of Fifth Avenue: *Rue du Rhône.* The suit was easy to find at the Hugo Boss shop, and they volunteered to have it delivered to our hotel once they completed the alterations. As soon as we walked out of Hugo Boss, Robin told me that because her dress shopping would be a much more prolonged and tedious process than mine, that I should explore the town and she would meet me back at the hotel. I agreed, probably more quickly than I should have.

"Be sure to visit Patek Philippe's V.I.P. room," our driver said, as I stepped out of the car. "It has one of the very best views of Lake Geneva!"

Rue du Rhône is Geneva's shopping district—a kind of Swiss Rodeo Drive that has storefronts representing all the world's most famous brands—from Baume & Mercier and Franck Muller to Piaget, Rolex, and Vacheron Constantin.

At one point, as I turned a corner I realized that I was seeing some shoppers and pedestrians over and over again—in front of me, behind me and across the street.

You're being paranoid...

Maybe it was because I had become so sensitized to paparazzi over the past several months that I knew when I'd grown a tail. In this case, they were men and women. But their reflective sunglasses were the dead giveaway. It was like a cartoon.

Losing tails on foot was never something I was too adept at, but seeing the Patek Philippe Salons directly in front of me, I stepped inside quickly, hoping to find a back exit.

Inside, I found myself standing underneath an antique chandelier of grand proportions. On each side there were hardwood and glass showcases with Patek Philippe's signature collections of watches and jewelry pieces. There was a room in back—a showroom that had marble walls, more chandeliers, and several salesmen and women dressed in suits. Stopping, more to see if I had successfully eluded those following me, a salesman told me the elaborate room was where they showcase their "historic collection." Only half-listening, I realized there was no rear exit, as I had hoped.

I quickly took the elevator to the fifth floor with a few customers, hoping to establish some additional separation from those who had appeared to be tracking me.

The door opened to a rather amazing—and beautiful—art-deco suite with hardwood floors, contemporary art, oriental carpets, fancy tables and comfortable chairs. The view outside at Lake Geneva and the spectacular fountain—*the Jet d'Eau*—was breathtaking.

Just as I was appreciating the view, vases and mirrors and windows began to shatter around me.

My first instinct was that it was an earthquake, except that the walls weren't moving, and the floor wasn't shifting. Everyone just seemed to look at one another for a split second, and then—bedlam: men shouting, women screaming in an arc of sound and shattered, flying glass. People ducked behind tables and chairs trying to find refuge.

I didn't hear any gunshots. Not the kind I was familiar with, anyway. All I could hear were thuds and twangs—a little like a reggae band practicing before taking the stage. I was distracted by a fast, stealthy movement, and felt a hand grab my arm and pull me down to the ground with enormous force. I felt a knee between my shoulder blades, pinning me down—the impact hurt badly. With my face plastered to the hardwood floor, I struggled to look up to see who was on top of me, but all I could really make out was a black .45 caliber pistol with a long silencer attached to the barrel, firing in the direction of the elevators.

Thud... Thud... Thud...

A second later, I was being pulled up with equal force, and the giant, silenced handgun was in front of me, still firing, ejecting spent, hot cartridges across my face. A hand was grasping my collar and pushing me to the building's stairwell. I saw two bodies on the floor. Very large men—one with a shaved head and thick brown beard, and the other clean cut with black hair. Both in slowly expanding pools of their own blood.

The hand holding the pistol caught my eye. It was not a man's hand. But a woman's—feminine and young, but strong and straining with every squeeze of the trigger.

"Get in there! Now!"

Before I saw my protector, I recognized her voice.

CHAPTER 25

IN THE STAIRWELL OF Patek Philippe Salons, I looked over to see Robin Nielsen holding the silenced pistol. Her left hand was tightly grasping the back of my shirt collar.

"No dresses at the other store?"

She pushed me forward, continuing to guide me. *"Move! They're trying to kill you!"*

Robin's voice belied a level of tactical competence and professionalism—her tone was urgent, clipped and steady. Seeing her now armed, and systematically shooting at people was really the last thing I expected.

As we descended the steps, I saw her holding her ear, as if speaking to herself.

"Coming down now. Meet us at the entrance of Patek Philippe. Two EKIA. None in trail."

"Who are you?" I heard myself blurt out, as we reached the first floor.

"Stand here," Robin ordered, positioning to one side of the doorway. "Wait."

She inserted another clip, pulled back the receiver, and loaded another round into the chamber. She opened the door, and stepped outside. A moment later the door reopened and Robin motioned me inside the store, her pistol now down to her side. "Okay. Quickly. Let's go."

Robin walked swiftly, a step ahead of me. I noticed that all-the-while she was actively scanning our surroundings, with the .45 extended and sweeping. As we approached the entranceway door, the alarm sounded. Two men with guns appeared in the doorway, and I saw Robin calmly fire at them four times through the glass...*POP, POP...POP, POP....* in quick succession.

The men dropped exactly where they were standing. More glass shattered, and the alarm steadily pulsed in the background. Just as I was about to back away, Robin grasped my arm and pulled me forward, shielding with her own body. In turning around, she saw the security guard running toward us from the back room. Without hesitation, she aimed at the top of the massive chandelier and fired five times at the mounting bracket on the ceiling before it came crashing to the ground—in front of him and behind us. A moment later, we were outside the store and I was being pushed head-first into a black BMW 740i.

As our car sped away down Rue du Rhône, weaving through traffic and narrow streets, I looked over at Robin who was sitting next to me reloading her .45, completely silent. Police cars sped past us.

"I think we need to talk," I said in the calmest, most understated way I could muster, while practically hyperventilating.

She looked at me and shook her head. "Are you okay?"

I nodded slightly as my frustration escalated. I turned toward her in the back seat, and spoke evenly. "Maybe you can tell me what just happened back there?"

"We hoped it wouldn't come to this, Daniel."

"*We?*" I asked incredulously. "Who the hell is 'We'? And who the hell are *YOU?*" I heard my voice raise an octave and I was waving my hands as if I were erasing from a chalkboard.

Just as I finished, we pulled up to the entrance of our hotel. Robin looked at me as our driver came around to open the door. "I'll explain what I can when we get inside."

I nodded. "That'd be just great," I said with more sarcasm than I intended.

Robin looked at me, but didn't respond. We rushed inside to the elevator and ascended to our suite in complete silence.

Once inside, Robin set her jacket, purse and holstered handgun on the dining room table. She turned to me and motioned to the sofa near the fireplace. "Okay. Why don't you sit down?"

CHAPTER 26

"DANIEL, I WORK FOR *the Central Intelligence Agency."*

I think those words from Robin were what caused our hotel suite to begin to swirl around me. I closed my eyes, and held the bridge of my nose in an effort to make it stop.

"Of course you are," I said, eyes still clenched shut, and then opening them. "Just glad I wasn't seduced by first impressions."

"And we believe you're being targeted by the Kremlin," she continued, ignoring me.

I shook my head. "Well, I guess that clears everything up!"

Robin's response was silence. But I wasn't finished. I leaned forward.

"Pardon me if I don't sound grateful for what you did for me back there, because I am," I began. "But here's the problem I have: up to now, I've been under the impression that you were a very smart, beautiful banker with language skills, *not a trained secret agent with a license to kill.*" I stared at her intently. "But thanks for saving my life back there anyway."

Robin brushed her hair to the side without saying a word. After several moments, she spoke calmly and deliberately. "Are you finished? Are you ready to listen?"

I took a deep breath and nodded. Slowly, knowing well the danger of jumping to conclusions.

"Much of it is classified, but we've been following several high-level threats out of Russia in the wake of their occupation of Ukraine.

Mostly dealing with Russian oligarchs and organized crime, but we believe there is a hard connection to the Kremlin. As the President of the Tory Foundation, you represent a significant threat to them."

"*I'm a threat to them?*" I asked incredulously. "How could I possibly be a threat when I don't even know what the Tory Foundation is?"

Robin nodded, with a look of wariness closing over her. "I believe you. But I had to be certain."

"That's why you didn't tell me who you really were?"

"That's one of the reasons, but not the only one," she said apprehensively. And after a moment's hesitation, "I'm still under cover. And now that you know that, we have a big problem."

"Well, the only big problem I'm seeing is that somehow I'm now the target of a KGB hit squad."

"FSB."

"Excuse me?"

"*Federal'naya sluzhba bezopasnosti Rossiyskoy Federatsii,*" Robin said in fluent Russian. "The FSB—the main successor to the KGB. Same movie. Same bad guys. Different name."

"Oh," I said blankly, and reached for the telephone without hesitation.

Robin reached out to intercept me. "Who are you calling?"

"Our pilots. Time to go home."

"Stop," Robin said, shooting me a narrow glance. "This is far more serious than you think, or could possibly imagine. It's larger than any of us, and it has massive implications for our national security."

"Why?

"Because it represents an imminent threat for the long term," she said. "Like it or not, you're now a player in this operation."

"When were you going to tell me all of this?"

"We weren't. We didn't believe you had a need to know."

"Oh, I see," I said, unbelieving, and with as much sarcasm as I could muster. "But now I do?"

"No, you don't. Nor, honestly, are you equipped to deal with the consequences of knowing. By telling you, I'm trying to salvage a significant compromise, and honestly I'm risking our entire operation by doing so."

"Okay, if you're under cover, is Robin Nielsen your real name?"

"Yes."

"But you're not really a banker, or a translator?"

"Not anymore. Those were my professions prior to joining the Company—and were skills that qualified me to work there. Having experience as a bankerallowed me to be hired under cover at the Lake Forest Bank and Trust. We never thought it would come to this."

"Well, you shoot well, for a bank clerk."

"You do a pretty good job of following directions, for a congressman."

Countless thoughts ran through my head as I struggled to make sense of what was happening around me, and to me. There was only one thing I was certain of—I was not in control of anything. Nor did I have adequate awareness of any of the activities, personalities, or agendas that were spinning around me.

"Just so I can be certain, can I see your CIA identification?"

Robin walked over to her purse, pulled an ID card out of her wallet and handed it to me. Against the background of a hologram-like State Department symbol was a color photograph of Robin with her name, issue date and expiration date. "We don't carry CIA identification cards—our cover is usually another government department."

I handed it back to her, and as the adrenalin began to diminish, I felt a kind of utter exhaustion set in. I looked up at Robin, my brows drawn together. "Why does a girl like you join the CIA?" I asked.

For the first time, I saw an annoyed expression. "For the same reason we sign up to be Chiefs of Staff for Congressmen, I suppose," she said thick with sarcasm. "What we do is important, Daniel. It's necessary."

I nodded. "Okay. Just out of curiosity, how did you transition so quickly from dress-shopping to body-guarding?"

Robin nodded and her eyes widened. "I knew they were following us—but I wasn't sure who they were following—you, me, or both of us. It turned out that it was you they were interested in—so that gave me the opportunity to follow them"

"And why were they trying to kill me?"

Robin shrugged. "We don't know exactly—but we do know that the Tory Foundation represents the single greatest private threat to the Kremlin's agenda and hold on power."

I eyed Robin carefully. "How could that be?"

"Authoritarian regimes are never quite as strong as their dictators would like us to believe," she answered. "They have plenty of vulnerabilities, and organized opposition is prime among them. The Tory Foundation is organized opposition—on steroids."

"How so?" I asked. "I still don't know what the foundation does!"

"The official version is that they advocate for democracy and civil rights around the world. They're quite active, and effective. But where they're most focused, behind the scenes, is in planning and executing regime change for those governments that are less than democratic."

"Like Russia?"

Robin nodded. "And its republics too, like Chechnya, Ingushetia, and Khakassia. Behind the scenes, they've also been instrumental in actively preserving western-style democracies on Russia's periphery—the Baltic States, Ukraine, Georgia and others. The Tory Foundation has been a prime force for their accession into NATO and the European Union as well. Much to the Kremlin's annoyance. They use unconventional means—currency dumping and speculation, media broadcasts, publications, banners, demonstrations, you name it—they fund it and organize it. They've been a major player in convincing OPEC to increase their production, driving down the cost of oil, and limiting Russia's influence."

"So now I'm their target?"

Robin smiled. "You are Jonas' designated successor as President of the Tory Foundation. And they know it."

"But according to Jonas' will, I have a sister in Moscow."

"Who the Kremlin would love to see as the sole heir to the Tory fortune."

"Just what they need—another oligarch," I commented dryly, looking up at the ceiling as if I were considering what color to paint it. "And what's the CIA's position on all of this? Aside from saving me from Bolshevik hit-men in expensive watch stores, what's *your* role exactly?"

Robin paused. "After what just happened, I'm not sure. They may call everything off once they receive my report, and—"

"Wait—" I interrupted. "Call what off?"

"A year ago, we received a tip from someone in the Tory Foundation that Russia is planning to invade and reoccupy Ukraine and the Baltic States—Lithuania, Latvia and Estonia. Ukraine was first, and they predicted that a full two months in advance. According to our source, the Baltic states are being actively targeted for hybrid warfare by the Kremlin."

"Why is the CIA so interested in the Baltics?"

Robin nodded. "If Russia attacks the Baltics, NATO will be obligated to intervene with force."

I shook my head. "I don't get it. Why isn't NATO intervening now?"

"Because neither they, nor Washington has the stomach for it. They don't want to trigger World War III. They're only doing the absolute minimum necessary. When Russian fighters are allowed to buzz U.S. Navy destroyers, that's an indicator."

"God forbid we should show we're committed to our allies."

"So we're investigating how reliable that information is before reporting on it. We have no other confirmation, but this source has always proven very reliable to us in the past." Robin paused and leaned against the fireplace, appearing to consider if she should divulge anything further. "Langley isn't convinced, and they won't like the fireworks display we just put on downtown. In fact, it may be just the excuse they need to pull the plug on the whole operation."

"Unless you provide them some proof of the Kremlin's plan," I said.

Robin shrugged. "Even then it may not matter. But there are already some indicators, like today's *Pravda* headline." She took the newspaper out of her shoulder bag and handed it to me.

My Russian was good enough to roughly translate it:

Lithuania's Policies Oppress Russian Population

"Every invasion needs a motive?"

"Something like that. This is what they've done in the past, and they'll do it again. They'll ratchet up the rhetoric every day. They'll show photos of poor, evicted Russians in the streets of Vilnius, Riga and Tallinn. And then they'll whip up a catalyst of some sort to galvanize public support for Russian tanks to come to the immediate rescue of their fellow countrymen. And they'll devise a trigger event, like the shoot down of one of their planes in Russian airspace to justify their actions."

"Would we let that happen?"

"We let it happen in Hungary in 1956, again in Czechoslovakia in 1968, and we've allowed it to happen in Ukraine. So the precedent is there."

"Why did they decide to target me so quickly—the minute I step foot off American soil?"

"You saw the funds under your name," Robin replied. "That was only a fraction of the Tory Foundation holdings. There are several hundred billion more dollars and Euros more under their direct control. Possibly as much as a trillion dollars in all."

"Trillion? With a *T*?"

Robin nodded.

My head was spinning, and I felt distinctly rudderless. "So now what?"

"Dinner at the Mayor's house," Robin said simply. "But I still need to buy a dress."

CHAPTER 27

THE MAYOR'S HOUSE WAS A SMALL turn-of-the-century mansion, or as Robin was quick to correct me, a "villa." Situated on the hills outside the city, it overlooked all of Lake Geneva with a view that could only be described as breathtaking. Robin wore a sheer back gold and black evening dress."

"You look stunning, by the way," I said, meaning it.

She smiled, placing her hand on mine. "Temperley London— only the best for you, Congressman. Langley isn't usually this generous."

As our car pulled up, I noticed Robin's cell phone lighting up continuously in silenced mode.

"Do you need to get that?" I asked, pointing toward her phone.

Robin nodded. "I'll meet you inside. Langley isn't too happy with me right now."

"Chandeliers," I answered.

"Pardon me?"

"I understand they're expensive these days."

"*Go!*" Robin exclaimed, with the trace of a smile.

I stepped outside the car onto the circular cobblestone driveway, and recognized the man walking over to greet me from our brief encounter at the airport— Mayor Rémy Recordan.

"Congressman! Welcome to our home!" He gestured toward the car. "We were also expecting Ms. Nielsen—has she accompanied you?"

I nodded, shaking his hand. "She's taking a phone call in the car. She'll join us as soon as she's finished."

Mayor Recordan nodded his understanding as we walked toward the villa. "We have several other guests who are here tonight. I will let them introduce themselves, but I think you will find it to be a fascinating group. This is the advantage of Genève—for centuries it has been an international crossroads, and so it remains."

I thanked him for the invitation, and was bracing for the inevitable pointed questions about the shooting incident at *Patek Philippe* just hours before, uncertain how I would respond, if asked.

Yes, Mayor, that was the cause of your shootout downtown—fortunately, I was rescued by my assistant, who is actually working undercover for the CIA assistant, and was still able to get my suit from Hugo Boss....

Thinking about it made me break out into a cold sweat, so I focused on not tripping on the driveway's thick square cobblestones.

Entering the house, I was struck by the villa's contemporary design—old growth post and beam construction, high ceilings, Chinese marble walls, grand stone fireplace, Oriental carpets on parquet flooring, and massive windows overlooking Lake Geneva. It was a spectacular setting. I could see a group of men and women had congregated in the living room, all conversing with wine and cocktail glasses in hand.

The first to greet me was Mayor Recordan's wife, Ruth—a stunning, tall blonde woman in her early forties with refined features, a practiced European manner, and a sophisticated, knowing smile. She wore an elegant black low-cut silk sheath evening dress tailored to an athletic figure that indicated a love of yoga or long distance running, or both.

"Welcome to Geneva, Congressman. We are honored that you could join us tonight."

I must have stopped in my tracks. I started to shake her hand, but she leaned forward to kiss me on both cheeks, and I caught the scent of what I quickly appreciated as very expensive perfume. In a somewhat awkward effort to recover my equilibrium, I addressed both the Mayor and his wife, extending my heartfelt thanks for their warm welcome and praising their beautiful home.

"You have chosen an interesting day to arrive in Geneva," Ruth Recordon said quietly, almost as if she were sharing a secret. "We had an attempted armed robbery downtown this afternoon that occupied Rémy until only an hour ago—"

"It was really nothing of consequence, Congressman," the Mayor said. "The police had it under control very quickly, and nothing was stolen, thanks to the store's tight security. Just some minor damage inside," the Mayor said.

"That explains the sirens." I heard Robin's voice behind me. I hadn't heard her come through the door.

Robin introduced herself to Ruth Recordan as my chief of staff, and apologized for her later arrival.

"A Chief of Staff's job never ends," Mayor Recordan said with a tone of certainty, half-joking. I could see many eyes were now looking in Robin's direction.

Robin nodded, meeting his smile. "Setting up a new office in Washington, D.C. has its challenges, as we're now discovering."

A waiter carrying a platter of champagne glasses approached. I quickly reached for one and drank from it, before realizing that I was on the verge of downing all of it in a single gulp. Robin sensed my anxiety as she walked through the foyer, and interjected her compliments to both of our hosts on the beauty of their home and the spectacular view of the lake and surrounding mountains. As we entered the living room, the other ten-or-so guests seemed to halt their own conversations and turn to us. Mayor Recordan stepped forward and provided an articulate, well-practiced introduction:

"Ladies and gentlemen, it is my great pleasure to introduce our guests of honor tonight: Congressman-elect Daniel Tory and his Chief of Staff, Ms. Robin Nielsen. Although this is our first opportunity to meet Congressman Tory, we certainly know of him through his superb reputation and wide media coverage in the United States. I would also venture to say that all of us here tonight feel that we already know him through his beloved uncle, Jonas Tory, who we knew well, and who spent many similar evenings here with us regaling us with tales of his storied past, fighting the Nazis and resisting the Soviets, even when the rest of the free world chose to ignore the plight of those subjugated peoples." Mayor Recordan turned to us with a broad smile and a slight bow. "And so, Congressman, Ms. Nielsen, please allow me to introduce you to our distinguished group of good friends…."

Mayor Recordan began introducing me to the people in front of us.

"Our American ambassador to Switzerland, Ambassador John Williamson and his wife Anna…the Chairman of the Swiss National Bank, Ernst Studer and his wife, Laura…Bjorn Boman, President of Interpol…Aksel Odin, the first Director for the European Union's Intelligence and Security Service, and his wife, Rane."

Robin and I shook hands with everyone as we were introduced to them. With each handshake, I had the distinct feeling that I was being welcomed into Jonas' inner circle—fast becoming clear to me to be a very exclusive club.

CHAPTER 28

ALTHOUGH THE MAYOR WAS MAKING the introductions, I knew this was really Jonas' party. I could hear him as clear as if he were standing beside me:

Danno! Meet my friends! Good people! Now they are YOUR friends!

I was beginning to realize that Jonas had scripted my every step up to that point—who I met, what I discovered, what I inherited. And I hadn't been able to predict any of it. So, here I was—in Geneva, Switzerland, in a house with a virtual "Who's Who in Europe" all there to meet me, at Jonas' posthumous behest.

Brilliant. But how will this end?

I felt a slender arm slip through mine just as the introductions were complete. I turned to find Ruth Recordan beside me, guiding me toward the U.S. Ambassador to Switzerland.

"Daniel, the first people you must meet tonight are Ambassador John Williamson and his wife, Anna. Of course he is your ambassador to our country, but behind his title is a truly fascinating man—and a dear friend of ours, and of Jonas as well."

I glanced over at Robin as I was being ushered away, and I caught her amused grin and an almost imperceptible wink. Ruth's grip on my arm tightened.

"Before John was an Ambassador, he was a Navy admiral and SEAL—he commanded the U.S. Special Operations Command. Your president offered him the ambassadorship for England or for France, but he chose Switzerland instead."

"Why?" I half-whispered.

"Anna is Swiss, and she was raised here in Geneva. We went to the same schools. She is a dear friend."

Ambassador Williamson stood out in the room. Impeccably dressed in a tailored blue pin-stripe suit, with closely cropped dark grey hair, straight posture and a controlled manner that exuded a quiet confidence, he was the picture of what you would expect (and seldom found) in an ambassador.

"Congressman, you honor us with your visit." Ambassador Williamson made a kind of laser-like eye contact with me as he shook my hand and introduced his wife.

I met his firm handshake. "The honor is mine, Ambassador. It's a distinguished group, and I'm humbled to be here."

"We all have Jonas to thank. We have been meeting like this several times each year for the past two decades—I dare say he is responsible for the high positions we hold today. Few would dispute that. We owe him a great deal."

"My uncle routinely surrounded himself with good people," I answered. "I'm not surprised."

Actually, I was stunned.

"He spoke about you often, Congressman," Williamson said. "So much that we have always felt like we know you, even if you have not known us."

I smiled, trying my best to repress Jonas' voice:

You see, Danno! I bring you only the best! They know you even before they meet you! Now you must get to know them, so you will be President!

"Congratulations on your election victory," Anna Williamson said. "Jonas told us only a few months ago how proud he was of you."

"We are excited, but we have an enormous amount of work ahead of us."

"The State of Illinois is the beneficiary, as are the American people," Ambassador Williamson said with finality. "The Tory Foundation" is very fortunate to have you continue where your father and Jonas have left off."

"My father?"

Ambassador Williamson nodded slowly. "Indeed. It was your father's sacrifice that ultimately made the Tory Foundation possible, and by extension, the enhanced security of our friends and allies around the world."

"His sacrifice?" I blurted the question, more than asked it. I saw everyone around me glance at one another for the briefest moment.

It was Ruth Recordan who spoke. I felt her squeeze my arm again, and pull herself toward my side, almost as if conveying a signal. "Daniel, there is much for you to learn about the Tory Foundation, and obviously about your family's circumstances." Her tone was somewhat hushed. I realized that she was being careful to ensure she was out of earshot of the wait staff. "When you look around this room tonight, and as we enjoy dinner, you should know that without your father's extraordinary and selfless courage, more than half of us would not be alive today."

----------- CHAPTER 29 -----------

HOW DO YOU RESPOND to a revelation like that—that your own father, who you never knew—had saved many lives? I did my best to recover quickly, but my surprise was obvious.

I turned to Ruth Recordan, and tried to maintain my composure. "I would be very interested to hear that story about my father."

"Of course!" Ruth replied enthusiastically. "But first, I am told dinner is ready!"

We moved into a large, modern, and very elegant dining room with a battery of wait staff lining each side of the table. Each setting had a name assigned to it. Ruth guided me to the center of the table. Aksel Odin, The EU Security Chief, and Laura Studer, wife of the Swiss Bank President sat beside me. Robin was being seated directly across from me, and from her own expression, it was clear that her own pre-dinner conversation had caught her by surprise.

Once everyone was seated, Mayor Recordan stood at one end of the long table, with both hands on the chair.

"If I may, I would like to offer a toast to the memory of our friend and our mentor, Jonas Tory." Recordan looked directly at me. "Even in death, Jonas continues to live through his legacy of courage, humor and love for his native Lithuania. Throughout his life, he fought bravely against oppressive regimes that sought to subjugate freedom. He never sought the spotlight—but worked tirelessly and selflessly for others. For those of us who know of his daring actions, Jonas Tory will remain a legend, and an example for us to emulate." He held up his glass and looked at everyone around the table. "To Jonas Tory!"

"To Jonas!" Everyone responded in unison. I noticed that Ruth Recordan had tears streaming down her cheeks as she and the rest of the table raised their glasses and took the first sip of wine.

Once the toast was complete, I turned to Aksel Odin and Laura Studer.

Throughout the main course, I learned that Jonas was the Godfather to all of the Studer children. It was an awkward moment, because I wanted to tell her that Jonas had spoken of them, but the truth was, he hadn't. Also during dinner, I discovered that Laura's maiden name was *Kalnietis*, and that her father had served with both my father and Jonas during World War II, and the Cold War resisting the Soviet occupation of Lithuania.

Laura Studer had asked about my mother, and how she was faring. I told her about the stroke she had suffered, the coma, and expressed my hope that she would recover. Laura Studer was a beautiful woman, in her early sixties, with grey hair that was once brunette, and kind eyes that appeared to have seen too much. She had an obvious abiding loyalty to her husband and children.

"When we depart tonight, I have something for you," she said softly.

My conversation with Aksel Odin was much different, fascinating, and somewhat unsettling. Odin was a larger-than-life personality. Standing at 6'6" with a muscular build, shaved head, a large angular face, and a cool Hollywood name, it would be easy to confuse Aksel for a WWF wrestler. Sitting beside him at dinner his massive hands could have been the centerpiece at our table. Appearances were deceptive though. Soft-spoken, with a baritone voice and accent a lot like Henry Kissinger's, Aksel Odin quickly established himself not only as a gentle giant, but had a professor-like understanding of international policy and strategy as well. Through our dinnertime conversation, I learned that his mother had first known Jonas and my father during World War II, and had helped them during the resistance. Following his father's death when he was only a young boy, Jonas had paid for his education from grade school to graduate studies at Oxford.

After a dessert of various handmade ice creams, international cheeses and dessert wine, Aksel rather spontaneously asked if I liked cigars. "I have two *habanos*, if you are so inclined, Congressman."

We stepped out onto the porch and walked toward the estate's winter garden overlooking an enclosed dock and a private beach on the Lake. Aksel lit my cigar and then his own. "You are arriving at a very interesting time for Europe and the Tory Foundation."

"I've noticed that, just this afternoon," I said in the most understated tone I could muster.

"It is an unstable and uncertain time for us. Our member nations are not in step. Many economies are failing, and our healthy nations— besieged with their own problems—are reluctant to help unless they agree to draconian austerity measures."

"Will Europe defend the Baltics?"

"Publicly now, yes," Aksel said, nodding. "But behind the closed doors, the discussions are far less cordial."

"So there is an actual threat?" I asked.

Aksel blew out a cloud of smoke into the darkness. "You will hear more details in our meeting tomorrow, but suffice it to say, the very survival of NATO is at stake."

"Does the EU leadership understand what's happening?" I asked, walking on the cobblestone walkway.

Aksel nodded tentatively. "A few enlightened people are concerned, but most ministers are in denial, and prefer to keep their heads buried."

"What about Washington?" I asked, still savoring the cigar's flavor and its sweet aroma.

Aksel stopped and shrugged slightly. "I fear Washington has lost the political will to lead. Your military forces have been drawn down to the lowest levels since World War II, and that has not been lost on the Kremlin. Regardless, anything they do now may be too late."

"Are we facing another Cold War?"

Aksel smiled. But it was a sidelong smile that revealed an in-depth knowledge of the situation that extended well beyond what was reported by the media. "If anything, the fall of the Berlin Wall empowered and emboldened the Kremlin rather than limiting them, as most would like to believe. It has taken even the Russians some time to realize it, but Moscow now has the ability to operate unencumbered around the world. Despite their current currency crisis, their cash and gold reserves are growing, but they know that it can't be spent domestically because it would end up in the wrong hands—"

"Who?"

"The mafia, oligarchs, politicians. Corruption is rampant in Russia. So for two decades they lamented the fall of the Soviet Union, until they came to realize the impact they could have abroad."

"Now they are focusing externally?"

Aksel nodded. "Not long ago, I was in Moscow and was invited to a speech by the Russian Prime Minister to KGB Veterans and current FSB officers. It was a large gathering with all of the pomp you would have expected during the height of the Cold War: long red banners, military bands playing victory marches, and men and women in military uniforms wearing medals and badges adorned with the Soviet-era hammer and sickle." He exhaled again, and paused briefly. "I believe I was the only westerner in the hall, but to hear the Prime Minister that day, telling these KGB and FSB veterans *"We're Back!"* was something I cannot forget. It was an omen of the direction he had planned at the outset, and it sent chills up my spine."

For a moment, I was captured by my own thoughts until I realized that my cigar had extinguished itself. I asked Aksel for another light and he continued. "No one understood the Russians more than your Uncle Jonas, Daniel. He clearly saw their trajectory of events well before the rest of us. It was easy for diplomats to dismiss him as reactionary, but all of his predictions have been eerily accurate. As your president was walking hand-in-hand with the Russian president in the Rose Garden, Jonas Tory was creating clandestine teams inside Russia to identify and, if necessary, disrupt or destroy the Kremlin's plans."

"Jonas never told me any of this," I interrupted.

Aksel shook his head slowly. "He wouldn't."

"Pardon me?"

"He would never tell you. He would never risk telling anyone unless they had a real need to know," Aksel said, continuing to walk through the garden on the walkway toward the beach. "But you should know that this effort defined him, because he—more than most—understood what the Kremlin is capable of doing."

I nodded my understanding. "Jonas was never one to stand still when he felt strongly about something."

There was a period of silence as we reached the rocky beach and blew cigar smoke into the cool air.

"This may not be the time or place to ask you the result of Jonas' efforts?" I asked.

I detected a wry smile from Aksel. "Only now is it delivering substantive results. *Dramatic* results. And the teams are still in place throughout Russia."

"Is this what the Tory Foundation really does?" I asked, somewhat experimentally. "Because I still don't have any idea."

Aksel looked up at the well-lit villa, and pointed up at it. "Daniel, inside that house are the Tory Foundation Board of Directors. All of those men and women who you met. In many ways, we are the private face of the foundation. Ruth Recordan is our board chairman. It is her role to explain everything about the Foundation to you."

"The private face?" I inquired with interest.

Aksel nodded and looked directly at me. "Yes, and tomorrow morning you will meet the *public* face of the Tory Foundation."

CHAPTER 30

"GOOD MORNING," ROBIN CALLED OUT.
I was in the kitchen, pouring a cup of coffee. It was 6AM, and I looked over to see her sitting at the dining room table in one of the hotel's robes, working on a laptop. Papers were spread out in front of her. Her tanned legs were crossed, athletic—muscular.

"I thought I'd be up first," I said.

"Jet lag," she replied. Woke a few hours ago, and I couldn't get back to sleep." She shuffled a few of the papers. "So I've been translating your father's journal."

I walked over and sat at the table, opposite her. "You don't have to do that," I said. "Obviously, you have a day job." I said too quickly, immediately regretting the comment. But it was too late to take it back.

Robin passed her fingers through her long brown hair, and I could tell that she was considering her response. She leaned forward again, and placed both elbows on the table. "I want to. If you'll let me."

I watched her sip from her coffee cup. Even without makeup, she was very beautiful, strikingly so…. "Of course," I answered.

"Langley is considering whether to pull me."

It took a moment for me to understand what she was saying. "Because of yesterday's events?"

She nodded. "Yes, but principally because I blew my cover."

"Well, I'm not going to tell anyone. Tell them that."

"It's not only you. There are security cameras throughout the store, and on the street. Our Station Chief is assessing the aftermath,

101

and trying to contain it"

"Well, if it's any help, I learned last night that our Ambassador is a card-carrying board member of the Tory Foundation, and so is Ruth Recordan. Between the two of them, I'm sure they could work something out."

Robin smiled for the first time. "Thanks. Those strings may be worth pulling, if it comes to it. So dinner was more than just chit chat?"

"I got the feeling there were more agendas at that table than there are KGB agents in Geneva."

"FSB."

"Pardon me."

"The FSB is the new KGB. Slightly different animal. Same gene pool."

"Oh."

"Well, this may be one of those agendas," Robin said, pushing the manila envelope over to me. "Laura Studer asked me to give this to you as we were leaving last night."

"What is it?"

"She said she mentioned it to you at dinner."

I nodded, recalling the conversation, and tore open the envelope. I pulled out several 8x10 black and white photographs. The first photo was grainy and showed two adults and two boys standing in front of a farmhouse. They were dressed nicely, and looked as if they had just returned from church. I flipped the photograph around to see a label with a bold-typed caption:

Paneriai, Lietuva – 1938: Danukas Tory, Saule Tory, Lucas Tory, Jonas Tory

I leaned back in my chair. The photo depicted my father, Jonas and my grandparents in front of their home—the same home that my father had described in his journal entries.

In the next photograph, two boys were arm in arm, one with a Thompson submachine gun and another with a .45 caliber U.S. Government Issue pistol. I turned the photo over the read the caption:

Antakalnis, Lietuva – 1940: Jonas Tory, Lucas Tory

I realized that it was taken precisely at the time of my father's journal entries—the Soviet occupation of Lithuania. Both Jonas and my father wore serious expressions and their eyes reflected a maturity far beyond their years.

The final photograph showed three men and a woman sitting on a truckload of bricks with machine guns and rifles in hand:

Leningrad, 1945 – Jonas Tory, Lucas Tory, Antenas Steponas, Tanya Klimas

Turėti Sovietų aukso, pavogta nacių. Atkurtas Lietuvos partizanų.

I handed all three photos to Robin. "Family photos," I said dryly.

Robin flipped through the photographs and read the captions for each of them. Her eyes widened when she reviewed the last one.

"Can you translate that caption?" I asked pointing at the label on the back.

She nodded. "The bottom line says, 'In possession of Soviet gold stolen by the Nazis. Recovered by Lithuanian partisans.'"

"Gold?" I asked, in complete disbelief.

"We just may be looking at the first deposit for the Tory Foundation."

CHAPTER 31

I HAD NEVER BEEN TO A CASTLE until I arrived at the Tory Foundation Headquarters, hidden away in the mountains high above Lake Geneva. After a long, winding drive, and ear-popping elevations, the 14th Century Schlossberg Castle seemed to appear from nowhere.

After a multitude of additional hairpin curves, we turned into a gated driveway with a guardhouse and two armed guards. Our driver showed his identification and spoke in Swiss, presenting both Robin and me as his passengers. Once cleared, we continued along a long evergreen-lined cobblestone driveway. In front of the castle, a man and woman stood, waiting to greet us. As we drew closer, I saw that the woman was Ruth Recordan. She was dressed in a black shoulder padded skirt suit; high heels and her long blonde hair combed back and put into a bun.

"Is that—?" Robin asked, visibly surprised.

The car stopped.

"Yes," I answered quietly. "She's the Chairman of the Board."

"Every castle needs a queen."

"Be nice," I whispered. Our driver opened the car door to a beautiful sunny morning and a spectacular view of Geneva and the lake. The air was substantially cooler at that altitude, with a steady breeze. Looking around us, I also noticed an abundance of security guards and surveillance cameras along the periphery of the castle grounds.

"Daniel, welcome to your Foundation!" Ruth announced,

shaking my hand and kissing me once again on both cheeks. "We have looked forward to this day for a very long time."

She turned to the man standing beside her. He was in his sixties, I guessed—medium height, with a slight build. He was balding, wore glasses and a distinguished face that had begun to wrinkle deeply with age.

"Please allow me to introduce you to our executive director, Laurent Abraham."

I was surprised at the strength of Laurent Abraham's handshake, and his virtually unaccented English.

"Welcome to Geneva, Congressman. Jonas spoke of you often, so many of us feel we already know you."

I thanked him and introduced Robin as my chief of staff. We followed both he and Ruth inside.

The Schlossberg Castle was as deceptive and impressive a structure as any I'd ever seen. The old world stone and ivy exterior could not have prepared me for the ultra-modern stainless steel, glass, and white marble interior: Large plasma screens, a contemporary Swedish-style gas-powered fireplace, smoked glass offices and a large conference room with an oval table constructed of gold Calcutta marble. The floors were a gleaming white, reflecting the overhead lighting as if they were ultra-modern mirrors. Above us were glass and stainless steel walkways that connected spacious offices.

"Ummm," Robin whispered. "Wow."

"Exactly," I replied.

"Jonas hired the finest architects to design our foundation's home. As you can see, he spared no expense, and hired the finest artisans. It was his masterpiece." Abraham was guiding us toward the glass-encased conference room. "Schlossberg began as a Roman outpost in the 9th Century, guarding strategic roads through the Alpine passes from Burgundy. It was later expanded to be a summer home to the Counts of Savoy, who kept a fleet of war and trade ships on Lake Geneva below. Two centuries later, it was used as a munitions and weapons depot, and then a State prison. In the 15th Century and those that followed, it was employed as a refuge for neighboring farmers and as an Abby for Benedictine monks."

"Swords to plow shares," I commented.

"Congressman, I know much of what you are experiencing since Jonas' passing has come as a complete surprise to you. You are seeking answers— answers about your family, about this Foundation and our agenda." Abraham opened the conference room door and stopped just inside, in close proximity to the large table. "And you are considering whether this is an organization with which you want to be affiliated."

Abraham paused, and I think I may have breathed a sigh of relief. Up to that point, I felt like I was being piecemealed information.

I smiled slightly. "Those thoughts had crossed my mind, Mr. Abraham."

Laurent Abraham smiled.

"Lor," Abraham replied. "Please call me Lor, Congressman."

"Daniel, our purpose here today is to provide those answers to you," Ruth said. "Jonas told us you would come to us essentially blind, and probably very surprised."

"Jonas was right," I replied simply. I looked over on the far wall and saw a map of the world lit up on a tall, ultra-modern translucent glass wall on the far end of the conference room. Small dots of green and red light were concentrated around the major metropolitan areas of the world, but the largest concentrations of dots were in the Baltic states and throughout Russia. It was no ordinary map, I thought. *More like an interactive piece of modern art.*

Laurent Abraham motioned me toward the head of the table. As Robin and I both sat down, a large high definition digital screen as wide as the conference table lowered from the ceiling in front of the glass map.

"I think the best way to begin is to show you a documentary that Jonas commissioned, and was completed only a few months ago. He specifically asked that you see it at the outset of your visit."

The lights dimmed and the video began with the sound of a solitary trumpet sounding in the distance. Black and white photographs of men and women faded in and out on the screen against a maroon background. With every photo, a drumbeat sounded. Slowly at first. A female English accented voiceover began after only a few photos had passed.

> *Sacrifice...courage...heroism...character...vision.   Qualities often sought, but seldom found; frequently taught, but rarely tested.*

The drumbeats quickened and the photographic sequence of faces picked up a more rapid pace, and I realized that all of those faces were certainly casualties of war.

> *On those occasions in our world's history, when the courage of ordinary men and women has been tested, those who step forward to defend their freedom, to oppose those who attempt to take it comprise a special coterie of men and women who are nothing less than extraordinary—many of whom willingly sacrifice their own lives for the freedom of others. We honor them today. Their spirit lives on. Nowhere has this spirit of courage and sacrifice been more prevalent than in the Baltic States since World War II.... Less than a year after the signing of the infamous Molotov-Ribbentrop Pact effectively partitioning the Baltic States, the Soviet Union invaded and occupied Lithuania on June 15th, 1940. One family recognized the imminence of a Soviet invasion and acted immediately to oppose it with all of the resources they could muster. Danukas Tory, a farmer who lived with his family on the outskirts of Vilnius, began a local resistance organization with his sons and neighbors, called "The Hawks."*

> *"Our father told us he would rather die than live under the Bolsheviks. So we began to make preparations to fight them. My mother told Jonas and I, 'Whatever happens, don't let them take you alive.'" [Jonas Tory Subscript]*

> *A storm of terror and violence was unleashed on the Lithuanian countryside. The Lithuanian flag banned. Widespread arrests,*

deportations, forced enlistments, torture, executions. Lithuanian political and cultural leaders disappeared, never to be seen again. In September 1940, Danukas Tory and his wife Saule were sent to a work camp in Siberia. Their sons, Jonas and Lucas narrowly escaped, and under their leadership, the resistance quickly gained momentum, and the Hawks Detachment they founded would become known as the Lithuanian Freedom Army—an organized underground national movement that would fight bravely against the Nazi occupation of Lithuania.

I glanced over at Robin. She was pursing her lips. She looked over at me, and I could tell that she, too, was just trying to maintain her composure.

I'm not ready for this, I thought.

I recognized a few of the photographs that followed from the Time-Life book that I'd found in Jonas' car. The first two photos in Laura Studer's envelope were also featured. But most of the photographs in that documentary, I had never seen before. Many of them were graphic in the violence—and in its aftermath. My mother was mentioned only later as a "fearless captain of the Lithuanian Freedom Army." The photographs of her with Jonas, Lucas and several others I could not identify showed all of them wearing Soviet and German uniforms alongside demolished military vehicles, and near the rubble of buildings.

While some Lithuanian resistance groups saw the Nazi invasion as an opportunity to revolt against their Soviet occupiers, and prematurely declare a restoration of Lithuanian independence, the Tory resistance refused to endorse the Nazi occupiers, and turned their operation against the Germans, publishing underground newspapers, organizing economic boycotts, and gathering arms. The resistance hoped that after victory the Western allies would insist on the restoration of Lithuanian statehood. The resistance bands under the Tory partisans continued to fight aggressively throughout Lithuania against an enemy of overwhelming strength. With the help of locals, their understanding of the dense forests throughout Lithuania provided an advantage to the Tory resistance over their Nazi invaders. In some cases, the Tory resistance collaborated with Soviet-sponsored undergrounds by staging military raids against German transportation, administrative, and economic enterprises.

"Many Lithuanians thought the Nazis were rescuing us from the Soviets, but we saw them as invaders of our homeland." [Jonas Tory Subscript]

Lucas Tory had come to hear that the Nazis and their Lithuanian collaborators were exterminating other Lithuanians, many of them Jews. Against the pleadings of his brother, Lucas infiltrated a Jewish workgroup at the Slobodka ghetto near Kaunas, Lithuania in an attempt to gather intelligence and convince the Jewish prisoners to revolt en masse. Lucas remained in the ghetto for several months, when the SS suddenly began to assume control of the ghetto with the intent to convert it into the Kauen concentration camp. In a dangerous effort, Lucas was smuggled to London to inform Winston Churchill of what was happening inside Auschwitz and in the Kauen camp. Lucas returned to Lithuania believing that the West would have no choice but to finally respond. But it became clear that his warnings and intelligence had been ignored. Ultimately, approximately 185,000 Jews, or 85 percent of the community's population, were massacred by Nazi death squads, with the overt assistance of Lithuanian collaborators. The experience only strengthened his resolve to resist Lithuania's invaders, at all costs.

I was transfixed. Hearing a complete historical account of my family's role in the resistance during World War II for the first time, complete with motion picture footage from the events was causing my heart to race. I removed my suit jacket. The detailed stories of my family's heroism continued—ambushes, raids, spying, assumed identities, POW rescues. All of them were so beyond what I grew up around, and so outside my realm of understanding, I wouldn't have believed any of it. But the photographs and film clippings that clearly showed much younger images of my parents and Jonas actively leading or participating in these operations was all the proof I could ever need. Seeing photos of your mother proudly standing over the dead bodies of Nazi SS Soldiers was surreal, and unnerving.

With German defeat imminent, the Soviet army reoccupied Lithuania in the summer of 1944. The NKVD quickly began arresting and murdering people, and the ranks of the partisans swelled. The Tory armed resistance in Lithuania was intensively targeted by Soviet counterintelligence, and became increasingly fragmented as partisans were captured, arrested, and often executed.

"After the war ended, life became much harder for all of the partisans. We were starving, and no one could trust each other. Our murdered partisans were put on display by the Soviets in the town centers. Their bodies were mutilated. We often could not recognize them." [Tanya Tory Subscript]

Lucas and Jonas knew their resistance would not survive without help from the West. Armed Lithuanian double agents—called "Smogikai"—working for the NKVD were able to infiltrate and destroy many of the last remaining partisan units. Under the leadership of Lucas Tory, and with only 20 partisans remaining, the Hawks were among the last organized Partisan resistance organization in Lithuania. The Soviets deployed thousands of security troops on search and destroy mission against The Hawks Partisans.

With the recognition that they may not be able to hold on much longer, Tanya and Lucas married in a quiet forest ceremony in

July, 1961.

"*I had one daughter, Tatyana, and found out I was pregnant. Lucas just said to me, 'I love you, let's get married.' But I always knew Lithuania was his first wife, and I was his second wife*" [Tanya Tory Subscript]

One evening in January, 1963, a former comrade who Jonas and Tanya had once rescued from a Gestapo jail, invited them over for dinner at his home. Jonas and Tanya went to the house with a bodyguard, confident that they would be safe, but unaware that he was a double agent for the Soviets. He ordered their capture, tied their hands, and shot their bodyguard. Jonas and Tanya were handed over to the KGB.

"*I begged them to kill me and let the others go, but they were Smogikai. We never knew who was Smogikai—they were traitors of the worst kind.*" [Jonas Tory Subscript]

Lucas Tory, upon hearing late of the dinner invitation, immediately set out for the house, and found the bodies of their partisans on full display. When he could not find Jonas and Tanya, a neighbor told him that they were being taken to a KGB prison in Vilnius. In a hastily executed plan, Lucas traded his capture if both Jonas and Tanya would be released. The exchange occurred, and later Lucas was reported to have been questioned and tortured.

Lucas Tory's submachine gun, military equipment and personal items are on display under glass in the inner museum of the Lubyanka Prison and FSB Headquarters in Moscow, which is closed to the general public.

"*I watched the crucifixion of my beloved country, felt the blood soaked soil under my feet. I could not stand by and do nothing.*"

[Lucas Tory Historical Footage]

The Sovietization of Lithuania was obstructed by the Tory Resistance Movement and others scattered throughout the country. From 1944 to 1963, 20,000 to 30,000 partisans were killed. With financial and operational assistance from the Tory Foundation, and enduring example of the partisan resistance, the Lithuanian people finally succeeded in regaining their independence as a free democratic nation in 1991.

1991 color film footage showed an older Jonas beside a fallen, dismantled statue of Lenin, holding a Lithuanian flag with many other Lithuanian citizens in celebration around him.

Jonas Tory founded the Tory Foundation in honor of his brother Lucas in 1970, seven years after Lucas Tory was believed to be killed by his KGB captors. To this day, the Foundation continues the legacy of the entire Tory Family.

The documentary ended with the same trumpet and drumbeat, ending with photos of Jonas, my mother and father, taken together and individually. More modern photos of Jonas and my mother standing alongside Queen Elizabeth, shaking hands with Presidents Nixon, Reagan, George H.W. Bush and Clinton, and with Jonas arm-in-arm with Princess Diana flashed on the screen to the beat of the drum. The final photograph faded in. It was a photo my father wearing a broad smile, chin up looking directly in the camera as if he were about to say something. The caption read:

Lucas Tory, 1925-1963
38 years old...

The lights turned on and I drank from the glass of ice water in front of me. Ruth Recordan sat down beside me. My throat was constricted, and I realized my face was wet with tears. I watched

Laurent Abraham walk over to the front of the room as the television screen retracted.

"Congressman, you can see that although Jonas was responsible for beginning the foundation, it was your father who inspired it. Jonas' interest was to create a living memorial to your father and your grandparents—to honor their ultimate sacrifice, and to continue their effort to support freedom and democracy where it is threatened." Abraham turned to the glass map with the light dots scattered all around it. "Here you see where we are located around the globe. The green lights depict single individuals. The blue lights depict our team locations. Today we have 13,453 people performing this work in 265 different countries."

I continued to drink ice water, and poured another glass. My conversation with Aksel Odin kept running through my mind: "*In many ways, we are the private face of the foundation. ...and tomorrow morning you will meet the public face.*"

Sitting at that conference table, I was more conflicted than I've ever been. My brows were furrowed, mostly because of the frustration of being the last to know about my family—and yet I felt a great sense of pride in knowing of their wartime service and sacrifices dating back to the Second World War.

I still had a lot of questions—how I came to inherit billions of dollars prime among them. But I always trusted Jonas more than anyone in the world. I was beginning to trust the people who made up the Tory Foundation—they were sincere and forthright, and obviously very loyal to Jonas and our family.

"Where did the foundation's money come from, Lor?" I asked abruptly.

Abraham nodded quietly and I saw him cast a fleeting glance over at Ruth, who nodded ever so slightly. "That too is complicated, but I can assure you it is all fully legal."

Ruth continued the answer for Abraham. "Some high profile figures and governments are unhappy about that still today, Daniel. During World War II, in the course of a raid, your parents and Jonas discovered information that the Nazis were moving a portion of stolen

Soviet gold reserves from Leningrad to Berlin by train on a specific night. With a large, well-equipped resistance party, they were successful in clandestinely boarding the train while it was still in motion inside a tunnel, and ambushed the Russian guard force taking them by surprise. 900 tons of gold was loaded onto waiting trucks outside Leningrad and stored in the basement of an Estonian barn for many years. After the war, the gold was recovered by your parents and Jonas. Some of it was sold and used to fund their resistance against the Soviet Union after they reinvaded Lithuania. The rest was stored."

"What is 900 tons of gold worth?" I interjected.

Ruth looked over at Abraham briefly. "900 tons of gold would be worth $3.27 billion today."

I swallowed hard, glanced over at Robin who stood wide-eyed.

Abraham continued. "The rest of those funds were invested and banked here in Switzerland and around the world, and has continued to accrue interest since. Once the Tory Foundation was created, the OSS and later the CIA—under Bill Casey and George H.W. Bush—employed us extensively to help them wage the Cold War behind the Iron Curtain and elsewhere. We were generously funded and resourced for three decades by your government. It is no accident that the Soviets were defeated in Afghanistan."

"I see," I said, groping for something further to say.

There was a momentary silence, which Ruth interrupted. "Our work is not finished, Daniel."

I shook my head, dumbstruck. "So what exactly does that mean? That we're still in the train robbing business?" I blurted, regretting it immediately. My attempt at humor wasn't acknowledged by anyone except Robin, who was doing her best to conceal her smile.

"Those people who work for us—represented by the dots of lights you see around the globe—generally do so at great risk to their own lives, Congressman," Abraham said evenly, pointing at some of the lights on the map. "They run a free press in Ukraine, cyber security teams in Moscow and Beijing, nuclear reporting in Iran and North Korea, economic reporting in Venezuela, Iraq and Afghanistan. It was not a game then for your parents and your uncle, nor is it now."

I shook my head. "No, I didn't mean—"

Ruth continued. "Since we were established in 1970, 14,576 men and women have died in the service of the Tory Foundation and their respective countries, fighting for democracy and freedom. It is an invisible war."

"I see."

"On occasion, through our sources and our people, we are able to see an international threat or situation develop far in advance of other intelligence agencies or media outlets. Becoming involved in those situations quickly and taking decisive action can often preempt the threat from maturing into something much worse."

I nodded.

Ruth Recordan was sitting straight in her chair. "We believe we have a situation at hand today."

CHAPTER 32

RUTH AND LAURENT WERE SILENT for a moment. It was Ruth who spoke up after an implicit nod from Abraham. "Daniel, we can provide you with either general or specific information on this threat. In general terms, as I mentioned to you last night, we are quite certain that the Kremlin is planning to invade and occupy the Baltic States of Estonia, Latvia and Lithuania soon—very soon."

"And what are you basing this on, specifically?" Robin asked

Laurent Abraham stepped forward slightly and addressed me. "Congressman, we can brief you on this information, but only you." He looked over at Robin. "I'm sorry, Ms. Nielsen, both the information and our sources are very sensitive. And we must protect them at all costs. I hope you understand."

Robin nodded and looked over, exchanging eye contact with me. "Of course."

Ruth opened the door to the conference room, "Daniel, please follow me."

We walked to a glass-encased elevator that allowed its passengers to see the castle's entire expanse as we ascended. Stepping off the elevator into a marble and glass anteroom, we faced a stainless steel door that looked like something out of the movie, *Goldfinger*. Abraham slid a card inside a slot, punched a code and then placed his chin on a grooved slot for a retinal scan. Upon successful completion of the sequence, the door unlocked into a large room with a multitude of computer terminals, Tandberg video teleconferencing machines,

116

digital world time zone clocks, recessed lighting, small glass offices in the back of the room, and coterie of people working and consulting with one another quietly. Digital television screens lined the walls. On the left side they played news sites from around the world and on the right side the video appeared to be from static surveillance cameras. On a full wall-size screen at the front of the room, an oversized military aviator-style map of the Baltic region and western Russia was displayed on a large television screen. It was the first real command center that I'd seen, and it was as impressive as anything I could have imagined.

Laurent Abraham motioned me to a chair behind an oval walnut table at the front of the room. Both he and Ruth sat beside me. A younger man, tall, short haircut and impeccably dressed in a grey suit, walked in from behind us and approached me.

"Congressman Tory, welcome to the Lucas Tory Operations Center—named in honor of your father. I am Augustas Valdemaras, the Chief Operating Officer for the Tory Foundation. I am briefing you today on a grave, imminent threat to the Baltic region by the Russian Federation."

Ruth interrupted. "Daniel, Augustas is the son of one of the original Hawks partisans, whose family was killed by Lithuanian *Smogikai*—Soviet double agents. His parents were dear friends of your parents, and Jonas."

"It is an honor," Augustas replied, and bowed slightly before continuing. "As you know, the Kremlin does not regard their invasion of the Baltic states as an occupation. In 2005, the U.S. House of Representatives passed a resolution requesting the Kremlin admit culpability for the occupation and denounce it."

Valdemaras flashed a quote on the screen:

"Now, therefore, be it resolved by the House of Representatives (the Senate concurring), That it is the sense of Congress that the Government of the Russian Federation should issue a clear and unambiguous statement of admission and condemnation of the illegal occupation and annexation by the Soviet Union from 1940 to 1991 of the Baltic countries of Estonia, Latvia, and Lithuania,

the consequence of which will be a significant increase in good will among the affected peoples and enhanced regional stability."
United States House of Representatives, July 25, 2005

"Despite the U.S. Congressional request, the Kremlin refused. Only a few months ago, the U.S. Senate passed a similar resolution, but it too was refused in the strongest terms. In fact, it elicited a visceral reaction from the Kremlin and from the Russian Parliament."

Additional quotes with the names and photographs of those who said them emerged onto the screen:

> *"To say that USSR had occupied the Baltic states is historical revisionism, and it is false. It is impossible to occupy a nation that already belongs to you—and where your people have lived and resided throughout history."*
> *-Russian Federation's Foreign Minister Sergei Andropov, May 7, 2012, in an address to Red Army veterans*

> *"What occupation? Absurd. The Molotov-Ribbentrop Pact stipulated that Nazi Germany was "giving back" Baltic territories to the Soviet Union in 1939. The Baltic countries therefore could not have been occupied, because they were already part of the Soviet Union."*
> *-Russian Federation President, Oleksandr Ivanov, May 21, 2012*

"The Kremlin's propoganda since the U.S. Senate resolution has continued, unabated, and it has worsened over the past several months in the aftermath of the occupation of Ukraine. The fact remains that Russia continues to view the Baltic states' accession into NATO as unacceptable. As recently as last month, the Russian Prime Minister called it "illegal" and said Russia did not recognize the Estonia, Latvia and Lithuania as viable members of the North Atlantic Treaty Organization."

Augustas Valdemaras directed his red laser pointer to Moscow, and then shifted it to the expanse of Western Europe. "Most of Russia's new leadership does not remember the strains of the Cold War and the economic and political costs associated with that period. They believe that the independence of the Baltics following the fall of the Berlin Wall was a historical mistake."

"This is all interesting, and even concerning," I interrupted cautiously. "But hardly a compelling case that the Baltics are on the verge of being reinvaded. With their occupation of Ukraine and their expedition in Syria and the Middle East, it seems obvious that they don't have the resources to invade the Baltics."

Valdermas nodded. "You should know that one of the distinct advantages possessed by the Tory Foundation globally, are our sources and operatives native to the countries we monitor and track. Nowhere is our network more sophisticated, with more breadth and depth, than in Russia."

Valdermas pointed to the digital map with photos of houses, apartments, warehouses and even a several Russian Orthodox churches, among others. "Through those operatives and sources we have obtained positive indicators of the Kremlin leadership's plan to launch an invasion to seize control of Estonia, Latvia and Lithuania—within the month."

I held my hand up to interrupt. "But what evidence do you have?" I stressed.

"The Russian Ministry of Defense scheduled a joint naval and ground exercise around the Baltic Region that includes a heavy naval presence in the Baltic Sea. That is a first indicator."

"The Russians do military exercises in this area every year, so that shouldn't qualify as a reliable indicator of an imminent invasion," I countered.

"This exercise is much larger than any other scheduled in over thirty years, Congressman. In addition, they have implemented a much more complex and secure field communications network. They have changed from radios to land lines for all traffic to and from Moscow, which is very unusual—really unprecedented for a field exercise. Our second indication was the movement of live ammunition, fuel, and food stockpiles from Moscow and Ekatrinaburg to Kaliningrad and St. Petersburg."

"Kaliningrad?"

"The Russian exclave here," Valdermas pointed the red laser just below Lithuania. "Between Poland and Lithuania on the Baltic Sea. It's geographically separated from the rest of Russia. Because it's the only Russian Baltic Sea port that's ice-free year-round, it plays an important strategic role in positioning Russia's Baltic Fleet."

"An exercise could still explain the movement of those stockpiles, could it not?" I asked somewhat skeptically.

Valdermas nodded. "It's possible; however, we have also learned that many Russian Army and Navy reservists have been recalled, all leaves have been canceled, and most training courses are being canceled. In addition, many of Russia's Spetsnaz units—their Special Forces units—have quietly been moved into Kaliningrad and St. Petersburg as well, and are positioned near large airstrips. By the end of the week, the Russian Federation will be capable of launching an invasion of the Baltic States with 20 divisions, and in three weeks will be able to increase the invasion force to 30 divisions."

I felt myself shudder, but even with these unmistakable signs, I didn't want to believe that the Kremlin would want to take such a dramatic risk on the international stage. "Is there a smoking gun, or are these just circumstantial indicators?"

Valdermas nodded to the computer operator who was controlling the slides on the screen in front of me. A shaky cellphone video began to play, obviously shot from the roof of a building, depicting a massive quadrangle below with thousands of troops standing at attention, flanked by tanks and other armored vehicles. Oversized Russian tri-colored blue, white, and red flags hung on the side of the surrounding buildings. A command was issued, and the entire formation shouted in unison. The English translation was sub-scripted.

"Victory! For the Motherland!"

After a brief pause, another voice in Russian could be heard over the microphone:

"Comrades! You are here today to prepare for a national day of reckoning! A day we never should have had to face, but one that we face with great pride and fervor! Three and a half decades ago, the Soviet Republics of Lithuania, Estonia, and Latvia were given away unlawfully with the mistaken belief that doing so would enhance our standing in the world, and lead to greater prosperity for Russia. Of course, that has not happened, and today, we face a significant threat from NATO in return. Our countrymen living in all three of these republics are being persecuted and discriminated against, for being Russian. They are being denied jobs, or even welfare, so they are unable to feed their children. Thousands of Russians have been arrested and imprisoned, with no trial. Hundred of Russians who dared to protest their treatment, have been gunned down in the streets of Vilnius, Tallinn, and Riga, and left to rot!

Comrades! Today, we begin preparing to take back what has always been ours, and to regain the glory of the Motherland! We have three short weeks to organize, arm, equip and train for this important event in our history! You will overwhelm and neutralize any resistance in a show of force unlike what NATO has ever before seen. Like lightning, you will strike by air, sea, and land!

Comrades! For the Motherland!

Thunderous and sustained applause followed. I turned to Augustus. "Who is that speaking?"

Valdermas nodded. "Marshal of the Russian Federation Igor Yegarov. He was just promoted to the rank, we believe to lead this invasion of the Baltics."

Ruth placed her hand on mine. "As bad as this is, unfortunately, there is more—and until that picture is fully developed, we are very reluctant to share any of it for fear that it will compromise our sources and our team members, and place their lives at grave risk."

"What else could there possibly be?" I asked, visibly alarmed.

"As compelling as this video may be, it unfortunately does not represent conclusive proof of Russia's intent to invade the Balkans. The video and sound quality is too poor, and the United States has resisted any actions that might offend Moscow—they would likely classify this as 'heated rhetoric,'" Valdermas replied. "Unassailable proof of an imminent invasion and threat to all of Europe will be required to gain NATO's support. Absent that, NATO will likely remain on the sidelines. Losing the Baltic States has very serious immediate and long-term implications—that extend from NATO's demise to...." Her voice trailed off.

"To what?" I asked.

Ruth turned in her chair to face me directly. "To an armed confrontation in Europe."

"But is that really possible?" I asked.

Ruth nodded. "In fact it is likely, and with NATO in a state of paralysis, it could escalate quickly, and it would be very difficult to contain."

"If NATO, the EU, and Washington remain complacent and don't see this as a threat, what can be done?"

"It is why we exist," Ruth said matter-of-factly. "A number of very sensitive operations will be required to address this threat. We are planning an operational surge throughout Europe and Russia that is unprecedented in our organization's history. It will be very expensive, and very risky—strategically and reputationally."

"You say we have people in Russia," I said, shifting the conversation. "I understand I may have a sister? Who I never knew existed until a few days ago."

Ruth nodded, and looked up at Augustas Valdermas. A color photograph appeared on the screen of a tall, older woman, brunette-gray, with once model-like features, stylishly dressed in a gray pin-striped business skirt suit. She wore dark sunglasses, which prevented a good view of her face.

"This is your sister, Daniel," Ruth said. "Her name is Tatyana Petrova. She lives in Moscow with her daughter."

"When can we pull them out of there?"

Ruth shook her head. "It's not at all that simple. We wish it were."

Aside from just being told I was an uncle, I was becoming visibly frustrated. "Well, what's so complicated about it, and when we can bring to bear all of the Foundation's vast resources? I have an airplane sitting on a tarmac just down the road that could go pick her up right now!"

Ruth spoke evenly, and calmly. The force of her response quieted the room. "Because Tatyana is the principal executive assistant to Russia's Prime Minister."

CHAPTER 33

WE DROVE OFF FROM the Schlossberg Castle in relative silence. Robin sensed that I was trying to sort through all the information that had been thrust at me, and didn't ask any questions. She mentioned that while she was waiting for me, she had a telephone call with the Congressional Member Services Office to let her know she would be their contact from now on, and to just copy me on their correspondence regarding my office set up. Actually, with that off my plate, it was a big relief.

"I told them we were only going to be starting off with a skeletal staff, and would build up over time," Robin continued. "Once we know your committee assignments."

I nodded. As our driver was about to pull into the President Wilson Hotel, I tapped him on the shoulder and asked him to drive us to a cafe that would offer some privacy. We ended up at *La Tour Carree*, a small, out-of-the-way café on the far left bank of Lake Geneva populated mostly by neighborhood locals. We sat outside under a clear, blue sky and could hear the waves lapping on the shore. In the distance we could see the *Jet d'Eau*—a massive, single stream fountain, and one of Geneva's most famous landmarks.

"I understand if you can't tell me what they told you back there," Robin finally said. "But I can't help you if I'm left operating in the dark."

I nodded. "Well, they did a pretty good job of proving their point."

"What point?" Robin asked

"Your point actually," I answered. "That the Baltic States are on the brink of a Russian invasion, and NATO's on the verge of collapse."

"Where are they getting their information?"

"They obviously have an impressive network of sources and their technical capabilities are state-of-the-art," I answered. "It's like another parallel version of the CIA."

"Oh," Robin replied shaking her head. "What could possibly go wrong with *that?*"

"Their reach and their information is impressive, any way you look at it."

"No one's going to listen unless you provide pretty compelling proof."

"They're massing on the borders of Estonia, Latvia, and Lithuania," I said. "That should be something your people could confirm with satellite imagery and other sources, right?"

Robin nodded impassively. "Yes, but the Kremlin does that all the time. Intimidating their former republics is a national past-time for the Russians."

"They promoted a guy to Marshal of the Russian Federation," I answered. "Just to take back the Baltics. I saw a video they smuggled out of him giving a pep talk to an entire Russian tank division. It's happening in the next several weeks."

Robin shrugged. "Something like that can be easily fabricated."

"What are you saying?" I asked, more than a little frustrated.

"Just that there may be some agendas here that we're not aware of," Robin answered. "They seem like nice people. Responsible people in high offices, held in high esteem. And they've seemed to advance a good cause. But they also have a clandestine side to their operation that isn't announced. In fact, it's pretty well-hidden from view."

"They're doing their best to draw me in to be their chairman," I said. "To replace Jonas."

"Are you?"

"What?"

"Drawn in?"

"I'm not sure yet."

Robin seemed trained to take in information, absorb and analyze it, and then fill in the remaining gaps. "What next, then?"

Before I could answer, the waiter came by our table and poured water in our glasses and gave us a basket of bread with butter. More to delay answering Robin's question, I ordered calamari and a '96 Pétrus Merlot.

"I came here to find out about my family, so that's what I'm going to do," I finally answered. "In three weeks I have to be in Washington, so this is my only opportunity."

"It sounds like we could be dealing with a full blown global crisis in three weeks. You'll be just in time."

"Or, too late."

The waiter returned with our bottle of wine and allowed me to inspect the label. I nodded my approval. He pulled out a black corkscrew and with the bottle on the table, carefully began to cut the foil.

"I'd also like to meet my sister," I continued. "Since I just found out I have one."

I could see her lips tighten with concern.

"And I understand she has a daughter," I said. "So I'm an uncle— who knew?"

The waiter pulled the cork out of the bottle of the Pétrus and poured a glass for me to test. After I approved, he poured a glass for each of us.

Robin waited for the waiter to leave. "The Company might have a problem with me going to Moscow, especially after the incident at the watch store yesterday."

"Tell Langley they have a rogue congressman on the loose," I said, tasting the wine. "And you're the only one who can possibly control him."

Robin smiled, shaking her head. "Can I?"

"What?" I asked, momentarily confused.

"Control him?"

"Probably not," I answered, smiling at the innuendo. "But that shouldn't deter you from trying."

"You'll need clearance to fly your plane in to Moscow, and visas—

preferably the diplomatic variety."

Robin pulled out the notebook that I recognized by now as my father's. "While you were in your briefing upstairs in the castle, I toiled in the dungeon." She paused and looked up at me. "Your father's diary is far more intriguing than any private Top Secret briefing they could have given you."

I took the notebook, and laid it on the table.

"Cheers," I said, raising my glass in a toast.

"So, to family," she said, suddenly in a more serious tone.

"To family," I repeated, clinking glasses.

We returned to the President Wilson Hotel after a few hours and more than my fair share of exceptional Swiss food and wine. That, compounded by lingering jet lag and the sensory overload of the past few days had taken its toll. When we got up to our suite, I laid down on the bed with Robin's translation of my father's journal.

September 3, 1940 – *They took Mother and Father away. A neighbor saw the Russians loading them into a truck. Jonas and I are trying to find where they brought them. Our house is ransacked. It's our fault that we were not here to stop the Russians. We could have put up a fight. One of our partisans believes it was the NKVD who took them with the help of Lithuanian collaborators, and that they will be taken to one of Stalin's work camps in North Russia in Siberia, like so many others we know. We are talking to many people and searching, but we are losing hope because we have no idea where they might be. Jonas tells me that now I must be the leader of the Hawks, but I told him it is the last thing on my mind, and I am not ready. He and others insist that I am now the commander.*

The next passage was dated, March 1941—nearly a six month gap:

March 3, 1941 - *We continue to fight and to resist the Soviets, but hunger, freezing cold, and sickness is causing many of us to die in great numbers. We bury our family members every day now. There isn't enough food for all of us. The young and the elderly are suffering. Tempers run high. Jonas is very sick with fever. We need medicines that we do not have. Father would know what to do if he were here. I think about him and Mother often. I miss them and pray for them, and wonder if I will ever see them again. The Russians are deporting more and more Lithuanians. We find a newspaper that calls those they send to Siberia, "Enemies of the People."*

June 16, 1941 – *We are seeing more and more Soviet trucks and trains taking Lithuanians away from their homes. As soon as people begin to see what is happening, they come to the forests to escape. Hundreds more have come to us when they find where we are. I am worried, because if they can find us, so can the NKVD. We now move our camps almost every day so at least we are a moving target. People complain about moving so much, but Jonas and I tell them our only other choices are to be deported or be killed. One of the men who just joined our group came from Vilnius. He tells me that the Kremlin is conducting mass deportations now so that they can move Russian colonists in to replace us to make Lithuania part of Russia.*

June 21, 1941 – *It is a very bad time. Our family in the forest grows quickly, and it is more and more difficult to feed and care for everyone, especially the elderly. The more people we have, the slower and more unwieldy we become as a group. The Soviets have taken people from their homes, and most farmhouses we go to are now vacant. But only recently, we have seen the Russian patrols less often. There are less military cars and trucks and tanks on our roads. Many of the Russian encampments are abandoned. We do not know why, except that they may be getting diverted to fight in Poland. Some say they do not trust the Germans. Many of our people think the Germans will invade Lithuania soon. At night we go to the abandoned Russian Army camps and take their ammunition and weapons they have left behind. As we bring in more supplies, I tell everyone to save what we have because we will surely need them later. Jonas and I agree we must continue attacking the Soviets wherever we find them. Keeping our fighters busy fighting is the best way I know to prevent unrest and arguing amongst ourselves, so we do not destroy ourselves from within. Many of our people want the Germans to invade, so we can declare independence— but I tell them they are as much an enemy to us as the Bolsheviks.*

I must have fallen asleep as I was reading, because several hours later I heard what I thought was a knocking on the door, and suddenly Robin was sitting on the side of the bed, shaking me, and urging me to wake up.

CHAPTER 34

HER TONE WAS URGENT AND DIRECT.

I sat up, rubbed my eyes open, and tried to focus.

"Daniel, the police are at Schlossberg Castle. There was an attack there about an hour ago. The chief of security here at the hotel told me everyone inside was killed. They say it was criminal, but I suspect it was an FSB assassination team."

"My God..." I whispered.

"Daniel, listen to me, we've got to get you out of Geneva and back to the States," Robin said calmly, but firmly. "You were likely their main target, and they missed."

"Who was there?" I asked. "Who was killed?"

"I'll give you the names, but understand—you're in grave danger. We've got to go."

I shook my head. "No, I'm sticking to the plan."

"That's insane," Robin said, shaking her head. "You don't really have a plan, and you have no idea what these people are capable of."

"I'm getting a pretty good idea." I picked up the notebook with my father's translated journal passages, and handed it to her. "Just a week ago, I would have run, but reading this, from seventy years ago, changed that. One thing I know now about my father is that he didn't retreat or back down. Neither did Jonas. And now, neither will I."

"I wouldn't advise it."

I shrugged. "Thanks for your advice."

"But if you're going, I'm going with you."

"Don't you need approval from your headquarters?"

Robin nodded. "Someone from our office in Bern is coming down with some alternate passports and visas."

I couldn't help but be amused. "So you knew I'd refuse to go back to the States?"

Robin shrugged. "Yes, I'm getting to know you pretty well, but you need to know that no matter what our passports and Visas say, they'll know exactly who you are when we land. We may have the element of surprise, because you coming to them is the last thing they'll expect. When they figure it out, we might not even make it past Customs. You won't reconsider?"

I shook my head. "You have a list of everyone who was killed, don't you?"

Robin nodded, and reluctantly handed me a piece of hotel stationary, folded in half. From the way she'd hurriedly written the names, I sensed they had been dictated over the phone:

Ruth Recordan
Laurent Abraham
Augustas Valdermas...

There were ten-or-so more names on the list that I didn't recognize. But I felt personally responsible for each of them. Their deaths were confirmation enough that Moscow saw the Tory Foundation as a threat to their agenda. I felt a surge of intense sadness, and anger.

"We're going to take care of families and bury our dead," I said, now feeling a conviction deeper than reason or logic overcome me. I reviewed the names on the list again and handed it back to her. "Aksel Odin isn't listed—we need to find him."

CHAPTER 35

AKSEL ODIN WASN'T EASY TO FIND. He'd flown to Luxembourg City earlier in the morning. An hour later, his office located him, and he called us back on his cell phone.

"I'll send a team of our own people down there right away," he said after a long silence. We agreed that he would be the interim Executive Director of the Tory Foundation, and his first task would be to disperse funds to support the families of our teammates who were gunned down.

About the time that I'd hung up, the telephone rang again. Robin answered it, and I could hear her speaking in a language that I thought was French. She hung up and turned to me. "It was a police detective asking you to come to their Geneva headquarters. I told them they would have to come here because of the risk, and that you were expecting a full briefing on the incident."

"They agreed?" I said.

Robin nodded. "We'll see how forthcoming they are."

I detected a distinct change in her voice, and I looked up at her. She looked anxious—even vulnerable.

"Despite what you think, I'm not used to this. In fact, I'm really worried."

"So am I, but I hope you'll see this through with me."

Robin nodded. "I can stay with you as long as I'm able to preserve my cover. Langley is working with State to provide you and me diplomatic cover with diplomatic credentials and passports—the

Full Monty."

"Okay," I replied simply. "I always wanted to be a diplomat-spy."

Robin scrutinized me with a rather searing look, and followed up with a scolding tone. "This isn't a game, Daniel. The moment we cross into Russia, you know we'll be crossing a point of no return, right?"

"We crossed that this afternoon when our people were murdered in cold blood." I said, looking at Robin intently. "Your agenda might be to collect intelligence on the Tory Foundation and anything about a possible invasion of the Baltics. But I plan to find out who's responsible for killing our people in cold blood."

"Those agendas aren't mutually exclusive," Robin said evenly.

"That would be good."

"And what will you do when you find their killers?"

"I don't know yet," I responded.

She nodded, pursing her lips slightly. "When the Geneva police come here, neither of us can reveal that we know anything about what happened yesterday at *Patek Philippe*. They probably already suspect you're involved in some way, given that both incidents occurred only a day apart."

"Don't they have closed circuit video coverage of the entire building?"

"That's been addressed," Robin said with a sort of vague confidence that disarmed me. "But they do have eye witnesses. Once they suspect you and I were there, I'm afraid we'll be stuck here for quite a while."

"What are you saying?"

"I'm saying that we can't stay here," she said. "We've got to go."

"I'm not afraid of telling the police what happened."

"Then you lose me," Robin answered matter-of-factly. "Langley will never go for it. They'll pull me the moment my cover is blown. But Daniel—"

"What?"

She hesitated. Her voice wavered. "You do realize that in doing this you're endangering your congressional career, not to mention your life?"

I nodded, suddenly doubting myself. I thought of my father and of Jonas—the responsibility both of them had taken on in the forests of Lithuania more than half a century ago. Just from my father's journal entries, it was obvious to me that they never backed down, even in the face of overwhelming odds.

I nodded slowly. "As soon as we're done with the police, I need to see Ambassador Williamson and Mayor Recordan—I'm going to tell them, because they both have a right to know. And our next stop will be the airport."

Robin nodded. "I'll call the pilots and tell them to get ready— where are we going?"

"East."

CHAPTER 36

I FELT LIKE ONE OF THOSE CRIMINALS on *Law and Order,* who's not yet a suspect, but who's as guilty as the day is long. Throughout their visit with us at the President Wilson Hotel, the Geneva *Polizei* detectives were very professional, almost deferential.

There were three detectives, dressed in suits. When the head detective mentioned the shooting at *Patek Philippe,* I shrugged and claimed ignorance about their theory that both incidents were likely connected. Robin served glasses of ice water to all of us as we discussed the incident.

Although the lead detective told me that they couldn't talk about any evidence they had collected from their investigation of the murders at the castle, it was all-too evident from our discussion that they suspected a team of professional hit men were responsible. He also told me that they believed I was on their target list, and that my life was in great danger.

One of the detectives began to stand, and then fell face-first onto the table.

Crack! …Crack! Crack!

The shots sounded a lot like bats hitting baseballs in quick succession. Without warning, I had three Swiss detectives dead, right in front of me with bullet holes in their foreheads. It was that sudden—that abrupt. I fell down on the floor and looked up to see Robin holding a stainless steel automatic handgun, with a silencer on its barrel.

I pointed at her gun, and asked somewhat ridiculously, *"What is that?"*

"It's a suppressed CZ 75 SP-01 Shadow," Robin said in a matter-of-fact tone, still holding her silenced pistol at the ready, while checking each of the men for a pulse.

"Jesus! They were Geneva Police! They had fucking badges!" I shouted. *"What did you just do?"*

"That's part of the FSB team responsible for the massacre at the castle. You and I were next." She pulled the lead detective from the table back into his chair, and handed me his notepad. "Look."

"At what?"

"Open the notepad."

I opened it and saw a lot of illegible cursive writing that I couldn't decipher, at all.

"I can't read it," I said.

Robin nodded. "You can't read it, because it's in Cyrillic. And you can't comprehend it because the language is Russian. I was able to get a glimpse of the notepad when I served them their water." She pulled out his wallet. "All of his identification cards are in Russian too." She walked over to the man who had fallen face-first onto the ground behind me, pulled down his collar to reveal a Russian Orthodox cross tattooed on the back of his neck. She rolled him over. He was still holding a silenced pistol in his hand, with his finger still in the trigger guard. "He was assigned to kill us. The other two were brought to distract us and back him up."

"That one had Geneva *Polizei* identification!" I argued, pointing at the dead guy in front of me. "He showed it to us!"

"It was either forged or it was stolen," she answered. "It's probably exactly how they gained entry to the castle."

I kept shaking my head in denial.

"This is what I've been trying to tell you, Daniel—they're trying to kill you. Not capture you—*kill* you."

I moved quickly into the kitchen as far away from the scattered bodies as possible. "Okay. I get that," I said flatly. "You obviously knew who they were before you saw the notepad—*how did you know?"*

"Russian Forest," she said matter-of-factly.

"Excuse me?" I said.

"It's a men's cologne by Novaya Zarya. A Russian favorite—has a distinct aroma of wood and soil. I smelled it when they came through the door. Swiss men don't wear it."

I nodded, and couldn't help but be impressed. "Okay, so now we have three dead guys in our hotel suite. What do we do now? Call the bell man?"

"Calm down, Daniel." Robin said in a hushed, urgent voice. "Better them than you. I'll get a team over here to clean this up."

I watched as she quickly began checking the pockets of the dead men. She removed their wallets and cell phones, quickly looked at the displays of each cell phone, and then held on to one of them, draping her wool coat over her arm to conceal the pistol with silencer.

"Stay here."

"Where are you going?"

"To see if there are any more downstairs," she answered. "Don't answer the door for anyone. Use the panic button in your bedroom if you have to. Understand?"

I nodded.

"I'll be right back," she said, holding up her card key.

I felt a wave of delayed, frenzied panic wash over me as the door shut behind her, leaving me alone with the corpses of three FSB hit men.

CHAPTER 37

THERE'S SOMETHING SURREAL ABOUT sitting alone with three dead guys in the same room.

I hurriedly began packing, throwing clothes into my bags and cramming shoes and toiletries into any corners where they would fit.

Without warning, everything had violently shifted—what began as a quest to learn more about my family had quickly turned into a bloody nightmare where preemptively killing people was just part of doing business.

I sat down on the bed holding one of my shoes in both hands, realizing that I had no control over anything. And worse, I didn't have any real clarity about the path ahead either. Everyone close to me was either dead, dying, or at risk of being killed. *Probably me among them.*

I looked over at the dead policemen in the living room, and threw a shoe at them out of sheer anger and frustration. I was reeling—never feeling so completely out of control.

My cell phone rang and Elena's name came up—I immediately answered.

"Daniel, your Mom is out of her coma, and she's asking about you."

"She's okay?"

"The doctors say that it wasn't an aneurysm, but a mild stroke. She should be fine—they'll keep her here for another week, and then allow her to go home. She just needs to rest and be removed from stress."

"Don't tell her I'm in Europe then," I instructed.

"I won't," she answered. "Where can I reach you?"

"I'm flying to Moscow, but will be back in a few days."

"Be safe," Elena said.

Suddenly, all the campaign promises I'd made over the past year seemed inconsequential compared to what I was now facing with my mother's condition and with the assault on the Foundation.

Part of the oath a congressman takes is like any other oath that someone in the military takes, or a president, for that matter. In that oath, defending "against all enemies; foreign and domestic," and "without purpose of evasion," wasn't just a suggestion, it was explicit. Although I hadn't yet raised my right hand to take that oath, the fact was, neither had my parents or Jonas. They just did what they had to do, armed with a value system that was uncompromising, and hard-wired into them from a sense of patriotism to their homeland, and their loyalty toward one another.

I wondered what Jonas or my parents would do if they were in my situation. But instinctively, I already knew.

"Never retreat..."

"Pardon me?" I must have said it out loud, because when I looked up, Robin was standing outside my bedroom door with the shoe I had thrown at the dead hit men.

"You're back," I said.

Robin nodded, handing my shoe back. She was holding the pistol by her right side. "You're already packed."

I stood up and zipped both suitcases. "So should you."

"I called the pilots," Robin said. "They'll be ready for us when we arrive."

"Were there any more downstairs?"

"Excuse me?"

"Bad guys."

She shook her head slightly. "No, but they killed two Geneva *Polizei* and stole their car. Their bodies were in the trunk."

"Why would they do that?"

"For their credentials," Robin replied. "So they could gain entry to this suite."

I shook my head. "$73,000 a night doesn't buy you much anymore, does it?"

"Security is always an illusion, no matter how much you pay for it."

"Okay, can we leave now?"

"We have to wait until our cleanup team gets here," she said, glancing toward the dining room.

"Everything okay with your bosses at Langley?"

"They weren't really happy with me, but yes..." She paused. "Daniel?"

"You should know that this operation is now at the top of the agency's priority list."

"What does that mean?" I asked.

"On the one hand, it means we'll have all of the resources that the agency can bring to bear, whenever we need it."

"And on the other hand?"

"We'll also be under extraordinary scrutiny. Not only by the CIA, but likely the FSB and potentially the media as well. And it means we're not alone—we'll be getting a lot of help whether we want it or not."

I nodded. "Slight change in plans, then. We'll be flying into Moscow first."

Robin's eyes were wide with surprise. "You mean tonight?"

"Yes," I answered. "Tonight."

CHAPTER 38

I'M NOT SURE WHAT I HAD EXPECTED a CIA "cleaning team" to look like, but it wasn't a group of silent Fortune 50 executives in Armani suits carrying black nylon suitcases.

"It looks like they're here for a business meeting," I observed.

Robin escorted them upstairs and as soon as they walked inside, she turned to me.

"Let's go, we need to hurry."

Our car was waiting for us outside as we exited the elevator. We loaded our bags into the trunk and headed straight to the airport. When we arrived, the plane's engines were running. One of our pilots, a steward, and a Swiss customs agent were standing at the bottom of the air stairs. Robin opened the car door and I watched her move back toward the jet center. Just about then, the driver handed me an envelope.

"From Aksel Odin, Sir."

I placed the envelope into the inside pocket of my sports coat. When I stepped out of the car, I noticed that Robin was talking to a man dressed in a khaki photo journalist's vest, cargo pants and dark aviator's sunglasses. As I removed our bags, I saw him handing her a large envelope and a bulging, blue nylon pouch. Our driver offered to take the pouch for her, but Robin politely declined and directed him to the other bags. The pouch, I noticed, was zipped and locked with a small metal seal.

She walked back and handed me a black diplomatic passport,

141

and a pen.

"You'll need to sign this before you see that customs agent."

I was surprised to see my current passport photo and that all of my personal data was completely accurate. "I'm impressed," I said, signing the inside page. "Why is the CIA doing this for me?"

"Because you already have a Top Secret-SCI Clearance," Robin said under her breath. She pointed toward the nearby hangar. "Ambassador Williamson and Mayor Recordan are inside the hangar. They want to talk to you."

I nodded and walked over to the hangar. Ambassador John Williamson had his hand on Rémy Recordan's shoulder in quiet conversation. They both looked up at me as I approached.

"Mayor Recordan, after meeting Ruth just yesterday evening, I felt like I had known her for a very long time. I can't fully express my sadness for her loss, not only as the Chairman of the Tory Foundation, but also as such a close friend of our family. You have my deepest condolences, and my personal pledge that we will find those responsible and hold them accountable."

Recordan nodded. "Thank you, Congressman. You can understand that my family and I are in shock. We will put Ruth to rest, and we will carry on with her memory to guide us. We sincerely appreciate your support."

I turned to John Williamson. "Mr. Ambassador, can I speak to you?"

Williamson nodded, and walked with me out of the hangar toward the airplane.

"You are aware of the attempt that was just made on our lives at the President Wilson Hotel?"

Williamson nodded. "I was just briefed," he said. "And I'm very glad you and Robin are safe."

"If Robin hadn't taken action when she did, at Patek Philippe and at our hotel, I would not be here."

"I am told by our Station Chief that she is truly exceptional," Williamson replied.

"We are flying to Moscow," I said directly. "I'm going to find out who was responsible for killing our people in cold blood—and I'm going to try to stop the Kremlin's invasion of the Baltics, or at least delay it."

I could see Williamson take a full breath before responding. "We would strongly advise you not to go, Congressman. We understand your intent, but your plan may be so ambitious that it will make the situation even worse. Behind the scenes, there is a determined diplomatic effort underway."

"I understand that's the official message you had to deliver to me, Mr. Ambassador. I have received it."

Williamson nodded. We walked over to where Robin was standing and he stopped, and turned to face both of us. "Personally, I want you to go find the bastards who did this."

Robin and I shook Williamson's hand. As we walked toward the airplane, Robin whispered, "What was that about?"

"John Williamson is obviously not your average ambassador."

We handed our passports to the customs agent, who stamped both of them. Robin presented a card to him, who then crosschecked the number on the lock's metal seal.

Our pilot extended his hand. "Welcome back, Congressman. We're set to go."

"No problems getting the flight clearances to Moscow?"

"None at all, Sir—probably the quickest flight clearance change I've seen."

I thanked him, and apologized for the last-minute change in plans.

I sat across from Robin at the plane's dining room table. She appeared visibly anxious. Not at all herself. Her eyes were almost clenched shut.

"Are you okay?" I asked.

She opened her eyes for a moment and looked at me with an expression of intense concern. "Actually, No, I'm not. We're trained for this, but until now, I've never had to actually kill anyone before. And frankly, if you have to know, your plan to go to Moscow worries the hell out of me. It worries me even more that Langley so readily agreed to it. We managed to have our visas ready for us when we arrive at Vnukovo, but we are pushing the envelope on everything right now."

The anxiety in her voice was obvious, and in a strange way, I felt responsible. "I know you didn't sign up for this."

"Actually, I did. I'm under orders from Langley to stay with you," she said evenly. "That guy I was talking to on the tarmac a few minutes ago? That was the station chief for Switzerland, he's a friend, and he just asked me if I knew what I was getting myself into. Along with—" She stopped herself.

"Along with what?"

Robin looked at me for a few seconds as if she were considering what she could reveal, and then picked up the nylon briefcase and put it on the table in front of me.

"Here."

"What is it?"

"It's a diplomatic pouch with two automatic pistols, and ammunition." She walked to the plane's master suite as we prepared to take off.

I closed my eyes with the hope that I would be able to fall asleep, to no avail. I moved over to the sofa and pulled the notebook out of my backpack with Robin's translated passages of my father's journal, and opened it to the place where I'd left off.

March 12, 1941 – We have learned of a camp not far from us that the Nazis created at Paneriai. Even though it is just ten kilometers from Vilnius, it is in Poland. The rumors we hear say it is worse than a labor camp because the people who go there never leave. No one knows what kind of camp it is, but it is close to railroad tracks, and we hear that is how Jews from Lithuania and other countries are moved. It is their destination, and I fear that the Nazi SD and SS are massacring them. I tell Jonas that we need to find out what is happening in the camp and then report to Britain and the United States what we find so they can liberate this camp and any others—but also convince them to help our resistance groups. Jonas says we could do surveillance on the camp or capture one of the guards. I tell him that would not be enough to convince leaders from other countries of the truth of what is happening. I know many Lithuanians do not want to do this because people we know well—other Lithuanians—are helping the Nazis and see them as our liberators. The Lithuanians who are collaborating with the Nazis are called the Ypatingasis būrys [Vilnian Special Squad]. There are many of them. Partisans from around Lithuania have become Special Squads. And even some of our partisans say they are part of our effort, and see the Nazis as liberators, but I get angry with them, and insist that the Bolsheviks and the Nazis are equally bad— that both are occupiers and that they are helping to murder our own people. If they do not see the Nazis as our enemy, I tell them to leave the Hawks. Jonas is angry with me because I told him that I want to infiltrate the camp as a prisoner and then escape. He calls me reckless and irresponsible and tells me that I will be killed because no one ever leaves the Ponary Camp. But I tell him it is the only way, and it is our responsibility.

March 21, 1941 – Our plan is ready. We are in the forest just above the railroad tunnel near the Vilnius-Warsaw road, only half a mile from the camp. Jonas is still arguing with me and trying to change my mind, but I tell him it is just another operation, like all the others we have done successfully. We will plan for it as we do an attack or ambush and we will be victorious. I know when I go into the camp, I will not be alone. He insists the odds are overwhelming, that it has never been done before and I have a death wish. That is why we need to do this, I tell him. We have created a plan so that I will walk into an area where Jews are being rounded up in the Vilnius ghetto and being arrested. I will escape 30 days later with the help of Jonas and the rest of our Hawks. When I am ready, I will tie a cloth to the top of a pole on a building, and they will cut the fence for me to escape.

The next entry stood out, not just because of its length, but also because of the obvious gap in dates—nearly two years later. The hairs on my arms were standing up.

December 2, 1942 – Nothing went according to plan a year and a half ago, except that I was captured by the SS in the ghetto. There was screaming and yelling, babies crying, glass shattering and shots being fired. In all of the chaos, the Nazis arrested me—they requested no paperwork, asked no questions, just a push to the rest of the group of Jews they had awakened in the middle of the night. They loaded us on a truck and then a train. But that is where everything went so wrong. The train did not go to the Ponari camp, but to another camp in Poland near Birkenau— called Auschwitz. At the rail station, they were requested to separate into two groups. They asked those of us who did not feel well to move to the trucks to be driven from the station to the camp. The rest of us who were well enough were requested to walk. I told everyone to stay away from the trucks, but many chose to ride because they were exhausted from the terrible train ride. I never saw any of those people again, and I fear they were exterminated with gas. Auschwitz is a large complex of separate camps named A, B, C, D. B2B are women's camps scattered around Birkenau. Camp A is the reception center, after arriving there by foot, they shaved my head, sprayed us down and had a tattooed registration number placed on my left arm below my elbow. Once I was in the camp, I saw some people with numbers tattooed on their foreheads. I was brought to Camp D.

A camp has 30 blocks. At Camp A, for example, blocks 5 to 18 are the hospital where inmates worked under the supervision of Nazi doctors. Block 25 is called the Death Block by all of us because that is where those selected for the gas chamber are kept. It is a beautiful building with marble walls, but nobody who sees it ever comes out alive. Block 2 is a children's block; Block 3 a block for patients to heal. Most of the other blocks are sleeping blocks.

Camp D is crowded with three or four thousand people. We lived in a brick building with a tattered roof over it. Every day, we were hungry, we worked until our hands bled, we were beaten and whipped by the guards, and we expected to die at any moment. On cold days, the wind whipped through our building. I could not see how we could survive in these conditions.

Reveille is at 0330; at 0400 everybody falls out to be counted, regardless of how bad the weather is. This usually lasts until 0530. By 0600 we were being taken to our places of work. Some of us worked outside the camp, others worked inside the walls. Every day, when we left for our places of work, the KAPO received orders from their bosses of the number of us who had to die while at work. There is a daily quota to be filled, and many prisoners are beaten to death in the fields by Nazi supervisors and collaborator gang leaders. Those of us who are healthier, try to help by distracting the guards.

From 1200 to 1230 we would be allowed our rest break to drink a soup of water and rotten turnips. Early afternoon, we fell out again to be assigned to work details. At dusk, the work stopped and we were given two slices of bread and, every so often, a little piece of sausage to eat— but this ration was our breakfast, too. Since it was so small, and other fellow prisoners would try to steal rations, I would eat it most of the time, then and go to work hungry in the morning.

Shake down inspections happen every day, sometimes a few times a day. When we returned from work they inspected us to see if we had brought in any food or clothing while outside the camp. We weren't to have any possessions but the worn clothes on our bodies and the small rations we received. Any mistakes or perceived act of misbehavior is punished with terrible beatings that often kill us.

Every four weeks on Saturdays, we were herded into the sauna to be deloused. On these days reveille was at 0200. We were beaten out of our cages, then led to the sauna where we had to sit naked all day long until our clothes were deloused. In the evening we had to march back naked to our blocks in columns of five under the supervision of SS guards. Not until night did our clothes get returned to us. After each day in the sauna, more and more people died.

Generalappell is held on Sundays. Everybody falls out and camp officials go around selecting people without any real reason—but I notice that Prisoners who are too thin or who appear to be very sick are most likely to be taken to death block. I hear constant screaming, crying, and moaning from that building — day and night.

There is a rumor that high-ranking Nazis often watch the gassings through special windows that allowed them to see a hundred naked men and women die by poisonous gas all together. It usually takes about ten minutes for everyone in the chamber to die. I am a part of the special detail that is forced to remove the gold teeth from mouths of the corpses with special instruments that they give us, then takes the dead to the ovens or bury them in trenches we have dug. A detail of girls sorts the clothes of our fellow murdered prisoners. I have become acquainted with one girl, who is a little younger than me. Her name is Tanya and she is from the Vilnius ghetto. No matter how bad things are for us, she laughs and has a beautiful smile. I tell her we will survive, and she tells me she believes me. One day I am re-assigned to work in the laundry service for the camp, washing all of the guards' uniforms and clothing. It is an easier job, and I still see Tanya almost every day.

One day, Evgeniy Euchev, a friend and fellow prisoner who works in administration and records tells me Tanya is on a list to be exterminated in two days. I am frantic and spend the next day collecting four uniforms from the laundry. Evgeniy is able to steal two pistols while cleaning the guard barracks. Another friend, Pranas Kadžionis, works in the motor pool fixing and servicing the trucks and cars, and I ask him for his help.

It was dark and cold, and it had snowed heavily the day before. I searched everywhere for Tanya, but I could not find her. Finally I hear her voice in a formation as I am passing by with a wheelbarrow. In the darkness, I was able to pull her back to the last rank where I know we will be on the outside and in the very back. She asks me what I am doing, and that we will be caught—but I tell her not to ask questions, to just do what I say. As we begin to march past a block of wood buildings near the fence, I pull her underneath one of the buildings. I know she is very scared because her eyes are wide, but she moves quickly. I am afraid someone will notice us, but by some miracle, they don't. There are spotlights that hit the building every 45 seconds. We make it to the cleaners, and I hide her in a closet. I tell her there is a Nazi uniform for her to change into, and to wait for me. I will be back in 30 minutes and to come out in uniform only when she hears a car horn. Evgeniy, Pranas, and I meet in the camp garage and dress in the SS uniforms I stole from the laundry. I am in the uniform of an SS Lieutenant, and have a Luger pistol—but no ammunition. We move quickly, and drive to the cleaners, and Evgeniy sounds the car horn. Tanya came out with eyes wide. We drive directly to the camp gates, but we see the guard is not opening them. Pranas tells me, "Do something or we will die!" I tell Evgeniy to sound the horn, and I begin shouting in German, and waving the Luger out the window at the guard. The gates opened, and after driving nearly an hour, we escape on foot into the forest.

I awoke in my chair as we landed at Moscow's Vnukovo Airport in a cold, driving rain—with the newfound realization that my mother and father had met at, and escaped from, Auschwitz.

CHAPTER 39

WE TOUCHED DOWN AT THE Vnukovo Airport, on the outskirts of Moscow. I vaguely remember filling out customs forms, the rapid fire Russian exchange between Robin and the Vnukovo Customs Officer, and the men in cheap dark suits standing around outside our plane, just observing. I had expected the exchange with the airport and Customs to be tense and difficult, but it instead turned out to be effortless and quick. I saw Robin gesturing toward the diplomatic pouch on the plane's dining room table. *"Mi diplomaticheskuyou pochtu, Ya kuryer. Vot moi zakazi kurerom i identifekatsi."*

The customs agent nodded, making an annotation on his clipboard. "Enjoy your visit to Moscow, Mr. Tory," he said, handing our passports back to us.

That's when I discovered that with diplomatic passports, quick and effortless is just the way you roll.

"Welcome to the Hotel California," Robin commented dryly.

A grey Bentley drove us under police escort to the Ritz-Carlton. Arriving there was a major event for the hotel staff—led by the hotel manager and concierge, with multiple bellhops hopping and popping all around us.

What I didn't quite remember was going to bed …in the same bed, with Robin. But when I awoke there she was. Sound asleep— beside me. She was wearing a white patterned silk nightgown and even in my drugged-like state she took my breath away. I struggled to remember any conversation we may have had that got us there, I was that exhausted.

Sitting up in bed, wearing only boxer shorts, I struggled to put everything into an orderly context.

I got out of bed and looked out the window to see a full view of The Kremlin, fully lit surrounded by its massive red brick walls—and for a moment, my mind was propelled to a time long before when my parents were struggling against both Nazi and Soviet occupation.

The suite we were occupying had five separate rooms. It was stunning. As I walked around the suite, the views of Moscow from every room provided a perfect window into Russia's fascinating, turbulent history, dating back to the Tsars. Even at 2AM, the city was bustling with activity. Massive commercial banners enveloped whole sides of large buildings. Ornate Russian Orthodox cathedrals punctuated the landscape, standing in stark contrast to new very modern commercial buildings.

Walking into the kitchen area, I found a bottle of water in the refrigerator, and wandered into the suite's study. It was a beautiful room with maple bookshelves and a mahogany desk. The chair had been pulled back from the desk, and on top of the desk was my father's journal and Robin's pad with her handwritten translations of the entries. She had obviously been working on it while I was passed out. I sat down at the desk and flipped to the page where I had left off on the plane.

March 30, 1941 – _I fear my reports to Great Britain about Auschwitz are being ignored. They will not allow me to talk to Churchill or Roosevelt. I am able to speak to one American in London. His name is Major General William Donovan. He is a very tough and honest man, who listens to me and takes notes about everything I tell him, never looking down, always looking me in the eyes as he writes. He has a group of men who are called the Office of Strategic Services—the OSS. He tells me he believes everything I have reported, and that he will show my report to Roosevelt personally. I believe him. He asks me how I feel about the Soviets, and I tell him that I believe they will return to occupy not only Lithuania, but also Poland, Latvia, Estonia and all_ of Eastern Europe if the West does not stop them. He nodded through our conversation, and told me he agreed with my assessment. He asked about The Hawks, and I tell him that we will fight anyone who occupied Lithuania, whether it was the Nazis or the Soviets. "Good," he says. "I would like to help you with that." He tells me that he is interested in a "long-term relationship" with us. As I write this, I am sitting on an airstrip outside of London, called Croydon Airport. I will be flown by the British and dropped by parachute into a field where Jonas and our men will be waiting for me. General Donovan just came to say goodbye to me, and gives me a small bag of Krugerrand gold coins to help us, and a radio operator to arrange for supplies and support. I am very surprised, and told one of his officers that I have never met anyone quite like him. The major shakes his head, smiles at me and says, "Neither have we. We call him 'Wild Bill'."

April 2, 1941 – Jonas just told me that Tanya left our camp while I was in London. He did not want to tell me why she left, but I made him. Finally, he reveals to me that she was engaged to a Russian partisan named Antenas Petrov, and that she had to find him. I do not say anything, but I feel like part of me has died. Jonas tries to cheer me up and keep me busy, but I am in no mood. Jonas tells me we can go find the Russian, shoot him, steal his woman, and drink his vodka. Then I laugh. Jonas knows how to make me laugh, even when I don't want to. I am beginning to feel healthy again, and Jonas tells me I look better, and my clothes actually fit. Tonight the OSS is dropping in guns and explosives and food for us. The morale of The Hawks is very high now, but not for me.

March 21, 1942 – We are the only group that sees the Nazis for who they are. Other partisans still believe the Germans are here to help us. We launch our raids against the Nazis every day, and they have been very successful. We conduct our operations independently, and that is why we have survived. Many partisan units are being decimated because other Nazi sympathizers—who are also Lithuanians, betray them. Jonas tells me that Tanya and her fiancé—the Russian—have a *partisan unit called "Margirio" from the Vilnius Brigade that is made up of Russians, Belarusians and Lithuanian Jews. I tell him that I don't want to have anything to do with them. The reason is our security, I say, but of course, there are other reasons.*

April 1, 1942 – Tanya just came to our camp unannounced. I tell Jonas that I don't want to see her, but she finds me. We talked in the forest for a while, and she tells me that she is with the Russian, Antenas Petrov, and they had a group of partisans who are fighting the Nazis. I tell her I already heard. She says that they wanted to work with us on a very big raid against the Gestapo headquarters in Vilnius. I tell her that I will think about it, but we work alone. She insists that I consider it— and that it would be a bold way to punish the Nazis for what they were doing to the Jews. It will make headlines that we desperately need, she says, and we can all take credit for it in the name of all those killed at the Nazi camps. I get angry with her, and tell her I am not fighting for the Jews, I am fighting for Lithuania. There will be terrible reprisals, I tell her. More Jews will die when they retaliate for a raid there. It is war, she says simply. She asks me why I infiltrated Auschwitz, and I tell her I don't know why, it was a big mistake because I found out now no one cares. Tanya is much more beautiful than I remember, but she is also colder now, I think.

April 6, 1942 – Tanya and Antenas Petrov come to our camp again with some of their partisans. Antenas Petrov is a big man, and very intimidating. He doesn't smile. He is very serious and I think he doesn't know what to make of me. Thank-you for bringing Tanya back, he tells me. I only nod, trying to make him out. He pulls out some maps of Vilnius. We are going to attack the Gestapo Headquarters in one week, he says. Good luck, I tell him. Antenas turns to leave and I can see Tanya is very angry with me. Stop! Listen both of you! Tanya shouts at both of us. We will not get this chance again! We have been told that in one week the headquarters will have much less security because they are sending almost all of the detachments to Poland to guard Hitler during his trip there. We should all be able to cooperate. Alone, none of us is capable of successfully attacking their headquarters. Together it is possible, Tanya says. I say it isn't possible. We will be risking too many lives. And what do we hope to achieve? Jonas is the one who answers this time. We achieve psychological advantage, he says. If we can break into their headquarters they know there is nowhere they are safe. There may be good intelligence we can obtain also. Antenas Petrov takes out one of the maps, but it isn't a map at all—it is a blueprint of the Gestapo building at Gedimino Boulevard 42. Inside, Petrov says, they are holding some of our people prisoner. All of them will eventually be executed. They are being held down here, in the basement. No one speaks for a while, but then Jonas steps up to me and says to me, we owe it to them to try to get them out.

I looked out at Red Square in front of me, and watched the Moscow night spool past. St. Basil's Cathedral and the red fortress of the Kremlin were on full display outside the window. I heard something faint and immediately sensed someone was watching me. I looked up to see Robin standing in the doorway in a thick white robe. She was stunning.

I pointed to her notebook. "I had no idea about any of this."

She nodded and didn't respond at first. She walked over to me slowly, and placed her arms around my shoulders from behind the desk chair. I felt her face against me, and the warm tips of her fingers brush against my arms and settle on my hands, our fingers interlacing together. The moment slowed and my face flushed. Pressing against me, her skin felt like silk.

In a convincing and seductive Russian accent, Robin whispered, "Welcome to Moscow, Congressman Tory."

CHAPTER 40

IT MAY SOUND ODD, but I felt safer waking up in Moscow than I did in Geneva. I suspect it had a lot to do with Robin. The truth was, I was falling for her in a way that, for me at least, was altogether unexpected. I wasn't sure how she would feel about that. When I awoke, Robin was up already and taking a shower.

I was starving and craving coffee. Sitting up in bed, I ordered room service for us, and while I was flipping through the dozen-or-so frantic emails from the House Administration Committee about deadlines to set up my Congressional office, I happened to glance over and notice the envelope in the inside pocket of my jacket that Axel Odin had given me in Geneva. I'd completely forgotten about it. I hung up the phone and tore the envelope open. Inside was a very fancy looking credit card—a Coutts & Co. World Card and a handwritten note:

Congressman Tory, this World Card has an unlimited credit limit. It is connected to the Tory Foundation accounts, and will be paid automatically on your behalf. You may use it freely. We are conducting our own investigation into the murders at Schlossberg Castle, and we will keep you informed. You will be contacted by one of our people in Moscow. Be very cautious—do not trust anyone.

Sincerely, Axel Odin

Unlimited credit limits...investigating murders....you will be contacted....trust no one.

They seemed like disparate components of a James Bond movie. But the difference was, this was real life. Axel's note stood in stark contrast to the hundreds of emails and rules I was receiving daily about creating my Congressional office that were designed to principally to constrain spending and keep congressional members on the straight-and-narrow. And yet, however surreal the contrast, it was now very personal. And direct.

When the phone rang again, I answered expecting it to be room service confirming my order. But it was the concierge.

"Mr. Tory, you have an envelope that someone dropped off for you. Shall I have it delivered to your room?"

"Who delivered it?" I asked.

"They did not identify themselves," the concierge replied.

My thoughts shifted immediately to Axel's note that a Tory Foundation representative would soon be contacting me, so I told the concierge to hold on to it, and that I'd pick it up from him on my way down. The fewer hands the better.

I'm not sure if it was a whim or an afterthought, but I stopped the concierge. "One more thing," I said. "Would it be possible for you find someone for me? She lives in Moscow—Tatyana Petrova. I believe she works at the Kremlin as an Assistant for the Prime Minister."

The concierge' response was immediate. "Of course, Mr. Tory."

Looking out the window, Moscow was bustling with traffic and bundled-up pedestrians making their way to work. The Kremlin wall and buildings seemed more imposing in the bright daylight. The sun reflected off the gold domes of the many Orthodox churches. It really was a spectacular sight. *The Tsars got this right....*

"Comrade Tory, I understand you need a Moscow Tour Guide?" Robin said behind me, with a very convincing Russian accent. She was drying her hair with a towel, standing just outside the bathroom door with a towel wrapped tightly around. Her skin glistened.

I smiled. "In fact, I do believe I'd be lost without you."

CHAPTER 41

***CONGRESSMAN TORY, AWAIT** our text message to you on this cell phone. You are in grave danger.*

Well, I can tell you, that note was a wake-up call, and it shattered any illusion of safety I had about Moscow. Standing outside the concierge's desk, and watching Robin approach from the elevators, I put on my bravest face as I placed the cell phone in my coat pocket, and threw the note and the envelope into the trash can.

"Are you okay?" Robin asked. "You look like you just saw a ghost."

I debated whether to tell her about the note and the cell phone, but didn't want her to get needlessly spun up, nor did I want to get into another debate about going home at this point.

I shook my head. "I'm good!" I said as cheerfully as possible. Where are we going?"

She seemed to study me for a moment. "To see a friend on the outskirts of town," she said. "In a Moscow suburb, called Sergiyev Posad."

"Who's your friend?"

"The Bishop."

"To confess?"

"Confession is only for you Catholics. We Orthodox far prefer the company of our sins," she said, smiling. "His name is Bishop Mikhail Chernigov. He has a better view of the dark underbelly of Russia's politics and inner workings of the Kremlin than anyone I know."

"How *do* you know him?"

"I stayed with a family at Sergiyev-Posad for a full year abroad when I was studying Russian at the University of Chicago. I met Mikhail early on when I was touring the cathedral there. I would meet with him nearly every evening, discussing Russia—speaking only in Russian. He was a strict taskmaster, but he and many of the other monks there are also dear friends."

Our chauffeured car drove up to the hotel entrance. It was the same Bentley that had picked us up at the airport.

I pulled out Robin's most recent translation of my father's journal. "I'm grateful to you for translating it."

"I've been riveted. It's the most fascinating story I've encountered."

"I never knew my mother was Jewish."

"Doesn't she have the tattoo on her arm from Auschwitz?"

"I've never seen it," I replied. "She may have had it removed. But she's always worn long-sleeve blouses and sweaters. She's never talked about Auschwitz. Or that she had a relationship with someone else beside my father—or that I have a sister for that matter."

Robin nodded unceremoniously. "I'll do my best to translate the rest quickly for you."

"Well, I've learned more about my family in the past week reading this than I have during the past four decades."

"We all have secrets," she answered.

"Not like this," I said. "Family secrets are usually well known within the family, aren't they?"

"Not necessarily."

"And what are your secrets?"

She laughed. "I think you have a pretty good idea, by now."

"Any more I don't know about?"

Robin smiled. "I'll be sure to let you know if I think of any."

"I'd-tell-you-but-then-I'd-have-to-kill-you?"

It was a joke, but I regretted the words the minute I said them.

Robin's glare was enough to make me fully retreat.

We drove in silence, northeast along Moscow's M-8 autobahn. When our driver detected heavy traffic, he activated a set of police lights that were installed into the Bentley's grill. What would normally have been a two-hour trip took us only 40 minutes. We approached the Assumption Orthodox Cathedral, and parked in front, at the entrance.

"I'm impressed," I said, looking up at the cathedral.

"It's the center of the *Trinity Lavra*—the most important of all the Russian Orthodox monasteries, and the spiritual center of the church. Ivan the Terrible commissioned its construction during the 16th Century."

"I always suspected he had a softer side," I said dryly.

"Okay, quick—listen," Robin explained. "You'll want to address Mikhail as 'Your Eminence.' When you meet him, bow by reaching down and touching the floor with your right hand, place your right hand over the left, palms up, and say: 'Bless, Your Eminence.' He'll bless you, and place his right hand on your hands. Then, you kiss his hand."

"Catholics just shake hands."

"That won't get you very far here, Congressman."

We entered the cathedral while the mass was still in progress. Deep chanting and religious chamber music echoed through the cavernous interior. The cathedral was austere and dark, and had a distinct chill to it. The windows were long and narrow in stained glass, with the haloed icons of the Trinity, the Last Supper, Crucifixion, Assumption and many other religious scenes. We moved forward slowly, but our footsteps still echoed loudly between the thick stone walls. Robin grasped my hand and arm and leaned into me in an effort to soften her steps. We positioned ourselves toward the back of the congregation, and kept standing. There were no pews or chairs.

The Baroque chamber choir music was beautiful and strangely calming, if not otherwordly. It may have been exactly what I needed at that moment to decompress. I closed my eyes, and allowed myself to become lost in it.

When the service ended, we made our way toward the door. Just outside, a large man with a white beard, wearing red and gold liturgical vestments and a richly embroidered, jewelry encrusted bishop's mitre stood, shaking hands with his congregation as they passed. We waited until everyone had passed and walked up to him. At the moment he saw Robin, his face lit up and he quickly approached her with open arms.

"Robin? Nyeuzheli eto vy? Vy vernulis k nam posle tak dolgo!"

Robin bowed and took the bishop's hand and kissed it reverently. *"Vysokopryeosvyashchenstvo, bylo slishkom dolgo. Moi izvineniya za prinyatie tak mnogo vremeni, chtoby vernutsya k rassmotreniyu etogo svyatogo mesta."*

The bishop shook his head, smiling broadly and turned to me. Robin introduced me in Russian, and quickly switched to English for my benefit. "Congressman Tory has just been elected to his position in the United States, and has chosen to come to Russia before he assumes his post. He is a very dear friend and I wanted him to meet you." Robin turned to me, "Daniel, please meet His Eminence, Bishop Mikhail Chernigov."

The bishop bowed his head. A large golden crucifix swayed from his neck by a thick chain. On his wrist, I noticed, he wore a Cartier Astrotourbillon Chronograph. And I did my best to go through the sequence of kneeling, touching the floor with my right hand and kissing the bishop's hand.

"Bless, Your Eminence," I said, hoping I'd gotten the sequence at least halfway correct. I felt his hand cover mine and then he performed the sign of the cross over my head.

"Welcome, Congressman," Bishop Mikhail said in his thick Russian accent. "We are honored to have you at Sergiyev-Posad and Assumption Cathedral." He smiled again at Robin, took a deep breath and exhaled it, still visibly surprised. "Please, come! Join me at the Abby for lunch!"

As we walked through the cathedral, a flurry of monks in brown robes circled seamlessly and silently, as Bishop Mikhail removed the mitre from his head and passed that and his robes off to them. We came to what appeared to be a basement doorway to a catacomb-like tunnel connecting to the cathedral from various other directions. Walking through that tunnel, I felt as if I'd been transformed into the 15th Century. The only difference was that gas lanterns had replaced what were previously lit torches to light our way on even intervals. Crypts with elaborate limestone faces and iron Orthodox crosses were built into the walls of the tunnel.

"Congressman, you are walking amongst the Tsars!" The bishop was pointing to my right. "Aleksey Mikhailovich Romanov rests there. He was Tsar of Russia in the early seventeenth century. The most attractive of Russian monarchs, and one of our most benevolent. He only wanted people to be happy and at peace. And there is Fedor, Tsar of Russia during the fifteenth century. He created what is today the Patriarchate of Moscow—our church. There are many others, just look around you."

Robin turned to the bishop as we walked. "I never knew this tunnel existed, Your Eminence. Why did you never show me?"

Bishop Mikhail laughed heartily. "*Moya doch' vo Hriste*, there are still many things you do not know. Many surprises await you!"

"We've had enough surprises, Eminence," Robin said, glancing over at me with a wry smile.

"Ah, you must tell me all about it!" the Bishop laughed. The thought crossed my mind that his Eminence was far more informed than he was prepared to admit.

We walked up a stone spiral stairway and into a massive room with a 40-foot ceiling, large stain glass windows and frescoed walls with scenes of the crucifixion and the assumption on one side and various portraits of the Russian tsars in reverent poses on the other. Large statues of male and female nudes occupied the middle of the room.

"They are Michelangelo's," Bishop Mikhail whispered to me. "Stalin, shall we say, 'reclaimed' them from Hitler. Both of these statues are believed to be Michelangelo's last works before he died."

He motioned us to the side of the male statue. "As you can see, the female side is complete, but the male side is still unfinished."

"An intentional omission, I'm sure," Robin said, deadpan.

The bishop let out a howl of laughter as he guided us through wide, marble hallways. The dining room was much different in style than the rest of the abbey. Massive white marble fireplaces stood at both ends of the room. The flooring was parquet and the walls were oak paneled. Three table settings were already prepared on the long table in the center of the room.

"Please!" Bishop Mikhail said, gesturing toward the table. Robin and I sat directly across from him.

"Do you feel all of our ghosts around you, Congressman Tory?" the Bishop whispered.

"Ghosts?"

"The Godunovs, Romanovs—princes, princesses, kings and queens—they have all eaten at this very table!"

"I'm honored to be here, Your Eminence," I said, glancing quickly at Robin. I detected a smile as she drank her glass of water.

"Even Lenin and Stalin came here to break bread with us!" the Bishop laughed, and then he lowered his voice. "We do not discriminate against our atheist leaders—because they need God most of all!"

Robin leaned into the table, toward Bishop Mikhail. "Eminence, what news do you have from the Kremlin?"

Bishop Mikhail stopped for a moment and shrugged. "You hear rumors," he said. "It is impossible to know what is true and what is not most of the time."

"We are hearing rumors too," Robin answered. "Some very concerning to us."

"There is a story of the Russian who was caught running through the Kremlin shouting 'Putin is a mad man! Putin is a mad man!' He was tried and sentenced to 21 years in prison. One year for insulting the Prime Minister. Twenty years for revealing a state secret!" Bishop Mikhail howled. "Behind its formidable red walls, the Kremlin is not as centralized or mysterious an institution as the outside world may think. The leaders are like any you find anywhere—they are lazy, driven, selfish, compassionate, corrupt, and a slight few of them are honorable."

"Who is in control now?" I asked.

The bishop smiled. "Today, many people are in charge. There are many sets of hands on the steering wheel, and not all of them have their offices in the Kremlin."

"We have been hearing of plans for an invasion of the Baltics," Robin said quietly. "Do you know anything about that?

Bishop Mikhail sat back from the table, his eyes narrowing. "How did you hear of this?"

Robin shook her head. "Rumors, Eminence."

The bishop smiled. Abruptly, he leaned over the table and whispered. "The rumors may be true in this case, I'm afraid."

"How so?" Robin asked.

"I have heard this report from two separate highly placed people. One in the Ministry of Defense. The other in the Kremlin. Both say it will happen in the next several weeks after a series of events."

"What events?" I asked. "Specifically?"

"I am certain you read the papers, Congressman," the bishop said. "It will soon be winter time, and Europe is forecasted to have their coldest winter on record. Now that the natural gas pipeline is complete, Europe is wholly dependent on Russia for its natural gas and heating oil supplies. In a few days, there will be an ultimatum to the EU to pay a higher price for both commodities. The EU will initially refuse. The supply will be disrupted by sabotage from within, and the Kremlin will accuse the West. Russian minorities have already begun to complain about being persecuted in Latvia, Lithuania and Estonia. Cyber attacks will black out communications in the Baltics."

"A diversion?" I asked.

Bishop Mikhail nodded. "One of many others, I suspect—to increase the noise, so that it drowns out the international furor."

"Why?" I asked.

Again Bishop Mikhail shrugged, and his gaze wandered off toward the stain glass windows behind us. "No matter if it was Tsar Alexander or Catherine the Great, Lenin or Stalin, Gorbachev or Putin—they have all sought one thing for Russia."

"*Uvazhenie*," Robin interjected. "They want respect."

Bishop Mikhail smiled at Robin and held up his index finger. "Precisely!"

"Surely they must know that an invasion of the Baltics will result in international condemnation well beyond what we saw with the

Ukrainian occupation—not respect."

"Congressman, you know one of our most famous sons of Russia, Anton Chekhov?"

"Of course," I answered. "Chekhov, the author?"

"Indeed! The very same! He once told us, 'No matter how corrupt and unjust a convict may be, he loves fairness more than anything else. If he does not receive it, he lapses into an embittered, extreme lack of faith.'"

Bishop Mikhail paused. "So one thing you must know about Russia is that fairly or unfairly, we have always been seen as the convicts of Europe. The feeling of bitterness has grown. Even the church has not been able to restore faith. When the Soviet Union fell apart, we lost a great deal of the international respect we previously enjoyed. Your leaked diplomatic cables calling Russia a 'Mafia State,' and other names have had a much more profound and enduring effect than you might imagine. It is Putin's goal to restore respect for Russia. To restore Russia's rightful status as a superpower. That, he believes will be his legacy, and most Russians support him on this."

"Surely he must know that shooting down passenger planes and invading neighboring countries isn't a good way to achieve respect?"

"That is the difference between us, Congressman. You focus on the means, while we focus on the ends. Legacy is what Russia cares most about."

Several monks served our lunch, quickly and efficiently. The first course was a beef goulash soup with bread and caviar, followed by the main course—a baked white fish on rice. Robin moved the conversation away from politics to lighter topics that included Bishop Mikhail's family, priests that she knew during her stay there, and on the expanded development around Moscow.

After lunch, we rose and said farewell to Bishop Mikhail, thanking him for his insights and hospitality. When Robin walked away to visit the bathroom, Bishop Mikhail took hold of my arm and led me to the door, away from anyone's earshot. His voice was a low whisper.

"Congressman, the questions you ask…you realize that if others hear them, they will place you and Robin in great danger?"

I nodded. "People have already been killed over this, Eminence."

"Robin is like a daughter to me." Bishop Mikhail took my hand with both of his. "I only tell you this because I do not want anything to happen to her. I could not bear it."

I nodded.

Bishop Mikhail whispered softly. "We all have choices, my son. The challenge is to make the right ones."

I nodded. Of course, that was my dilemma over the past several weeks. *What was the right thing to do?*

I put my hands in my coat pocket as Robin said goodbye to Bishop Mikhail. I felt the cell phone that had been delivered to me at the hotel that morning begin to vibrate.

I excused myself to go to the men's room and dialed the number that had been left for me, via text. I was surprised to hear a female voice.

"Congressman Tory, I will meet you tonight at 7PM. Café Pushkin. Boulevard Tverskoy twenty-six-A."

She had a slight Russian accent.

"Wait!" I said in an urgent whisper. "Who are you?"

"I am your sister," she said simply. "Please don't bring your girlfriend—come alone," she said peremptorily. And the line went dead.

CHAPTER 42

ROBIN RECEIVED A CALL on her cell phone during our drive back to Moscow. When the call ended she seemed unusually quiet.

"Ex-boyfriend?" I asked.

"U.S. Embassy," Robin replied, jabbing me in the side. "They're calling me in."

"Is that anything like being called to the woodshed?"

She shook her head. "We'll see. I shouldn't be gone long."

"You seem stressed."

She shrugged. "It's unusual for them to call me in when I'm undercover. Normally, they'd have me meet them at a safe house. But it's also an indicator."

"Of what?"

"That they're not too happy with me right now."

"Sorry I've put you in this position."

Robin exhaled. "Don't worry, you aren't responsible."

I watched the Moscow suburbs flashing by outside the window.

"Anyway, it's clear I won't be joining you for dinner tonight, unless it's late," Robin said.

I wanted to tell her about the telephone call I had at the monastery, and the meeting I was having with my sister in a few hours, but decided against it.

"No problem," I said. "I'll grab something."

"I'd be a lot more comfortable if you ordered room service,"

166

Robin said with obvious concern. She dug inside her backpack and pulled out a pad of paper with handwriting I now recognized as hers. "I translated more of your father's diary," she said, handing me the pad. "It should keep you occupied tonight."

I held the pad on my lap and rested my arms over it as if to hide its contents.

"Thanks," I said simply.

As we were pulling into the drive of the Ritz-Carlton, Robin grasped my hand. "I'm going to continue on to the embassy. I'll see you later tonight."

I nodded and kissed her.

"Room service—okay?" She reminded me.

I nodded, and stepped out of the car.

April 12, 1942 – The raid on the Gestapo headquarters was successful. We had the advantage of total surprise. We drove into their courtyard with one of their trucks and forged Nazi papers wearing their uniforms. Jonas and I were deep in their headquarters, planting our explosive charges all over the building, on all of the floors. We found the basement prison and presented a list of names of our partisans to the guards on duty, requesting that they be released to us for a high level interrogation. We were prepared to kill the guards if required, but the papers were enough to convince them to release their prisoners to us. We loaded onto the trucks and drove out of the Gestapo complex without encountering any problems. When we are far down the road, we hear the explosion and feel the ground shake. We are told that the entire building is in rubble. I am worried that other partisans will be killed with the detonation, but Antenas assures me that there are no others. We are in an abandoned farmhouse now. Tonight, Tanya came to my room and showed me some papers that she found on a desk in one of the offices of the Gestapo headquarters. She hands them to me and I could see from the stationary that it is official Nazi correspondence.

My German is not so good, but I could see that it was stamped "Top Secret," and that it was a notification of a cargo shipment from St. Petersburg to Berlin by armored train in two weeks. The cargo is two rail cars of gold. Tanya tells me that she has told no one, and she asks me, "What do we do?"

April 16, 1942 – We are making a plan to interdict the rail shipment of gold the Germans are transporting to Berlin. Jonas and Tanya are excited to hear my plan, but Antenas refuses to participate. He says it is too dangerous and that we will all be killed. He is angry that Tanya supports my plan, but she tells me to ignore his protests—she will take care of him. Jonas, Tanya and I know that if we are successful, we will have a way to fund the resistance and expand our operations so that we can operate not only in Lithuania, but in Estonia and Latvia too. Even though Tanya says not to worry about Antenas, I do worry. He has a very bad temper and I don't think he likes Jonas and me. Even though we helped free Tanya from Auschwitz, it seems like he resents us. Jonas tells me we should not trust him.

April 30, 1942 – We ambush the train fifty miles outside of Vilnius by placing explosives on the tracks and detonate them just as the train was inside a tunnel. From the documents Tanya found, we know the cars carrying the gold would be at the end of the train, and that they would be in armored cars each guarded by a squad of Waffen SS each. Rather than just stop the train, we decide to derail it so as many Nazi soldiers as possible will be injured and caught by surprise. Based on where we plant the explosives, Jonas accurately predicts where the train will finally stop inside the tunnel, so our partisans are ready to board the train and kill the guards quickly. Tanya waits with our trucks on the road adjacent to the tracks. We are able to quickly overtake the guards with our machine guns and grenades. One or two of the SS soldiers are able to pin us down from positions they take on the opposite side of the tracks, but after a few minutes, I hear the sound of a machine gun volley and explosions, and see Tanya come out of the tunnel telling us the problem is solved. Jonas' demolitions team blows the doors of the two cars where we believe the gold is stored. I am with the security team and get the call from Jonas to come to the last two cars immediately. When I find him, one of the cars is off the tracks. The doors are blown off both of the cars. "Come here, Lucas!" Jonas says to me on top of the car that is on its side. Climbing up and standing by his side, I look down at the wooden crates. Gold bars are packed from floor to ceiling with the crates. One of the crates has been smashed open and is filled with large gold bars. Jonas hands me one of them and I nearly fall over from the weight. "Look at the bar, Brother!" Jonas says, very excited. When I pick it up closer to look at it, I see why he is so excited. All the engraved markings on the gold are in Cyrillic Russian and translate to "Central Bank of the Union of Soviet Socialist Republics." I look at Jonas, and see him smiling broadly. "My Brother! We are very rich!"

May 2, 1942 - We store all of the gold in multiple places around Lithuania and Poland, in the underground bunkers where we store our weapons, and in the barns of farms that we control. It is a great victory for the Lithuanian resistance, and everyone is celebrating. But I am worried that because we have the Russians gold reserve in our possession, that it will drive a wedge between the Lithuanian resistance and the Russian resistance groups. I tell Tanya of my concerns and she tells me that it will be difficult to keep as a secret. Antenas knows, I tell her. She only nods her head at first. "He refused to participate, Lucas. This was your operation. The gold now belongs to you and Jonas," she said. "No," I correct her. "It belongs to us and we will use it to resist the invaders who are trying to enslave us."

I awoke to the sound of my cell phone ringing, and with Robin's translation of my father's journal on my chest. I immediately recognized my mother's home number.

"Elena? Is Mom okay?"

"She's better, Daniel," Elena replied over a lot of static. "They let her come home this morning. They say she'll make a full recovery. She's asleep now—I just wanted you to know."

"That's a big relief," I replied.

"She's still asking about you—can we call you?"

"Elena, it may not be a great idea now," I said reluctantly. "In a few hours, I'll be meeting my sister here in Moscow."

There was a long silence. "I understand. I'll let her know you called and that you asked about her."

CHAPTER 43

ENTERING THE PUSHKIN CAFÉ, it's easy to feel as if you've walked through a time warp. Plush, dark leather chairs, antique books in floor-to-ceiling bookcases, dimly lit, cigar smoke-filled rooms with oil portraits of Tsars and Tsarinas, Dostoevsky, Pushkin and other historical Russian notables, looking down at you from oak-paneled walls. The clientele was a healthy mix of expatriate businessmen, diplomats, oligarchs, bodyguards and high-class prostitutes sitting around the bar, drinking expensive cocktails.

"Gospodin Tory?"

I turned to see a receptionist directly behind me. She was thin, with long blonde hair. Wearing a short, black skirt and a tight white cashmere sweater, she looked more like a runway model than a member of the wait staff. I nodded.

"This way, Mister Tory," she said matter-of-factly, switching to heavily accented English.

As I followed her, I couldn't help but notice that she walked like a runway model too. She led me up a flight of stairs to a booth.

"Your party will join you soon, Mister Tory."

I thanked her, and checked my cell phone for any text messages or emails from Robin. One text was waiting for me, initiating a quick exchange:

U OK?

Yes. Where R U?

@Embassy—back soon.
Pls w8 for me.

K. Be safe.

Because I was planning to be back at the Ritz-Carlton in an hour's time, and just to keep her calm, I decided not to tell her that I'd ventured out without her. It did occur to me, however, that leaving the hotel alone to wander around Moscow could be perceived as stupid, even dangerous.

I checked my email and watched a series of messages download from "The House of Representatives Committee on House Administration," notifying me of my new office assignment: *510 Cannon Office Building, 283 1st St. SE.* The email went on to explain that I was also expected to pick out carpeting, drapes, furniture, paint colors, my website, parking and choice of stationary. And a reminder that my freshman orientation as a congressman was just two weeks from now. There was a postscript from the House clerk:

> *Congressman-elect Tory, your office has a very rich history. It was the first office of freshman congressman (and former President) Richard M. Nixon in 1947. Others to have occupied the same office are Tom Daschle of South Dakota, Norm Mineta of California and Brett Guthrie of Kentucky. We look forward to your arrival!*

At that moment, sitting in Moscow's Pushkin Cafe, the thought of assuming duties as a congressman was the furthest thing from my mind. And yet, I did feel some level of guilt. My constituents deserved to have a congressman-elect who was hard at work, choosing his staff, transitioning with the outgoing congressional staff, and picking his draperies. Instead, I was wandering around the European continent, trying to make sense of how I'd exceeded Warren Buffett's net worth overnight, and figuring out how to prevent World War III.

So, everything else seemed to pale in comparison.

But I felt completely inadequate when I compared my experience to what my family had gone through. What disturbed me most was that neither Jonas nor my mother ever found it within themselves to tell me personally.

Why hadn't they?

Again, I could hear Jonas whispering, *"Danno, some things in our lives—the people we knew, the things we've done, the mistakes we made—they go with us to our graves."*

I understood that. But where Jonas and my mother never told me about their past, my father had taken the time to do exactly that in a handwritten record that he had written through the years. To Jonas' credit, he had preserved it, knowing that I would eventually read it. *But only after his death.*

That was the critical distinction. And those revelations were likely the cause of my mother's stroke.

A female voice interrupted my wandering thoughts. "Daniel Tory?"

I looked up to see a striking woman standing above me, who at first glance appeared to be in her mid-to-late fifties. Her hair was a light grey, almost white, and contrasted with the black full-length mink coat she wore.

I stood immediately, and as I rose from my seat, I saw that she was probably older than fifty—perhaps in her early-sixties. But she carried her age with the grace and elegance of a woman who was certainly drop-dead gorgeous in her prime.

"Yes, I am," I replied.

She extended a hand with two large diamond rings. Her gaze exuded a discerning wisdom, and her expression was calm and contained. As I felt her hand clasped in mine, I realized that I was looking into the eyes of my mother.

CHAPTER 44

"I AM TATYANA PETROVA," she said directly.

She was slender, composed and sophisticated—and I struggled to maintain my composure, hearing the uncanny echo of my mother's intelligent, perceptive voice and confident manner. She seemed bemused by my own stupefied reaction—and again I saw the essence of my mother's smile transposed several continents away. As unnerved as I was, I somehow managed to invite her to sit down.

There was a long silence between us before either of us spoke, each of us seeming to examine the other with concealed, yet intense, interest.

I tried to look like the disarming, sincere politician. I'm pretty good at that. But she seemed to look right through me.

The waiter came, and she ordered a Henri Jayer Richebourg Grand Cru, without looking at the wine list. Seeing that I didn't yet have a glass, she revised the order for the entire bottle—a vintage I knew to be extremely expensive and rare.

"I believe we're related," I said abruptly, out of options.

She seemed to smile, as if she was amused. She reached into her purse and took out a cigarette from a pack in her purse. "You are my step-brother. We share the same mother."

We share the same mother. Her response seemed so clinical, and I was immediately taken aback. There was an undisguised shortness in her tone as she peered thoughtfully at me.

I groped for something to say, and elected to be judicious in my

174

response. "I wasn't aware I had a sister until recently, you know."

Her eyebrows rose. "I've known about you my entire life," Tatyana said, lighting the cigarette.

"Do you know my...our mother?" I asked cautiously.

She nodded and exhaled the cigarette smoke. "I remember her from when I was a girl of thirteen or fourteen. When she left us. And I remember you, when you were born."

"In Lithuania?"

"In Vilnius, yes," she replied.

"I still don't know the full story of what separated us," I said.

The waiter delivered her wine to the table, and she held her glass up.

"To family," she toasted in a subdued voice. I returned the gesture, and repeated, "To family."

"Can I call you Daniel?" she asked.

I nodded. "Of course."

"Daniel, I am certain you are discovering that our family is far from…" Her voice trailed off as she searched for the right descriptor.

"Normal?" I interjected.

"Yes, 'normal'. We are far from normal. I have learned to accept that."

"I'm only just now beginning to realize it."

"I'll try to help," she said. After a brief pause she looked at me directly. "Why are you here?"

"In Moscow?"

"Yes, in Moscow."

"I was hoping to find you."

She shook her head. "That is one reason. Why else?"

Suddenly, I felt more than a little intimidated by Tatyana Petrova. She seemed to know everything about me, while I knew very little about her. The realization that she was my older sister, and looked like a younger version of my mother had something do with it as well. In that moment, I was a ten year old being disciplined for playing hooky.

"That should be enough, shouldn't it?"

"How is our mother?" Tatyana asked.

She doesn't know.

I shook my head. "She's not well. In fact she had a stroke after Jonas died, and—"

Tatyana looked at me with noticeable surprise. "Jonas is dead?"

"Two weeks ago." I said quietly.

She exhaled smoke, extinguished her cigarette in the ashtray, and looked away at the bar. After a long moment of consideration, "He was my friend."

"And your uncle."

She shook her head. "He was your uncle, but not mine. To me, he was only a friend—someone who cared."

"He was a great man," I said. "I never knew my father, so Jonas was the closest thing I had to one."

"Your father is a hero to Lithuanians," she replied matter-of-factly. "And a rogue—how do you say? ...*Desperado* to Russians."

I nodded my understanding. "Who is your father?" I asked already knowing the answer.

"Antenas Petrov. He and our mother were married once."

I nodded, remembering Antenas Petrov's mention in my father's journal. But I wasn't aware they were ever married.

"Our mother never mentioned my father, did she?"

"No," I said simply.

"Or me?" Tatyana asked.

I hesitated, not wanting to hurt her feelings. "I'm not sure why—"

"She is ashamed of her past," she interjected. "And I am part of her past."

"I'm sorry," I replied, suddenly overwhelmed by guilt. "I didn't—"

Tatyana shook her head and touched my hand from across the table, her diamond encrusted watch glinted brilliantly. "It is not your fault. We can only try to make some sense out of our parents' decisions."

"I'm only now becoming aware of what they were involved in during the war," I said.

"Their activities are now legendary in the Baltics," Tatyana said.

"But they are infamous here in Russia—as is your name."

"Tory?"

"Your father's sub-machine gun is on display in the FSB headquarters," Tatyana replied. "Along with many other of his belongings, and pictures of his capture."

I felt the oxygen rush out of the room, and I struggled to take a deep breath. *"On public display?"*

Tatyana nodded. "Your father, Jonas and our mother were the most wanted people by Stalin, only after Hitler. Once Hitler was dead, he was obsessed with neutralizing the Tory resistance. He failed. But they remained on the KGB's 'Most Wanted' List, and where Stalin failed, Khrushchev succeeded partially, by capturing your father in 1963. My father was the KGB officer responsible for his capture. Our fathers were rivals."

I exhaled heavily, never expecting the candor, let alone the details Tatyana was conveying to me. "What happened to him in prison?"

She shook her head and looked at me directly. "My father was not your father's executioner. Oddly, he had a great admiration for your father's tenacity and skill as a resistance leader, but my father was—still is—Russian."

"He's still alive?"

Tatyana nodded. "He is in his nineties, and living in an old warrior's home in St. Petersburg with his friends—Soviet-era admirals and generals of the Army, NKVD, KGB and GRU. Still in reasonably good health."

"Can I meet him?"

Tatyana looked at me, for the first time, with an expression of frustration that bordered on anger. "No. Do not ask again."

I held my hand out, to placate. "I didn't mean—"

"Daniel, you should know that I do not share your affiliation with the Tory Foundation. They do not trust me, and I dare say the sentiment is entirely mutual."

"They believe Russia is on the verge of re-invading the Baltic States."

She shook her head in obvious disapproval. "They believe many things."

"What do you think?" I had the distinct feeling she might know more than she was willing to say. At nearby tables, I noticed, eyes were following her every move.

"I would urge you to reject your inheritance as President of the Tory Foundation now. Its foundations are built on the blood and fortune of the Russian People."

"So it's not true?"

"The Tory Foundation has always disguised itself as a philanthropic organization. It is the furthest thing. They have been funded through the CIA's Durham Trust as a surrogate to destabilize Russia. They are delusional, and they are dangerous, and—"

She stopped herself in mid-sentence, gauging my reaction.

"And what?"

"You should be very careful about who you are seen with, and where you go while you are in Moscow. I dare say, you will not be safe, anywhere—not just here," she said.

"That doesn't leave me any options, does it?"

"We Russians have a saying—'When the ice is thin, one should move very quickly.'"

"I'll move quickly then."

"You are drawing entirely the wrong conclusion."

I took a sip of the wine, savoring it—and I looked at Tatyana intently. "You know, I read a book once—by Tom Stoppard. In it he said, "We cross our bridges as we come to them and burn them behind us, with nothing to show for our progress except a memory of the smell of smoke—"

"And the presumption that once our eyes watered," Tatyana interjected with a wry smile, continuing the quote.

"*Rosencratz and Guildenstern.* I know the story well. Jonas obviously gave us the same book to read. It may fit your circumstances well—both characters are childhood friends of Hamlet. Do you remember?"

I didn't.

"Rosencrantz is a simpleton, and takes things at face value," she continued. "While Guildenstern is the thinker among them who constantly worries about the consequences of their actions." She paused to take a sip of wine, clearly enjoying the repartee. "The question, Brother, is: which are you? Guildenstern, or Rosencrantz?"

"You'll have to tell me," I answered, wishing I'd actually read the book closely, and not just remembered the quote.

Tatyana shrugged. "It doesn't matter," she replied. "Hamlet outwits them both in the end—they are executed, and he lives."

"Can you bring me to the FSB headquarters?" I asked, trying my best to change the subject, but realizing the absurd irony.

She looked at me with an expression of mild disbelief. "Why would you want to go there?"

I rubbed my knuckle against my temple. "To see my father's things—to smell the smoke."

Tatyana looked over at the fireplace beside us, and seemed to stare into the fire. I sensed that she was retreating from whatever entrenched position she'd assumed, and was seeking to understand the purpose of my visit.

At that moment, a man in jeans and a brown corduroy sports jacket, sitting alone at the table beside me stood up and positioned his chair beside us, handing me a business card. "Congressman Tory, you'll forgive me—I'm Tony Cochrane, with the *New York Times*. I'd like to ask you a few questions about why you were in Geneva during the Patek Philippe shooting, and why you're here in Moscow, if you don't mind."

Tatyana looked at the reporter calmly, and then back at me, collecting her purse and mink coat. Rising from the table, she said simply, "I will see what I can do."

—————— CHAPTER 45 ——————

WALKING OUT OF THE PUSHKIN CAFÉ, there was a large crowd assembled on each side of the restaurant, along the sidewalk—contained by the Moscow Police on foot and horseback. I weaved between the people in the restaurant who were looking outside. A woman fell against me and jammed me with the point of her umbrella. I felt a sharp pain in my calf, as I did my best to escape the pandemonium. I tried to ascertain the reason for the crowd and police presence, when I noticed that the majority of those in front of the crowd were holding large cameras. Without warning, the flashes of the cameras began going off, and I realized they were directed at *me*. I felt a rush of adrenalin through my head and managed a smile before jumping into the Bentley.

I checked my iPhone for any text messages from Robin, but there were none. So, I wrote another to her:

> Went to dinner @ Pushkin Café.
> Heading back 2 hotel now.

Almost immediately, I received a text reply back from her:

> V. Bad idea. Can U pick me up
> in front of US Embassy?

The U.S. Embassy in Moscow is a tall, imposing building, with an expansive compound that dominates an entire block. There in front of the security station, Robin was leaning against the gate, wearing designer blue jeans and a red North Face parka.

She didn't wait for the driver to open the door. She sat down beside me and glared at me.

"What happened to room service?" she said in a quiet, stern—almost icy—tone.

"I got lonely."

She shook her head. Now she was looking at me directly. "Why the Pushkin Café?"

I hesitated, but decided not to lie to her. "I met my sister."

She inhaled and her eyes widened disquietly. "You had dinner with Tatyana Petrova?"

I nodded. "She's an interesting woman, to say the least."

"She just called you up out of the blue and said, 'let's meet'?"

"Something like that," I said, not wanting to get into the details.

"And how was your family reunion?"

"She was very nice," I said.

Robin rested her head against the seat. "Did she tell you she's an avowed member of the Communist Party? Or that back in the day, at the height of the Cold War, she was a KGB spy based in Berlin?"

I began to sweat, and suddenly felt clammy with the sudden revelation. "No, she didn't mention any of that."

"Well, she must have liked you then—what else did you talk about?"

"Literature. Hamlet," I said quietly.

I mumbled something about Shakespeare and Hamlet, when the interior of the car began to spin around me. Robin's face was suddenly distorted, as if I was sitting in a revolving house of mirrors. My right calf and shin began to itch almost uncontrollably. A sharp pain exploded at the base of my spine, and I was drenched in sweat.

"Daniel!" I heard Robin's voice, now strident, and saw her distorted image over me.

"My leg...it's...like it's on fire." I held it tightly.

"Let go. Let me see." Robin picked up my pants leg and turned on

181

the interior light.

Robin's scream was more like a muffled roar. *Voditel! Poluchit nam Moskva Holnitse ceychas! Bistro!* – Get us to the Moscow Hospital now! *Fast!*"

"Listen to me! You've been poisoned. Do you understand? I'm not sure what it is, yet— you've got to stay awake!"

I nodded, blinking my eyes frequently in an attempt to regain focus. My vision swam, and the interior of the car seemed to spin around me. I can honestly say, I was never more afraid in my life. Suddenly, I felt disembodied, with no control whatsoever. The burning sensation began to shoot up through my spine and into the back of my head.

Robin was on her cell phone, shouting at full volume. "*Trumpet has been hit with an embedded capsule fired into his right calf. Symptoms consistent with Ricin poisoning. Dizziness, nausea, burning, blurred vision, profuse sweating. Enroute to Moscow Central Hospital's ICU. I need a poison specialist on site now!*"

The breath stopped in my lungs.

So, this is what it feels like to die, I thought. Not long thereafter, I felt another chill radiate through my body, followed by a sharp pain shooting through my head, and then utter darkness.

CHAPTER 46

I HEARD A SERIES OF BEEPS and guttural breathing before I could open my eyes. As they fluttered open, I was eventually able to determine that the sound was coming from the respirator and breathing tube that was in my throat. The electronic beeps were from the life support system that was attached to me. The room was only partially lit from the bathroom light. I must have made some kind of noise, because suddenly Robin was there, standing beside me, holding my hand. I struggled to speak, but quickly realized it was an impossible task.

I squeezed her hand. I hadn't ever given much thought about dying, but realized that I was dangerously close.

"Daniel, be calm. You've got to rest, okay?" The relief in her voice was palpable. "You've been poisoned with Ricin. Fortunately, they weren't able to get the full dosage into your bloodstream."

Who was "They?" Who did this to me? How did this happen? How long have I been here?

I couldn't ask any of the questions because of the breathing tube, but Robin was a step ahead.

"You were injected with some kind of pneumatic injector that was fashioned to look like something else—an umbrella or a cane, for example."

The woman with the umbrella...who ran into me at Café Pushkin....

"You're not safe here. As soon as you're stabilized, we're leaving.

183

It was a mistake to come to Moscow."

I tried to think about it clearly, but I felt as if I had awoken to the mother of all hangovers after a solid month of binge drinking. *Maybe it was a mistake,* I thought. When you've gone through life without a scratch, you have a tendency to feel immortal. But as I lay there, unable to talk, and barely able to move, all I could think of was that this was a game changer—at least for me it was. A feeling of panic reached out of my chest and seemed to envelop me.

The fact that the FSB had my father's belongings on display after they'd captured and executed him, like some big game trophy, was more than I could accept. So I was damn angry. Angry that they would treat my father like that even after he had died. And angry that now they were coming after me, and weren't willing to confront me, face-to-face.

I looked over at Robin, who was now sitting down beside my bed. Her iPad was on the table next to her. I pointed at it.

She turned the iPad on and handed it to me with the Notepad application. I typed the one question that mattered at that moment.

Who did this?

I handed the iPad back to Robin and watched her read my question.

She inhaled deeply and looked at me with a sad expression. "We believe Tatyana Petrova was ultimately responsible."

I looked up at the ceiling and closed my eyes in search of anything from our dinner conversation that conclusively proved—at least in my own mind—that Tatyana had planned this. Tatyana's disdain for the Tory Foundation seemed apparent, but that wasn't enough to prove that she was involved in an attempt on my life.

I groaned, and typed again, fighting through the fog of intravenous fluids, seizure drugs and the remnants of ricin that were coursing through my veins.

Am I going to die?

Robin shook her head and smiled. "No—you were lucky, this time. It takes 500 micrograms of ricin to kill an adult. That would be about the size of the head of a pin. They managed to get the pellet out of your calf that they estimate contained 2000 micrograms altogether. They're not sure, but they think about 20 micrograms made it into your system, so you'll be fine. You're lucky because there's no known antidote for ricin poisoning."

I tried to nod my head, but all I could do was groan again and blink my eyes.

Luck. This is how my luck always goes. Blind luck, usually. The newspapers said that's how I won my congressional seat.

'Lucky' is better than 'Good', Danno! Jonas would always tell me. I suddenly felt vulnerable with this tube down my throat, and my body essentially pinned to that hospital bed.

Pls get me out of here.

She read my note and smiled again, holding my arm. She took the iPad from me, brought up a document in a separate application and handed it back to me. "Get some rest, Daniel," she said, rising to her feet. "They're kicking me out of here—visiting hours are over. They have a guard assigned to you just outside the door. When you feel up to it, I did some more translating of your father's journal. It's all right there," she said, pointing at the iPad.

She turned back at me. "By the way, Happy Thanksgiving."

After Robin had left, I drifted off into what seemed to be a drug-induced sleep.

The ring of my cell phone woke me up, and I realized my breathing tube had been removed. Seeing it was Elena, I answered with a very hoarse voice—and sore throat. But the voice on the other end wasn't Elena's—it was my mother's.

"Daniel, it's me. I heard what happened to you. Are you okay."

"I'm just fine, Mom," I said as reassuringly as I could.

"If you're still in Moscow, I want you to leave now," she said simply.

"Mom, I'm fine," I replied. "How are you?"

"Don't worry about me," she said. "I'll be fine when you are home."

The next voice was Elena's. "Daniel, I'm sorry—she insisted we call you. She saw the news."

"Not a problem, I'm fine."

"Where are you?" she asked.

"Still in the hospital for a few more days, I think," I answered. "How is Mom doing?"

"Weak," she said. "And very stressed after hearing about your situation."

"I'll be fine," I repeated, and thanked her for being there for my mother.

I must have fallen asleep again, because I was awoken this time by the loud ticking of the clock overhead. I laid there, thinking about the conversation I had with my mother, and listening to the relentless passage of time—looking up, I saw it was exactly 2am. I roused myself from my immobility, still faint. In the dimly lit room, I saw Robin's iPad and turned it on to find random texted photos of a log cathedral and antique icons from a tourist agency, and Robin's translation of my father's journal entries:

February 3, 1943 – *Events are moving too quickly. Both the Russians and the Germans are actively hunting us now. Both know that a Lithuanian resistance group was responsible for taking the gold. The Nazis want it and have been searching for it, and the Soviets want it back. We hear that the Germans were defeated yesterday in Stalingrad. The Nazis have captured and tortured some of our resistance members and now they know who we are by name.*

May 2, 1944 – *We have learned that Antenas is the Russian NKVD officer who is leading the search for us now. The Nazis are being expelled from all of the Eastern European nations they occupied. A few weeks ago, the Soviet Army occupied Estonia and we believe it is only a matter of days before they enter Riga. The NKVD is hunting down anyone who is escaping to Sweden and Finland. In Estonia, we hear that some fighters are resisting the Russian occupation by killing Soviet senior officers of their army and the NKVD. We, too, continue to resist, and will do all we can to stop the Soviets from reoccupying Lithuania.*

July 30, 1944 – The Soviets have occupied Vilnius and instituted conscription for all Lithuanian men. Those who do not answer the conscription will be executed. Still, only a few of those eligible are showing up to join the Soviet Army. In retaliation, the NKVD is arresting hundreds of men and boys of draft age who did not show up to join the Soviet Army and they are executing them publicly. It has caused hundreds more of our people to seek us out in the forests and join our movement. In the darkness of our forest, the smell of death is fainter than on the streets of Vilnius, where the bodies are left to rot on the streets. There is a vile stench there. Bodies are covered with large black swarms of flies and covered with maggots.

August 15, 1944 – The NKVD are running organized search parties for our group, and we have found papers in one of our ambushes that shows they are looking for Jonas and me by name. They capture partisans and grant them clemency to turn them into double agents—Smogikai. The true members of our resistance do not allow this to happen and blow themselves up rather than be captured. But now, we don't know for sure whom we can trust. Many partisan groups in Lithuania are gone.

CHAPTER 47

I MUST HAVE DOZED OFF, because something caused me to suddenly wake up. The room was in semi-darkness. The heat was thrumming. I was still holding on to Robin's iPad in the dim light. Someone had texted a series of photos of old Russian churches made of logs, with the comment:

Посещение!!

With the mass of cords, wires and tubes that were attached to me, I felt like I'd been assimilated by the Borg. I'm sure it wasn't altogether wise, but I was restless—and for the first time I didn't feel like I was on death's door, so I removed all of the tubes but the IV. I placed my feet on the ground and took a single step before falling back onto the bed, writhing in sudden, sharp pain. A sudden rush of nausea overwhelmed me. I struggled to take several long, deep breaths before attempting to stand again. If it were possible to feel like a heroin addict going through the initial phase of detoxification, this must be it, I thought. I stood again and holding on to the bed rail, I struggled to stop the room from spinning. Regaining my balance, I found slippers and a blue hospital robe to cover my half-naked body, and walked into the hallway holding onto my rolling IV stand. Russian hospitals, I learned, don't have in-room bathrooms. Only rusty bedpans.

The surgical coldness of the room didn't seem at all compatible with healing. In fact, you got the feeling the blood had just been washed away prior to you occupying it.

The entire hospital floor seemed deserted and cold. It was dimly lit, and smelled of antiseptic. No one was at the front desk, which seemed odd to me. I found a bathroom directly across from my room, and once inside, I felt a wave of nausea and dizziness wash over me. I sunk to the ground and clenched my eyes shut in an effort to regain my equilibrium. I began dry-heaving into my bedpan.

So this is what it's like to be poisoned....

There were footsteps outside and the sound of a door squeaking open.

I realized it was the door to my room. I didn't move a muscle.

They just realized their American patient was no longer connected to his life-support systems. Now you're really in trouble....

I lifted myself up, using the IV stand to steady me. Preparing myself to be chastised, I thought up a litany of objections I'd use if they attempted to reconnect me to all of the machines that kept me pinned to that bed.

Net truby! Net mashiny! Ya horoshi! ...No tubes! No machine! I am good! It was at least a reasonable translation that I hoped would get my point across.

I came out of the bathroom and into the hallway, face to face with a twenty-something girl with sharp Slavic features that any man would notice—black hair, angular features, and familiar expressionless blue eyes. I immediately recognized her as the same woman who passed me, and looked at me so intently—carrying the umbrella at Café Pushkin.

Rather than holding an umbrella—this time, she was holding a handgun with a long silencer affixed to its barrel. I knew I'd caught her by surprise. Much more by instinct than advantage, I swung my rolling IV stand at her as if it were a baseball bat. At that moment, I saw the woman's face suddenly contort in anger. I felt my IV being ripped from my left arm in the process as I ran—or lumbered—toward the main doors.

Running past the front desk, I noticed the two nurses lying on the ground in a pool of blood, with frozen, opaque stares. My heart raced at full speed, but my legs were heavy. I breathed shallowly, and heard distinctive cracking sounds, and shattering glass around me.

She's shooting at me...

My balance gone, I couldn't feel my legs as they buckled and I fell headlong down the flight of stairs. At the base of the stairs, a hospital security guard was lying in a pool of his own blood, with a single shot to his chest. I saw the holstered revolver on his waist and managed to pull it out.

Trying to hold my breath, I heard footsteps—above me or below me, I couldn't tell which. I pointed the pistol up in a wild, uncontrolled movement, and pulled the trigger twice. I felt myself blacking out, the stairwell lurching and undulating around me, and I fired once more. The sound was deafening, and my ears were ringing loudly. My chest was heaving, and my legs felt like lead. The sound of sirens, shouting and pounding came from outside the stairwell as I collapsed on the steps beside the dead security guard.

"Daniel!"

I saw the vague outline of Robin above me as I regained consciousness. I did my best to straighten up in bed, and squinted up at her. Gradually, she came into focus, and she repeated the question: "What happened?"

"She was trying to kill me," I said slowly.

"Who? Who was trying to kill you?" Robin asked in an urgent tone bordering on panic.

"The same woman who had the umbrella at Cafe Pushkin," I whispered hoarsely, struggling to speak. "She killed them all—the nurses and the security guard."

"Whoever she is," Robin replied, "She's long gone."

"Who was she?"

Robin shrugged. "They're not sure, but I have my suspicions." She sounded indignant, and even angry.

I looked away, knowing that she was implicating Tatyana—but

somehow I just couldn't believe it—or at least I was refusing to believe it.

"I have to be at the embassy," Robin said. "They expect to release you as early as tonight, but the police will want to question you first. I'll come pick you up. In the meantime, you'll have police protection just outside your room—I'm trying to get you a diplomatic security detail." She pointed at the window sill where my cell phone was charging.

"I'll call you, okay?"

I nodded.

She handed me a copy of *The Herald Tribune*. There I was, above the fold, with the headline, **Assassination Attempt on U.S. Congressman-Elect in Moscow.** "Light reading." The author of the article was Anthony Cochrane—the same reporter I'd met at the Pushkin Café.

"At least it's not *People Magazine*," I replied dryly.
She withdrew a stack of other newspaper articles and magazines and laid them on the bed. There, on top of the stack, was People Magazine with a full-page cover photo of me from several days ago unconscious with a breathing tube down my throat.

Congressman-Elect Daniel Tory Poisoned in Moscow!

"Oh," I said feebly. "How did they get this photo?"

"You aren't in Kansas anymore, Kemosabe—this is Moscow," Robin answered, and kissed me on the lips. "I'll be back soon, okay?"

"Okay," I answered. "Can I ask you a question?"

She turned to me, eyes raised.

"Why are they trying to kill me?"

"Because, as the heir to the Tory Foundation, you represent the single biggest threat to their hold on power at the Kremlin."

"That's comforting," I said. "Funny—I don't feel like a threat to them at all."

"Behind those red walls, they're suffering from a massive insecurity complex," Robin answered. "They're far more vulnerable than it may appear on the surface, and that's when they're most dangerous." She smiled. "I'll be back, okay?"

I nodded. After she had left the room, I found myself wondering if the policeman who was stationed outside my room was placed there not so much to protect me, but to keep me from leaving. I felt a familiar sense of dread and foreboding—that, combined with the drugs and poison still in my bloodstream, were enough to create a feeling of euphoric depression, if that were at all possible.

Disequilibrium was the end result, but whatever I was feeling at the time, the ringing of my cell phone interrupted it. There was a moment of silence when I answered and then a familiar voice. Urgent, insistent.

"Daniel, we need to talk."

It was Tatyana.

CHAPTER 48

"DID YOU TRY TO KILL ME?" I asked directly. The muscles in my stomach tensed, and I realized I wasn't ready for her answer, whatever it would be.

There was a long silence on the other end. "Is that what they told you?" She asked, finally.

"It's been mentioned—yes."

"And you believe them?" Tatyana asked. Her tone was even and dispassionate.

"I'm not sure who to believe anymore."

"Do you want to stay in hospital, or get out of there?" Tatyana asked, knowing the answer.

"Tatyana, it's not as simple as that," I said evenly. "Someone tried to kill me, not just once, but twice—when I was outside the Pushkin Café *with you*! The other time was here in the hospital. Same killer. And whoever she is, she obviously wants me dead pretty badly. If you know anything about any of this, I'd appreciate your insights."

"As brother and sister, I had hoped we could have trusted one another more, Daniel."

"Yeah, excuse me if I'm not exactly feeling the love right now."

"I warned you," Tatyana replied after another long silence. "I told you Moscow was not safe for you. Why would I advise caution if it was my intent to kill you?"

"There are a lot of coincidences," I said, finally.

"Coincidences?" She said in her accented English. "Or events

193

made to appear as coincidences?"

"I don't know what to believe."

"I set up a personal tour for you of the museum at the FSB's headquarters in Lubyanka Square, but if you are too sick to leave…"

I laughed, looking at my unshaven face in the mirror, wearing hospital scrubs. My hair was matted and unbrushed. "I'm not exactly in any condition for a museum tour."

"Today at four o'clock. I understand if you cannot make it."

"I have a police guard outside my door," I replied. "I don't see how…."

"We arranged for him to step away from his post at three o'clock. Fresh clothes will be delivered to your room. You will have fifteen minutes to leave the hospital. That is all."

"Who is 'We'?" I asked.

"Excuse me?"

"You said '*We* have arranged," not "*I* have arranged.'"

"I'll meet you in front of the hospital's main entrance. Look for a black BMW." She paused. "Daniel?"

"Yes?"

"I was not the one who tried to kill you," she said. "You should know that."

"Who then?"

"I will see you at three-fifteen this afternoon, *da*?"

"*Da,*" I repeated.

The line went dead, and I dropped back down to the bed in a pharmaceutical fog. The thought that I was a lamb who just made a date to visit the lion's den only seemed to further confirm that I wasn't thinking clearly—reinforced by Jonas whispering in my ear.

Danno, don't give up! Never give up! I am behind you!

"I could really use your help right about now, Jonas…" I whispered to myself.

My cell phone rang again and I heard Axel Odin's distinctive voice and accent on the other end.

"Congressman, I heard what happened to you, and we are obviously very concerned."

"I'll be fine," I assured him in a strangled tone. "Obviously there are some people here who don't want me freely wandering around Moscow."

"Have you met Tatyana Petrova?"

"Yes. And she wants to meet again. I'm told she may be behind all of this."

"No, I would not think so," Axel said. "Despite her background in the KGB, she is a moderate voice in the Kremlin. Moderates do not generally resort to assassinations."

"Well, from our dinner conversation, it was clear that she's no fan of the Tory Foundation."

"That is understandable," Axel replied. "Can you appeal to her as her brother?"

"I'll try," I said. "But she seems pretty entrenched in her beliefs, and in her loyalty to the Kremlin. She did say she liked Jonas, and that he was her friend—so that's something we both have in common, aside from the same mother."

"Solid friendships have been established on far less than that, Congressman," Axel assured me.

September 14, 1945 – the West has abandoned us. All of the promises made to us during the war, have proven to be lies. Churchill and Roosevelt have made a deal with the devil, Stalin. Lithuania, Latvia, Estonia, Poland and other countries have been abandoned to the domination of the USSR. The NKVD continues to hunt us down. Sometimes, they are successful in arresting some of our partisans, but we move every night. We move freely throughout the forests, and while we have many friends throughout the Baltic states, we also have many

enemies and do not know whom to trust. *Smogikai* are everywhere. A week ago, we were told that an NKVD agent had infiltrated one of our resistance cells. Jonas and I dressed up in Russian Army uniforms and raided the cell in the middle of the night while they were sleeping. We lined all of them up and acted like we were going to execute them by firing squad. The traitor among them stepped forward and told us not to shoot him, because he was our informant. We dismissed the rest of the cell and shot him immediately. He was Lithuanian, not much older than me. We dumped his body in front of the NKVD headquarters in Vilnius, with a note that said "NKVD Traitor!" pinned to his shirt. Jonas was excited afterwards, but I am worried because I know that the Soviets will now redouble their efforts to find us through any way they can.

January 1, 1947 – I have not written in this diary for a very long time. The Soviets have tightened their grip on Lithuania and the other Baltic States, and the situation for us is very dangerous every day. As more Russian Army, GRU and NKVD come into Lithuania, we have moved frequently into Estonia and Latvia. We have melted some of the gold and made our own coins to pay those who support us. The gold also pays for our clandestine radio and press. One of our partisans is a professional artist, and he created a very beautiful design for the molds to cast the coins. Each coin says "Lietuvos Laisvės Kovų Sąjūdis" [Movement of the Struggle for the Freedom of Lithuania]. Jonas calls it our first national currency, and tells me now that he has money, maybe some ladies will finally agree to have dinner with him.

March 23, 1948 – We have made arrangements to move the gold from our underground bunkers to safe houses in Europe so that it can never be recaptured by the Soviets. Jonas is in charge of this operation. The first shipment will leave in one week. It is a very dangerous operation and I am very worried, but I know that it is important that we do this for the future of Lithuania and our movement. Jonas has convinced me that, if we do nothing, it is not a question of if the Russians will find the gold, but when. I will stay to direct our operations here. We now have *over 30,000 partisans in Lithuania alone. We are combining our forces with other resistance groups in Latvia and Lithuania because together we will be stronger and more effective against the Soviets. As a group across the Baltic states, we are now called, "The Forest Brothers."*

CHAPTER 49

TATYANA PICKED ME UP on schedule, and we drove through central Moscow in her black BMW M6 Coupe, weaving effortlessly between cars, and running yellow and red lights as frequently as she shifted gears. She didn't make any effort to talk as we raced through traffic. A uniformed officer placed yellow cones in front of and behind our car as we stepped out. I noticed the attendants stood at attention as Tatyana passed them.

"Are you sure you're ready for this?" she asked directly.

"I don't know," I said uncertainly. "What should I be ready *for*?"

An elderly, stocky gentleman with a glistening, bald head approached us. His eyes were unblinking gray, and finely wrinkled at the corners. He reached out to Tatyana with obvious recognition and kissed her on both cheeks. His voice boomed.

"*Tat'yana Petrova! Moĭ dorogoĭ drug! Ya skuchal po tebe! Dobro pozhalovat'!*"

Tatyana hugged the man warmly and then drew back. "Mikhail Nikolovic, it is very good to see you as well my dear friend."

She turned to face me and gestured in my direction. "Allow me please, to introduce Congressman Daniel Tory." She turned to me. "Daniel, this is my good friend and former colleague, Mikhail Gasparov. He is a retired Colonel of the KGB."

I met Mikhail's firm handshake and greeted him by his rank.

"Congressman, it is my pleasure to welcome you to the Chekist Hall of the KGB of the USSR," Mikhail said with obvious pride.

"Otherwise, and more commonly known as simply the 'KGB Museum.'"

He extended his hand as he opened the doors of the building and motioned us through. "Please!"

"Your English is excellent, Colonel," I responded, genuinely impressed at his near total lack of an accent.

Mikhail laughed and cast a knowing, yet amused glance at Tatyana. "Yes, well, Congressman. I was raised in the United States. I went to your schools and I was in charge of our office in New York for twenty years." He smiled broadly. "Breakfast at Sarabeth's and dinner at Le Bernardin. I miss those places very much. The cuisine was exquisite and the service impeccable." His voice turned to a near whisper as he looked over at Tatyana and smiled. "Those were very good days for us!"

I nodded and smiled, and attempted to release my grip from Mikhail's hand, but I noticed that he maintained the handshake for another second—forcing his intimate familiarity with New York city to sink in—before releasing his own grip.

"Thank-you for agreeing to show me your museum on such short notice," I said, swallowing nervously, attempting to regain composure.

"It is my pleasure!" Mikhail replied loudly. "You are in the building of the Federal Service of Security—or FSB—formerly, the KGB. Yuri Andropov who was then the Chairman of KGB created it. His original intent in building this was to orient our counter-spying officers only. But in 1989, with *Perestroika*, it was opened for more public viewing. Still, it is used today for historical training purposes, and for special ceremonies like awards, oaths of office, promotions and retirements."

We walked into the building and I was immediately struck by the architecture—a distinct throwback to the late Soviet era. As we walked along the granite floors, the cast iron and brass decorative wall frames left me feeling as if I had walked into an ornate prison. Although I was certain the goal at the time was to impress visitors and trainees with a contemporary interior design, the actual effect was nostalgic. Suddenly, I felt like I was gradually being transported to another time.

I heard Colonel Mikhail tell me how the museum covered the

period from Peter the Great to the current day, and how the four halls of the museum contained more than two thousand exhibits. Tatyana walked behind us as Mikhail first walked me through the glass display cases on the walls of documents that progress from the beginning of the intelligence services to the current day. As we walked, we passed more display cases with Soviet-era badges, portraits of Lenin and Stalin, helmets, flags of the USSR complete with hammer and sickle, radios, Nazi SS uniforms, brass knuckles, boots, ammunition and weapons.

Mikhail stopped at a large glass display case with a Thompson submachine gun, Browning automatic rifle and several pistols. There was also a canvas backpack, a map, and a small notebook with cursive handwriting in faded blue ink. Above the display was an enlarged black and white photograph of a man in a white shirt and handcuffs being placed into the back seat of a large, dark sedan. The exhibit was labeled only in Cyrillic print, but I could read enough Russian to understand what it said:

1963 – The Capture of Lucas Tory, and the End of the Lithuanian Forest Resistance

I closed my eyes and felt my heart begin to race with the realization that this was the moment that my father had lost his freedom, forever. When I opened my eyes, I found my glasses in my coat pocket and after placing them on, I leaned forward to read the annotations on the page displayed in the notebook. Everything was in nearly illegible Lithuanian. Through the corner of my eye, I saw Tatyana whisper something to Mikhail—who immediately summoned one of his many assistants and sent them away on an errand.

I looked at another glass case filled with black and white photographs from throughout the Cold War era—of captured and killed resistance members, weapons, ammunition caches, maps, message encryption devices, and safe houses. The curator was handed a folder, opened it, glanced at its contents, and gave it to Mikhail. As I looked over at him, I saw an enlarged photograph in a display case behind him of a man with features that were vaguely familiar. The caption in Russian,

Лукас Тори - Арестован 25 января 1963

was easy enough for me to translate:

Lucas Tory – Arrested 25 January 1963.

There's something surreal about seeing the mug shot of your murdered father in the KGB Museum. I must have been staring at it for a while, because the next thing I knew, Tatyana was holding my arm gently. Mikhail and his entourage were standing a respectful distance away.

Tatyana handed me a folder, and whispered, "Daniel, this is the English translation of your father's interrogation there in the display." She pointed briefly at the case. "You can take it with you and read it in privacy."

Interrogation...

I nodded absently and looked back at the enlarged photo of my father. Although it was black and white, through the panic and resignation, his eyes conveyed a piercing, defiant expression to his captors. For a moment, standing there, I felt he was looking directly at me.

What are you trying to tell me?

I looked away through the iron frame into the large granite stairwell where employees of the FSB were streaming in both directions, and something—some sixth sense—caused me to look over at the stairway's landing. There I saw her—short black hair, wearing a long cashmere overcoat, black gloves, standing still, talking on her cell phone.

The same woman who tried to kill me—twice, to be exact.

CHAPTER 50

I TASTED AN ACRID TENSION at the back of my throat, and my knees felt like they were on the verge of buckling. Tatyana saw my complexion turn an ashen white, and asked if I was okay.

"I need to use your bathroom—WC," I said suddenly, turning to Mikhail.

Mikhail nodded and walked me to the first hall and pointed toward the entrance. "Go downstairs. The *tyalet* is in the basement, at the base of the stairs."

"*Spacebo*," I said, thanking him. But a cold sweat ran down my back with the recognition that my would-be assassin was, from all appearances, an agent of the FSB.

I didn't trust most of my instincts at this point, but this seemed like too much of a coincidence. Her finding me was one thing, but me randomly finding her in this massive city was quite another.

Had she seen me? I tried to think clearly as I negotiated the maze of display cases in the museum. The connection to Tatyana, while not definite, was not something I was prepared for. I walked quickly—almost running—down the staircase, noting that the exit, while in close proximity, would require me to walk around and past the security station.

I heard voices as I descended to the basement floor. One of them was a woman's voice, directive and strident, shouting orders in Russian.

I entered the bathroom and saw several coats and suit jackets hanging on the wall. A few of them had official FSB IDs clipped to their pockets. I washed my hands at the sink and through the mirror was able to identify one coat that I thought might fit my frame. I grabbed it in a quick motion and slipped it on, walking as rapidly and decisively as I could along the granite hallway, past offices and conference rooms. At the end of the hallway, there was another ascending stairwell and some double doors. Waves of people were filing inside. I stood at the doors for a moment, irresolutely, and then joined the steady inflow, doing my best to blend in. A few steps later, I found myself moving with everyone else into a massive auditorium.

I glanced around the large room. The backdrop to the stage was a blue and red Maltese-like cross with an official double-eagled emblem in its center. I saw the sign on each side of the stage:

ВЫХОД

EXIT.

The distance to those doors, although short, seemed like an impassable chasm because of the line of security guards who were posted at the base of the stage.

What event fills an entire auditorium with FSB agents and also calls for heavy security?

The answer came an instant later when an event coordinator directed me to an aisle seat near the stage. Applause erupted as a man in a dark blue suit walked across the stage smoothly and comfortably. I did a double take—from the enlarged photograph on the wall beside me to the stage, and realized the man just yards away from me was the Director of the FSB, General Aleksandr Bortnikov.

I didn't understand much of his speech, but I did see that the entire assembled group viewed him as one of their own. He freely walked around the stage. I looked back quickly during the enthusiastic applause to see if any of my pursuers were lying in wait.

I couldn't see anyone, but then I realized that the only two people I would have recognized were Tatyana and the FSB agent that had been trying to kill me. In an audience of FSB agents being whipped up by their Field Marshal, I felt like I had positioned myself a far cry from any forlorn hope.

For someone who didn't understand any Russian, the General's speech was both mono-toned and monotonous in its delivery, but that didn't stop the wild applause at the end of every nearly every sentence. I was able, however briefly in the midst of it all, to catch my breath. There were a few times, when I thought he was looking right at me, probably wondering who the Western imposter was—but I realized that it was my own now well-developed sense of paranoia, combined with poison-induced vertigo.

At one point, the crowd stood in an extended, raucous ovation that I decided to use as an opportunity to cover my advance to the exit door, just a few steps away. One of the guards motioned me to return to my seat, but I remembered Mikhail Gasparov's word for the bathroom.

"*Tyalet!*" I shouted amidst the noise, along with some compelling, exaggerated body language conveying my urgent need to get to a bathroom. He nodded and allowed me to exit through the door. There were more stairs, but these led up to the southeastern side of the building. The red circular sign for the Lubyanka Metro. I followed it like a beacon, practically speed walking down the escalator to Moscow's extensive underground. I had a 20 ruble note in my wallet that I now vaguely remembered Robin giving to me the night we had arrived in Moscow, "just in case."

The attendant sitting in a cage slipped a metro ticket to me through the glass opening, and I walked into the sea of Muscovites awaiting the arrival of their train.

CHAPTER 51

MOSCOW'S METRO SYSTEM WAS unlike anything I'd ever experienced. The escalator ride down was long and steep, transporting me an the thousands of other Muscovites into an elaborate chandeliered hall with giant piers, pylons, sculpted walls, archways, and colonnades of brass and plaster, and domed ceilings above. I was struck by the grand Soviet-era revolutionary scenes that were still painted on the walls, and being nearly 300 feet underground was enough to enhance my growing sense of panic.

An intense claustrophobia started to overcome me. Not because of the enclosed space, or from being several stories underground, but because of the nearly relentless stream of events over the past week. The subway was literally overflowing with people. And a fair share of them were eyeing me apprehensively.

I inhaled deeply, and felt the folded papers in the inside pocket of my suit jacket.

The English translation of my father's interrogation.

Sitting there on the train, I pulled the sheaf of papers and unfolded them. All of the pages appeared to have been manually typed on a typewriter years ago, well before the advent of desktop computers.

```
Interrogation record of Lukas Tori, Commander
of Forrest Brothers Resistance in Lithuania
Statement of charges for war crimes
```

27 January 1963. Moscow

Tori, Lukas, born 1922
native of the town of Vilnius, Lithuania,
secondary school education, none
Commander of Hawks Resistance, Division of
Forrest Brothers Lithuanian Resistance

Interrogation conducted in Lithuanian.
Translator for the Investigations Section of the
2nd M[ain] Adm[inistration] MGB USSR, Lieutenant
Makeyev, had been advised of his responsibility
in conducting a correct translation according
to Article 95 of the Criminal Code of the USSR.

[MAKEYEV]

Interrogation beginning at 1355 hours
Interrogation ending at 1645 hours

Question: You have been charged according to
points 1 "a" and 1 "b" of Article II, Law No.
10, of the Control Council in Lithuania. Do you
understand?
Answer: I understand the charges.

Question: Do you acknowledge yourself guilty of
the charges brought against you?
Answer: I acknowledge myself fully guilty of
the charges brought against me.
Question: In what specifically do you acknowledge
your guilt?
Answer: I acknowledge my guilt first of all in
that being a career officer in the Lithuanian
resistance and occupying a leading position

in it. I led a resistance group during the war against Nazi Germany, alongside Soviet resistance forces. I acknowledge the fact that I fought against the Soviet Union in the wake of their occupation of Lithuania before the war and after the war up to the current day. I dispute any actions on our occupied territory that could be interpreted by anyone as an atrocity. While other resistance groups fought with the Soviets, I admit that the Hawks Resistance Group refused any possibility of collaboration, or any of your personal requests to do so.

Question: Why did you refuse my invitations and requests to collaborate against our common Nazi enemy?

Answer: I refused to associate with any group, Nazi or Soviet, which actively pursued the destruction and the subjugation of Lithuania and the other Baltic States for their own gain. I was 18 years old when the Nazis killed my parents. My brother and I continued to fight against them through any means possible. But we also clearly saw the designs that the Soviet Union had for Lithuania, Latvia and Estonia. So, all these years, we resisted. Now you have me. But we will continue to resist.

Question: Did you and your group steal a train shipment of gold belonging to the USSR during the war?

Answer: We heard about a shipment of gold that had been ambushed by another resistance group, but it was not ours.

Question: Whose group was it, if it was not yours?

Answer: I do not know.

Question: Describe your active participation in the Forest Brothers Resistance aggressive campaign, in particular, against the Soviet Union.

Answer: In the early days of the aggressive war against the Soviet Union and Baltic States, my father commanded a group of men who took part in the fighting against the Nazi Army. My brother Jonas and I took part in the fighting against the Nazi Army as young men. After my parents were killed, Jonas and I continued the resistance by attacking trains, vehicles, convoys, supply shipments and headquarters. Gradually, we gained large weapons and supply caches that helped us to feed the very large population of women, children and elderly who sought to escape in Lithuania's forests. From January 1942, we gained in numbers. I infiltrated the Nazi concentration camp in Auschwitz Poland and delivered a full report to you and to Winston Churchill. My report was a full record of the atrocities that the Nazis were committing against the Jewish people throughout Europe. But the Soviet Union and England ignored my report, and hundreds of thousands of innocent people were murdered as a result. I continued fighting against the Soviet Army as the Nazis withdrew. I took no part in other atrocities committed against the civilian population or against Soviet prisoners of war.

Question: Who is your family?

Answer: (To Interrogator). You had a daughter with Tanya Klimas. You abandoned both of them in 1958 to pursue your career in the NKVD. I married Tanya in the woods outside Vilnius on 24 April 1960, and I adopted your daughter. When you found out, you intensified your efforts to find us. Despite the atrocities you committed yourself in trying to capture us you were not successful until yesterday when I was taken prisoner. You have me now. You have assured me that my wife, my children and my brother are safe and will not be harmed. Do with me as you wish.

Question: [Curtain to window in adjacent room opens.) Do you recognize this girl?
Answer: (Profanities, attempts to Jump from Seat and Lunge, followed by Screaming at Interrogator) Tatyana! No! What have you done with my Family? (Loud Crying, Shouting).

(Curtain Closes).

Interrogator: They are dead. Shot in Vilnius as they boarded the ship. Because Tatyana is my daughter, her life was spared. I will raise her. The Soviet Courts tried you in absentia, and a judge ordered your execution upon capture. That sentence will now be carried out. Do you understand?
Answer: You will burn in hell, and I will be there waiting for you!

WEIDLING

Interrogator: Dep[uty] Ch[ief] of the 5th Section, 2nd M[ain] Adm[inistration] MGB USSR, Major Antenas Petrov

Translator: Translator for the Investigations Section of the 2nd M[ain] Adm[inistration] MGB USSR, Lieutenant MAKEEV

I finished reading the transcript as I emerged from the Teatralnaya Metro Station. I shielded my eyes and attempted to maintain my composure in the face of what I'd just read. A cold sweat enveloped me, and I was unsure if it was a result of the poison still in my system, or the anguish and torment of reading my father's last words transcribed in the same building complex where he'd been interrogated and executed. Rage mingled with anxious desolation as I thought about his final hours in that KGB prison—believing his entire family had been killed. I felt his fear pounding against my temples, like a vice slowly closing—imagining my father's fury and his cries of anguish—and I felt myself straining under their weight.

The department stores, advertisements and traffic spun around me in a hazed pulsating swirl. I felt myself stumble slightly before catching hold of a light pole, and turned the corner to see the Ritz Carlton just across the street. Black Cadillac Escalades and men in dark suits and earpieces occupied the hotel's front entrance, like Army Ants deployed in force.

I pulled my cell phone out and dialed Robin's number.

After just one ring, I heard her voice.

"Daniel?" Her voice was excited, almost frantic. "Is that you?"

"Yeah," I replied. "I'm in a lot of trouble."

"Meet me at Turandot," Robin said immediately. "It's on Tverskey Boulevard. Any taxi will know it. *Don't* come to the hotel. Do you understand?"

I looked behind me and saw two men in black overcoats approaching. One of them was smoking a cigarette. In front of me and across the street, two more men appeared, dressed exactly the same.

I realized I was sweating profusely, and there was nowhere I could escape. "It might be too late," I told Robin lowering the phone.

At that instant, I heard a screech of tires beside me and a black Lada Granta pulled up beside me with its door open. I recognized the driver right away as the *New York Times* reporter—Tony Cochrane.

"Get in, Congressman," Cochrane said evenly.

I looked at the men begin to run toward me.

"Hurry," Cochrane said insistently. "We don't have time."

CHAPTER 52

"WHERE ARE YOU HEADING?" Cochrane asked. "I'll drop you off."

"Where did you come from?" I asked. "How did you know—"

"I'm staying at the Ritz," Cochrane answered. "I was just driving up and saw them following you. Not too subtle, the FSB goons, you know."

I nodded, my relief fully evident. "Thanks."
Cochrane was dressed in a blue Columbia TurboDown Jacket, quickly maneuvering the gear shift and glancing in the rear view mirror.

"No problem, Congressman. Glad to help!"

"Turandot," I said absently. "Drop me off at Turandot."

"You obviously know your Moscow restaurants," Cochrane said. "Maybe you'll consider talking to me now?"

"Look, I appreciate your help, Mr. Cochrane—"

"Tony," Cochrane interrupted. "I go by Tony."

I nodded. "Okay, Tony. I'm grateful for the ride. But, you have to believe me—it's a lot better for me and for you right now, if we don't talk. You could end up dead."

"Can you let me be the judge of that?" he asked. "I already know you were onsite at the Patek Philippe showroom, as well as at Schlossberg Castle the day before the massacre there."

I paused, admiring Cochrane's adept driving skills, as he weaved through the Moscow traffic. "Alright, why don't we do this—I agree to a full series of interviews with you—first and exclusively—in return for not publishing any story. I have your card."

"Can you give me something to start with?" Cochrane asked.

I hesitated before answering. Cochrane's keen intuitive sense as a reporter was obvious to me now. I considered my response—grateful, and with the knowledge that his involvement could actually be a great benefit, I relented with a big question I had at that moment. "Antenas Petrov was involved with my father's arrest and imprisonment," I said. "He's in his nineties, and is in an Old Soldiers Home either here in Moscow or in St. Petersburg. Find out where he is, and let me know."

"Okay," Cochrane said, stopping the Lada, and shifting into "Park." He extended his hand and I shook it.

"Turandot," he announced, pointing at the ornate building. "It's one of Moscow's truly great restaurants. It took more than six years to build at a cost of around $50 million."

"Thanks," I replied. "I'll be in touch."

Turandot is not only one of Moscow's most well known restaurants, it's also only a few steps away from the Pushkin Cafe. Returning there, in the daylight, in the midst of everything that was happening was strangely calming. Turandot's greeters open their doors to you and welcome you in your native language. When you step from the street through their doors, you find yourself in an altogether different world.

Robin was waiting for me in the marble Venetian courtyard, dressed in a black sheath dress—standing between a statue of Neptune and some mandarin trees.

"Come here often?" I said, my attempt at humor failing to conceal my obvious relief.

She shook her head slightly, kissed me and quickly took hold of my right arm, intertwining hers with mine. We walked past a pair of expensive boutiques and into a virtual Baroque palace that was almost hypnotizing in its design: rich tapestries and frescoes, Japanese porcelain fireplaces, antique Venetian mirrors and colonnades, all crowned by a sky-blue dome and a massive crystal chandelier directly overhead. It wouldn't take much more to convince you that you had been transported back in time to Marie Antoinette's private residence. We were seated directly in front of a rotating stage with a harpist and harpsichordist dressed in period costumes and powdered wigs playing the classics of Mozart, Bach and Beethoven.

We sat there for a moment, just looking at one another.

"I went to the hospital this afternoon, after my appointment at the embassy," Robin said calmly. "You can imagine my surprise when I found out you weren't there?"

I nodded. "Yeah, sorry about that."

"You met up again with your sister?"

I nodded slowly.

Robin leaned forward. "You have a death wish, don't you?"

I didn't respond directly, but instead explained what had happened at the KGB Museum, and my narrow escape. When I had finished, she was silent.

Amidst the tension, the head waiter welcomed us, filled our glasses with water and brought us our menus.

A Chinese-sculpted grandfather clock gonged six times.

"What are you trying to achieve?" Robin asked evenly. "You're not in Chicago anymore—you're in Moscow. The rules are different here."

I shrugged. Of course she was right, and I'd ignored nearly every warning she had given me over the past couple weeks. And she'd saved my life on more occasions than I really wanted to think about.

A hostess in an 18th Century silk gown filled our glasses with water. The delicate chatter of Arthur Price silverware on Bauscher porcelain completed the other-worldliness of this place—ingeniously, completely contrived, harkening to a simpler, more elegant time.

"I found out how it all happened."

She cast a perplexed look as I passed the interrogation translation to her across the table.

Her eyebrows rose as she scanned it. "They just *gave* this to you?"

"Well, I'm not sure they exactly planned for me to leave the building with it."

She continued to read, flipping the pages rapidly. When she was finished, she looked up, wide-eyed.

"I'm so sorry," she exclaimed, reading it over again. "I don't know what to say. I—"

"You don't have to say anything," I said quietly. "It's clear to me that nothing much has changed here during the past seven decades—"

At that moment, a gilded peacock on the circular stage, previously static, spread its golden tail feathers dramatically. I jumped in my seat, and Robin laughed.

"It's a reproduction of an 18th-century original that's in the Hermitage, in St. Petersburg."

"Please have it removed," I said dryly.

"What can you possibly do about it?" she asked, suppressing a smile.

"The Peacock?"

"No, the Kremlin," she answered. "No one ever said they were saints."

One of our waiters placed gold-embossed leather menus in our hands. On the back page, one of the offerings was a 200-year-old Heritage Marie Domain Cognac.

"Come here often?" I asked.

"Whenever I'm in Moscow. It's my favorite restaurant."

"I think this may be my last trip," I said.

"In that case, I'd recommend the jasmine tea smoked pork and a glass of Roero Arneis," Robin answered with a slight smile, still reviewing the menu.

"I want to go to St. Petersburg tonight," I said abruptly. Not a question.

Robin looked up, and back down at the menu. "There may be a better time to see The Hermitage."

I looked around the room. Hostesses in 18th-century-style silk gowns floated around our tables.

Robin set her menu aside. "Why Saint Petersburg?"

"Tatyana told me her father is in a Veteran's home up there," I said. "I'd like to try to talk to him about my parents."

"We've managed to upset a lot of people during our short visit here, Daniel. Not only in Russia, but in the United States too," Robin said. "Does Tatyana know about your plan?"

"Who, exactly?" I asked.

"Excuse me?"

"Who else have we upset?"

"The Secretary of State, Director of Central Intelligence, for starters," Robin said. "They're practically lining up."

"Well, they're not the ones being poisoned and shot at," I said, pretending to review the menu. I looked up at her.

"I noticed," Robin said simply.

"I'll take the smoked pork then."

Robin leaned into the table, toward me. "Listen to me, Daniel. We are in way over our heads here. These people will kill us, and no one will ever find a trace. We'll just disappear."

"Like my father did."

My response had caught her by surprise. "Look, I—"

I shook my head and held up my hand to placate. "Over the past few weeks, I've learned more about my family and myself than I have in the past three and a half decades. What I've learned is that my family put their lives on the line for what they believed in—and not just some of the time—*all of the time*. They didn't hesitate. They took risks and they achieved results against all odds."

The head waiter took our order, which Robin provided in flawless Russian.

"You're a congressman," Robin said quietly. "Not a soldier. Not a spy."

The waiter came with the bottle of wine, opened it, and poured a sample in my glass. I tasted it and gave my approval. "No, but that's why I have you."

Robin paused. "They're pulling me from you."

I leaned back, watching the wine being poured into both of our glasses. "Then, quit."

She blinked, unable to disguise her shock.

"Excuse me?"

"Quit," I repeated matter-of-factly. "And stay with me."

Her cheeks flushed, and she frowned at me, because the answer was manifest. At least to her.

"It's not that easy," Robin answered with clear frustration. "And not fair of you to suggest it."

"I already hired you as my chief of staff, and you agreed," I said. "Remember?"

"I was under cover. You know that."

"And since then, you've been compromised," I said. "Once that happens, you're taken offline, right?"

"How convenient. Is that all I am to you, Congressman?" Robin asked, propping her elbow on the table and rested her chin on her hand. "Your spy-turned-bureaucrat?"

"I think you know that's not the case."

"What exactly is your end game?" Robin asked pointedly. "Can you tell me? Because I'm not even sure at this point."

I hesitated, momentarily disarmed. "I thought you would be the one person who would need no explanation.

"You've got the answers you were seeking regarding your family in that KGB document, didn't you?"

"Some, but not all."

"I'd like to know who killed the Tory Foundation team, how they plan to invade the Baltics, stop them from doing it, and—" I stopped mid-sentence.

"And what?"

"And I'd like to find where my father is buried...hopefully, with your help."

CHAPTER 53

WE BOARDED THE TRAIN close to midnight, drained—physically and emotionally. A throng of passengers with wet winter coats speaking rapid-fire Russian pushed past us, rubbing their hands together and fighting with their luggage.

The night train may be the best way to travel from Moscow to St. Petersburg, especially if you're able to grab a first class ticket. The Red Arrow's "Lyuks" carriage exceeds anything that Amtrak could possibly conceptualize—it wasn't the faded maroon, velvet-tassled, smoke-filled cabin that I expected. Instead, we were guided into an ultra modern cabin of stainless steel Scandinavian design, with round-the-clock service, two full-time attendants, and a full menu from the dining car.

The steward demonstrated the flat-screen television and stereo mounted directly across the double bed, and showed us the kitchenette and a full modern bathroom with gilded fixtures, heated floor and even a bidet.

Once inside our car, I pulled out the bottle of 2003 Chateau Latour that we had purchased at Turandot just for the trip, along with two complementary crystal glasses that the chef—a friend of Robin's—had wrapped up and placed into the bag with the wine. "There!" he had said with genuine enthusiasm. "Now you have everything you need!"

He could not have known how prophetic his words were only hours later.

At the moment our steward left the cabin, and to my own

218

surprise, Robin began stripping out of her clothes.

I confess that I stood there and stared unabashedly.

She saw me and smiled. "I hear the shower's to die for."

"Not exactly comforting words."

The train jerked to motion, and Robin's naked body collided into mine. She laughed, and kissed me. I watched her walk to the marble bathroom and glass-encased shower. She was stunning when she came out of the bathroom in the white terry cloth robe. Between us, we drank the entire bottle of Latour.

"Chateau Latour was the only wine that Jonas would drink," I commented. "That should have been an indicator that there was more to Jonas' blue collar persona than met the eye. *"Danno! When you drink wine, you drink Latour!'* he'd tell me whenever I had dinner with him. *'Latour is power. When you drink it, you are drinking the same wine from the same vines planted five hundred years ago. When you drink this wine, you think of your family.'"*

Robin laughed, and raised her glass. "To the Tory family then—your uncle had very good taste."

"He picked you for me," I said.

Robin touched my glass with hers and leaned back, smiling. "That should have been your first sign that he was much more well-to-do than he made himself out to be."

I nodded. "I should have listened more. Paid attention."

The rumble of the train, combined with the wine and with Robin there opposite me—it all had a rather relaxing, if not hypnotic, effect.

Robin lifted her laptop from her backpack, opened it and passed it to me. "I finished translating your father's last diary entries," she said matter-of-factly. "They're all there."

"After all this wine, I'm not sure I'll be able to make sense of it"

"When you're ready. You know—," she said quietly, and stopped.

I looked up at her.

"You really do have a remarkable family."

April 17, 1959 – *Jonas tells me that Tanya has a daughter, six months old, from Antenas Petrovic. She has not seen Antenas for six months and she told Jonas that they are no longer together because she discovered that he had her family deported to Siberia when he joined the NKVD.*

August 2, 1959 – *Tanya has come to our camp in the forest, and I tell Jonas I do not want to see her, but she finds me. I don't say anything to her—I sit and she talks about the mistake she made trusting Antenas. She says after experiencing the horrors of Auschwitz, and seeing them kill so many innocent people, she wanted revenge and saw her relationship with Antenas and his status as a Russian officer as a way to fight against them, not realizing that the Soviets were just as bad, if not worse. She tells me that she has always been grateful to me for saving her life in the prison camp, and helping her escape. She tells me she always thought her family was exterminated in the camps, but found out that Antenas sent her parents and older brother to Siberia. She tells me she has never stopped thinking about me but Jonas tells me I can't trust her.*

May 3, 1960 – *Jonas urges me not to fall for Tanya, calling her a Bolshevik sympathizer, but I know she is sorry for leaving us for the last ten years. She tells me that she is willing to prove her loyalty to us, and I believe her.*

June 24, 1960 – *Tanya is leading raids and ambushes on the NKVD around Vilnius, and I have never seen a more fearless fighter since we began this effort 20 years ago. Yesterday, I watched her walk into an NKVD regional office, dressed in a Russian officer's uniform, and personally kill 4 NKVD officers armed with pistols and machine guns. Even Jonas is quietly impressed now.*

August 7, 1960 – *Jonas, Tanya and I conduct a raid on the NKVD headquarters to free one of our partisans, Bronius Valdemeras, captured by the Smogikai. We placed explosives on one side of the headquarters building to create a diversion, and we are able to find him. Tanya hears one of the NKVD guards say that there is a meeting with a few Smogikai and the NKVD Major. She forces her way into the room, and kills the entire Smogikai team, but then sees that the NKVD Commander is Antenas. She lets him go, she says because he is the father of her daughter. I tell her that he will one day not hesitate to kill us.*

November 2, 1961 – Tanya tells me she has been pregnant for a month with my child. I could not be happier, except that we will be bringing a baby into a very violent and terrible time for Lithuania. I tell her we should get married as soon as possible. Jonas asks me if I am sure what I am doing, and I tell him I have never been more sure of anything in my life. "I feel happy when she is around," I say. "It's that simple."

December 20, 1961– Tanya and the other women take care of the children, teaching them in our bunkers and in the forest. Still, she insists on also handling the logistics of our operations and in helping to plan our raids on the Russians. There are very few left of us who continue to resist the Soviets. Jonas tells me we may be the only resistance that remains in Lithuania.

January 10, 1963 - The KGB captured Tanya, Jonas and the children in Vilnius. Bronius Valdemeras did his best to defend them, but was killed. I offer myself in exchange for the release of Tanya, Tatyana, Daniel and Jonas. Antenas agrees to be my go-between as he is Tatyana's father. He tells me they will agree, if I surrender myself, and if my family leaves the Soviet Union for good. We are the last of the resistance, and as the leader they know they can make me their trophy. I will only surrender when I receive a phone call from Tanya and Jonas, telling me that they are safe in England or the United States. Antenas says they will only agree if one of the children—Tatyana or Daniel—is left behind as "collateral" for my surrender, and that the child will be sent to her mother when I am in custody. Daniel is only a year old and needs to stay with his mother. I think about organizing a raid to rescue all of them, but I know it would be suicide for everyone.

January 12, 1963 – I meet Antenas at an abandoned farmhouse last night, and tell him that my decision is for Tatyana to stay with him during this time, since he is her biological father. His eyes are the coal black that I remember.

January 13, 1963 – Antenas tells me that Tanya has refused to leave the country without Tatyana, that she would rather die than leave her behind. Jonas also speaks to her, but she refuses to consider any other solution—even if Antenas gives her his personal guarantee that he will send Tatyana to the United States when I have surrendered. I know she does not trust Antenas, and that she hates him now, and says she wishes she had killed him in Vilnius. I tell Antenas that he must find a way to convince her. I am writing notes to Jonas and to Tanya. Antenas says he will make sure they receive them.

January 15, 1963 – Antenas gives me a note from Jonas saying that they are leaving Moscow. He gives his personal assurance that Tatyana will be sent to her as soon as I surrender. Jonas insists that he should be the one to stay with the KGB, not me. I tell him that I am the one they want, and he must take care of Daniel and Tatyana now.

January 24, 1963 – I have just spoken to Tanya and Jonas on the telephone. They are in London, and safe. Tanya remains distraught, and screamed at me, Don't surrender to those fucking bastards! Get Tatyana! Over and over. Finally Jonas came on the line and told me they were safe and not to worry about them anymore. He says he will take care of Tanya and the children. I tell Jonas I am proud to be his brother and that our days together fighting for freedom are the best of my life. I tell him I am at peace, and my final thoughts will be of him, Tanya and my children. Antenas now says Tatyana will stay with him, and that Tanya has agreed to give him full custody.

My hands were visibly shaking when I read the last line of Robin's translation. It was now clear to me why Jonas and my mother rarely spoke to one another—each for their own reasons based on circumstances and events that occurred more than half a century ago.

I stepped outside the cabin and walked down to the dining car. Something—still to this day, I don't know what—stopped me before I opened the door. Through the window, I saw her—the same female FSB agent that had been trying so hard to kill me, sitting down at a table at the far end of the car. My eyes widened.

I'm not sure how long I stood there staring at her. I think I was more dumbfounded than scared.

How could she have known I was on this train?

And yet there she was, drinking a cup of coffee, typing something on her iPhone, completely unaware that I was only feet away, staring at her through the door.

Maybe it was morbid fascination, but I realized she was actually quite beautiful, even with her rather sharp, angular features. She had a professional athlete's build, and a quiet confidence that belied the deadly tenacity I'd witnessed at the hospital. She was wearing jeans and a turtleneck sweater under a leather jacket. Inside her jacket, I saw the distinct bulge of a holstered pistol.

I was unprepared for the voice behind me.

"Daniel?" It was Robin, in her robe, arms crossed.

I must have visibly jumped.

"What are you doing?"

I pointed silently through the door window. "There, against the wall."

Robin glanced through the window and drew her pistol from the pocket in her robe. "Let's go," she said quietly. "Now."

She led the way back to our cabin.

"Grab whatever is important to you. Nothing more," she said with a tone of urgency.

"Where are we going?" I asked, stuffing my already full backpack with whatever I had removed—the museum transcript, my passport and wallet among them.

"Off the train." She reached into her own backpack and pulled out a Kimber .45 Automatic, checked the ammunition in the magazine, then locked and loaded it with a finality that was jarring.

"You pack differently than I do," I said.

"Get dressed," Robin said, hurriedly getting into jeans and a sweatshirt. "And open the window."

"Why—?"

"Just do it," she said evenly, now placing her sneakers on her feet. "Open it all the way."

The moment the window opened, the cold air rushed in. She put her head out the window and looked upward. When she ducked back inside, she placed her .45 into a holster and grabbed me.

"Okay," she said decisively. "Get ready."

"For what?"

She pointed at the open window. It was already freezing inside the cabin, and the blackness outside was moving swiftly—and loudly—by.

"Are you crazy?"

"There's a handle just above the window. Pull yourself up."

"I can't—"

"You can, and you will, Daniel," Robin ordered. "Or we'll both be dead very soon. I'll be right behind you. Now *GO!*"

It's hard to describe the feeling of leaving the comfort of your own luxury rail car and climbing out the window to the top of a moving train in the frigid cold. I pulled myself up, nearly losing my grip and footing a couple of times. Robin made the ascent effortlessly. Once atop the car, she pointed toward the rear of the train, and led the way in a brisk crouched walk. The wind whipped with a vengeance, and with the train moving underneath us, I felt like I was running at the epicenter of an earthquake in a hurricane. When we reached the last car of the train, we descended down a ladder.

"Now what?" I asked Robin, my chest heaving, realizing we couldn't hear one another's voices. I felt like I was in the middle of a tornado that followed our every movement.

"Jump!"

I can say now, conclusively, that jumping from a train at night is not as easy or as painless as it appears to be in the movies. In fact, it's a lot like blindly jumping off a cliff and then having the rug swept out from underneath you as you land—full force. I hit the ground on my side, and felt a sharp pain in my shoulder. And everything went black.

When I regained consciousness, Robin was holding my head. I must have winced or groaned because her first words were, "Did you break anything?"

I felt like I'd been pinned to the ground, paralyzed.

"My right shoulder," I said. "I can't move it."

Robin placed her hand inside my shirt, and I felt her pushing against the front, side and back of my shoulder.

"You dislocated it," she said matter-of-factly. "Can you stand up?"

"I don't know."

"Try."

I rolled and gasped for breath as she gingerly helped me to my feet. Just as soon as I stood up, my shoulder popped back into its socket. But I felt as if every ounce of my energy was now drained.

I looked around. The grass was tall and wet around us, and the dense line of a birch forest stood only a few yards beyond. The interior lights of the train were still visible at a distance.

"Now that I've done that once, I can honestly say I don't want to do it again."

"Can you walk?" Robin asked.

I nodded; my first attempt was more of a stagger than a walk. "Yeah, I think so."

"We'll backtrack along the outskirts of the forest," she said pointing behind us. "I saw the lights of a village from the top of the train before we jumped."

"How far?"

I realized that she had pulled the .45 from her pocket.

"A couple miles," she said quietly, checking the ammunition in her clip and reinserting it back into the handgun. "Maybe more."

CHAPTER 54

THERE'S A HAUNTED FOREST, with real ghosts, halfway between Moscow and Saint Petersburg. I've seen it for myself.

Admittedly, I may have been a little delusional after drinking a bottle of Chateau Latour and then jumping from a train in the dead of night; but at that hour, a forest of Birch trees swaying over you in a howling wind creates the illusion of many ghosts hovering around you. The white bark of the trees reflected the moon's glow, and the rich cloying scent of the winter soil inhabits you, giving the overwhelming sense that you're in the presence of something supernatural. When you emerge from that forest, though, the moonlight fractures, and you see a village entirely of log houses that have been painted a dark incandescent orange. At that point you feel like you just entered a parallel universe, where everything is just slightly off-kilter.

"There has to be a soundtrack for this movie," I said.

She didn't respond, but I could tell she was carefully surveying the unfolding scene.

My shoulder was screaming in protest every time I moved it to push away even the smallest branch. Once in the village, I felt as if we'd been transported back in time to the days of Stalin's reign of terror. The streets were unpaved and rutted with frozen mud. The log construction and "Soviet Yellow" paint that covered every structure and every doorway was otherworldly. Most of the chimneys had smoke wafting from them. Dark soot layered the old snow. There were no cars or trucks. Livestock—cows, horses and sheep—freely roamed

226

the streets and alleyways. A dog barked.

"We're the children of the corn," I whispered to Robin. She was now holding on to my arm to balance herself on the ruts as we walked between two log homes.

"Stop it!" She punched my shoulder lightly—the one I dislocated. I winced, and I could faintly see her smiling as she checked the signal on her iPhone.

"Okay," she muttered to herself. "Maybe it's enough."

"Excuse me?" I asked.

"To send a text message."

"Who to?"

"Our embassy team," she replied. "They'll send a car to pick us up, wherever we are."

"Katrinaberg," I answered, pointing up at the large sign in Cyrillic, in the town center.

"Thanks," she said, typing out her text message. I walked over to a park bench and sat down, waiting for her to finish.

Rather than sit, Robin wandered the area.

She finally returned and sat down beside me.

"All okay?" I asked.

She nodded and leaned her head back. "Yeah."

"Any response from the embassy?"

She exhaled. "Not yet."

There was a prolonged silence between us.

"Can I ask you something?" I said.

She turned to face me. "Nothing too philosophical I hope?"

"Why did we have to jump from the train?"

She laughed quietly. "That's a serious question?"

"Yes," I said. "In every other case, you've shot first and asked questions later."

Robin seemed to consider her response, and then began without turning to me. "For every gunfight we've been involved in, at the jewelry store and the hotel in Geneva, there wasn't a way out for us. There were no other options, and using lethal force has always been a last resort. This time, there was. If I had come out with guns blazing

227

aboard that train, there's no way we would have gotten away, and we would have had to jump anyway—can you understand that?"

"Yes," I said simply.

"Do you think I enjoy this, Daniel?" Robin said in a now exhausted tone. "Because I don't."

"Why do you do it?" I asked.

"Why did you run for Congress?"

I immediately regretted the turn the conversation. She had saved my life on several occasions, in as many weeks.

"What if I hadn't asked you to come with me?"

"To St. Petersburg?"

"On this trip."

She smiled slightly, and turned to me. "Then I would've had to find a way to ask."

"Ah," I said, amused. "I see. The hard sell?"

"But for the record, despite everything we've been through, I'm glad you did ask me to come along with you."

"Me too," I said smiling. "If I hadn't, I'd probably be dead."

"Hopefully that's not the only reason?"

I shook my head, smiling.

"Nice recovery," she replied. "You know this is just as personal for me, as it is for you, don't you?"

"In what way?" I asked.

"I told you my family is first generation Lithuanian," she said. "But what I didn't tell you is that they and their families were deported to Gulags in Siberia. My grandparents died in the Gulag in Steplag—also known as Special Camp No. 4."

"I had no idea," I said.

"There's no way you could," she answered. "It's really the reason I joined the agency's Special Activities Division."

"How did that happen?"

"They found me. Mostly because of my financial background and language fluency, I think. But I always thought Jonas may have played a role in them recruiting me."

"Jonas?"

She nodded. "I learned he was one of the CIA's original Paramilitary Group members in Vietnam. And he knew my family." She saw my stunned reaction. "You didn't know, did you?"

"I heard stories growing up, but I never paid any attention to them."

She shrugged. "I'll never know for sure, but you don't normally get brought on right out of college to be a Russian analyst in the Political Action Group doing covert stuff."

"What kind of stuff?"

"Everything from psychological and information operations to economic and cyber warfare," she explained. "At the time, none of the operational positions were open for women. But they began to realize women could do just as much as men, and often times do things men couldn't, and that's when I raised my hand."

I looked over at Robin. "So you were one of their first female operators?"

"There have always been some women in SAD, but not many— now we're growing. And that's another reason why I really don't want to screw any of this up."

We sat beside one another in silence for a while, both of us shivering. "If it means anything, I admire you for what you've done."

"It means a lot, actually," she said, and then turned to me. "When this is over, what happens?"

"To whom?"

"To us."

"That depends."

"On what?" she asked tentatively.

"On whether you're coming with me."

She leaned over and kissed me. It began as a brief, thankful kiss, but evolved into a long, romantic one that left both of us forgetting how cold we were.

"I'm with you," she whispered, sitting on my lap facing me. "Whenever and however this trip ends."

As we embraced, I realized the completeness I felt when I was with Robin. She was confident, strong and brilliant—and I knew implicitly that her concern well transcended the operational role and mission she'd been assigned by the CIA. I also knew I had placed her in a difficult, if not tenuous situation with her handlers.

The vibration of her iPhone interrupted the silence. Its glow lit up her face as she read the text.

"Our ride's a few minutes out."

CHAPTER 55

"DANIEL, THIS IS STEVE OMNIVIC," Robin said, removing her coat.

Wiry and weathered, and dressed in a locally made wool sweater and worn pair of Levi's, Omnivic extended his hand to me.

"Steve's my boss," she said simply.

I nodded, meeting his handshake. "I hear you guys aren't very happy with me?"

"Welcome to Saint Petersburg, Congressman," Omnivic said, ignoring my comment.

"Not the way we planned to arrive," I answered tactfully. "Sorry for pulling Robin into this mess."

Omnivic spoke very calmly, and paused to clear his throat. "It's never clean. This is what we do. Although I admit we prefer to do things with a lower profile."

"You're the Station Chief here?"

Omnivic smiled slightly. "No, I'm the director of Langley's Special Activities Division. The station chief isn't too happy right now. He's got an angry ambassador to contend with."

"Why are you here, then?"

Omnivic nodded. "Well, Congressman, Langley's interested enough in what you're doing to send me over to meet with you, personally."

"I'm flattered," I said. "You're here to send me home?"

Omnivic smiled. "No. At least not yet. For the moment, we're

231

trying to keep you alive, among other things."

"Robin's done a pretty good job of that," I said.

"I've been lucky, Daniel," Robin interjected. "And quite frankly, so have you."

I wasn't quite prepared for Robin's sudden, professional bluntness. I turned to Omnivic. "What else are you trying to do here, besides run interference for me?"

"Discern the Kremlin's intent."

"So you agree that Moscow is preparing a large scale invasion of the Baltics?"

Omnivic looked over at Robin and then to me. "Two days ago, we would have rejected the idea wholesale, but now we're not so sure."

"What's changed your mind?" I asked, looking up at Omnivic, and then over at Robin. "May I ask?"

Omnivic handed me a stack of 8x10 black and white photographs. "These satellite photos," he answered. "They clearly show a massing of forces along the borders of Latvia, Lithuania and Estonia, and a large number of ships and submarines docked in St. Petersburg. We haven't seen anything like it since the Cold War. Not even in Ukraine."

"Timing?"

"If the invasion of Ukraine and Georgia are any indicators, mass cyber-attacks against all three countries will precede the physical invasion by a few hours," Omnivic said. "Banks, government infrastructure, military command and control sites—all of it will be disrupted."

"And the tank formations follow?" I asked rhetorically.

Omnivic shook his head. "They'll send in Spetsnaz and mercenaries for the first phase. We're also anticipating that the cyber-attacks will be directed toward NATO countries as well—including the United States—to keep us occupied. They've stationed submarines along each of the 16 transatlantic cables connecting Europe to the United States. If they go through with severing them, it will be a significant disruption."

"We still would have our satellites though, wouldn't we?"

"Russia launched five anti-satellite spacecraft from the Plesetsk

Cosmodrome in northern Russia a week ago," Omnivic said. "These ASATs, as they're called, have only one purpose, and that's to kill other satellites. We're tracking all four of them, but its very worrisome."

"Why hasn't the President said anything?" I asked.

Omnivic shrugged his shoulders. "We've presented the information to him. He hasn't acted on it—we're told it's because he doesn't want to spook the markets, or further alienate the Kremlin. The Secretary of State is at the Kremlin now, working behind the scenes."

"It seems now would be a good time to go public, then, wouldn't you say?"

Omnivic inhaled. "You could do that, of course, but we can't. And it's not for us to say. There's one other thing that may work though."

I raised my eyebrows expectantly.

"The Tory Foundation gold," Omnivic said. "Give it back to them as a conditional token of good will. At least the portion that was taken from them during World War II.

"You're the only one who can find out, and who can authorize the return," Omnivic answered. "Once located, we would ask that the President personally make the gesture of returning the stockage."

I was surprised, up to that point biting my tongue not to interrupt. "Why do I hear my father and uncle screaming *'Bullshit!'*?"

"We've run out of options, Congressman."

"No," I said, shaking my head. "No you haven't. We could stand up to them. That's an option, isn't it?"

"Not a good one, and it's not a fight we could win in the short-term," Omnivic replied, shaking his head, eyebrows knit together. "Most of our forces are focused on the Middle East and the Pacific right now. Shifting to the Baltics would take months, and by that time, it would be too late. Western Europe will condemn the attack, but they won't take any real decisive action because they're afraid their natural gas supplies will be shut off just in time for winter. Moscow is well aware of all those gaps."

"It stinks of appeasement," I said. "When has that ever worked?"

Omnivic shook his head slowly and uneasily. "It'll buy us time," he said. "The diplomats have told us they need to give the Russians a face-saving concession."

"A concession?" I asked. "For what"

"To do the right thing."

"Well," I began slowly, looking up at Omnivic. "There's just one problem with that."

"What would that be?"

"I don't know where the gold is," I answered matter-of-factly. "Do you?"

Omnivic shook his head. "No, but if you agree with our approach, we'll make all of our resources available to you."

I laughed and shook my head. "Even though we stole it from them, fair and square?" I looked over at Robin. "Pardon me if this doesn't strike me as completely bizarre...all of it."

"We have a starting point for you, but—" Omnivic hesitated.

"But what?" I asked pointedly.

Omnivic looked over at Robin, who on cue, pulled out a yellow folder marked in bold red letters: **TOP SECRET.**

Robin glanced over at Omnivic with a concerned expression. Omnivic nodded silently.

"Daniel," Robin said tentatively. "We believe your father may still be alive."

CHAPTER 56

"WE BELIEVE YOUR FATHER MAY BE ALIVE."

Robin's words echoed, and my mouth was open in heavy incomprehension. My mind raced in indignant rebuttal as I tried, in vain, to reconcile what I'd just heard.

"*When*, may I ask, were you planning on *fucking* telling me this? Before or after we jumped off our train?" I had managed to not raise my voice, but had visibly lost my composure.

Omnivic blinked at the obscenity and waved his hand to placate. "We don't know with any degree of certainty, but we have an eye-witness account from a KGB defector who says your father was not executed as it was widely reported."

I did the quick math in my head. He'd be ninety-four years old, if it were true.

"What did your defector say happened to him?" I asked.

Robin handed me the folder labeled TOP SECRET. "The translation of his Company debrief is there on the right."

Omnivic pointed at the brown leather sofa by the fireplace. "Have a seat, Congressman. It'll take you a little while to digest it all."

I held the folder up and looked over at Robin. "Does everything that's in here sync with what you've already translated from my father's diary?"

Robin nodded slowly and apologetically. "It could align with everything we've already seen, but—"

"But what?" I asked pointedly.

"But this account is over three decades old," Robin said quietly. "If your father is alive, the chances—"

"Jonas died at ninety-three," I said, trying to keep my voice even. "I get it. But what I don't understand is why even try to build up hope where there isn't?"

Robin pointed at the folder in my hands. "You need to read that."

I opened the folder, and with one hand on the original document as I flipped the pages.

```
London,   111133Z July 1984
Debrief   of:   Vasiley   Sheremetyov,   Colonel
General, KGB
Debriefed by: Richard Albright, Special Agent
in Charge
```

RI: This debrief is being conducted in the secure conference room at U.S. Embassy London on 11 July 1984. Colonel General Vasiley Sheremetyov, the KGB's Deputy Commander responsible for the United Kingdom has voluntarily defected to the United States in exchange for asylum for him and his family. He has voluntarily submitted to this debrief and has also volunteered to have his statements corroborated through multiple means, to include polygraph testing. This is his initial interview. It will be conducted in Russian.

General Sheremetyov, welcome. As you know this is the first of several debriefings as we consider whether to grant you political asylum in the United States.

VS: I will tell you all that I know, as long as you take care of my family.

RA: We have granted full asylum to you and your family, General. You have our promise that that you will all be well taken care of.

VS: [Nodding]

RA: For simplicity, we will proceed chronologically. When did you begin working in the KGB, General?

VS: [Brief pause, then smiling]. It is not simple. I joined the GRU in 1947 as young lieutenant. In 1950, while I was in training as captain in Moscow, I was recruited into KGB.

RA: What was your first posting and your first case as a KGB officer?

VI: I spent one year in training learning field craft and Lithuanian. The following year, I was sent to Kaunas. My job, along with many other of my colleagues was to facilitate the new Soviet sponsored government in Lithuania. We were directed to seek out points of resistance, subversion and sabotage, investigate them and neutralize them expeditiously.

RA: These "Points of Resistance" were people, I assume?

VI: [Laughing]. Yes, they often were expressed to us as "situations to be dealt with," but in the end, people are the ones who create situations, are they not?

RA: Who were the subjects of your investigations?

VI: [Waving his hands]. Too many for me to remember. Politicians, bankers, newspaper reporters and editors, professors. They were easy to identify, because we had many Lithuanians who collaborated with us for their own benefit, and they guided us to them. They were called Smogikai. There was only one group that was a persistent challenge for us—" [Inaudible].

RA: Could you repeat that, General?

VI: The Tory Family—their guerilla group, "The Hawks" continually harassed the Soviet occupation, subverted us and evaded us at every juncture. Their chief, Lucas Tory, seemed to know our every move in advance. We would raid a reported headquarters where he and his people had just been seen, and they would be gone. The Lithuanians loved him and his partisans, and protected him. We called him "The Ghost" because we always heard about him, saw the aftermath of his raids and ambushes, but we never saw him. We had intelligence that he had masterminded the hijacking of one of our gold shipments by train. Thirty tons of gold.
RA: What happened to the gold? Was it ever recovered?

VI: [Shrugging]. Gone without a trace. How is that possible? But Lucas Tory knows.

RA: You use the present tense.

VI: Excuse me? I do not understand you.

RA: You said, "Lucas Tory knows." Where the gold is.

VI: [Shrugging. Shaking head.]. Lucas Tory, his wife and brother were captured by the KGB and brought to Moscow for interrogation, trial and execution. As far as I know, that is what happened, but—" [Pausing].

RA: "But" what, General?

VI: I only heard rumors.

RA: What are the rumors you heard?

VI: I heard rumors of a deal between the KGB and Lucas Tory. That they captured his pregnant wife, two-year-old daughter, and his brother, first. But Lucas volunteered to surrender himself to the KGB if his family was set free. The KGB colonel in charge agreed, but only if the daughter stayed behind, and if the wife and brother left the country, never again to return to the Soviet Union. Lucas agreed to the terms. He gave himself up once his family was confirmed to be in London. He was interrogated, tried and sentenced to death. But the sentence, I heard, was never carried out.

RA: Why?

VI: Because the Kremlin knew that if they

executed Lucas Tory, they would never find the stolen gold. Lucas made that clear to them. He was tortured severely, through the most inhumane methods, but he never broke. Midway through one of those torture sessions, a year or so later, he told them.

RA: Told them what?

VI: Well, I heard that at one point in his interrogation, Lucas Tory had seemed to break. But then he smiled, and began to laugh at his torturers and his interrogators. Loudly. He said that no amount of questioning or torture, no matter how cruel, could cause him to reveal any information about the Soviet gold. Because the only one who would know where the gold was stored was his newborn son.

RA: How is that possible?

VI: Lucas Tory informed his interrogators that the gold reserves and the location of the storage site would never be revealed, but a payment in gold would be made in exchange for allowing him to live.

RA: Lucas Tory established his own ransom?
VI: [Shrugging]. His own ransom? Yes, maybe. Or his own life guarantee. Ingenious, was it not? But it's only a rumor, and probably a folk tale to further the Tory legend.

RA: Who told you about this?

VI: A number of different sources, which makes me think it may be true. The most reliable source was a trusted friend, GRU Colonel Antenas Petrov. Antenas was also the arresting officer of Lucas Tory.

RA: If Lucas Tory is alive, where is he now?

VI: [Shrugging]. He is dead for all that I know. Antenas Petrov may be the only one to have the true story.

RA: Debriefing Paused. It is 11 July 1984, 12:05 Zulu.

My hands were shaking uncontrollably. I realized I was standing up and pacing. I felt the oxygen leave my lungs in short, imperceptible gasps. I looked at Omnivic, and then over at Robin with an obvious expression of disbelief.

"Is this some kind of elaborate hoax?" I asked, hearing my voice raise an octave. "Because if it is, it's a *particularly* fucking cruel one!"

"It's an actual debrief, Congressman," Omnivic said calmly. "We've authenticated it several times."

I looked up at Robin. "Antenas Petrov was my mother's boyfriend, and my sister's father. You translated his journal entries. He arrested them all, do you remember?" I realized my tone was sounding a little desperate, but this went a long way in explaining what had transpired so long ago, just before I was born.

Robin nodded. "I do remember."

I inhaled deeply, and looked up at both of them. "Well, is he alive then? Is my father still alive? Or is this just more intolerable bullshit?"

Robin spoke up. "On the original copy of the debriefing

transcript there is some hand-written Cyrillic script. We believe it to be an address in Vyborg."

"Vyborg?"

Robin nodded. "It's a sanitarium, hidden away on the grounds of Monrepos Estate. 170 kilometers or so northwest of here, near the border of Finland. Where Russia's elite are institutionalized."

"Can I get there?"

Omnivic nodded. "We've arranged a van to take you. You'll need to go undercover, as a stroke patient to be admitted. You won't have any need to speak, and Robin will be your attending physician." He paused, and looked at both Robin and me. "It's dangerous. We have no idea what you'll find there, or what kind of reception you'll get. It might be better to send someone else in your place."

"Think about your own situation," Robin pleaded. "You're in no shape—"

I looked at Omnivic directly. "No, I'm going."

CHAPTER 57

THE DAWN CAME GRAY, with gusts of driving snow. The van was already waiting for us—the same blue panel van and same driver that picked Robin and me up in Katrinaberg.

"This doesn't look much like an ambulance," I said to Robin under my breath, squinting through the snow.

"It's completely normal," Robin replied quietly. "This is Russia. A horse-drawn cart can be an ambulance. It's all they had available."

"Just how sick do I need to look when we arrive?" I asked.

"Like you have the worst hangover of your life."

"Okay," I said, feeling the combined lingering effects of the 2003 Chateau Latour, Ricin poisoning, and a dislocated shoulder. "That won't require much acting."

I awoke from a deep sleep, with Robin shaking me, saying that our driver had taken a wrong turn into an abandoned Soviet Army base, and our van was stuck in a snowdrift. Massive flakes of snow were falling outside, and accumulating on the ground.

"Okay. Get out," Robin said abruptly.

The van door was open.

"Excuse me?" I said.

"And help push," she said. "I'll get behind the wheel."

No sooner had I stepped out of the van and the entire glass windshield splintered, and then shattered. I looked over at the driver on his back surrounded by splotches of red soaked snow.

"GET DOWN!" Yelled Robin.

I looked into the vacant stare of our driver. A single bullet had entered through his right temple. Blood stained the snow beneath his body in a bright red crimson. I could not save him. *Someone was shooting at us, but who?* There were no sounds to accompany the shots, except a plinking sound that echoed off the buildings around us. Bullets were hitting the side of our van in rapid succession.

"Can you see anything?" Robin asked, almost conversationally.

I looked up at her, hunched into the seat, on the floor of the van, with her handgun drawn, surveying the area around us.

"No," I replied, but just as I'd uttered that, I caught the glint of metal, followed by movement inside an abandoned building to our immediate right front. "Wait...look at that—two o'clock, third floor... one, two, three windows from the right. See him?"

"Yeah, I see him," Robin answered calmly. "Don't move."

"How do you want to handle this?" I asked.

"They've got a high-powered rifle with scope. If I step foot outside this van, I'm dead," she said matter-of-factly.

"I'll do it," I said impulsively.

"Do what?" Robin asked impatiently—the first outward sign that she was worried, or at least stressed.

"I need your gun," I answered deliberately, peering up and over, trying to gauge the angles. "I think there's a blind spot where I am, behind the van."

"Okay," Robin said after an extended pause. "Give me you coat and your hat."

I stripped it off and handed it to her, as she locked and loaded a full clip of ammunition into her Colt .45.

"Here," she said, handing it to me. "I'll distract him. Crawl low to the ground...." She pointed. "To that tree line." She peeked above her seat, just barely. "You need to take him by surprise, or it's not going to work." She paused and looked at me intently. "Are you ready for this?"

"No one gets off Planet Earth alive," I replied, repeating Jonas' oft-repeated adage.

"*What?*" Robin asked, noticeably alarmed.

I shook my head and smiled reassuringly. "Don't worry, I'll be fine."

It was my first time I'd done anything like this, and I realized I was woefully unprepared. I put both my palms into the snow and tunneled, as if I were doing the breaststroke, through the largest drifts—for cover, however slight. The tree line wasn't far—half a football field or so, but it seemed much further away.

Just as I was starting to feel sorry for myself, I would hear the *plink* of high velocity bullets hitting the van, shattering more glass. And then it occurred to me that what I was facing paled in comparison to what my family had dealt with.

I plowed through the snow, practically tunneling into it with my bare hands, doing my best to keep my head turned and snug to the ground. The Blue Spruce and Birch forest approached with every push forward. Robin's .45 was in my pant pocket and occasionally fell out into the snow, forcing me to reach around and cram it back in. I was feeling unprofessional and disorganized, and distinctly unprepared for the task of taking another life.

Once inside the tree line, I pulled myself up behind a large pine tree, gripped the pistol in my now frozen-blue hands, and ran deeper into the forest. Snow had crept into my shirt and accumulated, and I could feel it melting onto my chest and stomach.

I sprinted across a clearing to the front of the non-descript building that appeared to have been a soldiers' barracks, crouching near the staircase, trying to catch my breath, and doing my best not to collapse. My lungs burned, and I realized I was soaking wet, and nearly hypothermic. My fingers were numb around the pistol grip, and I was shivering uncontrollably. I leaned against the entrance wall with the weight of a deteriorating situation bearing down on me.

Another shot rang out above me. I ducked reflexively, but then realized it was coming from one of the rooms on the second or third floor. I pushed the safety on the pistol to "OFF." Stepping around broken bottles and trash on the stairway, my heart raced wildly.

My stomach was gaseous and tight, and I questioned my ability to actually do what I said I would.

Another rifle shot echoed through the building from the third floor above, and I thought about Robin pinned down in the van—and that provided all the impetus I needed to move quickly. I thought about my parents and Jonas.

I heard Jonas' voice clearly.

It's up to you now, Danno. Everything depends on you.

On the third floor, I stepped silently over the remnants of mattresses, chairs and old vodka bottles toward the door of the only room I saw that would provide an easy vantage point to our van. Another shot rang out. Louder, more immediate. No echo this time. The distinct scent of burnt gunpowder, with a mix of ammonia and sulfur wafted through the doorway.

Step into the room, aim, and shoot.

I did just that. Everything but the shooting part, because I wasn't prepared for what I saw in the instant I entered that room.

CHAPTER 58

I'M NOT EXACTLY SURE what I expected as I turned the corner, but I know I didn't think I'd see a woman wearing white snow suit, with a high-powered sniper rifle trying to kill us.

Stop!

She spun around from her position in the window with a surprised, malevolent expression—pointing the rifle in my direction. The intensity of her stare and her sudden sneer remains indelible to this day. Fear captured in my throat, and she fired a shot that passed in close proximity to my head.

I don't remember firing the Glock at all, but I do remember her incoherent cry, the rifle dropping, and her expression of complete surprise as she sank to the ground.

I lowered the pistol and walked over to her, and kicked the rifle away. She was still alive, but her breathing was labored and shallow. A crimson stain began from the center of her chest and was expanding outward.

The color was quickly evaporating from her face, and her eyes were glazed.

"Why?"

It was the only question I could muster.

She coughed up blood and gasped soundlessly. Her breathing became shallow—then stopped altogether.

"We have to go." It was Robin. She was standing in the doorway, and breathing heavily.

"How long have you been standing there?" I asked.

"Long enough," she said matter-of-factly. She walked over to the sniper rifle, picked it up, and ejected a round from the chamber. "Come on, let's go."

I noticed she had taken the box of ammunition and spare magazines. "Are you expecting to have to use that?"

"We need to find the vehicle she came in," she said. "The van's completely shot up."

I checked the KGB woman's coat pockets, and found a set of keys and her iPhone. "Look for a Lexus," I said, holding the keys up.

I draped her coat over her head, and followed Robin down the stairway.

Outside, I heard the sound of a horn, and realized Robin was pressing the door lock button on the set of car keys.

"Over there." She was pointing behind an adjacent building, at a black SUV parked just inside the woods.

The abandoned compound was quiet, and so was the forest surrounding it. The snowfall seemed to insulate us from the outside world. In the midst of our isolation, seeing the Lexus SUV parked there in the forest was at once unsettling and welcome.

Robin drove the Lexus SUV in four-wheel drive through the snow to the main roadway.

"Her name was Natalya Sergeyev," Robin said "She was an FSB Major and worked directly for Putin's Chief of Staff. She's been on our watch list for the past three years."

I leaned back in my seat, pulled out Natalya Sergeyev's iPhone, and turned it on.

"She sent a bunch of text messages on her way over here, but they're all in Russian."

Robin put her hand out. "Let me see."

She scrolled through the exchange, all in Cyrillic script, and leaned over to me. "Okay, this is interesting. No name of the other party, but it's an international number—looks to be U.S.. We'll have it traced."

"Yeah, that's the interesting part," she pointed at each line in each text cloud. "It looks like these are her messages to the right, and the person she was texting are here to the left."

> They jumped off the train. Found
> out too late

> Assume they are enroute to
> Vyborg

> On my way now

> They cannot be allowed to arrive
> at Monrepos

She typed something on the phone, and handed it back to me. "Now they'll believe she was successful in killing us."

I admired Robin's deception strategy, but couldn't help but feel that was the *only* strategy we had at the moment. I watched the snow covered Russian countryside slide past. I thought about the KGB transcript of my father's interrogation more than half a century ago, and the defector's transcript twenty years later.

"Why didn't you tell me?" I asked quietly.

Robin looked over at me, realizing what I was asking. "I didn't know about that debrief until we were on our way to the safe house," Robin answered.

"I feel like I'm occupying a parallel universe," I said quietly. "I really don't know what to believe anymore."

The Lexus suddenly slammed to a halt just as we were about to get on the asphalt road. Robin threw the gear into "Park."

Her voice was strained, but even. "Listen to me. I understand you're upset, and confused. Rightfully so. But it was *your* decision to come here. *Your* decision to meet Tatyana. You came looking for the truth. But now you need to ask first if you're ready for the truth, and second, if it's worth the cost?"

"The truth is all that matters to me," I said. "The alternative is to live a lie."

We drove in silence, and I thought about the possibility of my father still being alive. However remote or improbable, even the possibility was enough to push me forward, regardless of the consequences.

"Why would they allow my father to live?" I asked rhetorically. "What does that get them?"

Robin shook her head. "He still had something they valued more than his life."

"Beyond the gold, what?" I asked, thinking aloud. "They could easily make him reveal that information through torture, blackmail, or physical threats."

"One thing I've learned in translating his journal, is that Lucas Tory was unbreakable," Robin said, looking ahead at the snow-swept road. "The things he cared most about were his family and his country."

"God."

"Excuse me?"

"He wasn't religious, but he was God-fearing," I answered, and pointed at the brown Orthodox Church just ahead of us, constructed entirely of wood. It stood alone, with no other structure in the vicinity. "Stop there."

"We don't have time—"

"Please," I said, insisting. "Pull in here. You can stay in the car, I'll be quick."

We parked in front of a sign in Cyrillic that read, **Church of the Resurrection of Christ. 1776.** Constructed from piled interlocking logs, its roof had an intricate aspen design, and the bell tower was a large ornate octagon. The church was as impressive as any structure I'd seen from that era. Looking up at the walls and down at the floors, I could not see a single spike or nail. I walked inside to the faint scent of spruce, and a wooden screen covered with religious icons hung on the log walls. Colorful linen scarfs draped over the icons. An arched log entrance led to the small gift shop. Hundreds of icons and orthodox crosses lined its walls. A quiet, elderly woman who spoke only in Russian attended the shop. When she realized I was American, she pantomimed what I could not understand.

I picked up a medium sized religious icon and showed it to the old lady. "Do you have any antique icons...very old?"

The lady nodded, laughed and pointed to herself. "*Staryy!*" And then pointed to me. "*Molodoy!*"

I nodded enthusiastically. "Yes! I need a Staryy icon! Your starriest"

"*Antichny!*"

I nodded once again. *Antichny.*

She held up her finger, signaling me to wait as she shuffled out of the room. A few minutes later, she came back with a middle-aged man dressed in black, with a long grey beard. He was carrying a shallow wooden box.

"You are American?" He asked in a thick Russian accent.

I nodded. "I'm looking for your oldest icon. As a gift for my father."

"The old ones," he said with noticeable skepticism. "They are very expensive, you know."

"The expense is not a concern."

"Then this would be the one you should see. It is fifteenth century, and very unique. It is called, 'Sterling Forest Triptych'."

The priest opened the box, and the extraordinary beauty of the icon immediately struck me.

"You can see that it has three silver frames, connected by hand-made silver hinges that are 400 year old." He turned the icon around. "The back is made from linden wood." Opening the icon in front of me he said, "Here you see the images of the Madonna, a scene of the nativity and a line of saints with a forest of trees as the backdrop, all painted with egg tempera on linden wood with gold leaf, and gilt in silver.

"Made in the year 1600," the priest said. "There is simply no other like this." He then proceeded to fold all three connected frames together into a compact box that locked with an iron swivel latch. "It is very expensive, though."

"I'll take it."

CHAPTER 59

"ARE YOU FINISHED SOUVENIR SHOPPING?" Robin asked, eyes raised.

I nodded, and pulled the icon out from one of the two bags and unpackaged it. "I think you'll be glad we stopped."

I unlatched the icon, and unfolded the three-boxed panels. A wax paper envelope that had been inserted between the panels fell out on my lap. Inside the envelope was a color photograph of an elderly man, with contemplative blue eyes and a heavily wrinkled face, looking out a window. The family resemblance was unmistakable—the sharp angular jaw line, the rounded nose, and thick eyebrows. On the back of the photo, there was a label in typed Cyrillic,

Лукас Тори

"Lucas Tory," I read aloud.

Robin looked over with an expression of combined surprise and disbelief. "How in the world...?" Her voice trailed off.

"When I was at the Schlossberg Castle in Geneva, I was shown a map with the Tory Foundation network in Russia," I explained. "There was a digital photo of this church on the map. And then, while we were at the Ritz-Carlton, I received a text photo of the same church from someone with the words "Antique Icons." I thought it was spam, but when I saw the church, I remembered it."

Robin nodded. "It's the nearest town to Vyborg. It makes sense for the Orthodox clergy to be a part of the Tory Foundation network—while the clergy will never openly oppose the Kremlin, they aren't adverse to subverting it either." She paused to look at the photo, and up at me with a smile. "You look like him."

"Well, if he's still alive, at least we know generally what he looks like," I answered. "And we'll know who to look for."

"Daniel, you know this may not work out," Robin said quietly.

I nodded absently, lost in my own thoughts. "I know, believe me, I know—but I have to see for myself."

Driving on a cobblestone roadway into Vyborg, it was easy to feel like we were entering a time warp that had thrown us back centuries, into a bygone era. The new snow seemed to temper the decay of the town's Finnish nouveau art buildings. The shores of Vyborg Bay led to a circular grey medieval castle that dominated the town center. The whole city had a ghost town like feel — there were no cars, and there were no people. Just stray dogs searching for food.

"Don't be fooled," Robin said, reading my mind. "People do live here, they're just not foolish enough to come out in these conditions."

"How do you know all this?" I asked.

"When I was at the University of Chicago, I studied a semester abroad here." She pointed at the water. "One of the largest naval battles in history—the Battle of Vyborg Bay—was fought there, not long after our Declaration of Independence," Robin said, pointing to the iced shores.

The cobblestone street rattled the SUV as we drove through the deserted town. "We're only thirty kilometers from the Finnish border. Over the centuries, the city exchanged hands between Russia and Finland more than a few times. The last time the Russians got their hands on it, they deported all of the Finns, which turned out to be a wise move."

"Why?"

"Well, you can't see it now because it's winter, and so we're out of season," Robin answered. "But in the spring and summer, the Finns come here by the boatload."

"Why here?"

"The women come for the shopping," Robin said, and then pointed at one of the many pubs along the main street. "And as expensive as alcohol is in Finland, the men willingly come along for the cheap booze."

Robin nodded at a sign on the outskirts of Vyborg.

Monrepos Park

"That's it."

"It doesn't seem real," I said.

She reached into her backpack, and handed me the same pistol I had used only hours before. "But whatever or whoever's here, we know the Kremlin doesn't want us to find out."

The short drive from the Vyborg town center to Monrepos Park was icy and treacherous, but the entrance to the park, situated on a frozen inlet, was well kept, and the setting remarkable. Huge rock outcroppings and trees lined the winding parkway. Italian, Polish and Scandinavian sculptures of poets and literary figures alternatively dotted each side of the road leading to a series of buildings. We passed a cliff top memorial chapel, a sculpture garden and a mausoleum with the remains of the former owners of the estate.

"Not what I expected," I said to myself.

Robin smiled. "It's one of my favorite parks in Russia and Europe—its like walking into the18th and 19th Century—different European cultures, all whispering their most closely held secrets."

"Well, I'm interested in only one of those secrets," I said. "They can keep the rest."

Robin pointed past the yellow and white manor, toward a manned gate inside the forest. "The Sanitarium is through that gate. We have to get past the guard."

I unzipped my backpack and opened out the other bag given to me by the priest at Church of the Resurrection of Christ. Inside was a medium-sized wooden box. I lifted it up to show Robin.

"What's this?"

"*Marusya.*"

Robin's expression was perplexed. "Pardon me?"

I took the box out "The best vodka in the world, if you like Vodka, that is. You can only find it in Moscow and it's made in small batches, that's what the good father told me at least." I handed the box to her. "This should get us in the gate."

For the first time, I saw Robin Nielsen rendered momentarily speechless.

Robin pulled forward and transitioned quickly—talking to the middle aged guard in flirtatious tones, laughing and smiling. She gestured to me, and from what I could make out; she was talking about my grandfather as a patient. He began to smile and shake his head, and when it appeared that he was requesting our papers, Robin pulled out the box of Marusya and showed it to the guard before setting it down in her lap. The guard looked around tentatively, almost furtively, and then nodded. Robin put the box back in the bag and handed it to him. In turn, he handed a vehicle pass for us to put on display, inside the windshield.

She raised the window and turned to me. "That was brilliant."

"Honestly, I was hoping we could keep it for ourselves," I said. "I understand it's that good. And I'm not even a vodka drinker."

Robin nodded with a sardonic smile. "Thank you for your sacrifice, Congressman."

CHAPTER 60

THE TREE-LINED ROAD LEADING to the Monrepos Sanitarium was snow packed. Long, thick icicles hung precariously from the branches like knives waiting to drop. The road was not plowed, but the Lexus SUV cut through the ice and snow with little effort.

"I thought the days of sanitariums ended a century ago?"

"Not in Russia," Robin answered. "But they are starting to rename them 'Health Resorts' and 'Spas' to address the stigma that 'Sanitarium' conveys."

The road ended at a small complex of modern buildings surrounding an older Napoleonic mansion. At the far side on the cliff's edge, a chapel overlooked the water—the Gulf of Finland.

"How should we go about this?" I asked.

"We tell them you're here to visit your father," Robin said.

"Really?"

"There's an advanced stage Alzheimer's patient your father's age in Room 152, East Wing. His name is Evgeniy Euchev," Robin said. She reached into her backpack and pulled out an envelope. "Your passport, Daniel Euchev."

It was an American passport complete with my photo, and several stamps from Russia, Germany, England and Switzerland.

"You've thought of everything, haven't you?" I said, placing the passport in my coat pocket. Nonetheless, I had this prickling sense of familiarity come over me that I couldn't account for.

"Everything but the booze," Robin said, parking the SUV in front of the mansion. "But you covered that requirement nicely." She turned to me. "What I don't know is what we'll encounter once we're inside."

"Well, let's find out," I said, opening the door.

Robin stepped out and put her arm in mine. "Once we're in, I'm your wife."

"Is that a promise or a threat?" I joked, immediately regretting it.

"Right now, it's a survival strategy," Robin answered.

We walked up the steps and through the doors to the sanitarium. The floors were clean, white granite and the walls were a mix of the original centuries-old limestone and dark oak. A middle-aged woman with white hair, glasses, angular features and a stern expression stood behind a desk. Robin smiled and began speaking a rapid-fire, sing-song flurry of Russian that took me by surprise—an approach that seemed so contrived, in fact, that I was certain it would raise suspicion. But as I saw the receptionist's severe demeanor dissolve into a wide smile and a conversational tone, I realized that it was actually working. She pointed down the hallway. I nodded, smiled and proceeded down the hallway beside Robin.

"Well, I'm not exactly sure how you did that, but I'm impressed," I said under my breath.

"We're looking for Room 152," Robin said out loud, pretending to ignore me, now fully immersed in her role. "It's so good that you will finally be able to see him after all these years."

I simply nodded, not knowing quite how to respond. I noticed that despite Robin's apparent calm, her eyes were darting in all directions. Her head stayed straight, but she was actively surveying our surroundings.

Passing the rooms, most of the doors were opened, but a few were shut. Each room was a small one-bedroom apartment, some with hospital beds visible from the hallway, and others with a simple sofa and chairs. The tan and brown patterned wallpaper was the common feature in each, along with the name of its occupant on a nameplate in Cyrillic script above the door.

"There," Robin pointed. "Room 152. When we go in, you are

Evgeniy Euchev's son, so play the role, and actively converse with him. I'll excuse myself to search the building, and we'll switch off so they don't get suspicious. Obviously, Mr. Euchev won't know who you are, and we can blame that on his condition."

"I'm sure he'll just be happy to have visitors," I replied quietly.

We knocked on the door and walked in to find an elderly man of medium, sinewy stature, bald head, and with a deeply wrinkled face watching a Russian talk show on the television. He looked at us with a slight smile and turned his attention back to the TV.

Robin sat beside the old man and took his hand, speaking quietly in Russian. Her tone was calm, reassuring—even soothing. Periodically, he would look over at her and smile at her, motioning to the television.

"*Gospodin Euchev, eto Daniel,*" Robin said in a loud voice, motioning toward me.

The old man sat there like a man in a dream, never taking his gaze off of the television, even as I sat down opposite him.

"We came from the United States," I said conversationally, but in English. "Chicago."

Evgeniy Euchev looked over at me with bluish eyes smudged of memory. He nodded. "Chicago?"

I nodded. "Yes, Chicago."

"Al Capone!" The old man remarked, extending his right hand toward the television as if it were a pistol.

I smiled, overjoyed to have gotten a reaction out of him. "Yes, Al Capone."

"Whiskey!"

I nodded again. "Yes, exactly, whiskey in the Windy City."

The man pointed at me with hands speckled brown with age, and spoke in broken English. "You have whiskey?"

I pulled out the remaining bottle in my backpack. "Yes, Sir— in fact, I do!"

Robin looked over at me, visibly surprised. "You brought whiskey too?"

"Balcones Brimstone Resurrection," I announced with pride,

rising to find some glasses in the kitchenette. "Only the best for Gospodin Euchev!"

"I won't ask," Robin said, shaking her head. "I'm gonna leave you boys and take a walk."

I nodded, holding up the bottle of Balcones. "Shut the door, just in case we get too loud. This whiskey's from Texas."

"Daniel, please don't drink too much," Robin pleaded. "I'm pretty sure having that bottle here is against every policy they have here."

"Whiskey!" Euchev shouted excitedly, pointing at the bottle with clear anticipation.

"Shhhh," I said pouring the whiskey into our glasses with a broad smile, feigning the need to be quiet.

CHAPTER 61

NOT MUCH OF ANYTHING Evgeniy Euchev said to me seemed entirely coherent, but in the short time I was with him, I enjoyed his positive, happy demeanor; and for his interest and persistence in trying to communicate with me, virtually ignoring our language barrier.

At some point, as I felt the whiskey beginning to have its effect, I pulled out the photographs I had of my father, Jonas, and my mother and handed them to Euchev.

"My family," I said simply.

Euchev flipped through the photographs of Jonas, an early photo of my father, and pointed at the black and white image of my mother when she was in her 30's, wearing a dark dress that was fashionable for the time.

"My mother," I said with a smile. "Before I was born."

"Ji yra labai gražus," Euchev replied, nodding. "Very beautiful...."

Euchev lifted up a photograph of my father and mother together.

"My parents," I said.

The next photograph was one that I had taken of my mother a few months prior to her stroke, with Elena—her nurse. Elena was smiling, and my mother's eyes that at once conveyed a regal mix of confidence, caution and kindness I had always known.

Euchev sat back in his chair, staring at the photo.

"My mother today," I said. "Before she fell ill."

A thought seemed to form in his mind; he looked at the photo, and then at me, inhaling, as if he were about to speak, but he said nothing, nodded, and downed the rest of the whiskey in his glass.

"Good!" he exclaimed. Handing the stack of photos back to me, he extended his glass, and motioned for more.

"Only this much more, Gospodin Euchev" I said pouring half a glass. "Or we'll get in a lot of trouble."

Euchev waved his hand laughing. "Trouble!" He pointed at himself. "I always in trouble!"

"Cheers," I said, touching his glass to mine. "Here's to lots of trouble."

"Much trouble!" he shouted hoarsely. His English seemed to improve with each drink.

We sat there in silence for a while looking into our whiskey, and out the window together. I sipped from my glass, and Euchev tended to gulp, always demanding more.

The door opened, and Robin entered. She looked over at me and shook her head.

"No luck?"

Robin exhaled, "No men your father's age."

"Mr. Euchev and I have had a good meeting anyway," I replied, unable to hide my disappointment."

"We should go, Daniel," Robin replied. "Before they figure things out."

I nodded, corking the bottle of whiskey and placed it in Euchev's kitchenette cabinet. "We'll leave you the bottle."

Euchev smiled and lifted his glass in a toast. *"Mano noras, jums gyventi "Dievų miškas," dangaus mėlynė!"*

"Where have I heard that before?" I asked.

"It's Lithuanian," Robin replied with surprise. "Roughly translated, it means, 'My wish, for you— to live in Gods forest, under blue skies.'"

I leaned down to pick up my glass and raised it up. "To God's Forest!"

Euchev shuffled over to the closet, picked up an oversized coffee book, and handed it to me.

"For you, Danno!" Euchev said with a glint in his eye.

I thanked the old man, and we gave each other a hug. On our way out of his room, Euchev gave Robin a hug, and whispered, "Thank you for the whiskey!"

"I'm sorry we didn't find your father, Daniel," Robin said, as we drove out of Monrepos.

I shrugged, "I didn't really expect we would, but it was worth the attempt."

"I'm going to make one stop on our way out of town," Robin said.

"Where?"

She pointed ahead. "Right up here. In the city center," she answered. "I won't be long."

"Can I help?"

She shook her head. "There's a package I need to pick up"

Robin parked the Lexus in the parking lot of the Pribaltiskaya Hotel. As she opened the door and began to step out, I reached out and touched her arm. "Be careful, okay?"

Robin looked at me momentarily and smiled. "I'll be right back. Call the pilots. Keep the engine running, and we'll head to the airport."

I nodded, and as I waited, I pulled out the book that Evgeniy Euchev had given to me, entitled "Gražus Lietuva!" *Beautiful Lithuania!*

A paperclip marked one of the pages, and opening it, an envelope fell out.

I glanced at the headline on the page—also in Lithuanian—that read, "Dievų Miš kas." *Forest of the Gods.* A full-page color photo of a dense forest with large rock outcroppings was positioned below.

I realized that the expression "Forest of the Gods" was a recurring theme in some variation or the other. My mother had also uttered the expression after I had confronted her with the World War II photo of her, Jonas and my father together during their days in the resistance. "Sunki situacija Dievũ mìško padángėj." *...Under the sterling garden*

263

of the forest of the Gods.

Opening the envelope that had fallen out, I noticed meticulously neat handwriting on the paper inside, neatly written in English. A color photograph was paper clipped to the page, with three men smiling, arm-in-arm. The backdrop was at the base of the obelisk I had seen at Monrepos Sanitarium.

Evgeniy Euchev was one of the men in the photo, and the other I was my Uncle Jonas, in the middle. Both men were noticeably vibrant, and a decade or so younger. I was struck by the other man's resemblance to Jonas. Like Jonas, his hair was snow white, and his features were dramatic and strong. His eyes were kind, and yet seemed to reveal a deep intensity. There were several other old black and white photographs of Jonas, my mom and dad and their resistance members in forest encampments, holding guns in individual and group poses. I held the stack of photos as I read the handwritten letter.

Daniel,

You have arrived! I am sorry I was not here to meet you, but I am glad you met our friend Evgueni Euchev. Ev fought with your Uncle Jonas, your mother, and myself in the early years of our resistance against the Nazis. He is one of the few who have survived. By holding this letter for you, and giving it to you today, he has delivered upon my final request—a letter that he has kept at great personal risk to himself and to his family. He is a man of great courage, and I have personally entrusted him with my life many times. His loyalty to our family and me has always been absolute. Although he has been very healthy and strong, he has remained with me, as a patient at Monrepos for all of the decades I have been here. By walking with a cane, talking to strangers and appearing to drink too much, he has feigned his own dementia. In truth he is lucid as a hawk, protecting me, and our family's legacy. We owe him a great debt for all he has done for us. After reading this letter, you will likely want to return to see him at Monrepos, but I ask you not to do so—with his long service to me, and his mission complete, his identity and purpose is now compromised, and by the time you would return, he will have departed. Do not worry about him—he will be well cared for.

Only then did the realization hit full force, and headlong. *Of course....* I muttered to myself, finally recalling what had been so familiar. It was the name. I reached back to my pack and pulled out my father's journal, and found the passage recalling my parents' escape from Auschwitz:

...One day, Evgeniy Euchev, a friend and fellow prisoner who works in administration and records tells me Tanya is on a list to be exterminated in two days. ... Evgeniy is able to steal two pistols while cleaning the guard barracks.... We move quickly, and drive to the cleaners, and Evgeniy sounds the car horn. Tanya came out with eyes wide. We drive directly to the camp gates, but we see the guard is not opening them. ... "Do something or we

will die!" I tell Evgeniy to sound the horn, and I begin shouting in German, and waving the Luger out the window at the guard….

I continued to read my father's letter, completely transfixed….

Daniel, I have watched you from afar, following you, observing your great success, celebrating your triumphs, and I have been so proud to be your father. As much as I wished all this time, I could have been physically with you, I knew well that was impossible if you and your mother were to remain safe.

Since World War II, our family has always been at risk. Our desire has been to shelter you and protect you. It was our sincere hope that with the end of the Cold War, our mission would finally be complete and we could fade away and go about our lives.

We stood by, watching the Berlin Wall fall, as former Soviet republics declared their independence, and as Lithuania and our sister states—Latvia and Estonia—were welcomed into NATO and the European Union. All these years we had resisted the oppression of Nazism and Communism. We fought for freedom, and we had every reason to be optimistic. Any hope we had, though, was fleeting. The new Russian state quickly emerged, not as a democracy, but as a corrupt oligarchy.

I am surprised I have lived this long. I am 94 years old as I write this to you. Decades ago, I surrendered myself to the KGB in return for the release of Jonas and your mother, so they could live and raise you. I expected a swift execution in prison, but I was allowed to live, at first in prison, and then here at Monrepos. My reprieve was granted under many conditions—prime among them, that I not attempt to leave, and that I give back gold and silver we captured from them during the Great War.

I knew the NKVD Colonel, Antenas Petrov, well from our days in the resistance against the Nazis. We fought beside him and his partisans. He was very brave, and a loyal Soviet officer. I had rescued his fiancé from a Nazi concentration camp. They never legally married. They had a daughter, Tatyana. While our world views were very far apart, we had a common enemy, and we fought together against the SS—and we even rescued him when he was captured by the Gestapo. Soon thereafter, he was recruited to become an NKVD officer, and was brought to Moscow. He left Tanya behind. Over time, your mother and I became very close. I married her and loved her daughter, Tatyana, as my own.

War is a terrible scourge. Not only for the lives it takes, but for the fate it brings to those who survive. After the war, Petrov learned that Tanya had married me and he was very angry and began to hunt us down. We only met again the day we were face to face when I surrendered to him in exchange for the release of Jonas and your mother.

Petrov demanded other things for their release— that his daughter, Tatyana, be returned to him, and a guarantee that Jonas and Tanya would never return to either the Baltic States or Russia again.

I agreed to both conditions so they could survive. It was the hardest thing I have ever done in my lifetime.

It is a decision I still struggle with to this day, but I know that in the end I had no choice if they were to survive.

On the night I was to be executed, I was walked handcuffed, with a hood over my head, through the prison corridors, and then placed on the back of a lorry with my guards. When my hood was removed, Antenas Petrov was sitting directly in front of me. He held a revolver in his hand and was smoking a cigarette in another. While we drove, he gave me a final ultimatum: to turn over the gold to him, in return for my own life, where I would be placed under house arrest at Monrepos Sanitarium. I knew I had no other option except to be killed.

We had taken 10 full boxcars of gold that night in 1946. We stored more than half in Lithuania. Under the cover of darkness, we placed the rest in a cellar close to where we had conducted our raid, at a collective farm near Leningrad. I gave Petrov the location of the farm and the cellar. He never asked me for the remainder of the gold, but he did tell me that if I were to ever leave Monrepos, the

KGB would not only kill me, they would kill Tanya, Jonas and you immediately. I believed them.

The Foundation has kept me informed, has shown me photos and videos of you. Now that Jonas and I are gone, it is up to you to take this great responsibility, and through the Tory Foundation, to lead our resistance against this terrible scourge.

It is a very big responsibility, but I know you would be the best person to lead our resistance to the tyranny, and to promote freedom, democracy and all of the values we have fought so hard through the years to protect.

Regardless of your decision, the Bolshevik gold remains untouched and is protected. It must be used in the best possible way to maintain the independence of our beloved Lithuania and our neighbors. It remains where we left it, į sterlingų sodas dievų miške...

Daniel, everything that now follows must be your decision, and yours alone.

With Love, from Your Father,

Lucas Tory

CHAPTER 62

MY HANDS WERE TREMBLING, and I was attempting to catch my breath when Robin stepped back into the Lexus.

"We need to go, now."

Intuitively, I knew the reason for Robin's directive—further reinforced as she zipped up the black diplomatic pouch. We were likely being pursued.

I drove for several minutes, and turned to her. "Everything okay?"

"We haven't got a lot of time," Robin replied. "I was expecting a dead drop, and instead Omnivic was there, waiting for me. He warned me that the Police just found Natalya Sergeyev's body, so it's only a matter of time before they connect her to us. We've got to get out of Russia as soon as possible. Your jet is meeting us at the airport in St. Petersburg."

I nodded. "We need to call the pilots and tell them there's a change to our flight plan," I answered.

"What are you talking about?" Robin asked, surprised.

"We're heading to Vilnius," I said, handing her the letter.

I watched as she unfolded the letter, and added, "The sanitarium wasn't such a dead end after all."

Driving through the increasingly heavy snowfall, I glanced over at Robin as she read the letter. Her expression shifted gradually from curiosity to surprise, bordering on disbelief.

Her eyes held him. "I never imagined—"

I nodded, looking back at the road ahead. "If it's authentic, everything is beginning to make more sense. But why don't I feel better about any of it?"

Robin exhaled. "It's the past," she said matter-of-factly. "Nothing more powerful or complex than the ghosts of ancestors."

She flipped through the book as I drove through the snowstorm, and toward the back of the book, she pulled out a small card.

"A business card," she said, handing it to me.

The card was green with the outline of a fir tree in white on the right, and the Lithuanian coat of arms on the left. The name on the card read:

Fr. Tomas Kadžionis
Genocido aukų muziejuje

Aukų g. 2A,
LT-01113 Vilnius, Įm. kodas 191428780,
tel./faks. (+370) 5 249 81 56,
el. p. TKadzionis@genocid.lt

"The Museum of Genocide Victims," Robin said.

"You've heard of it?" I asked

She nodded. "It's small scale, as far as museums go, but their research arm is powerful and their library of historical accounts, photos and artifacts is impressive."

"Research arm?"

Robin nodded. "It's a pretty eclectic group, made up of elderly veterans of the resistance dating back to World War II, in addition to museum curators, academics, lawyers, recent college grads, and others who don't want to see the past forgotten, or…." Her voice trailed off.

"Or what?"

Robin looked over at me. "Or see it repeated."

"This is no accident, then?" I asked. "Is that what you're saying?"

"No," Robin replied. "I don't believe it is. But the only thing that concerns me is the timing. It's almost too perfect…like it's been scripted."

I took my cell phone out of my pocket, and found the phone number for Axel Odin.

"Who are you calling," Robin asked.

"Someone we can trust."

Axel Odin answered immediately, on the first ring. The exchange was short and direct. "I'm sending you a business card—need your report as soon as you're able."

"Yes, no problem," Axel replied. "You are okay?"

"Yes," I answered. "Meeting some interesting people, and about to get on a plane. See you there tonight."

I ended the call, and suddenly saw the litany of increasingly urgent emails from "United States House of Representatives Liaison Office" requesting information from me, with meeting dates prior to my swearing in ceremony only a week away.

"What if I'm not there to be sworn into office?" I asked hypothetically.

Robin shrugged. "Hopefully, we'll have you back in time."

"It's funny," I said. "A month ago, I couldn't have been more excited about the prospect of being a congressman. Today, it's the furthest thing from my mind."

"Life has a way of reordering our priorities." Robin shifted in her seat. "Axel Odin is meeting us in Vilnius?"

I nodded as I took a photo of the Tomas Kadžionis business card, and texted it to Axel's cell phone. "We can't do this alone," I said. "With everything that's happened, and the direction this is heading, I believe we're going to need all the help we can get."

"Who can you trust?" Robin asked directly.

"I trust the Tory Foundation," I answered. "And I know Axel was someone Jonas Tory trusted, so that's all I need."

Robin nodded. "You know we're on very dangerous ground right now?"

"Is there something you're not telling me?"

"Some of my friends at Langley are beginning to believe your case that we're getting closer to a major confrontation with Moscow,"

Robin said. "They believe the Kremlin has its back against the wall, and nothing to lose."

"If the Baltics is just a means to an end, that makes them capable of anything."

"It's a game of three dimensional chess," she answered. "They know the United States will probably not intervene with force, and neither will Europe. No one cares enough to start World War III over a few former Soviet Republics."

"What's checkmate then?" I asked.

"After Brexit, they see the EU on the verge of collapsing. Ultimately, their strategic goal is to reestablish their buffer states, and cause NATO to dissolve."

At that moment, a convoy of semis hauling tanks and self-propelled artillery began to pass us in a loud procession that seemed unending. Robin snapped multiple photos and video footage of of the convoy with her iPhone.

"Where are they heading?" I asked.

"That road leads into Estonia," Robin answered.

CHAPTER 63

OUR PLANE HAD ITS LIGHTS ON and engines running when we arrived at St. Petersburg's Pulkovo Airport. Our pilot, Captain Mike Ryan, greeted us in the VIP lounge with a concerned expression, and led us out to the jet stairs before he spoke.

"We're not exactly sure what's going on here, but we received the third degree from some official goons when we arrived here several hours ago, and I don't think they're finished," Ryan said looking around as we walked. "If it's all the same to you, I'd like to be wheels up as soon as possible."

I nodded, and glanced over at Robin. "We're in full agreement."

A female Russian customs agent met us at the air stairs and asked to see our passports and visas. Robin handed her our diplomatic passports and conversed with her in Russian. In a matter of seconds, I watched as the customs agent began shaking her head and Robin's voice raised in a direct, then strident tone. Off to their side, a separate group of men in field paramilitary-style uniforms were standing as if in reserve.

"They want to search the plane, before they allow us to take off," Robin said. "I told her it was highly irregular, and that I would be reporting the incident and her through our Embassy. But she isn't relenting, so it's clear these orders are coming from much higher than their Customs Department. Make sure we have all of our documents, phones and equipment in the diplomatic pouch. Everything else is subject to search."

The search commenced with a full squad of customs agents in green uniforms boarding the plane and removing all of the contents of our aircrew's luggage.

"Where is your luggage?" The head customs agent asked. I saw her inhaling and exhaling, almost rhythmically. The fog of her breath was like smoke in the air.

"We have none," Robin answered. "It was lost by our hotel."

The Customs agent made an annotation on her notepad, and turned to speak into her sleeve microphone. Layers of condensation had frozen on her gray fur hat. She approached us again, with a distinctly confrontational demeanor.

"Your car?" She asked in a clipped tone. "The black Lexus you arrived in, it is in the parking lot according to our security camera footage."

Robin crossed her arms and shook her head, speaking in a flurry of Russian I could not decipher.

The Customs agent turned and spoke again into her sleeve.

I turned to Robin and whispered. "Now what?"

"For the first time, Robin's expression conveyed real concern, if not worry. "Let's see how far they want to push this."

"What happens when they find out the Lexus belongs to the FSB?"

Robin shook her head almost imperceptibly. "That can't happen. Not now."

The Russian Customs agent approached us again, her voice directive, thick and menacing. "Please, take us to your car. *Now.*"

Robin began speaking slowly and calmly at first, and then faster and more loudly. This time I could make out the words, *"nyet vremeni"* (no time), *"yerunda"* (nonsense), *"diplomaticheskaya pomyeka"* (diplomatic interference), and *"soobshchit v posolstvo"* (report to the Embassy). She dialed her cell phone, and just as she began speaking, she looked up at the entrance to the terminal, ended her call abruptly and looked over at me with eyes wide in surprise.

The reality of what was unfolding in front of us didn't register for me, even as the silver BMW M5 Coupe drove up beside the plane. I almost didn't recognize Tatyana when she stepped out of the passenger door, dressed in a full-length black mink coat and hat with dark sunglasses.

She didn't look over at Robin or to me. Instead, she walked directly to the female customs agent, with an official Kremlin ID displayed in a red leather ID holder, and handed her a set of documents. Their exchange was quick, and I could see that the customs agent was sufficiently shaken and chastened as she ordered the search team out of the plane, and they immediately withdrew.

Tatyana then walked over to me and Robin, speaking loud enough to be heard by everyone around us. "Congressman Tory, you are free to go. We apologize for any inconvenience. There has been a very unfortunate misunderstanding."

I exhaled my relief. I must have been staring at Tatyana, because I suddenly felt Robin interlacing her arm into mine and guiding me to the air stairs. "Let's go. Quickly, before they change their minds."

Tatyana was now beside us, speaking so only we could hear her. "Those documents were falsified, Daniel. You have possibly twenty minutes before Customs and the FSB discover what has happened."

Our eyes met, and I could make out a subtle smile from Tatyana. As we walked up the stairs, she handed me a zippered black nylon case. "You have to stop them, Daniel. Everything you need is in there."

"Why are you doing this for us?" I asked.

"I have my own reasons," Tatyana replied, then looked over at Robin. "You are in great danger. The reason they have been trying to kill you is because of me—and now will be coming after both of you."

"What about you?" Robin asked.

"Come with us!" I insisted.

Tatyana shook her head slightly, and smiled. "Here, this is for you," she said, handing me a book. It was Tom Stoppard's *Rosencratz and Guildenstern Are Dead*.

I held the book to my chest, remembering our first encounter. There was a mass of sirens sounding in the distance.

"Now, you must go."

We began to walk up the air stairs. When she looked back up at me, her eyes were filled with tears, and I could see she was struggling to maintain composure, but she managed a smile for her farewell.

CHAPTER 64

"*BRACE FOR IMPACT... BRACE FOR IMPACT...*"

Those words, clear and deliberate, came over the airplane's speaker system from the pilot, less than ten minutes after we took off from St. Petersburg. Suddenly, and without any explanation.

I honestly didn't know what was happening until I saw our flight attendant rush to her seat and frantically buckle her seatbelt, lean forward, and interlace her fingers behind her head. Robin and I followed suit, and looked at one another, with our own expressions of terror. At once, our airplane banked hard to the left, and began a steep dive that caused the airplane to shake violently and everything seemed to go silent. Oxygen masks dropped down from the ceiling and the silence was interrupted by a high-pitched alarm that sounded throughout the cabin. Glasses, papers and bottles flew off tables and crashed onto the ceiling walls and floor in a slow motion symphony of broken glass. I was pinned to my seat. Amidst the cacophony, I reached over and grasped Robin's hand and held it tightly, awaiting whatever was to happen next.

Please, God, let this end quickly...

Robin remained very calm, and just squeezed my hand.

We seemed to level off, lurch to the Starboard side, and then straighten out. I looked over at the flight attendant, who was struggling to hold the handset to her ear.

"*What's happening?*" I shouted.

The flight attendant said a few more words into the handset and turned to me. "We're being pursued by two Russian PAK fighter jets," she yelled. "The Captain doesn't know what their intentions are—they haven't made any attempt to communicate with us—but we're not far from Finnish airspace, so that's where we're diverting—toward Helsinki—to try and get away from them."

I looked over at Robin. "How convenient for them if our plane crashed right after takeoff?"

"They have to want something pretty badly to do this," Robin said.

We went into another steep dive. The plane dropped and pitched ferociously to the side. My stomach clenched and I was pinned to the seat. We began to roll, and I held my oxygen mask tightly to my face, and saw Robin bent over, doing the same. I've never been one to pray, but I did then—an *Our Father - Hail Mary* hybrid, along with some personal expletives for good measure. The engines roared and our plane pulled up and banked sharply, righting itself.

I looked out the window and saw that we were only a hundred feet or so off the icy sea below, flying at full speed… just avoiding the water.

A loud boom seemed to envelop the cabin, and I saw the flash of another jet flying overhead. Two other military fighter jets settled off on both sides of us, and I could see from the tri-colored roundel on the wings that they weren't Russian.

"Finland Air Force!" Robin shouted through her mask, pointing at the planes now on both sides of us.

"*Congressman, our apologies for the rough ride, but we were being harassed by the Russian Air Force. A few friendly F-18 Hornets from Helsinki just came to our rescue. They've volunteered to escort us the entire way to Vilnius. Recommend you keep your oxygen on a bit longer. We'll be landing in about 20 minutes.*"

Ignoring the Captain's recommendation, I removed my oxygen mask, and turned to Robin, handing her the key Tatyana had given me on the Tarmac in St. Petersburg. "Let's take a look at what's inside that pouch."

CHAPTER 65

ROBIN UNLOCKED THE ZIPPER to the briefcase, and pulled out a thick folder of documents and photographs, with a thumb drive attached to the binder. All of the documents were printed in Cyrillic, with official Kremlin seals and handwriting on the margins throughout.

She paged through the folder, slowly at first, blinking from time to time—as if in disbelief—and then sped to an almost furious pace. "Take back any criticism I ever said about your sister...."

"What is it?" I asked, now very concerned.

"It's a copy of the report from Russian Minister of Defense to the President outlining the plan to commence the re-assimilation of Poland, Estonia, Latvia and Lithuania to the Russian Federation."

"Re-assimilation...I'm assuming means Invasion?"

She continued to flip through the documents. "Okay," she said, finally, handing me one of the pages. "Here's an English translation of the actual order. It's signed by Pavel Demidov, the Russian Minister of Defense, three days ago."

I read the memorandum quickly and felt my heart racing as the full impact of the words hit me.

СОВЕОWЕННО (TOP SECRET)

25 October
From: Minister of Defense

THE STERLING FOREST

To: The Deputy Chief of Staff

The Chief of the General Staff has directed General Nikolay Tarasov to have primary responsibility for the conduct of Operation "BLUE STAR" and has set the date for the invasion of the Baltic States for 1 December. BLUE STAR will have the following immediate objectives, as directed:

a. Capture the vessels of the Estonian, Latvian and Lithuanian navies in their bases or at sea;

b. Capture the Estonian and Latvian commercial fleets and all other vessels;

c. Prepare for invasions and landings in Tallinn, Riga and Vilnius; follow-on to other metropolitan areas and military bases.

d. Close the Gulf of Riga and blockade the coasts of Estonia, Latvia and Lithuania in the Gulf of Finland and Baltic Sea;

e. Prevent an evacuation of the Estonian, Lithuanian and Latvian governments, military forces and assets;

f. Provide naval support for an invasion toward Rakvere, Estonia; and Klaipėda, Lithuania

g. Prevent Estonian, Lithuanian and Latvian aircraft from flying either to Finland or Sweden.

h. Assume control over all Estonian, Latvian and Lithuanian media communications, to include social media sites and other non-standard means of communication through the Internet.

Pavel Demidov
Minister of Defense
Russian Federation

Robin flipped to the end of the folder, and pointed at the handwritten annotation. "That's the Prime Minister's signature, and beside it his comment, "Approved. Commence Operations 7 December."

"My God, that's three days from now," I exclaimed.

"Happy Birthday," Robin commented absently, flipping through the pages, and stopped at one. "This is far worse…more insidious than I thought even they would be capable…."

"What is it?" I asked.

She continued to read, shaking her head. "The FSB is going to blow up six apartment complexes that are occupied by Russian nationals," she said breathlessly. "As a subterfuge, to justify a Russian invasion in force. It's the same method Putin applied to become President of Russia in 1999. The FSB blew up Russian apartments and condominiums, killed hundreds of innocent Russians in their sleep, and he used the domestic outrage to consolidate his power. It's brutal, and unthinkable, but for him it achieved his desired result, and now he's desperate, so he's doing it again."

"Can we stop them?"

"Maybe. But we have a much more immediate problem, Daniel," Robin said, looking out the window at the Finnish F-18's still flying beside us.

"What would that be?" I asked.

"If the Kremlin knows we have this plan—and we have to assume they do—the FSB will be waiting for us the minute we land in Vilnius, and they'll have orders to get it back immediately, regardless of cost or risk." Robin leaned toward me. "They'll come out shooting, with everything they've got."

I sat there for a moment weighing everything Robin was saying. I picked up the inflight telephone, and pressed the intercom button marked "Pilot." After one ring, Captain Ryan answered. I thanked him for his excellent flying and redirected with a request for us to change airports at the last possible moment. If not in Lithuania, in Latvia or Estonia.

"Understand," Ryan said simply. "We'll see what we can do."

I hung up the phone to see Robin taking photographs of the Russian documents with her iPhone. "What are we doing now?"

"Scanning all of the pages into a single document. I'll email it to Langley. This is the conclusive proof we've been looking for—the one document is in English, but others are still in Russian, so they need a little time to translate all of it and then analyze it for the President to act on it."

I nodded. "Well, I'm not sure where we'll be landing, but hopefully a last minute change will throw our FSB friends off our track."

"Whatever we do will be temporary," Robin said. "So we'll need to move quickly." She pointed at the diplomatic bag—navy blue, zippered nylon, about the size of a grocery bag—and handed me a key. "Open it."

The diplomatic bag had official State Department markings, and an attached numbered tag, marked:

From The Embassy of the USA, Moscow, Russian Federation
TO THE SECRETARY OF STATE, WASHINGTON, D.C.

It was stamped with an official U.S. Embassy stamp, and dated and signed by a "Pouch Supervisor." I unzipped the bag and saw the hard plastic case inside, and pulled it out. While continuing to snap photos of documents, Robin turned to me. "Use the same key to unlock it."

Inside, embedded in cut there were two .45 Automatic handguns, six magazines, two silencers, two boxes of ammunition, a map of Lithuania, Estonia and Latvia, and a small cell phone.

"I understand the guns, I guess," I said. "But why the cell phone?"

"It's a secure satellite phone," Robin said. "Untraceable, and can't be intercepted."

"Load the magazines," Robin directed. "I'm not sure what we'll be facing once we're on the ground."

The intercom phone beside my seat rang with a pleasant ring

that belied the tenuous situation we now faced. When I answered it was Captain Ryan.

"Congressman, we're going to touch down at Vilnius International Airport, and immediately lift off again. We'll land at Šiauliai Air Base— a Lithuanian Air Force Base in Northern Lithuania that has an airstrip that was designated as an alternate landing strip for the Space Shuttle several decades ago. A car will be waiting for you."

I thanked him and provided the details of the plan to Robin, who simply nodded her understanding, as if it were fully expected. I looked out the plane's window. Churches, farmsteads, towns and villages dotted the thickly forested rolling hills and verdant landscape below.

"How can you stay so calm through all of this?" I asked.

Robin looked up at me and shrugged. "I should ask you the same question."

"I'm about the furthest thing from calm," I answered.

"Okay, good. That makes two of us."

I nodded, wishing silently that at least one of us were truly brave and unafraid.

CHAPTER 66

AFTER LANDING, CAPTAIN MIKE RYAN came out from the cockpit and asked us to wait before disembarking. "Before you go, we have something for you."

I looked over at Robin who shook her head unknowingly.

Captain Ryan proceeded to lift the carpet off the floor in front of us, and lifted a compartment door that was packed with long, green hard plastic cases. He removed two of them and handed them to me. "Courtesy of your Uncle Jonas," Ryan said simply. "For circumstances like this."

"You're not just a pilot are you, Mike?" I asked, unable to conceal my surprise.

Ryan shook his head. "I've been with the Tory Foundation for over a decade. I was flying C-17's for the Air Force, and your uncle convinced me to join him. I haven't looked back—and it's been high adventure ever since. Today, maybe too much so."

"What didn't Jonas think of?" Robin asked rhetorically.

"Keep these with you," Captain Ryan said, handing her one of the assault rifles and an ammunition box.

Robin nodded. "Let's go," she said abruptly. "We don't have much time."

We descended the air stairs, and hurriedly packed the awaiting black Land Rover with the silent assistance of several very serious looking men and women.

Captain Ryan approached Robin and me, as we were preparing

to depart. He handed me a piece of paper. "From Aksel Odin. He's advising that you not to go to a CIA safe house, but recommends you go here instead. It's one of our facilities, and is much better equipped. He said he'll meet you there in three hours."

Robin nodded. "Okay. Let's go."

We drove in silence through narrow forest roads, and then through small Lithuanian villages and towns. I had programmed the Land Rover's GPS to avoid main thoroughfares and autobahns, in favor of the smaller roadways. What caught our immediate attention, at first, was not what we saw, but what we didn't see—people, cars, and traffic. And then, just inside the wood lines we passed, we saw the military hardware—tanks, artillery pieces and anti-aircraft guns, rocket launchers, 5 ton trucks, all under camouflage nets pointed toward the roadway in full defensive positions. A military convoy passed us, and we saw the Lithuanian Army markings on the bumpers of the trucks. A group of military helicopters flew over us, headed eastward toward the border of Russia.

"The rest of the world may not care about the Baltics, but they're obviously taking things very seriously here."

"I don't see any NATO equipment or troops here yet," Robin said quietly. "Lithuania can't hold back a Russian invasion alone. Nor can Poland, Estonia and Latvia."

"Surely, your bosses at Langley will show those papers to the President."

"They'll do their jobs," Robin said. "But I can't say the same for the White House. The last thing this President wants is to become directly involved in a war with Russia."

"Apathy's the real enemy then?" I asked.

"It's rampant and ubiquitous," Robin replied, nodding slowly. "We gave the White House more than three months advance notice of Moscow's intent to seize Eastern Ukraine, and they did nothing except ratchet up their rhetoric and threaten international sanctions. There's nothing that leads us to believe they would do anything differently in the Baltics and Poland. All the Kremlin has to do is threaten nuclear war, and we'll do whatever it takes not to become involved. We did the same thing in Hungary in 1956, and in Czechoslovakia in '68, despite all of our encouragement and promises. When it comes to intelligence analysis and predicting behavior, actions are what matter. Not words."

I considered her commentary. "Well, maybe that's the reason I was elected to Congress," I said.

Robin diverted her attention from the road and looked over at me. "Only if you're willing to sacrifice everything, Daniel. You put it all on the table, and bet everything. That's the only way it works," she said directly. "They'll do everything they can to discredit you. Not just the Kremlin. The whole Washington establishment."

"How do you fight complacency?"

Robin shook her head. "You do a full, frontal assault with everything you've got. You go public—reveal their plans, their lies, and show what's happening on the ground, in real time. You take a stand, and you remain relentless."

"What about you?" I asked. "Where do you stand?"

"Me?" Robin asked as she drove in silence for at least a minute or two. She pulled out her iPhone and did a quick Google search, then passed her phone to me. "I've already told you some of this, but here."

The article was entitled "Chicago Lawn's Witness to Soviet Genocide," published in the *Chicago Tribune* in February 2015.

It is an atrocity that has been all-but-forgotten, except in the memories of those who witnessed what their friends, neighbors and family members endured.

On May 22, 1948, as part of the Soviet mass deportations, Laura Me kaus and her family were taken by Soviet NKVD agents from their farmhouse and loaded into cattle cars. At the

time, Laura was only 8 years old, and her brother, Janus was 6 years old.

Her father and grandfather were separated from the rest of the family, and she later learned were transported to a Siberian concentration camp in the Krasnoyarsk territory. She would never see them again.

Laura, her mother, and grandmother were transported to the Altai Mountains. They were given very little to eat throughout the train ride—some water and rancid soup. With only a few small barred windows, there was little air to breathe. A hole in the floor served as a toilet for them and fifty others throughout the terrible journey. Along the way, Laura's grandmother died on the train, along with many others. The NKVD pushed their bodies off the train to the side of the tracks.

Weeks later, their train arrived, and the NKVD immediately marched them into the forest to cut trees. They worked in deep snow, and bitter cold. They built their huts from the trees they cut. The small ration of bread they were given to subsist on depended on the work they accomplished. Suffering from constant hunger and malnutrition, Laura watched her mother die from starvation and her brother die from disease. To this day, she remembers digging shallow graves for them in the frozen earth.

In 1948, the Soviets started to implement mass collectivization, appropriating land and livestock throughout Lithuania's countryside. This resulted in establishment of kolkhozes, or collective farms. In 1950, 90 percent of Lithuania's land was given to kolkhozes. Mass deportations continued until the death of Josef Stalin in 1953.

In 1956, Soviet leader Nikita Khrushchev directed the deportees to be released. In late 1959, Laura was the only surviving member of her family to return to Lithuania.

Life was not easy for those who survived and returned to Lithuania. "We were placed in an impossible situation. The government required us to register with the local municipality or face renewed deportation. In order to register, we needed an employer, but no one would have courage to give work to a former deportee. I lived and worked illegally for many years with the help of relatives," she said.

Laura was able to move to Chicago through an Amnesty International program that offered vocational training to victims of political prosecution. Her memories of the horrors she endured remain vivid.

The survivors of the Gulags and deportations can speak openly now.

Now former political prisoners, deportees and partisans receive an additional pension, which is managed by the Lithuanian state. Russia, officially proclaimed inheritance of all

> international rights and obligations of the USSR,
> and shows no will to pay compensation to them.
> The Russian Federation has never said a word
> asking for forgiveness for the Soviet terror in the
> occupied Baltic states, but Russian dissidents
> have expressed their regret on behalf of all
> Russians.
>
> Virtually no one has been called to account for
> what was done. The West has chosen to forget.

I finished reading and looked over at Robin.

"Laura is my mother," she answered, without being asked. "So while that may be something our country has forgotten, I can't forget what she endured. So if you have to know, I was "All In" well before I met you or your uncle."

"But Jonas knew, didn't he?"

Robin nodded. "Better than most ever could."

CHAPTER 67

"GRAB ONE OF THE M4s from the cases behind the seat," Robin directed, glancing repeatedly in the Land Rover's rear view mirror.

"Why?"

"We're being followed—I don't know who it is," she said, pulling the .45 Automatic out of the diplomatic pouch.

I crawled into the back seat, and felt my heart pounding through my chest. Robin gradually sped up, and began to weave between lanes, and I could see the black BMW sedan staying in close proximity to us...well beyond a normal or safe distance.

I unsnapped the hasps of the black resin case, and pulled the M4 Carbine out from the shaped foam that surrounded it.

"Now what?" I asked.

"It's already locked and loaded. Just switch it off safe."

Just as I was about to utter some inane protest, all of the windows rolled down in unison. The rush of frigid air into the Land Rover caught me completely by surprise.

"If they try to pull alongside us," Robin shouted. *"Shoot!"*

I nodded silently, hoping a gunfight wouldn't be necessary. I looked back and saw Robin collecting up several magazines of ammunition with her free hand, and place them in the seat beside her.

When I looked back, there were suddenly not one—but two— large BMW sedans. And they were attempting to drive alongside us on both sides simultaneously.

Robin saw them coming and jerked the steering wheel to the right and then left, slamming into both cars. The sound of metal scraping on metal at high speed was loud, jarring and caustic.

"Get ready!" Robin shouted. "You take the car on the passenger side. I've got the one on this side!"

I pulled the trigger to the M4 repeatedly. The noise was deafening. We were both shooting through the open side windows. Because of their heavily tinted windows, it was impossible to see inside the BMWs until the windshield of one of the BMWs splintered across its entire width, and the car lost control, veering off the road, crashing into several pylons. When I looked over to the driver's side, Robin was still shooting and driving. The remaining BMW slammed into our side with enormous force, throwing me against the seat, and I heard the plinking of bullets impacting our car. The Land Rover swerved violently. Regaining my balance, I aimed the M4 out the driver's side window, and emptied the remainder of my magazine into the BMW. Quickly losing control, the car turned, and flipped several times behind us, landing on its roof.

Robin glanced back at me back at me through the rear view mirror, changing magazines and driving at full speed.

I changed the magazine to the M4, locked and loaded it before turning the selector switch back to "SAFE."

"Are they gone? I asked.

Robin nodded. "Reload this too," she said, passing a .45 magazine back to me. "It's not over."

"Can we get off the autobahn?" I asked, reloading the magazine and handing it back to her. "It'll be crawling with the police in no time."

Robin nodded and pointed ahead. "We'll take this exit." After a brief moment, she looked back at me several times in silence. "Daniel?"

I realized I was sweating profusely, and shivering intensely from the cold. I felt my teeth clattering. "Yeah?"

"You're getting to be good at this."

I shook my head as we turned off the autobahn. "I'm definitely *not* good at this," I answered, still gripping the handle of the M4 tightly, my eyes darting around like someone just released from an asylum. I was shivering uncontrollably from the rush of frigid air inside. "Can you raise the windows?"

CHAPTER 68

"YOU ARE SAFE!" Aksel Odin exclaimed.

"Barely," Robin replied, surveying the severe damage sustained to the Land Rover.

Aksel nodded. "I heard what happened," he said quietly.

"My ears are still ringing," I replied, turning around to see what I could of the estate grounds, but it was already becoming dark. We were somewhere on the outskirts of Vilnius, surrounded by dense forest.

"This is Pavilniai Regional Park," Aksel explained. "One of Lithuania's oldest forests, and in all of Europe."

Aksel Odin led us into a large mansion made entirely of glass and steel. Armed guards were posted at various spots around the estate, and the perimeter of the home.

We entered, and our steps echoed on the black slate floors, against antique brick walls. A large brick fireplace was the centerpiece of the home, rising up two floors. As we walked up the stairs, I could see the glow of the Vilnius' Old Town illuminating the Vilnia River Valley below.

"Congressman, this is the forest where your parents and Jonas lived and operated throughout their resistance to the Nazis and the Soviets—where they hunted and were hunted." He motioned for us to sit down. "We understand what you have both just gone through, and we are bringing all of the Tory Foundation resources to bear to help resolve this crisis quickly."

Robin nodded, and pulled out the set of documents that Tatyana had given to us. She placed them on the table, and spoke to Aksel directly. "We need to get these documents translated from Russian into English," she said. "Quickly."

Aksel scanned the first several pages of the Kremlin operational plans, and looked up at both of us in obvious surprise. "Where did you get these?"

"From Tatyana—my sister," I answered.

"We had significant questions about her allegiances," Aksel said. "But if these documents are genuine—as they appear to be—there can be no doubt."

"I want to see if we can get Tatyana out of Russia, Aksel," I said directly. "If she's still alive."

Aksel turned his iPhone on, searched and found an email. He seemed to hesitate before passing it to me.

"What is it?" I asked.

Aksel nodded at both Robin and me. "Tatyana Petrova—your step-sister—was sentenced to death, and executed yesterday in Moscow."

I went cold the moment I heard that, and inhaled deeply. My heart constricted—fighting off a wave of anger, tears, and memories that were still way too fresh. I scanned the email—it appeared to come from one of the Tory Foundation's agents operating under deep cover in the FSB:

> _Subject Name_: Tatyana Petrova
> _Action_: Expedited Trial and Sentencing at Kremlin Direction
> _Charge_: Espionage
> _Sentence_: Death (Execution Immediate, Carried out at 12:01am, Moscow)
> _Comments_: U.S. Congressman Daniel Tory, and CIA Agent Robin Nielsen are actively being sought for possession of highly sensitive and materials with the highest classification, using all available covert and overt means, with immediate priority. Tatyana Petrova admitted to

covert communications by email and SMS messaging to Daniel Tory with opposition and underground contacts, aiding and abetting the Tory Foundation activities.

I handed the Aksel's iPhone to Robin, who held her hand to her lips and looked back at me. "Oh, Daniel, I'm so sorry...."

Robin handed the phone back to Aksel, visibly shaken. I felt like I'd been punched sharply in the gut—realizing that it was Tatyana who had sent me all of the anonymous messages and warnings during the past weeks, to include the photo of the Church of the Resurrection of Christ, where I received the antique icon containing the photograph of my father.

"Tatyana died attempting to stop an impending World War," I said evenly. "We need to get those papers to the media, and wherever else they can make an immediate impact."

Aksel nodded. "The translation will be ready in the morning."

"Are you staying here?" I asked.

Aksel shook his head, and handed me a map. "Tomorrow at 7AM, you will meet me here," he said, pointing at a spot on the map circled in red. "You can sleep soundly—and safely—here tonight. We have also arranged dinner for you—it is ready now."

"Aksel?" I said, suddenly remembering.

Aksel looked back at me.

"Tatyana had a young daughter, I understand," I said. "I'd like to see if we can get her out of Moscow so she doesn't have to live in an orphanage."

I could see Aksel contemplating the request silently. After a moment, he nodded. "Yes, I'll see what we can do."

"I feel like I'm back on the train to Saint Petersburg, blindly preparing to jump off," I said to Robin quietly in bed—her head on my chest.

My mind continued to race as I considered everything that was now happening in what seemed to be hyper-speed.

"It's not too late, you know," Robin said.

"Not too late for what?"

"To jump off."

"No, I'm committed," I said. "Especially now, after what they did to Tatyana."

"Even if it derails your congressional career?"

"The two shouldn't be mutually exclusive," I answered.

I shifted to face Robin. With the ambient starlight that shone through the windows, I could see the radiance of her face. "Do you think I'm making a mistake?"

She looked at me for an extended moment before responding. "My mother used to tell me, 'there's a fine balance between honoring the past and losing yourself in it. The mistake, she said, is not moving forward.'"

Are we moving forward? Or am I lost in another generation's struggle? Whatever the answer to those questions, one thing I knew with certainty was that there was no middle "safe" position in any of this.

As I drifted off to sleep, the faces of my father, Jonas, and my mother returned as if in Technicolor—vivid and full volume. Laughing and celebrating together, planning and fighting together, mourning their dead, and picking up the pieces of their lives—in the face of dramatic world events well beyond their control.

"What's important to you, Danno?"

Jonas was standing in front of me. And suddenly everything was clear—through my father's journal, they had been providing their counsel to me all along—through his words, and through their own example. In the midst of all the turbulence and in the face of overwhelming odds, their consistent approach was to take back control of those things they could, live life day to day, and defend what was most important to them.

I awoke with a start, drenched in my own cold sweat. Robin was beside me, holding on to my shoulder.

"Are you okay?"

I nodded. "Yeah. I think I just saw a ghost."

CHAPTER 69

WE WALKED OUT OF THE HOUSE at 6AM, dressed warmly in jeans, sweaters and hiking boots, to a new black Mercedes G550 SUV in the driveway. The air was as cold, clean and crisp as I've ever breathed. Looking around, there was no sign of our wrecked Land Rover.

Robin looked over at me, equally surprised, and held up the map Aksel Odin had given to us the night before. "You drive. I'll navigate."

As we drove along the narrow road, I noticed Robin staring at me and smiling.

"What are you thinking?" I asked.

"You're a good man, Daniel Tory," she said simply.

I shook my head. "I'm not feeling that great right now," I said. "They just killed my sister, and I didn't do a thing to stop them."

Robin didn't immediately respond, except to announce a turn into the entrance of the Aukštaitija National Park.

"She made her own decision, knowing exactly what the consequences would be. You tried to get her on our plane—we both did—and she refused."

We continued to drive through the park along a road that bordered a large lake. Robin pointed ahead where the road split. A black Jeep Grand Cherokee was parked on the shoulder of the road.

"That's Aksel," Robin said, glancing back at the map. "This is where he said he'd meet us."

We pulled alongside the Jeep, and the window lowered. Aksel

was wearing a black cap and sweater, and talking on his cell phone. He smiled at us, pointed ahead, and said simply, "Follow me."

In less than a mile, we passed by a large field of old traditional wooden crosses of all sizes, and were waved through a high security steel gate by two private security officers. At the gate, signs in Lithuanian, Russian, Estonian, Latvian and English read:

RESTRICTED – NATIONAL PARK ESCORT REQUIRED

"Welcome to *your* National Park," Robin quipped.

We followed Aksel's Jeep, winding through the dense forest along a narrow gravel road that ended at a large lake and boat ramp, where a small barge was parked. A dense fog had settled overnight on the lake, and was struggling to lift.

A man waved Aksel's vehicle forward toward the ramp onto the barge.

"Interesting—the map doesn't show a ferry," Robin said, looking at the map. "But there are quite a few islands in this lake."

The ferry master waved us forward, and signaled us to park directly behind Aksel Odin's Jeep. Aksel walked over to us. "Welcome! Enjoy the ride and the beautiful scenery. It is a fifteen minute trip."

"Where are we heading?" Robin asked Aksel.

"You will soon see. For us, it is our sacred ground," Aksel replied. "And the place that both Lucas and Jonas have wanted Daniel to visit, for many years now."

A congregation of starlings floated through the slate gray fog. Small waves slapped against the steel hull.

"I wish I could have come under different circumstances," I said. "While they were both alive."

"That would not have been possible without endangering your life, and your mother's life," Aksel said. "Neither Lucas or Jonas would even consider the possibility, and they went to great lengths to protect you and your mother."

"What's changed?" I asked, looking ahead as we progressed almost silently through the fog, across the lake. The lake's water, I realized, was crystal clear.

"Everything," Aksel replied. "But also nothing."

"Thanks for clarifying," I said.

Aksel pointed across the far end of the lake. "You can't see it this morning because of the fog, but there is a village over there called "Trainiskis," where a large, very old tree stands, believed to be 800 years old—and said to have been used by the Pagans for human sacrifices."

"Sometimes I wonder if we've evolved at all since then," I responded.

Aksel continued, smiling slightly at my comment. "We were fortunate to have the leadership of Lucas and Jonas to guide the Tory Foundation for so many years," Aksel explained. "And they did so at great personal sacrifice, and risk. Their achievements are legendary, and their legacy can now continue through you."

"I'm not sure I can live up to their example," I said.

Aksel nodded and smiled. "It's natural, I suppose, but you should not doubt yourself."

I chuckled. "Doubting ourselves—that's one thing we politicians are generally incapable of doing, even when it would be wise to do so," I said. "What did my mother have to say about all of this?"

Aksel paused before answering. "Tanya was very much opposed to you knowing about the Foundation, much less leading it. She has always been concerned about your safety, first and foremost."

I laughed and shook my head, looking over at Robin. "I can understand her concerns now."

"The security now provided to you is the very best available anywhere," Aksel said, to reassure. "It is unobtrusive, and most of the time you will never know it is present."

"Right here? Right now?" I asked looking around. "Sorry, but I don't see it."

Aksel nodded, and spoke into his sleeve. "We will show you."

After only a brief moment, a series of multi-colored strobe lights began to flash through the shroud of fog, and underwater, all around us, in a silent, almost psychedelic cacophony of lights. A moment later, the lights disappeared.

I looked over at Robin, and could see that she was as surprised as I was.

"Although the fog obscures our vision, the men and women assigned to protect you, can see us perfectly through state-of-the-art optics, hardware and technology."

"We could have used them a few times over the past couple weeks," I said dryly.

"Why didn't you have this kind of security at your headquarters in Geneva?" Robin asked directly.

Aksel nodded. "We failed," he said simply. "We learned many lessons from that terrible event, and have taken actions to prevent, and even preempt other attacks in the future. This is the emerging reality of what we face today. All of us now understand that we cannot assume security and safety."

The scent of pine on the lake was refreshing. A full variety of birds were singing around us, and I could hear the water splash against the ferry. Security, I had begun to realize, was really nothing more than an illusion.

The ferry connected with the concrete dock, and Aksel directed us back into our cars. "Only a short drive, and we will arrive."

We drove along the island's perimeter for a short distance, and then into a modern steel-fenced compound on a small driveway that led us through an old growth forest of pine, oak and ash trees. To our right, we passed by what appeared to be an ancient fortification on a hill with buried mounds and old thatched cottages.

Three guards on duty waved us through the gates into a spectacular, otherworldly setting completely invisible from the island's shore.

At the end of the driveway, we both gasped in unison at the ultramodern, cantilevered structure in front of us.

"I'm not sure what I was expecting," Robin said quietly. "But it wasn't this."

Constructed of opaqued, brushed steel, titanium, and glass, the building reflected a full array of colors that seemed to change in unison from golds and greens to deep reds and purples with the changing azimuth of the sun.

Aksel led us to the stone steps at the entrance. A Franciscan monk greeted us in heavily accented English.

"Congressman Tory, Miss Nielsen, I am Father Tomas Kadžionis. Welcome to Sterling Monastery."

I shook his hand, and as we walked alongside Father Tomas, and up the stone steps, Aksel provided his own commentary. "As we pass through the metal façade, this is the original stone entrance of the Capuchin monastery that was destroyed by the Soviets in 1967. The ruins were reconstructed using the same original stones, and reinforced with contemporary impressionistic architecture of titanium, steel, and glass that symbolizes the immortality that is conveyed by faith, and the rebirth of freedom."

Robin stopped at the entrance, and held my arm. She reached into one of the pockets of her backpack, and handed me the business card for Fr. Tomas Kadžionis that had fallen out of the book. "Coincidence?" She whispered. "I can honestly say this is the first monastery I've seen that's surrounded by an electrified security perimeter equipped with high end intrusion detection, defensive lasers, and a Franciscan Friar as its welcoming committee."

I realized Aksel must have overheard her. He smiled calmly and motioned us to step inside. "Please, all of the answers to your questions are inside."

If we were unprepared for what we saw outside, our surprise was redoubled by the interior. What began as an old world cathedral with a soaring stone gothic ceiling complete with stone piers and arches, the traditional design ended there—not abruptly, but gradually. As we walked down the main aisle, we began to notice the long, rectangular stained glass windows engraved with distinctly modern, impressionistic designs that allowed sunlight to flood inside in broad, rainbow-like beams. Our footsteps echoed on the white Carrara marble floor.

Approaching the altar, Father Tomas led us to a side doorway. Almost immediately, we encountered another doorway that resembled a bank vault with hand and retina biometric access scanners. Father Tomas handed us personalized access badges with our photographs already affixed. He turned and submitted to the hand and retina scan, and the door opened into a red carpeted foyer manned by two security guards holding automatic weapons at the ready. The guards checked our badges, and we were waved through a thick glass and steel door. As it opened, we felt the steady stream of pressurized air on our faces.

"The breeze you feel is part of the countermeasures we employ in case of a chemical or biological attack on our facility," Father Tomas said, leading us to an elevator. "We are fully self-sustaining in either scenario."

Aksel smiled at Robin and me. "Now you see, there is much more to our church than meets the eye."

Tomas motioning us down a flight of stairs, through an glass entryway, with 3D etchings of trees, labeled in English on top and Lithuanian below:

The Tory Foundation
The Sterling Forest of the Gods

Father Tomas opened the doors and led us into a large room with dark green carpet, stone walls and elegant recessed lighting. Large framed high resolution photographs covered one wall, depicting the Lithuanian Resistance during World War II, and the Soviet occupation. Along each of the walls, freestanding museum display cases of various shapes and dimensions showcased a full variety of machine guns, rifles, pistols, knives and military uniforms. In the center of the room, a large circular unit logo was embroidered into the carpet that I recognized from my father's journal as the official unit crest of "The Hawks."

Tomas stopped us there. "Over the past decades, we have collected many artifacts of the Tory and Forest Brothers' Resistance. As much as this place is a center of operations for the Tory Foundation, it is also a living memorial to all of the brave men and women who died for freedom, and who fought against tyranny through the years. You can see the weapons of resistance, the faces of those who fought and dies for all of us, and hear their stories here." Tomas stopped and looked over at Aksel.

Aksel nodded. "Congressman, everything began here in this forest, and it is where our effort continues."

"Why was this constructed here?" I asked.

Aksel nodded. "Part of the reason is symbolic—the resistance spent much of their time hiding and planning, quite literally, under ground—in bunkers and cellars where they could not be easily detected. And that provides the other, more practical reason—this facility is far more secure and survivable under ground than above ground. Your father, uncle and your mother played a leading role in designing this facility. No expense was spared, and no detail was overlooked. One day, they knew that you would come here to visit, and come to learn all that they experienced and fought for through the years." He paused, and looked at Robin and at me, gauging our reactions. Both of us were transfixed.

He led us over to a display case with a large black and white framed series of three photographs: one of a smiling young girl dressed in a school uniform, another somewhat grainy close-up of a gaunt-faced teen wearing a striped concentration camp uniform, and the third young woman wearing a Lithuanian Army uniform, submachine-gun in hand. It took me only a short second, even before I read the inscription, to realize that all three photographs were of my mother. I looked down and saw the actual clothing items from the photograph above laid out in the glass display case: the girl's school uniform, the striped concentration camp uniform, the Army uniform, and the AKM submachine-gun she was carrying—all meticulously arranged in the same succession as the photographs. The inscription read:

Tanya Tory was the sole survivor of her family, who escaped from the Auschwitz Concentration Camp with other members of the resistance movement and joined the partisans in the forests of Lithuania against the Nazis. Rather than "keep house" back at their bunker like other female partisans, Tanya demanded active duty assignments alongside the men. Tanya Tory participated in hundreds of subversion and sabotage missions, to include raiding

Gestapo headquarters in Vilnius, infiltrating other resistance cells to identify Nazi collaborators, burning down bridges, blowing up railroad tracks, and ambushing Nazi road and rail convoys. Following World War II, Tanya Tory played a leading role in the underground resistance against the Soviet occupation of Lithuania during the Cold War.

I felt Robin grasp my arm gently as I considered all that my mother had experienced through the years. Realizing now that I could never fully know all of the pain and suffering she endured, I felt my anger at her refusal to tell me about our family's history quickly dissipate to a visceral understanding that no longer required explanation.

I looked over at the separate display beside us, and saw a larger-than-life black-and white image of a youthful Jonas Tory, with his characteristic wide smile, standing inside a rail car in front of a mass of pallets—stacked from ceiling to floor—holding a pistol in one hand, and what appeared to be a large brick in the other. The inscription beside the photo read:

Jonas Tory was the Co-Founder of the Hawks Resistance Movement—one of the few Lithuanian Resistance forces that fought against both the Nazi and Soviet occupations. Jonas participated in countless raids and ambushes against Nazi forces throughout Lithuania and the Baltic States. He and his brother, Lucas Tory, planned and executed the legendary raid against the Nazi rail convoy carrying captured Soviet gold reserves. 21 rail cars carrying gold ingots were captured by The Hawks and funded their resistance through World War II and much of the Cold War. One of these armored rail cars was dismantled and reassembled here to commemorate this daring raid.

I pointed at the last sentence, and turned to Tomas. "What does this mean? 'One of the rail cars was dismantled and reassembled here to commemorate the raid?'"

Tomas looked over at Aksel, who simply nodded his permission.

Tomas pulled out what initially appeared to be a TV remote, and pressed one of the buttons. At that moment, both Robin and I jumped slightly as the floor we were standing on seemed to draw back in a noiseless mechanical sequence.

Aksel smiled. "Do not worry, we are standing on very thick structural glass flooring. It is completely safe!"

Through the glass, I recognized the armored rail car on top of a section of actual track and travelled ballast, perfectly reconstructed, with the exception that it had only a fraction of the roof intact so the interior would be visible from above. Two heavy machine guns were situated in iron turrets on both ends of the car. Inside, the pallets were stacked as they were in the photo with Jonas with long, thick gold ingots stamped with a hammer and sickle and the Cyrillic letters "CCCP."

"This is an exact replica of one of the captured armored cars from that raid," Aksel said. "The gold ingots are the very same that were captured there. In addition to serving as a display for the Tory Foundation, this facility is also one of the most secure vaults in the world—more than seven hundred million dollars worth of gold and currency are stored in this facility. The rest has been distributed in deposits and securities throughout Asia, Europe and North America. As CEO and Chairman of the Board, you have veto authority over all expenditures. With majority approval and oversight of the Board of Directors, you are authorized to recommend and execute all expenditures."

"Who are the Board directors?" I asked Aksel.

"After the recent tragic events that occurred in Geneva, you and I are the only ones remaining. Our search is now underway to identify new Board Directors who are committed to the ideals and values that made the Tory Foundation possible."

I nodded. "If appropriate, I'd like to extend board positions to the spouses of those directors who were murdered in Geneva."

Aksel nodded. "We will include them for your consideration."

I looked over at the opposite wall, and saw the large oil portrait of a younger version of the man I recognized as my father, in Lithuanian uniform, gripping his signature Thompson submachine gun.

As I walked toward the painting, Tomas said, "It was painted by one of Lithuania's most famous artists. She knew your father as a little girl, and painted this portrait from memory."

"It's excellent," I said quietly, looking into my father's eyes.

"You look like him," Robin whispered, beside me. Standing there, I finally saw the distinct physical resemblance with my father, for the first time—in a painting.

Looking down, I saw the army uniform and Thompson submachine gun in the display case below the painting. Also included were a dagger, a compact leather-bound bible and a hand-knotted rosary made from string. The inscription beside the painting read:

Lucas Tory was the co-founder of The Hawks Resistance Movement—the operational foundation of what became the Lithuanian Freedom Army. His fearless leadership and inspirational example throughout World War II and the Cold War in resisting the tyranny of the Nazi and Soviet occupations are legendary. He is recognized as the only resistance leader to break into the Auschwitz concentration camp, and free the woman who would become his future wife. Lucas and Tanya were two of only 144 Auschwitz prisoners to escape in one of the most audacious prison breaks in the camp's history. He orchestrated his own infiltration into the camp, and joined the resistance movement in the camp. With his ability to speak fluent German, he convinced the SS to become first work in the camp's laundry. He began planning a mass escape, until one day, through a fellow prisoner with access to the administrative records, he learned that his friend, Tanya Klimas was scheduled to be murdered in two days. With the assistance of several other prisoners, he immediately implemented an emergency plan for he and Tanya and several other fellow prisoners to escape the camp by commandeering SS uniforms from the laundry service, and a staff car from the motor pool. Lucas carried the plan out rapidly and with authority, even getting out of the car at one point to shout at the SS Gate Guard for hesitating in opening the gates for their departure. They drove for 35 kilometers, to a rendezvous point with Jonas Tory and other Hawks partisans. Lucas and Tanya broke out of Nazi-occupied Lithuania to Sweden where he met with General William O. Donovan, Commander of the Office of Strategic Services (OSS), providing photographs of the Auschwitz Camp, prisoner rosters, and personal accounts of the atrocities that the Nazis were committing there.

"Your father saved countless lives," Father Tomas said reverently. "He was fearless in his pursuit of freedom for Lithuania and all people."

I turned to Robin. She nodded, intuitively understanding my request. She reached into her backpack, and handed me my father's journal and the complete translation, along with the translation of his KGB interrogation, which I slipped inside the journal.

I held the journal in both hands, feeling it's rough, worn texture. "This is the diary of Lucas Tory, and the English translation, Father," I said extending it to Tomas. "I believe he would have wanted to have it be on display here."

Tomas nodded and smiled, and held it to his chest. In many ways, turning my father's journal over to the Tory Foundation felt like finishing a portrait that had taken decades to draw.

"We have one more room for your to see," Aksel announced, turning to Father Tomas.

"Please follow me," Tomas said, leading us to a large elevator.

The elevator walls were stainless steel and the floor was the same white Carrara marble. The ride down lasted at least a minute, and caused our ears to pop several times during our descent.

The doors opened to reveal an ultra-modern command center in the round, with stacked flat screens surrounding two massive ceiling-to-floor Planar screens opposite one another. Recessed lighting lit the room in dull red and blue hues. Computer terminals and workstations surrounded a touch screen "Board Room" digital glass tabletop that occupied the center of the room. The room was bustling with people at their stations, crowded around maps of each of the Baltic States—

many depicting full order of battle schematics. Other screens displayed aerial surveillance photos of Russian tank and artillery formations that were lined up on the borders of Estonia, Latvia and Lithuania. A surveillance video seemed to be on a continuous loop showing a bird's eye view of roads filled with Russian model T-84 Tanks. Other screens depicted news shows from around the world—volume off—with streaming subtitles and closed captioning.

"This is our most capable headquarters, Congressman," Father Tomas said. "And well-placed for us to see the situation as it develops on the ground."

"We have satellites?" I asked Tomas, pointing at the large screen in front of me.

Father Tomas nodded. "And we have the most advanced drones—all of them are state-of-the-art, and in use along the frontier with Russia. This feed is from one of our Predators."

"*One* of *your* Predators?" Robin asked, noticeably surprised.

Tomas smiled again, and motioned over to Aksel, who answered.

"Indeed, we have over three hundred drones in use around the world," Aksel replied. "Most of them are unarmed, for reconnaissance purposes, half of them are always airborne."

"*Most* of them are unarmed?" I asked. Now it was my turn to be surprised.

Aksel nodded. "Yes, but all of them can be retrofitted and weaponized on short notice. As we are doing now, to defend the Baltic States, in the event of a Russian invasion. One of those armed drones is patrolling the skies directly above us now."

"Is NATO aware of what we are doing here?" I asked, looking over at both Aksel and Father Tomas.

"Yes," Tomas answered. "And in fact, our existence makes these measures possible for them, because we are not part of any nation's budget, and we can act independently, while keeping Brussels fully informed." Tomas pointed at several desks, where men and women were sitting and monitoring multiple computer screens side-by-side, and talking on secure telephones. "Liaison officers from the intelligence agencies of NATO's leading countries are assigned here, and support our activities daily. We also have a cyber-security capability that is equal to any Western nation—with capabilities that are both offensive and defensive."

I turned to Robin. "Did you know about this?"

She shook her head. "I didn't."

"You wouldn't," Aksel interjected. "The mere existence of our facility is one of NATO's most closely guarded secrets. It's possible that you have heard of it by its code name, "Key Stone," but our many locations and our mission is compartmentalized at the highest levels."

"I've heard of Key Stone, but only as an ELINT source," Robin said. "Definitely not this, though—an active, armed, privately funded intelligence and cyber-operations center."

Aksel stepped forward. "We are much more than that," he said, turning to Robin, and then to me. "We exist first and foremost because of your family. The Tory Foundation had very humble beginnings—in the forests above us that we now own and occupy. Fighting against the Nazis, and then the Soviets—often at a distance, frequently in close quarters, and sometimes hand-to-hand. The Sijudis Movement had its origins with the Tory Foundation. With Perestroika, in order to rally popular support for demonstrations that had already begun, we continually emphasized the importance of peaceful protests. The demonstrations increased in size and frequency until March 11th 1990, when Lithuania was the very first of the Soviet Republics to declare independence. Jonas and your parents knew the Soviets would not stand idly by—behind the scenes; they helped create a strategy that ensured Soviet defeat. In January 1991, Soviet tanks and troops stormed the Vilnius TV tower, killing 14 unarmed civilians and injuring 700—and the Soviets had failed. By 2004, Lithuania was part of NATO and the European Union."

Aksel moved around one of the digital tables, and continued. "While the world was celebrating and the fall of the Berlin Wall, and our new independence, however, Lucas and Jonas Tory knew it was only a matter of time when we would face a resurgent neo-Soviet threat, and have to defend against it once again. Their warnings were prescient, and here we are."

"Okay," I said. "What's our strategy for dealing with *this* threat—here and now?"

"The papers you were given by your sister provide all the proof we need of the Kremlin's intentions," Aksel answered. "We have provided those papers to all of the Western intelligence agencies. However, the European Union's foreign policy chief is openly pro-Kremlin, and the question is whether they will confront the Russian President and Prime Minister with this incontrovertible proof. Even if they do, the Kremlin will certainly deny all of it. So that is why we believe we must move forward immediately with a full public release."

"Providing all the documents to the media, you mean?" Robin asked.

"Yes, with the context and detail that only the Tory Foundation can provide, leveraging all of our capabilities." Aksel waved his hand in the direction of the massive screens that depicted active satellite and drone video coverage of the Russian armor and artillery formations now spread along the borders from Lithuania to Estonia, and turned back to me. "We would very much like to have your voice in reporting the Kremlin's actions to the American people."

"Can I do that?"

"As Chairman of the Tory Foundation, speaking publicly about the humanitarian implications of Russia's planned actions would be a natural role for you," Aksel replied. "As an American congressman and member of the House Intelligence Committee, warning about an imminent invasion would make a very significant impact."

"I'm on the House Intelligence Committee?" I asked, turning to Robin.

She nodded. "We were just notified—normally they don't make committee decisions until February, but you already had a Top Secret-SCI security clearance from your previous work in the White House Chief of Staff's office."

"And as the son of Lucas Tory, nearly being killed by the FSB on multiple occasions would also be good front page fodder," I said. "Would I be more effective if I didn't take on a public role?"

"Ordinarily, that is what we would advise," Aksel replied.

"It would be very controversial. But these are exceptional, exigent circumstances. Of the likes we haven't seen since the height of the Cold War."

"I'll do whatever I can," I replied, but the words sounded hollow as I said them. But I also knew that my life was about to change dramatically, in a very public way.

"Very well," Tomas said.

"Before we do anything, I'd like to visit my father's grave if it's here."

Father Tomas nodded. "If you will follow me, we have something we would like for you to see first."

"I'd like to see my father's grave," I repeated quietly, insistently.

Tomas nodded, smiled and gestured behind us. "There is no need."

Through the door, I saw my mother being pushed in a wheelchair by Elena, with a tall elderly man—stooped in the neck, with thinning gray hair, wearing a grey tweed overcoat—standing beside her.

Mom was looking up at me, beaming with emotion, and tears I had never before seen from her. After a moment, she extended her arms. She was noticeably frail, but completely lucid and steady in her movements.

I rushed toward her, knelt down, and hugged her tightly.

"I had to come," she said softly, in a voice fainter than air. She motioned toward the elderly man beside her, and said the words that are forever ingrained in my memory. "Daniel, this is your father, Lucas Tory."

I stood up and looked directly into his piercing blue eyes, and the recognition was instant. Beyond any doubt, I knew that the man in front of me was my father. He was trim, several inches shorter than me; but even holding a cane, he fought mightily at that moment to stand straight and proud.

I was at a complete loss for words. He was smiling slightly—forlornly—and I could see the emotion welling in dark blue eyes that had been gray in all of the photos I had seen.

I shook my head in self-imposed denial, stammering.

Unbelieving. "But I thought—"

When he spoke, it was in broken, thickly accented English, mixed seamlessly with Lithuanian, with the same tenor I remembered of Jonas' voice. "Please forgive me, my son. I am sorry—it was impossible for me to leave until now. But I have never been too far away."

Mom continued, "We could not risk anyone knowing about his escape from Monrepos until it was complete, and that everyone—him, and both of you, were safe."

I nodded, regaining myself—and embraced him. I had a thousand questions rushing through my head, but in that instant, all I could manage was unconditional gratitude for a reunion I never thought would happen.

I looked over at Robin, and saw her smiling, doing her best to contain her own tears.

I turned to my mother, and held her hand, incredulous and unsure what to say. "You're okay, Mom?"

"I'm fine," she nodded, smiled and wiped away her tears. "Elena is taking good care of me."

"I begged her not to come all the way over here," Elena interjected with a wide grin. "But you know your mother can be very stubborn."

I nodded and laughed, knowing my mother's strong-willed nature all-too-well.

"Nothing could keep me from coming," Mom said, and then pointed at both my father and at me. To our entire assembled group she said, "You see, they look like twins, don't they?"

Everyone laughed, and my father turned to me, "You look very much like my father—your grandfather." He continued in Lithuanian, and Robin translated for him: "Everyone respected and looked up to your grandfather."

"And you are revered," I said, and asked Robin to continue translating, so it could be fully understood. "And I am proud to be your son."

My father laughed in much the same way Jonas did—I noticed they shared the same mannerisms as well. Their voices were very similar. "Jonas always told me you would be President of the United

States!"

I shook my head and laughed. "After everything I've learned about each of you, anything I've done seems insignificant."

He listened to Robin's translation, shook his head, and raised his index finger. "Not insignificant! We are proud of you!"

Our eyes met, and I said earnestly, "Welcome home."

There was silence, and I watched my father looking over at Mom. She was squeezing his hand in reassurance—and in that gesture, I understood how meaningful this moment was for both of them.

After a moment, she motioned toward my father. "Our fight for freedom comes first. Even before family. Your father has always reminded everyone of this, even while imprisoned and under house arrest. He insisted that you not be brought into this struggle when you were young, so you could live a full life, free from the atrocities and bloodshed."

I nodded my understanding and drew a deep breath.

My mother pointed to Robin, who was standing behind me. "You must be Robin," she said warmly. "Jonas told us much about you, young lady—you are even more courageous and beautiful than he described"

Robin stepped forward, and greeted them both with a warm embrace.

"Thank you for being a friend to Jonas, and for protecting our son," my father said, gesturing toward me.

Robin responded with a demure smile. I could see tears streaming down her face, and realized how profoundly affected she was by the sudden turn of events. She was clearly enjoying our family's reunion.

Mom pointed toward the elevator, and turned around to Elena. "Let's go outside now."

CHAPTER 70

STEPPING OUT OF THE CHURCH, the fog that was so heavy when we had arrived had dissipated completely. Robin and I walked beside both of my parents through the graves marked with tall sculpted crosses of polished Sterling steel, I found myself supporting my father by holding on to his arm as we entered the cemetery.

"This is the first time I see this," he said. "It is where souls of iron and steel still roam, so we call it the Sterling Forest."

In fact, the sheer profusion of crosses created the illusion of being in a dynamic, otherworldly forest. Walking among them, you found yourself surrounded by hundreds of beautiful, sacred monuments to men and women who had made the ultimate sacrifice for freedom. As the wind passed through the cemetery, the crosses released their own somber tones, rising and falling, depending on where you were standing. The net effect was a chorus of variegated tonality without any predictable scale.

"The entire cemetery is a soundscape," Father Tomas explained. "Each of the crosses consists of tubes and tuning strings activated by the wind, to create a unique, constantly changing harmony. No visit here is ever the same."

"It's exquisite," Robin remarked.

"We wanted to show how our partisans worked together," my father said.

Mom continued. "Even in death, as they had done when they were on this earth among us. Just one cross will not create this kind of

318

symphony. It takes all of them working together."

I felt overwhelmed at the sheer magnitude of what had been created to memorialize the men and women who had fought with my family defending Lithuania. It was obviously a solemn place, and it had a profound effect on my own perspective as I walked through the pathways, and saw the names, inscriptions and photographs of the dead. As we walked, my parents would occasionally look at an inscribed name, and put their hands on the cross marking the grave. Where hands had grasped the crosses, they were well worn. Each cross felt different than the last. Many had fresh flowers at their base. The sound of the wind passing through gave a ghostly voice to each gravesite.

Aksel led us to the front of the cemetery, where four large steel crosses stood, as if they were standing in front of a military formation. One of the Franciscan monks handed him an urn.

"We have Jonas' ashes with us," Aksel said quietly to me. "Your mother brought them with her."

"But Jonas was buried in Chicago," I said, turning to my mother. "I was there!"

"Half of his ashes are buried in Chicago," Mom replied in a half-amused tone. "In a casket—he wanted to be with his friends, in both places."

My father pointed at the large gold cross directly in front of us, and the brass marker at its base. "These are the graves of my mother and father—your grandparents. We place Jonas there, beside my mother. And when our time comes, your mother and I will be buried here too, beside your grandfather."

After placing the urn containing Jonas' ashes in the vault embedded within one of the crosses, Father Tomas tapped my shoulder and handed Robin and me four sets of large flower bouquets in ground vases that fit perfectly into the base of each cross. I knelt at each gravesite, ran my fingers across the engraved names, and said a prayer.

I stood, and as we walked, I held my mother's hand. Robin walked with my father and spoke to him in Lithuanian. Occasionally we would stop, and each of them would tell me about the person buried there.

The grip of memory was inescapable here. As they spoke, I realized that their reminiscences of their fellow partisans, the conversations they shared, the sacrifices they made together, their acts of heroism, their tragedies and triumphs—many as distant as seven decades past— were still fresh and often immediate. Events and personalities, once confused and disparate, were now taking on an unexpected, evocative order.

I found myself gripping many of the crosses as I walked by them, listening to the acoustic whispers and harmony through their pipes. This, I realized, looking at the sea of steel crosses reflecting the sunlight, was the actual Sterling Forest of the Gods.

"I'm very tired," my mother suddenly announced.

I saw Elena turn to Aksel with a concerned expression.

"We will depart now," Aksel said to me. "Your parents will be staying with us, at the same house in Pavilniai Park."

I helped my parents into the black Range Rover. Mom held my hand and squeezed it tightly, without saying a word. I looked over at my father now sitting beside my mother, as if he had never been away from her. Stepping back, I shut the heavy armored door.

The driver stowed the wheelchair in the trunk, and at Aksel's direction drove through the gates of the compound.

"You should get some rest also," Aksel said to both Robin and me. "Dinner will be served tonight at the house. Tomorrow, we will be at the Presidential Palace. A very important day."

CHAPTER 71

WE ARRIVED BACK AT THE SAFE HOUSE at Pavilniai Regional Park in a state of utter exhaustion. Too much had happened in those several hours at the Tory Foundation headquarters for either Robin or me to fully absorb.

"What I now realize," Robin said quietly in the back seat of the SUV, "Is that the Tory Foundation is as much about preserving stories of the past, as it is about promoting democracy and freedom."

"Maybe the two go hand-in-hand," I replied. "So as the world changes, when people die, their stories don't die with them."

As we were about to get out of the vehicle, Robin's cell phone rang.

"It's from Langley," she said looking at the number.

When she was forced to stay on hold, it became obvious to me that the caller on the other end was very high level...and when she scribbled "DCI" on a notepad beside her, I then knew it was the Director of Central Intelligence. The call was brief, and although I only heard Robin's responses, it was clear the conversation was one-sided and directive.

"Yes, Sir. I understand, but—"... "No, Sir, I can't guarantee—"... "I'm sorry, I won't do that." ... "Yes, I understand the consequences." "The source was his sister, and she was just executed by the KGB." ... "The Congressman isn't the one who's invading the Baltic States." ... "Absolutely. You'll have my resignation within the hour."

Robin took a deep breath, and turned to me. "Is that Chief of

Staff job you offered still open?"

"Apparently, the White House isn't at all happy with you—or me," Robin said.

"Why?" I asked, rhetorically. "We can't let them stop us in our tracks, or allow a Soviet invasion to happen as if it were a complete surprise."

"You're being blamed for everything at the moment," Robin said. "The State Department just learned that you were leading the joint press conference with all the regional Presidents tomorrow, and now everything's hitting the fan—Republicans are all over TV denouncing Putin, saying we should defend the Baltics against an imminent Russian invasion, demanding an immediate armed response. Democrats are urging restraint and diplomacy to reduce the tensions and avoid conflict."

"Well, that's why I'm an Independent," I said.

Robin referred to her scribbled notes. "The Kremlin just dismissed the U.S., Lithuanian, Estonian and Latvian ambassadors from Moscow, and all of the Baltic states reciprocated. Global stock markets are in complete chaos—Moscow and China shut down their trading for 48 hours. Spetsnaz border incursions are continuing across the Baltics, and both sides are reporting fatalities. Lithuania downed a Russian MiG-35." Robin was deciphering the notes she had scratched out during the call. "And now Riga, Tallinn and Vilnius are reporting cyber intrusions that are playing havoc with airports, hospitals and power stations. The internet is completely jammed, and so are many NATO radar capabilities."

"Does Langley believe this will just die down by doing nothing?"

"Doing nothing can sometimes be a strategy," Robin replied. "But it's not a good one in this case. Steve Omnivic just texted me that he submitted his resignation an hour ago to the DCI in protest against Washington's latest actions—or lack thereof."

I nodded. "At least you have his support."

"In their own way, Washington and the Kremlin are publicly blaming you for starting a furor over the Baltics, and the White House is warning you not to go anywhere close to tomorrow's press conference in Vilnius—let alone participating in it."

"Sorry for putting you in this position."

Robin shook her head, and smiled. "Don't give yourself too much credit, Congressman. I knew what I was getting myself into well before I met you."

That statement alone was unsettling.

"So I was just another CIA research project? Is that it?" I asked, immediately regretting the words.

"At the time, you were," Robin answered. "Yes."

How exactly do you respond to that?

Sensing an argument ahead, I chose instead to withdraw and go for a walk outside on the park's trails.

I walked along a pathway covered with a light dusting of snow, and feeling my strength returning, I began a slow jog. The air was cold and damp like the inside of a medieval church. Towering, centuries-old oak trees surrounded the path, giving the illusion of running through a tunnel. After a long uphill climb, I stopped along a dramatic cliff that overlooked the Vilnia River Valley and Old Town Vilnius. Doing my best to forget the events of the past day, I shut my eyes and took in the frigid, clean air.

"You are on top of Belmontas Hill, Daniel," a familiar female voice announced behind me. I turned around and saw Elena—my mother's caretaker—standing along the pathway. I hadn't seen a single person on my run at that point, and I was caught completely by surprise because she was the last person I was expecting to see up here.

"This is the Pučkoriai Exposure," she continued. "It's an ancient place where mammoths once roamed, and where your family hid out for a large part of the war."

"Elena!" I exclaimed. "Why are you all the way up here?"

"I was waiting for you," she said walking toward me. "The trail outside the house leads only this way."

Elena wasn't exactly young—in her late forties or early fifties. In the two decades she was with my mother, I never saw her as a walker or a hiker, so seeing her along this trail was odd. I walked toward her, and saw her pull out a very large automatic handgun, made larger with the silencer.

"Stop there, Daniel."

I felt a surge of shock and panic. "*Why*?" I shouted in utter disbelief.

"This is a fitting place for the Tory family story to finally come to an end," she said. "I've waited many years for this moment. Honestly, I didn't know if it would come."

"Who are you?" I asked, glancing back and forth to Elena's eyes, and into the barrel of her silencer. I looked around quickly and saw how isolated we were on top of the hill. "You are Lithuanian—*one of us!*"

"Half Lithuanian, half Russian," she corrected. "My father was an NKVD Colonel, and my mother was a proud member of the *Smogikai*."

My mind raced. I had heard that term—*Smogikai*—before, in my father's journal. Smogikai...partisans captured by the NKVD, who were granted clemency and turned into double agents. Used very effectively to infiltrate and to hunt down their former comrades, and to defeat the Lithuanian resistance. And they were extremely ruthless.

"So you're a spy, from a long line of traitors," I said.

Elena shook her head and smiled. There was a sinister depth in her voice I'd never before encountered. "Of course, you could never understand, Daniel. The FSB placed me with your family over 20 years ago, under deep cover, as part of the cell only to be activated in a time of war, or in the event of your father's escape from Monrepos. After today, my mission will be complete, and I will finally be able to return home to Moscow."

"You can't think you'll get away with this."

"Oh, yes! You see, our operation is now fully underway," she motioned down the hill. "The house has been surrounded, and everyone inside—to include your mother and father—are now being eliminated as we speak. I was hoping that we could have accomplished all of this while you were still in Russia, but that did not happen. You and your CIA girlfriend were far more of a nuisance than we expected."

"That FSB shooter was taking direction from you?"

Elena nodded. "Katrina was one of our best agents, very competent, and efficient—and she was my niece. You killed her."

"She tried to kill us," I said flatly.

Elena raised her pistol, aiming it at my head. There was an abrupt sound, like an extended burp from above and a large branch hitting the ground. For a split second, I thought she had fired, but Elena crumpled to the ground. The snow around her began turning a bright crimson, and a ghostly shadow emerged from the tree line. I struggled to see through the haze, but the identification slowly came, first from his imposing size, and then from his accented English.

"A very close call, Congressman," Aksel said, emerging from the forest's shadows. I could see that he was carrying a pistol at the ready. As he approached Elena's body, his eyes focusing intently on something in the middle distance.

"You shot her?"

He shook his head and pointed upward. "No, one of our aircraft did that."

My mind raced, remembering the briefing we had on the island about the Tory Foundation's arsenal of drones. "A drone?"

Aksel nodded, looking over at me. "You can thank Evgeniy Euchev for telling us you were leaving the house unaccompanied, and that you were being followed by Elena."

"She said there's a FSB squad surrounding the house," I said with urgency.

"The problem has been addressed," Aksel said conclusively. "Everyone in the house left through a tunnel, and Lithuanian special police are waiting inside house—quite a surprise for our Russian friends!"

Aksel effortlessly dragged Elena's body off the trail into the trees, and I noticed him receiving a call on his cell phone.

"Everyone is safe," Aksel said to me, as he hung up. "Everyone at the house has been evacuated into city."

As we walked through the forest, I heard a distant, prolonged exchange of gunfire. At a clearing on the ridge, we were able to look down at the Tory Foundation house—now surrounded by police cars with lights flashing, armored vehicles, and tactically dressed SWAT men with automatic weapons.

Only a short walk away, we were picked up in a black armored Land Rover top-of-line model, *Autobiography*. I immediately recognized Evgeniy Euchev as he opened the door on the passenger side.

The driver, wearing dark sunglasses, overcoat and a business suit, with a swing holstered Mini-Uzi visible under his overcoat.

"Thank you for the whiskey, Danno Tory!" Euchev said in a cheerful, enthusiastic voice. "Your father tells me 'keep an eye on you,' so I do!"

"I didn't think I'd see you again after Monrepos, Ev," I said as we stepped into the SUV.

"Your father knew for very long time we had mole in the Tory Foundation," Euchev said, "Too many coincidences. I trust no one, and then I see her following you from the house. Nothing worse than *Smogikai*, on this earth, Danno. Smogikai betrayed your father. She was the last of them—now they are gone forever."

I was momentarily taken aback by Evgeniy Euchev's cavalier approach to all of this, but then I realized that after 70-plus years, it was all a game to him. Like chess, only with guns. *Outsmart them. Kill them before they kill you.* Evgeniy Euchev, like Jonas, Lucas and Tanya Tory, was a survivor.

Aksel continued in an even almost journalistic tone. "After the tragic events in Geneva, we uncovered some discrepancies in Elena's background. We knew someone was reporting on us from within the Foundation, but did not know whom. She had been acting strangely since arriving in Vilnius," Aksel paused for a moment. "I am sorry for what happened, Congressman. We don't like to act impulsively, but we took immediate action once we understood what was happening."

"I have to say, I'm relieved you did," I said simply.

Weaving through heavy Vilnius traffic at high speed, I saw a rainbow of flashing colors reflecting on the windshield, and realized that our car was equipped with interior mounted strobe lights.

Aksel tapped my arm and pointed at the large tower high in front of us at a distance, set on a tall ridge of pine trees. "Look over there!"

I turned and looked. Euchev was speaking to him in Lithuanian. Aksel translated.

"This is where the Soviets tried to put down our revolution on January 13th, 1991. There were many tanks and Soldiers. They shot and crushed 14 of our unarmed protestors and injured 700 others who were defending the tower and Parliament, with their tanks and guns."

Aksel pointed to our right. "They are all buried here, at Antakalnis Cemetery."

I squeezed Aksel's arm, in an unspoken request for him to translate for me, so I was fully understood. I turned to Euchev. "Ev, it seems like a very big coincidence that the CIA had picked you as an Alzheimer's patient with no recorded family for us to meet at Monrepos."

After listening to Aksel's translation, Euchev laughed. His response came quickly, in English. "No coincidence! When the KGB tells Jonas he can't come to Lithuania again, that is just another obstacle for both of us. I chose to be with him at Monrepos. Jonas gave my name to the CIA as the safest patient to contact—knowing they will someday want to visit there."

Aksel pointed at the manor where the former President of Lithuania lived, and commented that we were now in the *Turniškės* neighborhood of *Antakalnis*—one of the oldest suburbs of Vilnius— driving along narrow cobblestone streets with townhouses tightly pressed together. We pulled into a gated square compound with a beautiful Baroque mansion as its centerpiece.

Stepping out of the Range Rover, I turned to Euchev. "All this time, you knew my father was alive? Why didn't you tell me?"

Euchev seemed surprised, looked over at Aksel, and then turned around to face me, directly—dramatically taking hold of both of my arms in his still powerful hands. "Lucas Tory—your father—best man I ever know! We knew the Kremlin would come after your entire family and kill you if your father left Monrepos."

"What changed his mind?"

"When we find out about Kremlin plan to invade the Baltics, that changed his mind," Euchev answered. "When Jonas died, and when he finds out you flew to Europe and Russia, that changed everything. Quickly."

CHAPTER 72

WE WALKED INTO THE MANSION'S elegant doorway, and before we could shut the door, Robin rushed toward me, and collided into my arms. When she pulled away, I could see her concern.

"You're okay?" She asked.

"A little shaken," I said. "But thanks to our friend Ev, I'm fine."

Robin looked over at Evgeniy Euchev and I could see that her recognition of him from Monrepos was immediate. She hugged him, with a quiet and sincere "Thank-you."

Euchev was clearly not prepared for Robin's hug, and waved his hands in the air. "You are lucky I am not 50 years younger, Danno!"

"Daniel!" I heard my mother's voice from the living room into the foyer. I walked into the room to find her and my father sitting on a sofa in front of a large, lit fireplace. A panoramic window extended the entire length of the living room, providing a spectacular view of the Neris River.

I hugged both of them, and assured them that I was fine, thanks to Evgeniy Euchev.

"Ev is one of our bravest partisans," my father said simply.

I nodded, and held my mother's hand, still trying to reconcile his use of the present tense. "I can understand why."

I was standing, still dressed in my running gear, and felt a sudden chill. "I'm relieved everyone's safe."

My father urged me to sit, and called Evgeniy Euchev to also come and sit down with us. Two bottles of wine were on the table—a La Tâche '42 and a Richebourg '42. Quite possibly the most legendary vintages of the 20th century. Dad passed them to me to open. "I have been saving these for a very long time, Daniel—since I came to Paris for the first time in 1945. They were both given to us by General William O. Donovan for a special occasion." Dad looked at Mom, and then at me and Robin, and smiled. "Today is that time."

He poured the wine and reverently passed a glass to each of us.

It's difficult to describe the scent of intense plums, floral aromas, and a cedar fire, combined with the panoramic view of one of Europe's oldest cities at night. Despite what was happening nearby, on the border with Russia, it was the first time I genuinely felt safe in weeks.

"I'd like to propose a toast to our founders—Lucas, Jonas and Tanya Tory—and to the freedom they have helped to preserve for all of us."

We all touched glasses, and listened to stories shared by my parents and Evgeniy about the years of resistance against the Nazis and the Soviets. Many of the stories were humorous, while others were tragic, and often harrowing. They recounted conversations with friends and enemies alike, described loved ones lost in their struggle, and their hope for a large-scale intervention from the West that never came. It was the first time I was able to listen to the stories first-hand—from those who lived them. I remembered my own late night conversations with Jonas, the way he talked as he poured Krupnik and wine, and his unbridled enthusiasm.

Robin squeezed my arm, looking at me, and I realized tears were flowing from my eyes. "Jonas left the world a better place," she said. "And he entrusted it to you."

"Have we heard anything about Tatyana's daughter?" I asked.

Robin handed me a folded piece of paper. "It's from the *Times* reporter you keep avoiding," she said.

Congressman, General Antenas Petrov is living in the Voronovo Nursing Home, 30 kilometers outside Moscow. Tatyana's daughter, Irina, is his only remaining descendent.

"Thank you," I whispered, folding the paper and putting it into my pocket.

"Tomorrow will be a historic day for Lithuania," Aksel Odin announced to all of us. "I can think of no more fitting place than the Presidential Palace to confront the threat from the Kremlin. Originally it was a nobleman's residence during the 14th Century. In 1997, it became the President's. Napoleon Bonaparte himself used the palace during his doomed advance to Moscow. Tsar Alexander the First also was an honored guest."

"To Lithuania," My father toasted, holding his glass up.

"To Lithuania," everyone repeated.

Robin's phone began ringing mid-way through the evening, and she ignored all of them, knowing they were from Langley and Foggy Bottom.

Robin opened the Facebook app on her iPhone, and showed me the hundreds of posts with articles, and my image on full display:

Congressman-Elect Fights Kremlin because White House Won't

Congressman Daniel Tory Defies President on Foreign Policy

Congressman Single-Handedly Resists Russian Invasion Plans

"I may not be a Congressman when I get home," I whispered to Robin.

"But, you'll be able to look in the mirror," she whispered back with light amusement, offering her own private toast.

CHAPTER 73

THERE ARE MOMENTS IN LIFE that you remember. And yet, however clear the memory, or seemingly preordained the outcome, it's usually true in hindsight that the path that led you there was never really defined or welcoming. Standing on the podium in the Presidential Palace with both of my parents, and the presidents of Lithuania, Latvia and Estonia, was one of those surreal moments as cameras flashed in a variegated array of blinding light. News cameras surrounded us, and reporters crouched below, furiously taking notes and pointing their iPhones at each of the heads of state as they delivered their prepared statements, revealing the Kremlin's war plans on the Baltic States, and reminding the NATO alliance of its collective security obligations to defend them against Russia's aggression.

"We thank the Tory Foundation and the pivotal role of Congressman Daniel Tory in thwarting the Kremlin's imminent plans to invade our Baltic States," the President of Lithuania said. "The evidence he has delivered to us is incontrovertible, and exposes the lies and disinformation—and so as the truth prevails, it mandates a forceful and immediate response from our NATO allies. Any attack on a North Atlantic Treaty Organization member State must be regarded as an attack on all of its members. As neighbors, we stand together ready to counter this very serious security threat to our countries, the region and Europe. As the world's strongest military alliance, we know that NATO will deal with this serious threat as it has throughout its history, in the most difficult circumstances."

She paused and looked thoughtfully over at me, and then at my parents.

"And finally, for all of us who love and treasure independent Lithuania, it is a great honor for me to welcome Tanya and Lucas Tory, who stand with us today. Over a lifetime of enormous courage and sacrifice, they personify our aspiration to create a strong, proud and united Lithuania. Tanya and Lucas Tory, like each of the former freedom fighters here today, are the defenders of our homeland, and they are the guiding lights reminding us of our collective personal responsibility for Lithuania. Over their lifetimes, they honored and cherished Lithuania's freedom more than personal happiness or even life. Our brave freedom fighters gave each of us a chance to live, talk and think as we want. The blood of their families and friends, spilled for the motherland, does not allow us to undervalue our independence. Please welcome Tanya and Lucas Tory!"

A thunderous standing ovation erupted, even from the members of the media. I watched as my mother and father waved at the crowd and stood for pictures.

And so that's what you learn about yourself in those moments when everything seems so predestined in retrospect—that the past is far from dead. In fact, it's very much alive. It occupies the hidden passages of our minds as dynamic memories that interject themselves as we react to the present-day events, and influencing us as we prepare for the future. Sometimes the effect of our past is subtle, other times it's those moments of *Déjà vu* that hit you like a Mack truck, when you least expect it. Then you realize the ghosts of your past—the men and women who raised and reassured you, sometimes warning you, were always guiding you. And those memories you once found so elusive were always holding you tightly, and you had the answers with you all along.

When it was my turn to approach the podium, I couldn't see much of the audience because of the intense lights—but I could see the first several rows of the audience—all former partisans. Each of them was looking at me intently, knowing that I was the son of Lucas and Tanya Tory. Seeing them—only them—directly in front of me caused me to fold up my several pages of remarks, place them back inside my inside coat pocket, and speak extemporaneously:

Three days ago, a very brave lady handed me Kremlin documents that prove Russia's plan to reoccupy the Baltic States. She understood the consequences of turning those documents over, but accepted her fate freely. She had the opportunity to flee Moscow, but chose to stay. The Kremlin executed her yesterday.

With the flooding recollection and realization, my own tears began to stream, and I suddenly found it difficult to speak or see clearly. Now remembering everything, my voice noticeably cracked. I paused briefly, regained control, turned to the elderly former partisans in front of me, and addressed them directly.

"You know, one thing I've learned is that none of us can slow or revise the passage of time. The events and stories that fill our time here on earth are what define us. So, I've learned that for a legacy to be fully realized, we must listen. Carefully. As the son of Lucas and Tanya Tory, and the nephew of Jonas Tory, I didn't do that growing up. I never understood the extraordinary service and sacrifices they made—and that each of you made over years—for all of us here today. Looking back now, I wish I'd listened more closely....

EPILOGUE

President Asserts Kremlin Risking War in Europe Because of Baltic Build Up. United Nations Warns of Peril.

By ANTHONY COCHRANE Special to The New York Times;
December 2,
Section 1, Page 1

WASHINGTON, Dec. 2—Following a dramatic press conference with all three Baltic Presidents, led by U.S. Congressman-Elect Daniel Tory (I-IL) showing alleged proof of Kremlin plans to invade the Baltic States, the Pentagon today deployed Carrier Strike Group 4 to the Baltic Sea today to counter a build-up of forces along the borders of Lithuania, Latvia and Estonia. President Wilson denied NATO was threatening Russia in any way, but was only responding to a substantial threat to the Baltic Region. "NATO has no quarrel with the Russian people. We do have a quarrel with Putin, or Russia, trying to change borders by force," the President said.

Moscow Warns Washington Action by NATO Risks Nuclear Conflict—Challenges U.S. Right to Presence in Baltic Sea.

By ANTHONY COCHRANE Special to The New York Times;
December 3,
Section 1, Page 1

MOSCOW, Dec. 3—The Kremlin challenged today the right of the United States and NATO to stage military forces in close proximity to the Russian frontier around the Baltic region. "Russia is left with no other option but to boost its troops and forces on the western flank," said Gen Yuri Yakubov. Congressman-Elect Daniel Tory (I-IL) held a press conference urging NATO solidarity in the face of what he called an "imminent Russian invasion of the Baltic States." Lucas Tory, Congressman Tory's elderly father and famed resistance leader against the Soviet occupation, said, "Lithuania has lived through horrific Nazi and Soviet occupation characterized by oppression, rape, looting, deportation and mass murder. The Kremlin continues to threaten the Baltic States with an imminent invasion that our NATO Allies must help us defend against." Tory said.

Baltic Crisis Deepens. United States and NATO Weighs Direct Steps if Kremlin Defiance Continues

By ANTHONY COCHRANE Special to The New York Times;
December 4,
Section 1, Page 1

WASHINGTON, Dec. 4—The White House made public tonight a new intelligence report showing the Russian build-up of military forces along the borders of Lithuania, Latvia and Estonia was proceeding at a rapid rate with the apparent intention of "achieving a full reoccupation and return of Cold War borders." NATO Ground Forces were now positioned in all three Baltic countries to counter potential cross

336

border incursions. Both Finland and Sweden have expressed a desire to join NATO, to demonstrate their commitment to deterring Russia's expansion in the Baltic Sea. Finland's Minister of Defense described the move as a "stabilizing factor that will further encourage the development of our own defense capabilities."

White House Urges Kremlin Stand Down and End Baltic Threat

By ANTHONY COCHRANE Special to The New York Times;
December 5,
Section 1, Page 1

WASHINGTON, Dec. 5— President Wilson revealed tonight that President Putin had offered an acceptable solution for the Baltic crisis but is now wavering.

President Urges Quick Action to End Tension and Press for Future World Peace

By ANTHONY COCHRANE Special to The New York Times;
December 6,
Section 1, Page 1

WASHINGTON, Dec. 6— President Wilson and President Putin reached apparent agreement today on a formula to end the crisis over the Baltic Region and to begin talks on easing tensions in other areas. Congressman-Elect Daniel Tory (I-IL), who raised awareness of the imminent Russian plans to invade the Baltic States, applauded the accord and stressed the need for "constant, unwavering vigilance for freedom to be preserved."

The old man shuffled quietly—head down, back hunched—into the Voronovo Nursing home, carrying a gift-wrapped package under his arm. Passing through the doors, he stopped momentarily to brace himself against the stench of urine, sickness and despair that hung in the air of the dilapidated building. Passing the front desk with an indifferent wave, he lumbered through the empty hallway glancing sidelong into the rooms with elderly men and women—many his age—lying silently in their beds, sleeping or staring blankly at the ceiling. It saddened him to see his generation treated this way—kept barely alive, ignored and overmedicated.

At the end of the hallway, he found the room he was seeking—Room 189. He knocked softly and entered.

At first there was no real recognition whatsoever. But as the old man came closer to his old acquaintance sitting up in his chair, looking out the window, he grew certain the man sitting in front of him was retired GRU General Antenas Petrov.

Lucas Tory sat down opposite Petrov, and once their eyes met, he began speaking in fluent Russian, still in a Lithuanian accent.

"*Moy General*, it has been a long time."

General Petrov nodded slowly, looking briefly at Euchev and then back out the window. "A very long time, Lucas," Petrov replied. "I never expected to see you again. Why have you come?"

"I have news for you," Lucas answered. "It is very bad news, I'm afraid."

"The news here is seldom ever good," Petrov said quietly.

"Three days ago, the Kremlin executed your daughter Tatyana by firing squad—for treason. Tanya wanted you to know."

Petrov inhaled deeply and sat in silence. Lucas watched a tear fall down his cheek. Petrov made no attempt to dry it from his face.

"You should know that she sacrificed herself for the cause of peace," Lucas said finally.

"Irina?" Petrov asked. "My granddaughter. Is she safe?"

Lucas nodded. "Yes. She is fine, and I have brought a gift from Tanya for you both to give to her. Both of our days are short, Antenas—but with this, Irina's future will be well secured."

Euchev handed Petrov the package, and Petrov nodded holding it tight on his lap.

"You and Tanya are together?"

Lucas nodded. "Yes, we are now reunited, along with our son, Daniel."

Petrov looked up from his lap to face Lucas. "Thank you, *Tovarich*. I am sorry."

Lucas Tory nodded, stood up, and placed his hand on Petrov's shoulder briefly before shuffling out the door.

Petrov opened the package to find an antique three-paneled icon—the *Sterling Forest Triptych*. He unfolded and extended the panels and found the large wax envelope affixed to the backside. Inside the envelope, there were a variety of cards, a passport, and a large key. One of the cards conveyed the details of a Swiss bank account:

Banque cantonale de Genève
Quai de l'Ile 17 - CP 2251
1211 Genève 2
Vault Holder: Irina Petrova
Vault 360

The passport was black—an American Diplomatic Passport—bearing the seal of the United States of America. Inside the passport was Irina Petrova's full name and photograph. The expiration date was listed as "Indefinite."

A handwritten note on a personalized correspondence card with the heading "Tanya Tory" read:

Irina,

You have a family in Chicago who loves you!

Your mother, Tatyana, was the most courageous person I have ever known. We are all very proud of her, and we are also proud of you.

Your Grandmother,

Tanya Klimas Tory

AUTHOR'S NOTE

Lucas Tory's description of Auschwitz and the camp's daily activities (journal entry dated March 21, 1941 on pages 150-152) is based on, and often directly applies text, from a SECRET classified report, "SEMI-WEEKLY INTELLIGENCE SUMMARY" from Headquarters, 12th Army Group, Report No. 3, dated 18 May 1945. Source: Hoover Library, Stanford University, Manuscripts Library: Daniel Lerner papers, box 36, "May [1945]."

The description of Lucas Tory's escape from Auschwitz with Tanya Evgeniy, and Pranas that follows (pages 153-154) is based on the actual account of Kazimierz Piechowski's escape from Auschwitz on 20 June 1942—one of the most audacious and harrowing escapes in the history of the notorious Nazi concentration camp.

Lucas Tory's infiltration of Auschwitz parallels the extraordinary exploits of Polish army captain Witold Pilecki, who intentionally entered the Auschwitz concentration camp to expose the horrors of the Holocaust. Pilecki's reports were the first to emerge on Auschwitz, and were universally dismissed as "too horrific to believe."

Lucas Tory's journal entries often reflect the extraordinary personal accounts found in countless letters and diaries of Lithuanian, Latvian, Estonian and Polish partisans who courageously fought their Nazi and Soviet occupiers throughout World War II and the Cold War periods.

ABOUT THE AUTHOR

JOHN FENZEL is a retired senior Special Forces officer who served on our nation's battlefields throughout Europe and the Middle East. He served on the personal staffs of the Secretary of Defense, Army Chief of Staff, and the Vice President of the United States. Following the Cold War, he led the first U.S. deployments to the Baltic States. He lives with his wife and three children in Annapolis, Maryland. He is the author of the international thriller, *The Lazarus Covenant.*

Visit the author online at www.JohnFenzel.com